Kellan MacInnes thinks he contracted the HIV virus in the summer of 1988. Diagnosed with AIDS-related cancer in 1997 he packed in his job, cashed in his pension, went home and waited to die... only he didn't.

Since not dying of AIDS, Kellan has worked as a befriender, a painter and decorator, a supermarket delivery driver and a bike tour guide. Kellan's first book *Caleb's List* was acclaimed by readers and reviewers alike and was shortlisted for the 2013 Saltire Society First Scottish Book Award, Scotland's most prestigious literary prize.

Also by Kellan MacInnes

Caleb's List: Climbing the Scottish Mountains Visible from Arthur's Seat

THE MAKING OF MICKEY BELL

KELLAN MACINNES

First published in Great Britain
Sandstone Press Ltd
Dochcarty Road
Dingwall
Ross-shire
IV15 9UG
Scotland

www.sandstonepress.com

Editor: K.A. Farrell

The publisher acknowledges support from
Creative Scotland towards publication of this volume.

ISBN: 978-1-910985-27-4
ISBNe: 978-1-910985-28-1

Jacket design by Two Associates
Typeset by Iolaire Typesetting Newtonmore
Printed and bound by CPI Group (UK) Ltd, Croydon, CR0 4YY

To Sam, Mercy and Hope

the cast

Mickey Bell	a benefits scrounger from Glasgow
Tyke	a wee collie dug
The Munros Book	a talking climbing book
Ryan	on the cute side of chubby
John Paul O'Malley	a psychotic Buddhist
Tamara Stricher	owner of The Love Shack
Dougal Anderson	a lecherous mountain guide
Carmen d'Apostolini	the advocacy worker at Face West and a high priestess of Avalon
Nige	a DSS snooper
Zelda	a wicked Queen
Mr Fuk Holland 2012	a gay Hell's Angel
Maggie	Mickey's Scottish aunty
Aunty Nora, Carol-Ann, Linda and Rita	the girls from Haberdashery
Ruiadh Bridge	a fictional Highland village located somewhere west of the A9
Malcolm	the font of all wisdom
Andrea	the barmaid in the pub
Fithich	a raven

DG Fraser	legendary Scottish climber and editor of The Munros Book
John Fraser-Smythe	Secretary of State at the Department for Scroungers and Skivers (DSS)
Sir Gideon George Oliver Brokenshire	the multi-millionaire absentee landowner of the vast Torran estate
Kyle	a bit of rough
Mr Tighty-Whities	a Scotrail employee

appearing as themselves

Sir Hugh Munro	a Victorian mountaineer
A________ S________	The First Minister of Scotland
The Innacessible Pinnacle	an improbable whalefin of rock forming the highest point of Sgurr Dearg
Bette Davis	a film star who made it big in the 1940s
Mr Alex Roddie	a writer of mountain fiction
Thomas Pennant	an early traveller in Scotland
M_______ M_______	The Gay Toon Planner
The Munros	the Scottish mountains over 3000 feet

tell us about last night?
well, we had a wee ferintosh and we lay on the quiraing.
it was pure strontian!

From *Canedolia, an off-concrete fantasia*
by **Edwin Morgan**

the coachman waits

White Bridge: 1908. The horses' breath steams in the cold night air and drops of rain glisten on sleek black flanks. Brass buckles on leather harnesses clink as the beasts shift uneasily in the shafts, unnerved by the angry white torrent churning beneath the arches of the old stone bridge.

The coachman waits.

He pulls his collar up against the night and the rain hurled on the grey wind. He holds the brass lantern aloft and peers into the darkness. The flickering yellow light gleams in the raindrops puckering the surface of the puddles as the blaeberry bushes along the side of the stony road flatten with each new gust.

A sliver of melted ice at the heart of the heavy drops of rain beating on the windows of the carriage, running down the glass and over the coat of arms and the painted, varnished gold letters that spell the name *Lindertis*.

A beam of lamplight through the rain-streaked glass falls on the velvet-cushioned seats of the carriage and on the wicker hamper: silver cutlery, a cold roast pheasant, a slab of Madeira cake and a bottle of claret. And beside it a copy of *The Perthshire Advertiser* lies on top of a sheaf of printed papers bearing the legend *Forfarshire Unionist Association*.

Four miles upstream two tweed-clad figures, hunched

over against the grey wind, battle into the storm along the south bank of the Geldie Burn. The threatening afternoon had quickly turned to stormy night: hours earlier, defeated by the wind and the rain and the cloud on the mountain top, they failed to get within one thousand yards of the summit cairn.

The shorter of the two men, square-shouldered, compact, wiry, stops and looks back. He runs a hand through his beard, the sourness of defeat in his mouth as the mountains stand a darker line against the black night.

His companion that wild day will be little remembered beyond his initials lingering on in Century Roman font at the end of articles on the yellowing pages of the Scottish Climbing Club Journal.

The bearded climber surveys the banks of the Geldie. He has a Highland name and, when he opens his mouth to speak, the words come out with a Scottish accent though he was born at number 27 Eaton Place, London.

'The burn's in high flood. At the stones we might—'

He shouts into the darkness but the wind seizes his words and hurls them away downstream.

After a few moments he steps into the swirling black water. He clutches his walking stick, trying to balance, hobnailed boots scraping on greasy granite boulders. Then, a third of the way across, the angry peaty torrent seizes his ankle.

He slips.

He sees the foaming white water snatch him and sweep his body downstream into the gorge.

A searing spasm of panic starts in his groin then shoots through his stomach and up to his chest. His hands grasp frantically at the dripping spindly branches of a rowan sapling.

He drags himself up the steep bank, the woody twigs of ling catching in his beard. His wettermantel is soaked and heavy, his breeches slimy with black, peaty mud. He lies on his back in the heather, gasping for breath, looking up at Carn an Fhidhleir, a three-thousand-foot-high black wall in the darkness.

He swears a silent vow to return.

The rain hurled on the grey wind beats down with a new ferocity as night closes in around the two figures on the banks of the swollen burn while the coachman waits at White Bridge.

Author's Note

Sir Hugh Munro, compiler of the list of Scottish hills over 3000 feet, never did reach the summit of Carn an Fhidhleir. At the time of his death in 1918 he still had two mountains left to climb: Carn an Fhidhleir and the Inaccessible Pinnacle.

Monday

the legal implications of love

Mickey Bell is lying on his back with his jeans and grey boxer shorts round his ankles. He's worrying about his appointment with the dole in the morning and he's wishing he was somewhere else.

He watches as Sharon pulls a purple latex glove over one hand. She's overweight and has red cat scratches up her arms.

'We can do a full sexual health screening while you're here,' she'd said moments earlier.

'Aye – OK then,' he'd stuttered.

'Just lie back. If you could undo your belt and slip your jeans down.'

He knows she's called Sharon. It says so on the laminated Greater Glasgow health board ID card clipped to her blue tabard.

She lifts his shrivelled cock, pulls back his foreskin and gently feels his balls.

Then she takes a three-millimetre-wide plastic strip from a pack, cellophane wrapper torn open on the trolley beside her.

This is the bit Mickey hates.

He winces in a spike of pain as she inserts the plastic strip into the eye of his penis then quickly slides it out again.

'That's the worst bit, eh?' says cheery Sharon. 'If you just turn onto your side now.'

He rolls over. The strip of paper towel covering the examination table scrunches up under his bare thighs. He lies there staring at the scuff marks and grubby fingerprints on the white clinic wall.

'I'm going to get a smear from your bum now.'

Sharon takes a swab and swipes it along his anus. Like someone scratching your bum with a toothbrush.

'Can you sit up now, please?'

Jeans and pants still round his ankles, he perches on the edge of the examination table.

This'll be over soon, he thinks, as the heavy buckle of the belt on his jeans clatters on the red, buffed shiny vinyl hospital floor.

'I'm just going to test for gonorrhoea.'

In her hand Sharon holds a wooden swab like the stick in the middle of an ice lolly. As she says, 'Open wide.'

My mind cuts back tae when I wis a kid... sun drenching the tarmac, weeds in the cracks between the paving stones and orange drips of melting ice lolly making ma fingers all sticky.

Sharon thrusts the wooden swab down the back of his throat.

He gags.

'Aw I hate that but,' he says as Sharon drops the swab into a clear plastic jar with a white screw-top lid.

'Can you just confirm your name and date of birth?'

'Mickey Bell – 3/5/79.'

The nurse scribbles in blue biro on the label on the side of the plastic jar.

'OK, that's you.'

He pulls his pants and jeans up.

'I'll do your bloods now.'

He sits on the edge of the hospital examination trolley. Under the strip of paper towel Sharon tore from a wide roll on a desk in the corner of the room, yellow foam rubber bursts through cracks and splits in the black plastic mattress cover. He breathes in a faint hospital smell of disinfectant.

'Just a wee scratch,' she says as she slides the needle under his skin.

He twists his head round and looks out the window at the branches of the trees in the park behind the clinic waving gently from side to side in the breeze. It looks like the rain has stopped.

The first plastic phial of blood, Mickey's blood, clatters into the silver foil tray as Sharon snaps it off the green rubber tube leading from the needle stuck in the thick blue vein on his right arm just at the elbow. He glances down at the phial of red, arterial blood, his blood lying in the foil tray.

'You've got good veins here,' she'd said, as she'd tightened the blue rubber tourniquet around his upper arm, his short-sleeved, twin-pocketed, checked shirt pushed up to his shoulder.

Dark-haired, snubby nose, average-looking but then – there's something in the broadness, the turn of his shoulders. He can't be much more than thirty, Sharon thinks.

He looks young and he looks anxious.

She just wants to give him a big hug.

'Just a couple more to do,' she says. 'I'm going to loosen the tourniquet off a bit.'

He watches as his blood oozes millimetre by millimetre into another plastic phial. With unconscious expertise Sharon quickly snaps the phial off and clips an empty one on.

'Do you want me to test for Hep C and syphilis too?'

Mickey knows he doesn't have syphilis but he says, 'Aye, go on then.'

Another phial fills with blood. Then she slides the needle out from under his skin and holds a cotton wool ball over the ruby droplet on his white forearm.

'Press hard.' Then, 'Are you allergic to Elastoplast?'

He shakes his head and she sticks a small circular plaster onto his arm.

'Could you manage a urine sample, d'you think?'

Sharon's holding out a small clear plastic jar with a white sticky label on it.

He frowns.

It's Monday morning.

He's a bit hungover, the stale taste of last night's cider still in his mouth.

'I'll get you a glass of water,' she says.

He sits down on the plastic chair by the desk. Sharon's left the door open and he can hear her footsteps disappearing along the corridor.

Alone in the treatment room with its tatty posters he reads about the importance of hand hygiene and the dangers of needle-stick injury. One door of a freestanding office furniture cupboard in the corner hangs open. Plastic-wrapped packages containing dozens and dozens of pristine new plastic phials have spilled out onto the floor.

Sharon comes back in and hands him a plastic cup of cold water from the chiller in the waiting room. He gulps it down.

'There's a toilet across the corridor,' she says.

He doesn't bother to lock the door. Someone's stuck a YES sticker on the cistern. As he stands there, holding the plastic jar, willing himself to piss, he can hear the rattle of plastic as Sharon sticks labels with his date of birth onto the plastic phials of red arterial blood.

He's pissing now and the jar fills rapidly then overflows into the toilet bowl.

'Aw fuck!'

He's dribbled on his jeans.

He screws the white plastic lid onto the jar and places it carefully on the edge of the basin. Yellow drops glisten on the shiny clear plastic and, as he wipes the jar dry with a paper towel, he marvels at its warmth.

He washes his hands and stands there gazing at the face in the mirror that looks back at him. Then he opens the toilet door and hands the jar to Sharon.

He's used to this routine now: it doesn't bother him.

He doesn't worry about it – now.

Not like the first time he came to the clinic, one bleak, still half-drunk Monday morning; black stubble and black rings under his eyes.

The young doctor had brought his face very close as he looked at the little purple spot just below Mickey's cheekbone. Then he slid his swivel chair back across the shiny buffed vinyl floor, back to his computer.

'I think we should do some blood tests,' he'd said before explaining, 'The lab's very busy today. The nurse can do them now but the results won't be back till this afternoon.'

All that was five years ago. Mickey's had time, lots of time, since then to get used to this routine and procedures.

You can get used tae anything in time, he thinks.

Sharon's sitting at the desk in the examination room leafing through a three-inch-thick file. Mickey's perched on the edge of the plastic chair between the desk and the door.

On the dog-eared brown cardboard cover, his name and, below it in black marker pen, SO54982Z, his hospital number, used to guarantee the anonymity of patients attending the clinic.

'When was your last sexual contact, Mickey?'

'Um—'

Of course he remembers.

'And was that your partner or someone you'd just met?'

Mickey doesn't have a partner.

Not since Jonnie.

'Do you understand the legal implications of having sex with someone who's HIV negative?' asks fat, cheery Sharon with the red cat scratches up her arms.

Mickey looks at the floor.

Aw gie us a break! The legal implications of... love? Fuckin hell! I havenae got a scoobie about the legal implications of love – bound tae be loads of fuckin legal implications for a man in ma position but. Na – I couldnae really say that in my heart I like grasp the legal implications of love.

'What are you doing today?'

'—are you going back to work?'

'Naw,' says Mickey, 'I'm no goin' back tae work.'

There isnae any work in Drumkirk – no for folk like him.

Naw.

He's not going back to work: in the afternoon he's going to take the bus to the terminus where the bungalows and the city end in the weeds and rosebay willowherb and red foxgloves and walk Tyke out along the path till he gets up to the reservoir. He's going to sit at the edge of the water and throw the old chewed and slimy-with-dog-saliva green tennis ball. Tyke'll bring the ball back and drop it at his feet and look up at him expectantly. And he'll think this is where it all began.

the journey of the pipes

The circular Elastoplast Sharon stuck on the soft skin on the inside of his forearm that morning is hanging half off now. Mickey scrunches it into a little ball and pings it into the metal bin next to the telly. Tyke's ears prick up and he lifts his shaggy head.

Home: level zero of the high flats in Drumkirk. At least being on the ground floor I dinnae have to use the lift wi' its fag ends and smell of piss. I jist have tae enter the numbers 3-5-7-9 on the tarnished metal keypad. Then the lock buzzes and I shove open the reinforced glass and steel door.

He lies there on the faded and frayed blue sofa, staring at the ceiling as darkness settles over the city, Tyke dozing at his feet. The sirens and shouts and sounds of night in the city streets as he reaches down to stroke the dog's thick coat.

The sitting room door's open and from the cramped kitchen of the flat, with its blooms of black mould in the corners of the ceiling, he can hear the drip drip drip of the leaky mixer tap. He's been onto the housing association to fix it but that was six months ago and nothing's happened. The tap's still dripping.

d
rip

after

d
rip

af
ter
glossy
swelling
drip

How many gallons have dripped away? He wonders sometimes.

In the cupboard below the sink, among the mouse droppings and empty bottles, there's a plastic bag of sprouty potatoes and a polystyrene tray containing a few wizened carrots and some limp broccoli with a yellow *Reduced to 17p* sticker. On the lower shelf, behind the empty carrier bags and the pile of Vote Yes For an Independent Scotland leaflets, the Value cream cleaner and the solidified lump of black shoe polish, the water rises through ¾-inch-bore copper pipes punched through the damp chipboard shelves of the sink unit.

From the kitchen the pipes run beneath the concrete floor of the early 1970s towerblock to join the watermain at a steel plate embossed with a W set in the paving slabs outside Mickey's bedroom window.

From there the water surges through bright blue plastic pipes installed a little over a year ago. Behind temporary traffic lights and plastic barriers workmen with pneumatic drills broke through first tarmac and then cobbles to expose the red, stony soil the city was built on.

The Victorian pipes had corroded from the inside and water was leaking away into the ground. The cast iron mains were cracked and choked, the city's arteries clogged with a century and half's build-up of rusty iron sludge.

Somewhere near Milngavie the one-foot-diameter pipes reach open countryside where water splashes into the southern end of Mugdock storage reservoir from a mossy stone aqueduct built by Victorian navvies.

To the north, eighty tunnels and two-and-twenty aqueducts channel the waters south from Loch Katrine; over many miles of birch trees and bracken and sheep-grazed fields. Stone aqueducts so well engineered the water supply is fed by gravity alone over the two dozen miles from Loch Katrine where alders and rowans fringe the rocky shore.

Through cross-connectors and trunk mains and valve junctions on engineers' plans, the blue plastic pipes and tunnels and stone aqueducts spread out beneath the city streets and on through the suburbs and out across the countryside to the edge of the mountains; like capillaries and veins and arteries under the skin.

Has the dripping tap in his kitchen caused Loch Katrine to drop half a tenth of a hundredth of a millimetre over the years? Mickey wonders.

He once took the journey of the pipes from the dripping tap.

That was how it all started.

One overcast June day four years ago.

Exploring…

Stifled…

Desperate to escape the city with its sirens and threatening overcast of violence and lust.

§

He'd been in the huddle of people crowded round the *Reduced* shelf of the chiller cabinet in the Morrisons on the corner of the Crow Road, trying to see the prices on the yellow stickers on plastic packs of mince, paper bags of mini beef pasties, tubs of cottage cheese and grey-looking lamb chops.

The old guy in the woolly hat was there of course.

He must live in the supermarket.

He's there every time Mickey goes in, standing chatting to the staff as they fill the shelves with bags of wild rocket and spinach, cartons of cherry tomatoes and cellophane packets of beansprouts. He overheard him asking the woman stacking the shelves in aisle one with red-stickered *Two for £5* ready meals, what time she finished at. Then he felt guilty, silently chastised himself, thinking of the old man's cold, empty flat, his loneliness showing through in the endless, empty days spent pacing the aisles of the supermarket.

When they sat in rows in school on plastic chairs at metal-framed desks with Formica tops and looked at books, the pages were full of pictures of what people did. Pictures of firemen, postmen, dustbin men, nurses, bus drivers, teachers and airline pilots. There was a sense back then the children could be anything they wanted. No pictures in the books of childhood of people jostling round a chiller cabinet in a supermarket aisle scrabbling to buy yellow-stickered, reduced-to-clear food items.

MICKEY: I'm one o' the lucky ones but. I know I am. I know that fine. 'Your HIV's very stable,' ma doctor at the clinic told me last week. My GP's the same: CD4 count in the low hundreds – below average but nothing tae worry about, she says. My life's been saved by twenty-first-century medical science. The meds and the NHS and all that wis there for me when I needed it. But sometimes I get tae thinkin' like whit's the fuckin point? WHAT IS THE FUCKIN POINT? It all seems kindae lacking in meaning sometimes.

I mean – whit am I on the fuckin planet for but?

Tae lie in my bed wanking and fartin' till three o'clock in the fuckin afternoon?

I dinnae think so.

Some mornings jist in case the DSS are watchin' like, I'll get up early and open the blinds and then go back tae bed.

Ha ha ha!

That's a joke – right?

OK, so I'll get up then. Whit am I gaunny dae like? Trail round the charity shops for tae get some crap tae resell on eBay, get a few quid in ma PayPal account. I'll be fuckin minted then like, aye right – then stay up all night talkin' tae folk in America and makin' non-friends on fuckin shite Facebook. Fuckin pointless but! Whit the fuck am I daein' with my life that I'm taking fuckin six tablets a day to keep alive? Maybe I should jist have a wank in the bath wi' a polybag over ma heid and fuckin be done wi' it. That's what I think – sometimes – in the long afternoons on the dole as the rain pours down on Drumkirk.

Outside the supermarket, he waited at the bus stop in Great Western Road. It was a hot day in the city and a balding long-haired man in filthy combat trousers and a worn leather jacket pedalled slowly by on a racing bike.

Across the street he watched a bare-chested, young guy with tattoos and white trainers and an inch of stripey boxer shorts visible above the waistband of his jeans, being dragged along the pavement by a huge Alsatian on a chain lead.

MICKEY: Scottish people go fuckin mental when the temperature rises – it's like the weather triggers something and they go back in time tae when Scotland wis near the equator and there were palm trees in Motherwell and fuckin dinosaurs in Fife.

Aw fuck. The bus pass routine: hold yer national entitlement card in front of Perspex screen protecting driver. It saves a fuckin fortune in bus fares – be stuck in the flat all day without it but never run for the bus mind. You're supposed tae be disabled but. That's why I've got a bus pass – right? The driver's looking at me. He's thinkin' I've seen him oot walking his dug. He's no disabled. He's no in a wheelchair. How come he's got a bus pass? Now walk slowly upstairs and sit down in the front seats where you used tae sit tae drive the bus when you were a kid. Sunlight shining on faded fabric seats. Dust specks floating in the air. Then get up again and open all the windows on the empty top deck of the bus.

The sun was beating off the pavements in Douglas Street in the centre of Milngavie when he stepped down from the bus in a haze of hot diesel exhaust and hissing air brakes. He stood, watching as the bus pulled away and, orange indicators flashing, turned right into Campbell Avenue.

He looked around at the 1930s bungalows, each one white-painted and well maintained, the gardens with lawns cut and hedges trimmed. A blue hydrangea flowered on a striped lawn among lazily swaying clumps of pampas grass.

Only three miles but it was a long, long way from the dandelions and knee-high grass littered with crisp packets, polystyrene fast-food cartons, Coke cans, empty torpedoes of cider and dirty plastic syringes choking the abandoned front gardens of Drumkirk.

He wandered along Craigdhu Road.

A woman walking a Golden Retriever passed him. 'Good morning!'

He smiled back at her.

Nae Staffies and Rottweilers and guys wi' biro tattoos here then.

Craigdhu Road broadened out into a wide semi-pedestrianised street. He walked past RS McColls, the British Heart Foundation shop and Costa Coffee. None of the shop windows were boarded up. And there was a Greggs. Mickey hadn't eaten that day and he headed straight for the shop with its inviting smell of lentil soup and pastry.

A black Labrador-like dog with strange orange highlights in its thick, curly coat was tied to a park bench outside Greggs. The dog watched him disappear through the glass doors of the baker's. The dog remained in a sitting position for about sixty seconds then its front legs slid slowly forward and it lay down, head resting flat on the pavement, staring at the door of the shop.

Five minutes later the dog wagged its tail as Mickey reappeared clutching a paper cup of soup and a steak slice and a sausage roll in a white paper bag already turning translucent with yellow grease. He sat down on the bench and tore a corner of pastry off the steak slice and dropped it at the dog's paws.

A grey-haired man in walking boots and a red North Face T-shirt came across and made a fuss of the dog. It rolled on its back, wriggling and wagging its tail.

'What kindae dog is he, pal?' asked Mickey through a mouthful of sausage roll.

'Labrador crossed with a poodle,'

The man rubbed the dog's tummy.

'Great dog,'said Mickey and he watched as the man picked up a large, heavy-looking rucksack and a pair of walking poles and, with the dog following at his heel, walked away, past the bench where Mickey was sitting.

Mickey looked round. Behind him a paved path led into the trees and above his head, spanning the gap between the brick buildings, was a steel archway. He twisted his head round to read the words on it.

When he'd finished licking the last flakes of puff pastry from his fingers, he got up from the bench and stepped through the archway.

And then everything was different.

Tuesday

the fifteen point question

'I'm training to be a high priestess of Avalon,' she'd announced at their first meeting in the basement office down the stone steps in Bath Street, where a never-ending stream of baseball boots, high heels, Doc Martens and Uggs tramped past the gaps between the black-painted railings. Forty-five-ish, Australian and blonde, the advocacy worker and benefits adviser at Face West rejoiced in the name of Carmen d'Apostolini.

'You daein' anything nice at the weekend?' he'd asked innocently enough, making conversation while they washed the coffee cups in the downstairs kitchen.

'I'm going to Glastonbury Tor – I've just about completed my first spiral of training—'

She chattered on but Mickey wasn't listening anymore. All he could see in his head was Carmen the white witch in flowing white robes with her coven dancing naked around a circle of standing stones.

§

GETTING TO YOUR WORK CAPABILITY ASSESSMENT

0803: Leave home. Walk 2 minutes east on Drumkirk Road.
0805: Wait at bus stop opposite John Paul II High School.
0814: Take service number 60. Provider: First Glasgow.
0843: Arrive opposite James Watt Street on Argyle Street. Walk 2 minutes.
0845: Arrive Corunna House.

The letter in a brown envelope that had dropped through the brushed-steel flap onto the doormat two weeks before had included a map and precise instructions as to how to get from his flat to Corunna House.

The appointment is for the seriously contrived time of 8.50 am. Carmen says it's deliberate: to see if he can get out of bed in the morning and to check he really is nauseous after taking his meds.

It's a bright, cold, sunny day and he's meeting Carmen outside a brutalist-style office block of black glass windows in Cadogan Street. Above the high buildings, pewtery clouds move swiftly across the sky and the wind sweeps the litter up and swirls it around the street.

The travel information turns out to be accurate to the minute and as scheduled he arrives at the bus stop opposite Corunna House at 0841 precisely and as instructed walks for two minutes to the nearby pedestrian crossing.

He hasn't shaved for a few days and he walks slowly along the pavement.

His stomach churns.

He woke drenched in sweat at 4 am.

'Are the night sweats the virus or like stress?' he'd asked his GP.

'Who knows?' she'd answered, chewing the top of her GlaxoSmithKline biro.

Fuckin shite day, he thinks, as he sits down on a bench outside Corunna House. The street is a busy thoroughfare and he watches as two women in dark-coloured, work-type clothes enter the building.

He bites his thumbnail. Carmen's a couple of minutes late now. He's hoping she hasn't forgotten or had a crisis with one of her kids or the poodle. But no, bang on 0847 he spots her stomping along the busy street.

They go straight into the building.

A security guard stands, arms folded, in the foyer of the '70s office block. ATOSA, the French multinational contracted by the Department of Social Security to carry out work capability assessments on people claiming health-related benefits, has been the target of several demonstrations and activists from RATBAG have twice attempted to storm the building with a giant inflatable plastic rat.

'Have you got your appointment letter there?' asks a second security guard from behind a perspex screen, 'I'll need to see some photographic proof of identification too please.'

Mickey slides his bus pass under the security screen.

Maybe some folk try to send a stand-in in a wheelchair to their assessment.

'"Disabled" is a relative term, Michael.'

He can hear Carmen's voice in his head: 'People living with HIV and cancer count as disabled from the moment of diagnosis – that's not just me talking – that's according to the terms of the Equality Act 2010 – being disabled isn't like being Oscar Pistorius and competing in the Paralympics. A disability you can't see can be just as restrictive and isolating as being stuck in a wheelchair.'

The security guard photocopies his bus pass. 'First door on the left, mate,' he says.

Mickey's careful to walk slowly along the neon-lit corridor to the orange-carpeted waiting room lined with plastic chairs. He's seen stuff on RATBAG's Facebook page about ATOSA medical assessors secretly videoing 'disabled' people on their way to assessments.

A middle-aged woman and a young couple are sitting in the waiting room. They don't appear any more 'disabled' than Mickey. After he's been waiting ten minutes a grey-haired woman with a walking stick enters the room and sits down heavily on one of the seats nearest the door.

The waiting room is decorated with notices about what to expect at your ATOSA medical assessment and the right of ATOSA employees to work free of the threat of harassment and violence.

He can hear Carmen's voice in his head again. 'It's the stigmatising attitudes of society and people's fear of a chronic, life-threatening, sexually transmitted medical condition that makes HIV disabling.'

A woman in a white coat with her hair tied back puts her head round the door.

'Desiree Campbell,' she calls and the young couple get anxiously to their feet.

After another five minutes it's Mickey's turn.

The medical assessor is a cheerful, red-headed, middle-aged Irishwoman in a blue nurse's uniform who ushers him and Carmen (scowling fiercely) into a small room with a desk, three chairs, a set of scales and a computer.

The medical assessor sits down at the computer and, without looking at Mickey, explains she is a qualified nurse.

'How did you find getting here today?' she asks conversationally.

'I followed the instructions on the letter yous sent me.'

The nurse starts typing on her keyboard.

Mickey glances at Carmen.

'I find going to the doctor stressful and I need tae have someone wi' me,' he explains.

Carmen nods emphatically.

A series of questions follow. Mickey sits slumped in his chair, head down, staring at his feet. The nurse types very quickly and hardly looks at him or Carmen who sits, like a smouldering antipodean volcano, by Mickey's side.

'Who does the shopping in your house?'

Mickey answers to the effect he does the shopping on days when he feels OK, Carmen nodding approvingly at the phrase 'fluctuating medical condition.'

'Do you live on your own?

'Yes.'

'Do you have a partner?'

'No.'

Mickey doesn't have a partner.

Not since Jonnie.

'Do you have any pets?'

Carmen's warned him not to mention Tyke – it's none of their business, she says.

And he thinks, *Fuckin right! Whit the fuck dae the employees of a French multinational know about whit it's like trying to survive HIV? Fuck all, but.*

'Do you watch EastEnders on TV?'

He hesitates. 'I dinnae like soap operas and if I try tae watch a film on TV I jist end up falling asleep on the sofa.'

This (truthful) admission prompts a renewed outbreak of furious clacking on the keyboard and clicking with the mouse.

Then something freezes on the screen and there is silence in the room for a good five minutes while the nurse tries to fix whatever the glitch is.

'Do you suffer from urinary incontinence?' she asks at last.

'Well I have tae pee a lot and I'm up like three times in the night. My GP says it's a side effect of ma meds – I've got high cholesterol see—'

Carmen interrupts him.

'It's a very common side effect of antiretroviral drugs,' she says impatiently.

The nurse doesn't type anything at all.

Good sign or bad, wonders Mickey.

'How's your walking?' continues the nurse.

'Normal,' answers Mickey.

But Carmen interrupts again.

'Don't forget, Michael – you get a very sore anus after bouts of diarrhoea and that can make walking very uncomfortable for you.'

When he got his first letter from ATOSA, Carmen had told him, 'I used to work for the DSS.'

And she went on to describe the lines of civil servants sat at desks in rows of low office blocks beside the dual carriageway, scoring benefit claims on a points system according to how claimants answered certain questions.

'I used to work for the DSS, Michael – you score 14 out of 30, you get zilch, mate,' she'd explained. 'But you score 15 out of 30 and you get to keep your benefits.'

A drop of sweat runs down Mickey's back. He stares at the wall. It's true, he does get diarrhoea a lot but he doesn't want to sit in this stuffy little room and talk about it with a total stranger and a charity worker. 'The doctor I see at the clinic disnae know if it's the virus causes the diarrhoea. He thinks it might a side effect of the medication I'm on.'

Then Mickey stares straight ahead and says what Carmen has told him to say.

The fifteen point question.

'In the – er – morning and after eating I suffer from sudden and unpredictable bouts of diarrhoea and have tae get tae the toilet in a hurry.' Mickey looks down at the floor. 'I dinnae always make it and – when that happens I have tae change my clothes and have a shower and it all leaves me feeling exhausted but…'

His voice tails off.

Still typing furiously on the keyboard of her PC and without looking away from the screen, the nurse asks, 'Do you use incontinence pads?'

She stops typing.

Mickey looks straight at the medical assessor as he says quietly, 'I'm a gay man. I'm no going tae use fuckin incontinence pads.'

A tense silence descends on the room. He can hear the traffic revving up outside on Cadogan Street and the bleeping of the pedestrian crossing outside the ATOSA office.

'OK then,' says the nurse, 'so your viral load's undetectable at below 40 – what medication are you on just now?'

Mickey's anticipated this question. The letter instructing him to attend the work capability assessment said to bring any medication he was taking with him.

He picks up his scruffy Karrimor rucksack from the green, carpet-tiled floor, tips it upside down and empties onto the desk six months' supply of meds given him the day before by the pharmacist with the short, black, bobbed hair at the clinic.

The orange and aquamarine cardboard boxes of Nevirapine and the small white plastic containers of Tenofovir spill across the desk where the nurse sits. There are half a dozen yellow packets of Abacavir and he remembered to include the foil-wrapped strips of Simvastatin too.

The nurse stares at the pile of medication on the desk in front of her then randomly picks up one of the boxes of tablets and writes down the name and dosage of the drug.

Tipping the rucksack full of meds out onto the desk had been Zelda's idea. Subconsciously the heap of boxes of pills and tablets spilling across the desk conveys the idea of a very sick person. Zelda, past mistress of the flamboyant gesture that she was, had said, 'My mother used to act in amateur traumatics and a wee bit of theatre always helps, dear,' as they sat one overcast afternoon waiting for Cash in the Attic to start.

MICKEY: I've got this memory but, from when I wis a kid. I got hame from school one day, done the usual stuff, watched TV. It wis fishfingers and homemade chips for tea. After tea I told ma mum – my throat's sair, I said. In the morning when I woke up in my kiddie's bedroom wi' the racing cars on the curtains, ma tonsils were all swollen like and ma mum said I could stay aff school for a couple o' days. Then she went off tae her work... I loved those days but – cosy under a tartan travel rug on the sofa watchin' Pebble Mill at One. And sometimes I think tae mysel' in the afternoons sitting in ma flat, I remember whit it wis like being a kid and no having tae go tae school. And then I think that's whit I'm like about work. Some folk love their work, jist like some kids loved school. But that's no me like. Think I missed oot somewhere. I've niver had a real job like – just fuckin exploitation at Poundland for six months then back on the dole. It's no I'm lazy and wantin' tae sponge off other folk aw the time. It's jist I've been living like this for so long – I cannae really imagine what it'd be like no tae be on benefits. I dunno in ma heart if I can stand on ma ain two feet like other folk seem tae manage. I know I've got the skills tae be independent. I mean – fuckin hell! – look at some o' the folk that manage to hold down a job but.

Maybe I jist need to take that leap in the dark.
Jump off that cliff.
But right now?
Tae be honest I'm scared as fuck.
Some mornings I wake up and I'm like 60-40 No I cannae

– Yes I can. On good days it's mair like 50-50.

But like if the virus has taught me one thing it's that I dinnae have to do nothing I dinnae want tae.

Silence fills the room. The nurse has stopped typing on her keyboard.

'OK, that's you,' she announces suddenly. 'You'll get a letter in four to six weeks' time informing you as to the outcome of today's assessment,' looking away from the computer at last as she stands up and ushers him and Carmen out the door.

the city of the stare

As John Paul O'Malley walked slowly along the path and over the frost-covered lawns and out the iron gates of the Murray Royal Psychiatric Hospital there was only one thing on his mind: Mickey Bell.

The hospital stood in wooded grounds on the east bank of the River Tay at the foot of Kinnoul Hill. Half a mile westward the river flowed sluggishly past the Georgian tenements in the middle of Perth before winding its way by the playing fields and the railway and the council houses of North Inch.

When the winter ice begins to melt in the big snowbowl, north-facing corrie high on Ben Lui, it swells the waters of the Fillan and the Dochart and they pour in brown spate beneath the oaks and rowans, past Auchessan and Luib before emptying into Loch Tay. Then fifteen miles east at Kenmore, at the outflow of the long, narrow loch, the River Tay rushes out under the silver birches.

On the morning of the 12th February 1814 the citizens of Perth awoke to the sight of icefloes blocking the arches of Smeaton's Bridge. The water level rose rapidly behind the dam of ice and the mighty Tay burst its banks and flooded the newly built tenements along the riverbank.

The Great Inundation of Perth, they called it.

Two hundred years pass, the climate changes, the planet heats as centuries of dark, soot-rimmed chimneys reek smoke and now the river floods once in every decade.

Unlike most of their neighbours, Jonnie's mum had kept up the payments on her contents. When the Tay burst its banks and the council houses by the playing fields at North Inch flooded and in due course, the insurance company's cheque arrived, she was able to buy a new white velvet-effect sofa as well as having some money left over for Jonnie who lived on jobseekers' allowance.

She helped Jonnie out from her sickness benefit money too. She'd found the lump herself one morning as she lay in the bath while the trailing leaves of the spider plant brushed against her face and the unfrosted upper section of the window steamed up. The lump had grown in the same cavity of her body where a quarter of a century earlier the baby John Paul had floated.

A sympathetic female locum GP sent her for a scan and marked her letter to the hospital 'urgent'. When she went back for the results of the scan one of the nurses had taken her aside. 'Can you wait here please?' she'd said, 'The consultant wants a word.'

Jonnie, in his mid-twenties, still living at home and devoted to his mum, took the news badly: chemotherapy might slow the progress of the disease but not reverse it.

She'd always doted on her youngest son. Indulged him when she came home early from her cleaning job at the college to find ten-year-old Jonnie sat at her dressing table, plastered in Boots number 7 lipstick and trying on her earrings.

Sometimes, though, she thinks meeting fifteen-year-old Jonnie wearing panstick, rouge and eyeliner at 11 am one Saturday morning in the St John's Centre was a factor in Sean, her partner of five years', subsequent decision to leave her to go back to his family in Belfast.

In the late afternoon, on the days she felt sick from the hospital treatment, in the bedroom with the flowery curtains pulled tightly shut and the wallpaper border peeling away at the edges, Jonnie would curl up on the bed and put his arms around his Mum as outside frost formed glistening white cobwebs on the streets of Perth.

§

It was Friday night in Glasgow. The city of the stare, a grey-haired man once wrote and it was a stare in Glasgow on a Friday night that changed everything for Mickey.

The Waterloo Bar on the corner of Argyle Street early on a Friday evening: the pub was empty, just the barman all pointy shoes and sharp angles and slim-fit shirt; baldy-heided, grey-haired wee Harry in his anorak sipping a pint of heavy at the end of the bar; and the retired Co-op windowdresser with the bad wig reading the *Evening Times*.

Jonnie was sitting on one of the sofas at the back of the Waterloo, looking at his phone, spinning out a pint of cider till it was time to catch the Megabus back to Perth, when Mickey Bell walked into the bar.

Jonnie stared as Mickey threw his hood back and shook the Glasgow rain from his jacket. He watched Mickey chat to the barman, before wandering over to waste a couple of pound coins in the puggy beside the sofa where Jonnie was sitting.

Stars lit up. A line of three lemons whirred round then froze. Mickey slid his second pound coin into the slot. The lights flashed again and then shone brightly. Three red slices of watermelon appeared in the window:

BAR – BAR – BAR
Three red hearts flashed!
BAR – BAR – BAR

He tapped the yellow nudge button – once – twice – then bells began to ring accompanied by electronic fanfares as the fruit machine spat out twenty-five quid.

Mickey squatted down and scooped the warm pound coins into his pocket. Jonnie stared at the gap between Mickey's hoodie and his jeans where his pants and the top of his arse crack were showing.

'Your luck's in – gaunny buy me a pint, handsome?' Jonnie camped it up from the sofa next to the puggy.

Mickey grinned. 'Pint of cider?'

'Aw cheers, doll.'

He'd clocked the camp young guy on the sofa when he was at the bar: short, dyed-blond hair, round black stud earrings, clear skin, nice-looking; even in the dimly lit Waterloo Bar Mickey could see the eyeliner.

From the off Mickey sensed –

Naw –

Who was he kidding?

He knew Jonnie was trouble.

Knew it from the first night they'd lain together on the mattress on the concrete bedroom floor in Mickey's flat.

Knew it from the way Jonnie clung to him in the night at 4 am, that darkest hour when you hear your heart pounding in the darkness. The time babies are born and people at the end of life slip away into the arms of death's final cold embrace.

Knew it from the way Jonnie blurted out, 'I love you.'

In the dark at 6.30 am just as the first faint light of dawn glimmered in the eastern sky and the block of flats slowly stirred to life and a new day. A door banged somewhere, footsteps walked across the ceiling, a distant flush of a cistern, the revving of a bus in the street outside, first birdsong.

'D'you like me being around?' Jonnie had asked him.

When Mickey hesitated, he said quickly, 'I was just thinking out loud, like.'

And yes for a month or two or three he had liked being with someone. He didn't miss sitting on his own at the bar in the Waterloo or lurking in the shrubbery among the gravestones in the overgrown cemetery where the broken stone angels' wings lay among the weeds and the purple pods of Himalayan balsam popped in the warm March sunshine.

Zelda had said, 'I think maybe he's got issues, dear.' Then, with a frown, 'A wee bittie unstable – low self-esteem, lack of self-confidence, that kind of thing – your Aunty's seen it all before, believe me.'

It suited Mickey though: for a while. But looking back with the clarity of the passing of time, like water over the stones on the bed of a Highland burn, he'd realised Jonnie was desperately clinging on, hoping he'd be the one.

The spring sunshine warmed the pavement slabs in West Nile Street. As they turned the corner into Killermont Street they passed a wee Glasgow drunk sat on a bench. He wore black Doc Martens, a cheap grey polo shirt, bleached jeans and a leather jacket.

A can of Special Brew sat on the bench beside him. His face was crumpled and lined, his skin the same yellow as his nicotine-stained fingers. He had a jaundice suntan all the months of the year. And as Mickey and Jonnie walked past he clapped his hands together in applause and raised the can of lager in a toast.

The corrugated brown concrete edifice of the Buchanan Galleries loomed along one side of the street. In the window of John Lewis, a girl with long blond hair, bright red lipstick and jeans with a spangly belt, was crouching down tying the shoe laces of a grey-faced mannequin dressed in tan chinos and a Ben Sherman shirt. The mannequin's stylised grey facial features stared blankly back at Mickey through quarter-inch-thick plate glass.

In the next window six hand-knotted Persian rugs hung symmetrically on a white background. Small green price tags were suspended below them: one price printed in black with a line scored through it and a new lower price £2,495 immediately below in bright signal red. In another window two stripy green and white deckchairs sat side by side.

They watched as the girl in the window knotted a cashmere sweater around the grey-faced mannequin's neck.

'I used tae love the Scalextrics in the window of Goldbergs in Sauchiehall Street but,' Mickey said. 'When I was a wee boy I spent hours watching the cars whizzing round and round.'

Mickey knew.

Of course Mickey knew.

The steel lift doors slid apart and they walked out onto the second floor of the Buchanan Galleries. Gleaming white floor tiles swept across to the steel rail and waist-high glass screen that curved around the fifty-foot drop to the atrium below. Jonnie shrank back against the magnolia-painted wall beside the lift doors. He began to shake, walking bent double. Passing shoppers pushing buggies laden with carrier bags cast curious glances as he trembled with vertigo, seeming to want to cling on to the glossy floor tiles.

'I'm funny about places like this,' he whispered to Mickey, drops of sweat glistening on his brow.

They ran across the road, dodging between scruffy black cabs and cut through a gap in the glass perimeter wall of the bus station with its illuminated advertising hoardings.

A man in blue swim-shorts with a perfect torso and neatly trimmed stubble ran hand in hand with a bikini-clad blond across a sandy beach. Beckham lay back in his Emporio Armani white underpants.

They reached Stance 52.

Yellow LED display: Service *M9 Perth*.

'Aw, he's awright but.'

'Who?'

'Him over there—' said Mickey.

A twenty-five-ish college boy type, all skinny jeans, Converse baseball boots and French Connection checked shirt, his blond-red hair fringing freckled skin and blue eyes, was getting off the Airport bus.

'Don't you be getting any ideas – I'll fuckin jab him if he so much as looks at you.'

Mickey saw the dark blank look on Jonnie's face. He saw the crazy jealousy in his eyes. Saw the way his hands gripped the strap of the messenger bag, twisting it round and round his wrist and in his stomach he felt a first twinging of anxiety.

Diesel fumes filled the air. Mickey breathed in particulates of nitrogen oxide as the doors of the Megabus hissed shut and it pulled out of Stance 52. Through a cloud of blue exhaust he saw Jonnie's crazy, jealous face pressed against the grimy, dusty, pockmarked-with-raindrops back window of the bus.

So he knew.

Mickey knew from the start.

And then there was religion, Buddhism to be precise. The next time they met, after the first time in the Waterloo, Jonnie talked a lot about the Temple.

'What temple?' Mickey'd asked, looking surprised.

Jonnie hesitated.

'It's why I'm here in Glasgow – to dae my mindfulness.'

He explained as they sat on a low wall in George Square eating chips with curry sauce from a polystyrene tray.

Then he unzipped his black canvas messenger bag: inside

were white robes edged with bright orange. Jonnie was the first and, come to think of it, the only psychotic gay Buddhist Mickey had ever met in Glasgow.

He'd been co-opted into Buddhism one January afternoon in Sauchiehall Street in the classic way recruiters for religion operate on the city streets. Mickey remembered the student types in glasses and geeky clothes, always a boy and a girl who used to stand on the steps of the Victorian building between Poundland and Pizza Hut, the one with the white paint peeling away from its façade and the tarnished brass plate on the door.

The steps raised the recruiters and their clipboards just above the height of the passing shoppers.

'Would you like to take part in a survey?' they'd ask, as Mickey stomped past, head down avoiding their gaze, as the buses and cars waited for the lights at the junction of St Vincent Street and George Square.

Jonnie, with his craving for any kind of human attention from any kind of person, was exactly what the Buddhists were looking for. He'd filled in the form, signed up, read the book, bought the T-shirt.

But then, if you had to have a religion, Buddhism's a no bad one with its creed of peace and not harming other people. Mickey and Zelda had once whiled away a long Tuesday afternoon on the dole, between the One O'Clock News and the start of Jeremy Kyle, with a debate about whether a Buddhist would kill a midge.

Zelda's posh friend Lesbian George had been a Buddhist for a while. George wasn't her real name and she wasn't a lesbian but Zelda had given her a camp name after seeing a photo of her sunbathing on a rock in Greece.

'She's got muscles like a wrestler,' Zelda had said. 'We'll call her George the Lesbian.'

George had given Zelda a detailed account of the weekend retreat she'd been to at Balquhidder. The taxi dropping her off at the white wooden gates of Dhanakosa as darkness fell on Loch Voil, the prayer flags fluttering in the wind, the timber meditation bothies on the hillside among the pine trees.

She hadn't lasted long as a Buddhist though, finding the vegan diet of chickpeas, brown rice, tofu and kidney beans seriously indigestible or as Zelda, who detested anything vegetarian let alone vegan, quipped, 'Who put the pulse in repulsive?'

It turned out the Buddhist Centre was just a few streets away from Zelda's flat in Govanhill. A good Buddhist has to spread the word: in the office of the Buddhist Centre there were dozens of cardboard boxes full of glossy softbacks with titles like *Change Your Mind, Principles of Buddhism* and *What is the Dharma?* All priced £8.99.

Jonnie and a girl he was friendly with would take a rucksack full of books to sell on a Saturday afternoon beside Donald Dewar's statue outside the Buchanan Galleries. If they got lucky and managed to sell a few copies they'd risk bad karma and spend the proceeds in the Horseshoe Bar.

Jonnie stayed the weekend, phoning or Facetiming his mum every second moment of the day, it seemed to Mickey, even texting her to say goodnight.

Sitting in the grey, harling-clad council house that backed onto the playing fields by the river in Perth she'd stub out a lipstick-ringed cigarette in the souvenir from Lanzarote ashtray. As she reached for the phone on the glass-topped coffee table the lump in her lower abdomen pressed gently but insistently against her pink nylon dressing gown.

'John? Where are you, son?'

Jonnie lay on the mattress, the duvet pulled up to his waist, the red pink of his nipples against the black stubble where he shaved his chest.

'Wi' ma pal in Glasgow.'

Phone pressed to his ear, he stretched across and kissed Mickey. His long girlish eyelashes wasted on a boy. Jonnie ran his fingers down Mickey's chest wall. Feeling his ribs, brushing the tips of his fingers lightly over the brown circular scar that stood out like a burn on his white skin.

'Fine—,'

'Aye.'

'No, I told you—,'

'He's not working just now. '

Mickey could tell from the one-sided conversation Jonnie had told his Mum all about him; guessed that to Jonnie his relationship with Mickey was far from casual.

'—Love you too.'

Jonnie put his phone down and turned his face to the wall. The muffled thump thump thump of music from the students upstairs filled the silence in the room.

Jonnie had told him how sometimes he would curl up on the bed with his arms around his mum, to eke out time even as the grains of sand emptied away through the narrow neck of the hourglass. As he spoke, the tears welled up, glistening in Jonnie's brown eyes.

The Sunday morning was grey and damp, the tops of the high flats hidden in the mist when Mickey went out to the shop with the steel shutters at the end of the road. When he got back Jonnie was sitting on the edge of the bed. Instead of putting on his usual skinny jeans and red hoodie, he pulled a white shirt edged with orange over his head, then wrapped a tablecloth-sized length of white cotton around his waist and tied it in place with an orange sash. Brown leather sandals on his bare feet completed the outfit.

Two strings of red sandalwood prayer beads hung around his neck and a fabric pouch containing his offerings for the Lama dangled from his left wrist.

'Gie us a twirl,' said Mickey from the sofa. 'You look quite pretty in yer robes, but.'

'Hey! Listen,' Jonnie said, 'one time I was on a retreat at Samy Ling and one of the other novice monks was really cute—'

Mickey coughed. 'I didnae hear you say that.'

But Jonnie continued, 'You were supposed to be celibate – it didn't work – after four days I started havin' wet dreams every single night.'

Mickey laughed. He picked up a cushion off the sofa and threw it at Jonnie. He liked the idea of just black boxer shorts and Jonnie's bare, hairy legs under the robes but apart from that the outfit didn't do much for him. In fact the apparition standing in his front room on a grey, overcast, slightly hungover Sunday morning just looked bizarre.

When Jonnie went for a piss, leaving the black velvet pouch containing his offerings for the Lama on the table, Mickey loosened the drawstring and slipped a strawberry-milkshake-flavoured condom in a shiny foil wrapper inside.

That should liven things up at the temple, thought Mickey, as he stood at the window watching Jonnie, resplendent in his white and orange robes, beads clattering as he walked across the car park outside the flats. At the corner by the bus stop, Jonnie turned and waved, the black velvet pouch flapping on his wrist as a grey drizzle of rain started to fall.

§

viral load: a term used to describe the amount of HIV in one millilitre of blood

CD4 count: a blood test to measure the relative health of the immune system – in a healthy adult CD4 cell count is in thc range 600-1500

nineteen seventy-four

September 1974: Gerald Ford is booed by crowds for pardoning ex-president Nixon. The Bay City Rollers are topping the charts with *Shangalang* and in his art deco office in St Andrew's House the secretary of state for Scotland, Mr Willie Ross, tips back in his chair, gazing out through the metal-framed windows at the spires and domes of the Edinburgh skyline. On his desk (unread) lie the Countryside Commission's plans for a 95-mile, long-distance footpath from Milngavie to Fort William.

giro bay

The stench of urine burns the back of his throat.

'Lift approaching the seventeenth floor—'

There is a whine and a rumble of cable motor then the lift shudders.

'Doors opening!'

The electronic voice announces.

Mickey steps out of the graffiti-smeared lift.

At the end of a corridor of bare breeze block walls he climbs a flight of concrete steps. His trainers crunch on little cubes of shattered glass. He reaches through a fist-sized hole in the wired security glass in a door at the top of the steps, turns the handle and steps out onto the roof of the high flats.

He walks across to the low wall that surrounds the flat roof and sits there, dangling his legs over the edge, looking down at the little dots on the tarmac pushing buggies towards the bus stop. Three hundred feet below is the wide expanse of muddy municipal grass in front of the high flats where he laid the aluminium poles and pegs out one hot July afternoon.

A fuckin Vango Storm Tempest – Ah couldnae believe it – I Googled it – as used by Reinhold fuckin Messner on Everest – it wis about ten years old but. I got it from the British Heart Foundation shop in Byers Road – some Granny must've priced it wrong. I pitched it and re-waterproofed it with Fabsil – £14.99 from Blacks – *cost me mair than the fuckin tent. It wis boiling hot that day and I like lay back in the sun in my white nylon Adidas football shorts, still tasting the glue-like smell of the Fabsil in my throat and waited for the flysheet tae dry, ignoring the wolf whistles from the two fourteen-year-old lassies on the balcony on the seventh floor.*

The surface of the roof is covered in a heavy duty roofing felt coated with tiny, smooth, rounded pieces of white gravel. An empty brown bottle of Buckfast stands in one corner among the torn pages of Razzle magazine: black suspenders and huge tits. A faint smell of burning plastic hangs in the air; the smell of Drumkirk is always the smell of burning. A rusty syringe, the plastic barrel cracked and split, lies on the low wall where he sits on the roof looking across at the smattering of YES posters in the windows of the adjacent towerblock. A saltire flag hangs limply from a top-floor balcony. Ben Lomond is a distant blue triangle beyond the slated rooftops, chimney pots, domes and spires, concrete bridges and motorway flyovers. There's heat in the evening sunshine yet and he pulls off his white T-shirt, the one with the rip in the back.

§

A morning some four years earlier: the end of August, almost a chill in the air, spiders' webs coated in dew draped the grass, the herald of autumn, devil's bit scabious in flower and the blackberries ripe and juicy. A robin pecked around looking for crumbs in the grass, as he zipped up the flysheet of the little orange tent pitched on a square of grass among the oaks, beeches and rowans in the corner of the car park near the shore at Rowardennan.

The curtains were still closed on the black hearse parked beside the pier. As he tiptoed past he glanced through the rear window. A couple of packets of green Rizla papers, lids torn off and an empty bottle of Smirnoff lay on the floor cushions scattered across the back of the hearse. He could hear the sound of snoring coming from the tent pitched next to it. An Irn Bru bottle half full of urine lay next to a blackened branch that still smouldered in a ring of stones.

Past the pier he followed a faint footpath along the shore of the loch. There among the birch trees he came to a ring of polished granite mounted on a circle of slate framing the vista of loch and hill. He stood there under the silver birches and he read the words carved in black letters on the shiny grey stone:

> This land, rising from the shore of the loch to the summit of Ben Lomond, is dedicated to those who gave their lives in the service of their country.

§

Newly demobbed workers stream out along the bomb-damaged streets of Clydebank. Hitching a lift on the back of a lorry out of the food-rationed city, climbing the mountain in ex-army surplus gear and soldiers' boots. Nerves shredded by the stray bomb that fell on the line of trucks, the day the Stuka strafed the convoy on the long straight stretch of road between the poplar trees south of Amiens.

Staying the night at the youth hostel with its red-painted eaves and the purple-pink rhododendron growing wild up the hillside behind the old Victorian shooting lodge; heads full of the dream of the new world they are building.

In Edinburgh Mr Tom Johnson, his majesty's secretary of state, has a plan. The seven wartime emergency hospitals constructed for the casualties of the expected widespread bombing will form the basis of a new National Health

Service for Scotland. All working people will pay a small contribution, National Insurance it will be called, and in return the unemployed, the retired, the widowed and the sick will be provided for. The system will be funded by employers and the government. The Victorian distinction between the deserving and undeserving poor will be banished and the New Welfare State will vanquish the five giants standing on the road to the New World: Poverty, Disease, Ignorance, Squalor and Idleness.

§

He walked on beneath the oak and beech trees to join a dirt track road at a wooden post carved with a thistle: the West Highland Way. The two Dutch girls he'd been speaking to the day before in Drymen, when the guys in the hearse stopped and offered them all a lift, greeted him with smiles.

He walked on and came to a little bay with a shingle beach and a wide view across Loch Lomond. Through the birch trees he caught a glimpse of the Sput Ban waterfall, a white streak high on the heavily wooded hillside.

A few hundred metres beyond the high, locked wooden gates of Ben Lomond Cottage, the West Highland Way crossed a low concrete bridge over a stream. But something drew Mickey and he turned off the track and onto a narrow footpath where, beneath the moss-covered branches shading the banks of the stream, the roots of ancient oak trees clawed through the surface of the path.

MICKEY: Sometimes yer life just turns in an instant. The steel archway beside the park bench next tae Greggs in Milngavie wis an unlikely looking portal tae another world. But it led out the city. Time and again it led me out the city. How good wis it tae be away from the cars and the concrete and the noise and the high flats breathing clean air from the hills that rose up at the edge of the Highlands. Then after, on the way back in tae town, bumping along, flicking through the *Metro* as the bus crawled its way along Great Western Road. Now – today – lookin' back four years at ma younger self walking under the steel arch and along the paved path beneath the sycamores and oak trees beside the Allander Water and out across the sundried heather moorland – it wis like I'd found the beginning of a way into the future. I didnae know it then but as I sat there at the edge of the reservoir skimming chuckies across the water, there was the sense of a beginning at the end of the journey of the pipes. The West Highland Way wisnae exactly the Yellow Brick Road – but for me, Mickey Bell, life would never be the same again.

Where the trees gave way to hawthorn and broom he came to the remains of a sheep fank; licheny drystone walls protruding from the bracken. A few hundred feet higher up the hillside he reached the waterfall. Redstarts, pied flycatchers and wood warblers flitted among the hawthorn, aspen and rowan as the path climbed up through the woodland beside the Ardess Burn. There was heat in the late August sun as Mickey gazed down on Loch Lomond.

He was sweating.

His heart was racing.

But he was happy!

And though he knew the shape of Scotland from tea towels and weather maps and shortbread tins and the STV logo, as he stood there high on the hillside looking down at the islands of Loch Lomond shimmering in the sun, he had this sense of living on the west side of an island in the ocean on a blue planet in space.

He pushed on through the bracken to the foot of an outcrop of small heathery crags. Eyebright grew by the path, the wild flower's petals like shining eyes among the deergrass.

High up, safe from the sheep grazing on the grassy ridge, a rowan tree grew out of the bare rock. To the left the hillside dropped steeply down to the quiet eastern shore of the loch. The latch on the wooden gate clicked shut behind him and he climbed on through patches of purple heather among the grass.

§

'Fuck man, how can you sit there like that? It gives me the shakes just lookin' at you—'

Mickey turns his head. It's the black guy from the sixteenth floor. He walks across to where Mickey's sitting on the low wall that surrounds the roof of the three-hundred-foot-high towerblock but keeps well back from the edge.

'At least you ain't got the fuckin dog up here with you this time!'

Mickey laughs.

'Hey – how's the supermarket, mate? You still goin' oot in the van but?'

'Aw it's crazy in Deliver and I've got exams next week—'

The black guy digs about in his pockets. 'You got a light?' Then with a smile, 'I got a blunt—'

And they sit on the roof of the three-hundred-foot-high towerblock, Mickey dangling his legs off the edge, stretching back to pass the spliff, wreathing themselves in sweet-smelling smoke while the sun sets orange and red tinged with green behind the Luma lightbulb factory.

§

The path, well constructed with stone steps and rainwater gullies, climbed up past four big slabs of rock heaped together. The sides of the boulders white with lichen, their tops capped with woolly fringe moss. At a hairpin bend, where the path twisted round to cross a side stream, alpine ladies' mantle grew by the burn and bright green cushions of sphagnum moss were scattered across the hillside.

He hadn't seen a single other person on the ridge that sunny Tuesday morning at the end of August.

The silence disnae bother me. I'm a bit of a loner, see. There's nothing tae be frightened of like.

The things that scared him, they lurked in the dark streets of the city.

As he gained height the ridge became more defined and began to narrow. A big circle of sweat, edged with a white halo of salt, formed on the front of his T-shirt and his back stuck to the rucksack.

As he pulled the damp T-shirt over his head he felt a small tear appear in the back of the soggy cotton.

He looked down at his white skin.

Mickey Bell, the man wi' a tan, he thought to himself.

Five minutes later the path, now a white gravel line in the short-cropped grass brought him to the first top of the ridge.

Tom an Fithich, the peak of the raven.

He sprawled on the grass gazing down at the islands glinting on the blue waters of Loch Lomond fifteen hundred feet below while the black ravens rolled and tumbled on the breeze.

In the distance he could see Dumbarton Rock and to the west lay the Luss hills, the Arrochar Alps, Ben More and Stob Binnien. A murk of pollution hung over the city and he could just make out white towerblocks rising out of the yellow haze over Glasgow.

He lay on his back, bare-chested, the scrub heath scratching his shoulders. His heart thumped. The big vein in his forearm where they slid the needle in, stood out green under his white skin. He turned his face to the mountain and the cobalt blue sky and the glistening loch, shouting out loud the words in his head, ‘Hey Toto, something tells me we’re no in Drumkirk any mair!’

§

viral load >128,000 copies/ml
CD4 count 168

MICKEY: Five hours I had tae wait. Five fuckin hours! I stood outside the clinic at the bus stop across the road. In a fuckin daze! I got on the wrong bus like and I wis halfway intae town before I realised and had tae get aff and get oan a different one. It was pissing down with rain but. I remember I went upstairs on the bus and like wiped a hole in the condensation wi’ my sleeve. And I jist sat there starin’ out at folk wi’ umbrellas hurrying along the street. All the car headlights blurry in the rain and I’m jist wishin’ it was jist anither day for me too. Five hours I had tae wait but. Five fuckin hours! How tae spend five hours like those? It wis like time had stopped... the second hand of ma watch crawled around the dial and I’m lying curled up like a baby on the sofa. And I’m thinkin’ what the fuck is gaunny happen if the blood test comes back positive? What’ll happen like? Then ma phone starts ringing and it’s some cunt wi’ a Liverpool accent wantin’ me tae claim payment protection compensation. I tried watchin’ the telly, lying there on the sofa... flickin’ thru the channels but I kept lookin’ at the green LED clock on the DVD player countin’ down the seconds, the minutes and hours while I’m clinging tae the sofa huggin’ a cushion. Thing is I’d always been pretty careful but. I knew the virus was out there, lurking among the bottles of poppers, sticky cans of cider and the ashtray of fag ends on the bedside table at four in the morning. Couldnae remember a time there weren't posters in the pubs and jars full of durex and sachets of lubricant. I'm lying there on the sofa thinking maybe it wis that Australian guy when I wis pished but I didnae think he'd cum. But maybe he had – and like apart frae that time and maybe one or two other times I'd always been careful, see. Used a condom like – anxiously checking for rips in the yellow latex stocking with its pearl-like globular contents before dropping it in tae the bin in the kitchen. I know but – it just takes a few wee particles o' virus tae get intae yer blood. And then I'm wonderin' – whit treatment will I get. Will there be side effects? Suppose the drugs dinnae work but? Fuckin all this stuff, birling around in ma heid. Fuck it, I thought. If it comes back positive I'll just no tell anyone. Ma secret like. But then suppose I meet someone I know in the clinic, they'll guess why I'm there. They'll know. Fuck! And aw the time the clock on the DVD player's daein' its green flickery countdown to when I've got tae go and get the bus. I must've fell asleep at one point cos I woke up and I was like where the fuck am I? Then this great black wave washed over me and I'm lying there greetin' intae the cushion cos I'll have tae go back in forty-five minutes. I'm thinking where's ma blood now? Is ma future on a computer print-out shoved in the top of some file? Daes the doctor know now? Dae the nurses know? Daes the crabbit receptionist know? It wis ma fault like. Just bein me, driftin' through life. Something wis bound tae fuck up. Its the kindae thing that happens in ma shitty life but.

fault
guilt
blame
shame
if only

if only
if fuckin only

I pulled ma sleeve up – looked at the fine black hairs on ma arms. I seen the tracery of green veins runnin' under the skin and wondered if particles of virus floated there in ma blood. I remember the rain had stopped and there wis a little warmth in the watery sunshine when I pushed open the glass doors of the clinic.

§

The path climbed on up the knobbly ridge in a series of zigzags and stone flights of steps edged with fir club moss. He paused beside a little lochan near the seven-hundred-metre contour line and looked across to the summit of Ben Lomond.The mist kept blowing in then clearing and tiny figures stood on the top of the mountain. He wanted the mist to stay just where it was. The way to the summit looked clear.

Beyond the lochan the path steered around a series of rocky bumps before crossing a line of stepping stones over green rushes and red sphagnum moss to reach the foot of the north-west ridge of Ben Lomond. He climbed up through mossy boulders, unperturbed by the steep, broken ground that fell away on his left down to Leac na Cailliche. He scrambled easily over the few little crags near the top, the path just seeming to steer him through them. He was just below the summit of Ben Lomond.

Suddenly, three feet away, tucked in among rocks seamed with white quartz and ochre lichen, two ptarmigan mottled grey and brown on top and white underneath. Like pieces of living rock, ptarmigan on the Ptarmigan ridge.

He placed a hand on a mossy ledge, squeezed between two boulders, his boots slithered on gravel, he glanced down at the big drop into the corrie and then he was up, standing by the trig point on the bare gravelly summit of Ben Lomond.

He was drenched in sweat.

His legs ached.

He was gasping for breath.

'Oo ya fucker!'

He stood there on the summit of Ben Lomond.

Hardly believing he'd done it.

'Yes!'

Climbed his first mountain.

He punched the air.

And then he shouted, 'Mickey Bell one – virus nil!'

§

viral load <40 copies per ml
CD4 count 289
treatment: combination antiretroviral therapy
munros climbed 1/282

caw caw caw

Caw!
Caw!
Caw!

(A harsh, rasping cry)

Fithich the raven speaks:

The ravens were here when a mysterious hooded figure stood by the lochside, quill pen in hand, sketching on parchment the name of the ridge Mealden Tarmachan.

Timothy Pont, the ravens remember him, the son of a priest, he stravaiged across Scotland in the sixteenth century mapping the land for reasons that are lost in time.

The year of our lord Anno Domini 1769: one day in late summer. The ravens are here tumbling and rolling in the breeze still. The hillside above Loch Lomond is now extensively settled and Thomas Pennant an early traveller in Scotland writes of fields of 'yellow corn' on the lower slopes of Ben Lomond. The zoologist clutching his watercolour drawings of mountain hares and alpine saxifrage will report of Ben Lomond, 'Ptarmigans inhabit its summit'.

The ravens were here when a township stood under the oak trees by the Ardess Burn and families lived and farmed, growing oats, barley and potatoes; grazing black cattle, sheep and goats.

And among the birch trees and where the shade falls on the path, the shadows of the past lurk between the dappled patches of sunlight. At the end of the street, in the gaps between the cobbles and in the cracks in the stone walls, lurk the shadows of the past.

The ravens were here in the time of the Clearances when the Duke of Montrose and his men came on their horses.

The ravens were here when the houses had been abandoned, falling into ruin beside the mossy banks of the Ardess Burn where birch leaves float on the water.

Tumbling in the air a hundred feet above the summit of Ben Lomond the ravens hang on the breeze. Far to the south, the dim green blur of the Cheviots.

The city by the river and the city on the hill.

Kings and queens and soldiers and princes fighting over the one green island.

The ravens see all.

The ravens see the fallen mossy stones among the head-high bracken. The ravens hear the footsteps tap tap tapping on the stones of the path by the Ardess Burn. The ravens see Mickey Bell from Drumkirk climbing the ridge like one of the children of the mist.

Caw!
Caw!
Caw!

Fithich the raven is my name.
They called the hill after me.

Caw!
Caw!
Caw!

Wednesday

The wonderful things in life are the things you do, not the things you have.

Reinhold Messner

Munro. *Pronunciation: /mʌn ˈrəʊ/ noun (plural Munros) any of the 282 mountains in Scotland that are at least 3000 feet high (approximately 914 metres).*

The Oxford English Dictionary

can I be your dog?

2 pm: He's twelve feet away from his front door on level zero of the high flats when Tyke recognises the familiar footstep and starts barking. A dog, a good burglar alarm, you need one of them round ma bit, he thinks as he unlocks both mortice locks then slides his key into the Yale.

The dog stands halfway down the hall, tail wagging in round and round circles, barking joyfully. Mickey crouches down and Tyke licks his stubbly, unshaven chin just like he did that first day outside the barn at Torbreac, in Assynt, where the waves lap the white sands of Achmelvich.

§

Maggie was his Scottish Aunty, his mum's best friend from college. It was the cars she used to drive Mickey remembers, the ancient Ford that jumped out of gear going downhill with (to a child's ears) a terrifying, juddering, roaring vibration. The white Renault 4 with the L-shaped gear lever and handbrake sticking out the dashboard. The Dormobile camper van – pure Scooby Doo.

Maggie used to go on holiday with them when he was a kid. That was before his mum moved to Saudi to work as a nurse for £800 a week. Maggie always seemed to have more money than his mum and took Mickey to Rothesay and bought taramasalata when it was new and trendy.

After a spell living in Hamburg, Maggie finally said goodbye to the Victorian upper villa in Hyndland that had been her childhood home, with its green plastic dial telephone and wall-mounted bell and Swiss-German cuckoo clock in the hall.

She'd gone to live at the Balnakeill craft village near Cape Wrath where she made miniature weavings of the bleak northern-lit, stormy landscape of Sutherland. After a couple of years Maggie'd had enough. She said the craft village had all the social problems of the inner city: from alcoholism to drug abuse to domestic violence. She moved thirty miles down the bare, rocky coast to Assynt and a grey stone cottage at Stoer.

Maggie had once been married for a few short years at the beginning of the '80s. On one of their few holidays between honeymoon and divorce the couple had been to Assynt. As Maggie used to say, 'We had an argument in Lochinver then another argument five miles up the road in Clachtoll.'

But she held the memory of the bleak austere beauty of the storm-crashed coast of Assynt as the decades passed. The white sands of Achmelvich and the ocean waves breaking and the seagulls swirling around the black cliffs below the lighthouse at Point of Stoer.

So at the age of fifty Maggie moved to Stoer to run the tiny post office which operated out of the front room of Shore Cottage. She bought a loom and planned to sell her weavings and do bed and breakfast to make ends meet.

Some eighteen months after Mickey's diagnosis, a message had come from Maggie, relayed via his mum in Saudi. Maggie, by then in her late fifties, had got itchy feet, wanting one last big trip to India to sit and smoke a spliff on the beach in Kerala. The problem was what to do with the post office and her two cats, Suilen and Lia, while she took a steam train from Mumbai to Jaipur.

Maggie worried about Mickey, knew he was HIV and living on benefits in Glasgow. Said she'd pay him cash in hand £20 a day for the couple of hours three mornings a week the post office was open. Mickey jumped at the chance.

§

He was the only passenger leaving the train at Lairg. The station was in total darkness as he stepped onto the platform. White gravel crunched beneath his trainers. After a few moments he caught sight of a rotund, shadowy figure in a wide-brimmed hat peering into the night from the footbridge over the railway line.

Maggie drove him the fifty miles to Stoer, her long scarf trailing over the gear lever of the six-year-old VW Golf, squinting over the steering wheel into the blue Highland night, trying to see deer on the road.

Stars speckled the cloudless sky two hours later when the car drew up outside Shore Cottage. In the darkness Mickey was dimly aware of a picket fence and a grey stone cottage. But he heard the low roar of the waves as they tossed and rolled the shingle on Stoer beach.

The first morning, with Maggie busy in the post office, he wandered down the single track road to the foot of the hill. He walked over short-cropped grass dotted yellow with tiny heart-shaped petals of tormentil to where a line of reddish, sea-rounded stones marked the edge of the steeply shelving shingle of Stoer beach.

From there he followed a narrow strip of turf between a barbed wire fence trailing yellowing tufts of wool and the wave of shingle at the top of the beach. He headed towards a low circular wall of stones on a little sheep-grazed grassy headland and climbed through a gap in the wall where a great triangular block of pink sandstone lay on the machair. He sat there on the fallen stones in the centre of the broch and smoked a roll-up, gazing out at the swelling grey Atlantic breakers, the light flimsy and filmy, the Outer Hebrides a faint blue smudge on the western horizon.

He walked on along the coastline, following the low cliffs round until he stood at the edge of the sea near the old fishing bothy on the shore at Clachtoll. The bothy had walls of stone and a rusty red corrugated iron roof. The machair under his feet was yellow with tormentil and clusters of sea pinks huddled among the shingle. Cara-mhil-a`choin, the men who once worked out of the fishing bothy called tormentil. It flowered all summer long and they used the roots of the plant for tanning the fishing nets.

Great sheets of Torridonian sandstone sloped down to the sea where the waves broke on the edge of this, the Vikings' southern land. The gulls wheeled overhead around the wooden posts where fishing nets once hung to dry.

An old black and white collie with a grey muzzle appeared from nowhere, sniffing along the brown kelp tideline. A simple white granite slab stood on the grass. The dog brought a stick and dropped it at Mickey's feet while he stood there in front of the monument:

To the memory of the Reverend Norman Macleod
Born here on 29th September 1780

Leader, Minister and Teacher

He led his people
Over 14,000 miles of ocean to
Nova Scotia, Australia and New Zealand.

The collie picked up the stick and threw it down on the machair. Barked and barked again, while Mickey read on:

Lean iad e ou iomall na talmhainn

They followed him
To the ends of the earth.

Looking out across the ocean swell, on the far north-western edge of Europe, it seemed to Mickey the people had begun their journey from the ends of the earth.

'Fetch it! Pal! Fetch it!'

He picked up the stick and hurled it across the green and yellow machair onto the shingle beach at the edge of the world.

Maggie spent that afternoon showing him how the post office worked: how to enter transactions on the computer, how to process the odd giro cheque and where the stamps were kept in the drawers with the brass handles under the long oak counter she'd bought from a hotel closing-down sale in Tongue.

The next morning a rainless gale rushed out of the west, flaying the salt of the sea across the shrubs in the garden of Shore Cottage. Lia, the small grey cat, rubbed around Mickey's ankles as he stood at the gate in the picket fence, tasting brine on his lips and watching Maggie haul her travel bag and rucksack into Sheila's rusty Volvo for the two-hour drive to Inverness and the train to London.

Maggie hugged him as he stood there at the gate. 'I'll miss you, son,'and he felt like a kid again at the end of the summer holidays. Then she cradled Lia in her arms. 'Remember there's extra cat food in the shed.'

'Have a great trip, Maggie. See you in October.'

Then he grinned. 'Dinnae get too stoned but.'

'I didn't hear that!' she called and then she was gone.

Mickey picked up Lia and stroked her grey fur as he watched the old green Volvo rattle off down the hill past the white houses at Clachtoll. The cottage and garden filled with silence. Beyond the peninsula, the place the Vikings called Assynt, land of rock, the mountains stood in a great line: Quinag, Conival, Ben Mor Assynt, Canisp, Suilven, Cul Mor, Cul Beag.

'Filed on the blue air—' Maggie'd said the night before as she sat on the frontstep, a roll-up in one hand, a gin and tonic in the other.

As the car disappeared around the last bend by the crescent of white sand at Clachtoll, he put Lia gently down on the garden path where wall flowers grew in the cracks and clusters of bell heather stood among the sea pinks.

He liked cats but what he really wanted was a dog. A dog like the dog from the fishing bothy at Clachtoll, a dog to stomp through the hills with, his dog at his heel as he tramped through the heather, a dog for a gay boy all alone in Assynt.

Aw well, he thought, as he went back indoors, he'd got all summer long to find a dog: saw himself driving round, checking out likely looking farms, imagined a red-cheeked farmer's wife with a basket full of puppies by the Aga. He'd be bound to find a good dog in Assynt.

The next morning he took Maggie's beat-up VW Golf the seven miles into Lochinver for supplies from the narrow-aisled Co-op where he squeezed between overweight German tourists and an ancient crofter with his trousers held up by blue bailer twine.

As he stepped out onto the pavement with his plastic carrier bags of shopping in his hands, the briney smell of the Atlantic behind the low sea wall, Mickey realised he'd forgotten to buy tobacco. He'd passed a newsagent's on the way into Lochinver, he could stop off there.

As he parked the VW outside the shop, a few drops of rain fell on the windscreen out of a grey-white sky. There were a number of posters and notices in the window of the newsagent's: the Rogart sheepdog trials, yoga in the village hall, a plant and produce sale in aid of Gaelic Toddlers, a meeting of the Assynt Crofters Trust.

But it was a handwritten notice scrawled in blue biro on the back of a brown envelope that caught Mickey's eye.

He pushed open the glass door of the shop. It stuck on the uneven terracotta floor tiles. The woman behind the counter had a London accent, frizzy grey hair and the wrinkled, lined smoker's face of WH Auden.

'That's £3.78 please.'

As she handed him a half ounce of Golden Virginia and two packs of green Rizla papers, Mickey asked, 'See the notice in the window – dae you know where Torbreac is please?'

'Yes – it's on the wee road signposted Achmelvich. Torbreac's one of the crofts along there. He'll be glad to see you. He's desperate to get rid of the last two puppies.'

And as Mickey pulled the door of the shop open, she added, 'They're driving him mad.'

On the way back to Shore Cottage he drove up a steep track to a gate with the name *Torbreac* on it and there was a house but it was deserted. The VW though was quickly surrounded by a herd of two dozen long-horned, shaggy, brown Highland cattle that seemed to be under the impression Mickey had come to feed them.

'Sorry, guys,' he said, backing nervously into the car.

He turned the VW carefully and the cattle lumbered slowly out the way, swishing their tails and lowing as he inched his way between them, back down the steep track to the road.

Back at Shore Cottage, after heating up a tin of tomato soup and making a corned beef and onion roll he put the *Closed* sign in the window of the post office and walked across the road and knocked at the door of Stoer House.

The owners of the Victorian villa across the road with the blue-painted eaves were a retired Dutch couple. He owned a tractor and liked to play at being a farmer while she seemed permanently depressed and looked as if she'd be happier watering tulips in a window box in a flat in Amsterdam.

Mickey'd christened her Miss Edam 1975.

'He doesn't live at Torbreac – he rents it out as a holiday let,' Miss Edam explained as she poured boiling water onto foaming Nescafe in the warm kitchen with its blue and white windmill tiles.

The next morning Mickey drove the beat-up VW back down the hill, past Clachtoll. Two miles along the unclassified byroad to Achmelvich, he turned up a potholed track beneath mossy beech and oak trees. He parked at a gate beside an old kennel built of three-quarter-inch plywood. Untreated and unpainted, the layers of ply had swollen and warped and split in the West Highland rain.

He opened the gate and found himself standing in a muddy yard. Two shabby static caravans and a tractor occupied one side of the yard. On his left was a half-finished stone building which looked like it might be a barn. Someone had taken great care in the way the irregularly shaped blocks of stone had been chiselled and cemented together. The first floor of the building was open to the sky but the ground floor looked wind- and watertight.

A wide wooden door was held shut by a faded white plastic fish box, its edges smoothed by the swelling, rolling brine of the sea and held in place by an old tractor wheel. From inside the barn Mickey could hear high-pitched yapping and squealing.

He walked up to the nearest of the two static caravans. One window was boarded up with a sheet of hardboard. Another window was open and a curtain flapped in the breeze from the Atlantic.

He knocked at the frosted glass door. After a couple of minutes there was the sound of shuffling movement from inside, then the door opened. A man in his late fifties, balding with grey hair, stood in the doorway, fastening the belt which held his frayed black trousers up. His shirt was unbuttoned and he wore a grubby white vest under it.

'Mr MacLeod? Ah've come about the notice in the shop in Lochinver – about the puppies.'

'Aye – right you are.'

MacLeod extended a nicotine-stained hand towards Mickey. He was unshaven and a smell of stale whisky lingered on his breath.

MacLeod led the way across the yard to the half-built stone barn. The squealing from within grew louder as he rolled back the tractor wheel and then pushed aside the fish box. The door opened a couple of inches and a black furry nose appeared.

MacLeod pushed the barn door open wide and a black and white puppy jumped over a brown puppy and charged up to Mickey who crouched down. The puppy stood up on its hind legs and licked his face.

The puppy had blue-green eyes the colour of the sea where it laps the white sands of Achmelvich. A flickering consciousness gleamed behind those bright sea-green eyes as the puppy licked Mickey's face again and again, then sat and looked up at him as if to say, 'Can I be your dog?'

Meanwhile the brown puppy and the other dogs from the barn rampaged around the muddy yard. MacLeod pointed out a white collie. 'Now, that's his mother—' he turned towards a curly bearded collie rooting in a black bin bag under a tree '—and that'll be his father. Which puppy will you be wanting then?'

Mickey didn't hesitate. 'I'll take the black and white yin, please,' he said.

MacLeod stood in the middle of the yard, hands on hips, shouting ineffectual commands at the wild bunch of farm dogs charging around the yard barking.

After five minutes he gave up trying to shepherd the dogs back into the barn. As the black and white puppy wriggled in Mickey's arms, Macleod fetched a battered steel dog bowl and filled it from a fifteen kilo sack of *Wilsons Original Mix* dried dog food.

On the crumpled, yellow paper sack Mickey could see a drawing of a shepherd with a crook. At his feet a black and white collie sat obediently, gazing adoringly up at his master.

Eventually, by walking backwards and banging on the battered, steel dog bowl with a spoon, Macleod finally managed to lure the collies back into the barn. Then he slammed the door and replaced the old fish box and the tractor wheel.

He walked Mickey to the gate.

Mickey opened the rear door of the car. The puppy whimpered as he lifted it onto an old blanket covered with straw on the back seat. He closed the car door and shook hands with Macleod.

Then he said, 'Sorry, I nearly forgot – that's for you, mate.' And reaching through the open window onto the passenger seat, he handed Macleod a bottle of Whyte and Mackay.

The puppy was quiet as the VW bounced down the potholed track and up the hill to Stoer. At the summit of the steep section of road Mickey pulled into a layby. A bend had been straightened out and he could see the line of the old road hair-pinning across the hillside. Grass sprouted along the middle and at the edges of the crumbling tarmac.

Below him lay the lochan and rock-studded landscape of Assynt. Canisp swept up like the sail on a Viking longship. Grey cloud capped the summit of Suilven the pillar mountain. The breeze rustled the heather and a scent of bog myrtle drifted in through the open window. It was silent, not a car on the road. Mickey got out and opened the back door of the VW. He buried his face in the puppy's fur.

'Yer a little tyke, aren't you?' he said.

It was dark when Mickey took the puppy out for the last time that first day. Tyke barked at the ice cream sign at the side of the road outside the post office. Then he looked up and stopped. The Milky Way blazed a ribbon of white muslin across the night sky. More stars in the universe than grains of sand on a beach, thought Mickey, as the puppy gazed up at the sky seeing the stars for the first time in his life.

§

As he stands up in the narrow, low-ceilinged hall of the flat on level zero and wipes the dog drool from his stubbly chin, he notices more of the embossed vinyl wallpaper has peeled away from above the sitting room door. He pushes open the chipped, white-painted hardboard door and drops his jacket and messenger bag on the sofa. He picks up the remote control and switches the TV on.

Grains of sand spill out of the corners of Karen Gillan's eyes.

'Don't take your eyes off the angel! Don't even blink!' shouts The Doctor as the screen fills with the twisted gargoyle face of a stone angel.

Tyke jumps up onto the sofa and Mickey sits down next to him.

'Whoa, doggums – remember when we saw the weeping

angels, T-T-T-Tyke,' he says, throwing his arms around the dog in mock terror.

§

CD4 count 424
viral load <40 copies
meds 5 tablets daily with or after food
munros 51/282

The needle on the speedometer of the VW Golf wobbled between 65 and 70 on the long straight stretch of the A835 south of Inchnadamph. The mountains stood in a great line between the brown moorland and a sea flecked with white: Suilven, Canisp, Stac Pollaidh, Cul Mor, Cul Beag and Ben Mor Coigach.

He slowed the car to take a chevronned bend then, as he slid the gear lever up from fourth to fifth and pushed the accelerator pedal down to the floor, the pure joy of being alive and here in the world welled up inside him as the car sped down the wide brown strath towards Ullapool.

At the sound of the indicator, Tyke, asleep stretched out on the back seat during the hour-long drive from Shore Cottage, was instantly awake, sitting up, recognising the braking car, alert to the change in tempo of engine noise, wondering what it meant.

Mickey parked up beside a deer fence in a layby by a stone bridge and a red telephone box. The only other car in the parking place was an eight-year-old, cream-coloured Renault estate.

As he swallowed a handful of pills, one blue, two tan-coloured, one large and beige, one small and white, one pink, all washed down with mouthfuls of hot, sugary thermos-flask tea and a Mars bar, he glanced through the windscreen of the Renault.

On the front seat of the estate car lay the torn open packaging from a box of Mr Kipling apple pies. But it was the dashboard that caught his eye. Stuck to the grey leather-effect plastic were two dozen or more furry fridge magnet figures. There were fluffy pink ones and green ones and blue ones.

'For fuck's sake,' went through his mind, 'what kindae fuckin weirdo—?'

The dark conifers crowded around the ruins of the house at Glensquaib as Mickey, with Tyke fifty yards ahead of him, climbed the eroded stony path to the deer fence at the edge of the moorland.

Whcre the forest ended he dropped the rucksack and began to gather twigs and small branches from among the bracken. Tyke, stick-obsessed, kept leaping up, trying to snatch the brittle, sunbleached branches of pine from Mickey's hands.

'Oi! Leave it!'

But after a minute he gave in and hurled a stick into the bracken and Tyke chased joyfully after it, tail in the air.

The bundle of firewood made the rucksack top-heavy and unwieldy as he tramped along the stalkers' path beside the Allt Gleann a' Mhadaidh. The peat was springy and spongey beneath his feet, a circle of blackened stones on a level patch of grass by a waterfall, river sand and white pebbles but he pushed on across the rising, open moorland.

TYKE: I'm the dog I'm the dog I'm the dog straw straw straw suckle suckle suckle puppies puppies puppies dogs dogs dogs growl growl growl big dog big dog big dog teeth teeth teeth snarl snarl snarl whimper whimper whimper

smoke smoke smoke car car car hard hard hard road road road paws paws paws smell smell smell grass grass grass ball

ball ball I'm the dog I'm the dog paws paws paws lick lick lick bed bed bed I'm the dog I'm the dog I'm the dog

sniff sniff snuff snuff sniff sniff snuff snuff yip yip yip mhadaidh mhadaidh mhaidaidh stink stink stink run run run yip yip yip man man man shout shout shout leave leave leave run run run man man shout shout leave leave leave angry angry angry back back back why why why I'm a good dog I'm a good dog I'm a good dog

I'm the dog I'm the dog I'm the dog stones stones stones grass grass grass sticks sticks sticks sticks paws paws paws up up up mist mist mist cold cold cold up up up man man man long long long paws paws paws mud mud mud sore sore sore paws paws stones stones smell smell wet wet mist mist I'm the dog I'm the dog I'm the dog sniff sniff snuff snuff stones stones meat meat under stones crisps crisps crisps drool drool drool eat eat eat

Next morning the deer were halfway down the hillside as he fried bacon under the flysheet in the tiny porch of the tent. Blatters of rain, swept in from the Atlantic on the fresh to strong westerly wind, clattered against the flysheet.

Mickey had pitched the orange tent beside the first of the Little Lochans, a string of three peaty pools threaded together by a silver ribbon of stream that splashed down from the heather and scree-streaked slopes of the Eididh nan Clach Geala. The mountain they call the web of the white stones.

To the west, across the high moorland and beyond the broken teeth of Stac Pollaidh, rocky tongues of land thrust out into the sea. Drops of rainwater glistened on the bundle of sticks in the wet grass. A headtorch, a woolly hat, a toilet roll, a bag of crisps, an apple and a pair of black boxer shorts lay scattered across the groundsheet of the inner tent. Tyke, curled up at the back, a furry ball snuggled into Mickey's sleeping bag.

‘Hey, doggums.’ Mickey crawled into the inner tent. ‘When yer curled up like that I cannae tell which end is the bitey end and which end is the smelly end but,’ he said as he stroked the dog’s warm coat.

Two hours passed and in the late morning they reached the edge of a line of broken crags, a thirty-foot step down to the wide black peaty bealach below. A smirr of light rain in the air; misty grey cloud scudded across the grassy hillside.

Boot on rock, hand gripping wet roots of heather, he climbed down. The dog left claw marks in the black peaty soil. Under Mickey’s boot a little brown frog hopped away into the long grass. He pulled out the compass that hung around his suntanned neck on its red cord. It felt warm. He crouched down, resting the map, snug in its clear plastic bag, on his knee.

He laid the transparent edge of the compass along a line from the gap in the crags to the northern tip of Loch a’ Chadha Dheirg. Like the Gay Toon Planner had shown him (remember red lines on blue lines, he’d said). Then spun the red dial and got to his feet.

Held in the palm of his hand, the compass needle floated in its little ocean then turned, fluttered and settled, pointing north-west. He’d thought it was that way. About one and a half kilometres, 200 metres of ascent: he should be at the top in about thirty minutes.

‘C’mon, pups.’

Mickey and Tyke huddled behind the circle of stones surrounding the summit cairn as the wind battered along Strath Oykell. June and the rain was turning to sleat on Seana Braigh, the old high place.

Q..w..e..rtyU..Y...But it will always be blue sky on the summit of Seana Braigh in the endless summer when DG Fraser climbed this hill********* he called it the remotest of all the Scottish mountains over 3000 feet. A climber stands on page 149 at the edge of the cliffs of Creag an Duine. DG Fraser lies back in the grass, resting his head on his rucksack, dozing in the endless golden summer of his younger self---------------------------))))

The wind lessened late in the afternoon and a blink of watery sunshine dried the flysheet of the tent pitched beside the Little Lochans.

It was dark outside when he unzipped the door of the tent. 'C'mon, Tyke – last round up!'

The dog stretched and pushed his snout out the nylon flap, sniffing the droplets of mist that hung in the air. Mickey walked slowly along the path towards the second of the Little Lochans, Tyke snuffling and cocking his leg at boulders.

In the mist the grey rocks and boulders surrounding the lochans took on the shapes of fallen statues and gravestones and obelisks.

Like the weeping angels from Doctor Who.

Don't blink! Don't look at them! thought Mickey with a shiver as he ran back to the little orange tent and curled up in his sleeping bag, arm around Tyke, face buried in the dog's warm shaggy coat.

§

The Tardis spins through the vortex and the credits roll to the scraping, grinding chords of the BBC radiophonic workshop. Leaving Tyke stretched out on the sofa, Mickey goes over to the window and gazes out at the drizzly rain falling on the wide expanse of muddy grass in front of the high flats. He scratches his chin. His five-day-old beard itches.

He jumps at the metallic clang of the letterbox: a second later Tyke races out the room barking furiously. He follows the dog out into the narrow hallway. Tyke is standing guard over a brown envelope on the frayed carpet.

Letters in brown envelopes – I fuckin hate letters in brown envelopes but. Most of the stressors in ma life come in fuckin brown envelopes: you must attend a work-focused interview, Mr Bell, we have overpaid your housing benefit, gie us our fuckin money back – fuckin brown envelopes. I fuckin hate opening letters in brown envelopes but. When I see one on the doormat I'm like heart racing, stomach flutterin'. Google social security – gaunny dae it now like – there's all this stuff on Wikipedia about the welfare state and that. The guy that set it all up, Aneurin Bevan was his name – he wrote a book – In Place of Fear *it wis called. Well there's plenty of folk living in fear now like, fear of a fuckin brown envelope comin through the letterbox.*

He picks the brown envelope up off the worn and stained carpet and, like he always does (*it's ma wee ritual see, superstitious behaviour for tae stop bad things from happenin'*), he takes the envelope through to the kitchen and sits down at the table to open it.

Strathclyde Housing Asociation
Darryl MacConnachie
Service Delivery Manager
SHA

Building 3
282 Munro Place
Glasgow
G13 UPU

FINAL DEMAND

Dear Mr Bell

This letter is notification that Strathclyde Housing Association will be raising proceedings for the possession of the dwelling house at 2 Drumkirk Court, Drumkirk Road, Glasgow due to outstanding rent arrears of £130.15.

I can advise you that I am required by law to serve a notice on you before starting court action. This notice will warn you that Strathclyde Housing Association will take court action to re-possess the dwelling house at...

The bedroom tax: he twists his hands together and bites his thumbnail. Under the kitchen table his right leg's shaking. He's been trying to forget about it. Push it away to somewhere at the back of his mind but now he can't. He doesn't have £130.15 to pay the arrears and they'll keep mounting up month after month. He knows what to do with the letter: take it to Face West. Someone at the charity will help him appeal it or whatever the fuck he needs to do.

The bedroom tax: Google it – *gaunny dae it now like* – introduced by a right-wing English cabinet minister who lives for free in a £2 million Tudor manorhouse on his mother-in-law's ancestral estate in the Chilterns with four acres of land, a tennis court and a swimming pool.

Mickey puts the letter back in its brown envelope and tucks it out of sight behind a glass storage jar and a pile of leaflets from the Yes campaign. Tyke comes trotting through, tail up. The dog knows the rattle of the biscuit jar. Tyke sits expectantly, gazing up at Mickey with bright eyes. As he looks down at the dog, an image flickers in his mind: him and Tyke under a blanket in the rain with a cardboard sign and a paper cup on the pavement.

He shivers.

'Brrrr –I'm feelin' cold and chilled, pups. And my back's sair – I'm gaunny have a hot shower,' he says, reaching down to pat the dog.

Ten minutes pass. In the damp, clammy bathroom, black, cloud-shaped blooms of mould spread across the ceiling. He never switches the immersion on. The extractor fan is silent: he disconnected it six months ago to save electricity. Soothed by the hot water, he stands naked at the basin warmed by the steam that fills the bathroom.

He takes a corner of towel, wipes the condensation from the mirror and fills the basin from the shower. He splashes hot water on five days of beard growth. A creamy-white blob of Value shaving foam drops onto the black hairs around his left nipple. Another lands on his stomach.

He dips the orange, plastic disposable razor in the water and draws it across his face, starting below his left ear. A razor blade's width of pink skin appears, furrowed by an inch-long, old red scar, as white shaving foam and black stubble froth over the rusty razor blade.

§

The Wheelhouse Bar, an ugly, low breeze block extension to the austere, grey granite Victorian Culag Hotel, between the harbour and the Lochinver Fish Selling Company, was never going to be a gay-friendly establishment, was never going to be the kind of place a boy could mince up to the bar and say, 'Two pink gins please, bartender.'

Still, during his six months in Assynt he'd been in a couple of times and the locals and assorted Dutch and Germans had seemed friendly enough.

He'd had a couple of pints. Bored with the sea and the sheep and the isolation of Shore Cottage, he'd not spoken to anyone but Tyke for three days and yearned for human company.

He'd been playing the fruit machine next to the Gents and just lost four quid when the three of them came into the bar. The one buying the drinks, thirty-ish, with a neatly trimmed beard, dirty jeans, workies' boots and an expensive-looking Helly Hansen jacket was talking loudly to a younger red-headed guy in blue overalls. But it was the cute dark-haired buzz-cut one with the tattoos he couldn't resist sneaking a look at.

'They're straight.'

He could hear Zelda's voice in his head. Fishermen off one of the handful of trawlers in the harbour perhaps; he sensed they were talking about him as he perched on a bar stool pretending to read a copy of the *Ross-shire Journal* one of the regulars had left behind.

He guessed the locals knew, that word had got around about him, the gay bit and some. He'd come into the kitchen of Shore Cottage one rainy morning early in April to find chain-smoking Sheila and Issy from the croft down the road sat at the kitchen table. They were always dropping in at first to check the post office was open and the cats fed. His meds lay glinting in their silver foil wrappers and brightly coloured cardboard boxes on the top of the dresser for all to see. Tenofovir and Abacavir like the names of the knights of the round table. He knew people see empty drug packaging in the bin and go home and Google it. So he reckoned half the folk in Assynt knew his HIV status.

Two pints later Mickey found himself standing next to the dark-haired young guy with the crew cut and tattoos at the urinal. He couldn't resist a quick downward glance as the cute one jetted a golden stream against the porcelain; a fleeting glimpse of white foreskin between suntanned fingers.

Mickey stood in the dark of the car park beside a rusty, blue Mercedes S class with German number plates. He leant back, a little unsteadily, against the grey, pebble-dashed wall at the corner of the Wheelhouse next to the redundant fish processing unit with its tarnished steel roller shutters.

Rizla paper, wedge of Golden Virginia. He rolled the tobacco between thumbs and forefingers; licked the adhesive edge of the cigarette paper. Put the roll-up between his lips, thinking half-seriously he'd always been orally fixated, since he was a kid, sucking thumbs – cigarettes – cocks.

Reached into his jeans pocket for his lighter and then drew deeply on the roll-up; exhaled a cloud of blue smoke.

'Dirty AIDS fucker!'

He hadn't seen the three men leave the bar.

'Fuckin poof!'

The empty Becks bottle cracked over his head, slicing into his cheek just below his left ear. The thirty-something one with the beard and the Helly Hansen jacket grabbed him by the hair and pulled his head down to crotch height. Two seconds later a paint-spattered, tan leather, steel toe-capped boot hit him in the face.

Mickey's nose exploded in a fountain of crimson. He was on his knees, tears welling up in his eyes, when the cute one from the urinals kicked him hard in the balls. Mickey curled into a foetal position, his face a mess of blood and salt tears, watching his bloodstained roll-up floating on the oily surface of a puddle.

'Let's get tae fuck out of here!'

Boots stomping… running on tarmac… car doors bang… the revving of a souped-up engine... screech of tyres. The noise of the car's throaty exhaust faded as it sped away east.

Silence fell as he lay there. He could see the little cracks in the surface of the tarmac. He could taste the blood in his mouth. He could hear the waves lapping around the barnacle and seaweed-encrusted concrete pillars of the harbour pier. Five minutes passed then Mickey pulled himself slowly to his feet and staggered back into the Wheelhouse Bar, covered in blood.

The ambulance men gave him a lift back to Shore Cottage, Mickey sitting in the front pressing a square of surgical wadding to his nose, a neat row of butterfly stitches just below his left ear.

Half a mile before Clachtoll the driver braked sharply. Just beyond the edge of the white beam of the headlights, a pair of dark hunched shapes trotted across the road: two badgers.

Parked up outside Shore Cottage, the ambulance men made him sign a pink form.

'Just at the cross there – it's to say you've discharged yourself.'

They'd wanted to take him to hospital in Inverness.

He'd refused.

'Make sure you keep the wound clean,' the ambulance man with the ginger beard told him, 'The medical centre in Lochinver's open weekday mornings.'

Mickey walked shakily through the gate in the picket fence and along the garden path as the red tail lights of the ambulance trailed off down the hill past Stoer beach.

Tyke barked when he put his key in the door. His hands trembled as he fumbled with the lock. Inside the house he sat down heavily on the sofa in the dark of the front room with its sanded floor and Georgian chest of drawers beside the fireplace.

'Aye, OK pups, you must be bustin', doggie, I'll take you oot in a sec.'

Tyke jumped up onto the sofa beside him, sniffed the coagulated blood in Mickey's nostrils and started licking his ear.

Mickey buried his face in Tyke's fur.

Then he began to cry.

CD4 count 456
viral load <40 copies
meds abacavir nevirapine tenofovir
munros 147/282

'They weren't from round here,' Sheila tried to reassure him.

They were sat at the wooden kitchen table, its drawers jammed full of 1980s recipe books, linen tea towels and tarnished silver cutlery.

He hadn't ventured into Lochinver in the two weeks since he was queer-bashed.

'Issy's son thinks the two young guys are fishermen from Kinlochbervie. They'd been down here working on the Kylesku Bridge for a contractor from Skye – industrial rope access work – painting the underneath of the bridge or something. He says the contractor's name is Dougal Anderson.'

Tyke shifted position on the checked, woollen blanket in the dog basket next to the red, oil-fired Rayburn.

Mickey put his head in his hands.

'There's nae point going on aboot it – it's just whit happens in ma shitty life but.'

'Aw, c'mon – you're too hard on yourself, Mickey.' Sheila tried to distract him, 'What about the Munros? How many have you done now?'

He didn't look up.

'A hundred and forty-seven and counting,' he said at last, 'I plan tae get the last two Filthy Fannichs next weekend.'

A
Chailleach
An Coileachan Sgurr Breac
Beinn Liath Mhor Fannaich
Meall Gorm Fionn Bheinn Sgurr Mor Meall
a'Chrasgaidh Sgurr nan Clach Geala Sgurr nan Each

He'd christened them the Filthy Fannichs on account of a mixture of horizontal rain, snow and storm-force winds encountered during the ascent of this range of ten mountains to the south of Ullapool and the A835 road from Garve.

The distances were getting longer now. He'd ticked off all the Munros within two hours' drive of Stoer. He'd driven north to Ben Hope and Ben Klibreck, south to Moruisg, Sgurr Choinnich and Sgurr a'Chaorachain and east to Ben Wyvis.

It was nearly October. He'd only got a few weeks left in Assynt. He stretched his legs out and leant back from the table.

'Fuckin homophobic cunts.'

He muttered.

An awkward silence filled the room.

'Sorry, Sheila – but fuck them – it's still been the best summer ever.'

He glanced across at the dog basket beside the Rayburn.

'Eh, Tyke? Whit'd you think?'

Hearing his name, Tyke jumped up out of his basket and laid his head on Mickey's knee. He stroked the dog's shaggy head and in a quiet voice said, 'Will you like it in Glasgow, pups?'

tyke

I'm the dog I'm the dog I'm the dog sniff sniff snuff snuff I'm the dog I'm the dog I'm the dog... see me, I wis born in a cold stone barn. The first thing I saw when I opened my eyes were the last leaves of autumn blowing across the yard and under the door.

It sleated that February night, a'ghraidh and my old master was away at a meeting up the hill. In Stoer. Folk crammed into the room. The printed papers on the table at the front. The yellow light blurry behind the steamed-up windaes of the village hall.

The night I wis born the dogs at Torbreac barked the news all along the coast:

North to the collies at Clachtoll and the lighthouse keeper's dog at Stoerhead,

The Alsatian on the fishing boat at Kinlochbervie snarled the news to

The whippet at the garage in Durness.

And to the south in Lochinver: the harbour master's black lab lifted his ears and bayed,

The bookseller's Westie at Inverkirkaig yelped,

And the beardie at Achiltibuie yipped,

The terriers at the caravan site at Ardmair Point yapped the news to

The Staffie tied up outside the Arctic Bar in Ullapool,
The collies on the quayside at Gairloch howled the news
To the Jack Russell at Lochcarron

And the old dog on the ferry moored at Kylerhea barked it across the Sound of Sleat to the wee collie all alone on the pier at Glenelg.

i luv u

4 pm: He sits on the frayed and faded blue sofa, Tyke's head resting in his lap leaving fine black dog hairs on the damp white towel wrapped around his waist. The dog licks the residue of soap off his skin. On the TV a robotic figure in a red frock coat with a gold clockwork face is chasing the Doctor.

§

pls tell me u didnt mean wat u said 😬

WHY MICKEY?????

WHY???? 😮

but I luv u……pls text me bac

I LOVE YOU

I don understand? 😢

it wudve been our 6 month anniversary 2day Mickey...

fuck u

fuck u

fuck u

pls pls pls pls dont finish with me!!! 

I LU

u patronising fucker 

u got a small cock btw mate

I LU

why u have 2 finish with me just when my Mums so ill

i love you Mickey U B SORRY

i luv u

u ve ruined my life

Then one night just after midnight: 'Ish me – let me in!'

It was Jonnie buzzing the entryphone: pished, aff his face, wasted, bevvied, guttered, oot the box, plastered, steamin', wrecked, hammered.

He staggered through the flat, incoherent, mumbling about being in the Waterloo. 'Shu got anything to drink?'

Mickey shook his head. It was true. He was skint. Four

days to go until he got his dole money. He'd finished the last of the half-full green plastic torpedo of flat cider in the fridge the night before.

Through his drunken haze Jonnie spotted a bottle on the worktop in the kitchen.

A plastic bottle with a B&Q label; Zelda had left it in the flat one evening a couple of weeks back with the explanation, 'I'm going to the pub on the way home and I don't want to look like a bag lady'.

Jonnie picked the bottle up.

'For fuck's sake! Ah said no tae dae that! That's teak oil but. It disnae have any alcohol in it,' Mickey protested.

But Jonnie didn't hesitate.

He unscrewed the red plastic safety cap, threw back his head and swallowed several large gulps of the cloudy, viscous, brown liquid.

Fuckin bampot, thought Mickey, losing patience as Jonnie staggered onto a plastic chair and sat slumped, with his head in his hands at the kitchen table.

Shouldae left the fuckin paint stripper oot too but!

Tyke gave a low warning growl from under the table; dogs don't like drunks. Mickey scowled and flicked the switch down on the kettle, put a teabag in a mug and got the milk out the fridge. It was 2.30 am before he heard the front door slam shut as Jonnie shambled off into the madness of the night.

the book

I wis daein' the charity shops that day, see. It wis grey Glasgow early morning, Tyke sniffing around the roll-up ends, chocolate wrappers and the blanket on the pavement where the glaikit beggar sits in daylight. Like I said I wis daein' the charity shops that day – ye have tae get in there first thing or the good stuff's all gone like. I dinnae ever bother wi' books mind. I dinnae like reading - havenae read a book for years like. Whit I was efter was games for the Nintendo that kindae thing. Stuff tae resell on eBay. Get a few quid in ma PayPal account - every little helps like. But this day, time tae kill, I pushed open the glass door of the charity shop, breathed in the fousty smell of second-hand claes, saw how the dust motes danced in the sunlight and looked along the shelves and that wis when I saw the Book.

§

Elena puts the cup of tea down carefully on the stained, wooden coffee table. She's young, twenty-four, twenty-five maybe and pretty with blond, shoulder-length hair cut in a side-swept fringe. She wears a green tabard and jeans with a glass bead-studded belt and white baseball boots.

'That's your tea, Donald,' she says in a thick Polish accent to the old man asleep in the tan-coloured Parker Knoll armchair.

The old man hadn't stirred when, moments earlier, she'd pushed open the door, its scratched white paintwork brushing across the furry, orange, nylon carpet of Room 17.

The room is the same as all the other rooms on the second floor: door, double window, high single bed on wheels with metal frame and headboard. An olive-green basin stands in the corner of the room with hospital-type chrome lever taps. Where the rooms vary lies in the choice of personal possessions the residents brought with them.

Donald, the occupant of Room 17 these past twelve years, brought with him a small, wooden writing desk. It is a solid rather than an elegant piece of Victorian furniture made of varnished walnut with six drawers and a sloping lid that folds down on tarnished brass hinges to form a leaf to write on.

A red anglepoise reading lamp and a cut glass vase of lilies stands on the tattered leather surface of the writing desk. The heady, sickly smell of the lilies lies heavily on the stiflingly warm, centrally heated air.

The scent of the lilies drifts to Donald's nostrils and, at the end of a bricked-up tunnel somewhere in his mind, mingles with the smell of the boys' toilets at primary school. The odour of institutional cooking wafting down the corridor outside; like the smell of school dinner mince.

Elena could write her name in the pollen from the lilies that lies, a thick yellow dust on the varnished wood of the writing desk.

The second piece of furniture the old man was allowed to bring with him was a small wooden bookcase which stands at the foot of his bed.

'You'll want your books in the home, Dad.'

The old man's son works as a teacher and comes to visit his

father every Tuesday evening and most Sunday afternoons (if he's not playing golf).

On the bottom shelf of the bookcase a stack of magazines lean against a dozen red photo albums and a Roberts radio, its once-shiny black buttons coated with house dust.

On the middle shelf, a row of green-fabric-bound volumes: *The Master of Ballantrae*, *Wild Animals I Have Known* and a 1960s hardback copy of *The White Spider* by Heinrich Harrer, its glossy paper cover torn and tattered.

Elena pulls a yellow duster out from the pocket of her green tabard and runs it quickly along the top shelf. Over the row of inch-to-the-mile Ordnance Survey maps (Sheet 56 Loch Lomond and the Trossachs, sheet 50 Glen Orchy, sheet 41 Ben Nevis) and the silver shield engraved with the spidery words:

D.G. Fraser
Scottish Climbing Club
President
1983-86

And over the pewter hip flask next to it:

Donald Fraser
September 17 1964
Compleat Munroist
Number 167

And across the spine of the 1991 edition of *The Scottish Peaks Over 3000 Feet*, edited by D.G. Fraser. The title printed on the cover in a red font below a picture of Ben Cruachan.

As she stands there beside the old man asleep in the armchair, she remembers today is her birthday.

They're going to go to the new pizza place in West George

Street, the one down the steps in the basement. When her boyfriend's finished his shift at the supermarket, he'll come and collect her. She'll listen out for his blue Ford Fiesta with the thick exhaust and alloy wheels; the scrunch of his tyres on the gravel car park.

She likes him. He's steady, reliable. She likes the neat tidiness of his one-bedroom flat. Likes walking through IKEA hand in hand with him, imagining the day they'll settle down in a bought flat. She likes his neatly clipped beard, likes the touch of his white Scottish skin.

The noise of TV, a daytime chat show interspersed with adverts for payday loan companies, plays on the widescreen telly in the corner of the room under the window with its white-painted frame.

Elena half hears the wailing moan from the old woman two doors along. It hardly registers, the weary sigh repeated every five minutes throughout every day.

She steps past Donald's chair, squeezes around the end of the bed with its neatly folded tartan rug and pushes apart the white net curtains draped across the double window.

She looks out across the trees at the edge of the garden of the nursing home to the grey bungalows and beyond the yellow haze of the city, to the Campsie Fells, a green blur on the horizon.

A dribble of saliva runs down from the corner of the old man's mouth and, in wiping it away with a tissue, she awakens him. His legs twitch and then kick out.

'Donald— Donald,' she says again though she knows he won't respond to his name, doesn't even recognise his own son when he comes to visit, his cerebral cortex a mass of neural plaques and tangles of abnormal protein.

The old man in the armchair is awake now but dazed.

'I help you with that. It's very hot,' she says.

She likes the old man. Something about him reminds the

girl of her grandfather back in Gdansk in the tiny flat decorated with Orthodox Christian icons of saints and smelling of pickled cabbage and Polish vodka on the twentieth floor of the towerblock with its view of the docks and cranes. She places the cup in the old man's wrinkled hands, dotted brown with liver spots.

The TV in Donald's room in the nursing home is digital high definition but his flickering memories all play in the Kodachrome tint of slide film. His mental maps are all Ordnance Survey one-inch-to-the-mile where shaded green hachures highlight the brown hillsides.

A'Mhaighdean and Ruadh Stac Mor.

Climbed one day in June long ago.

And now... and now... and now...

In one of his few remaining, still functioning areas of frontal cortex, there is a break in the cloud, the mist lifts from the hills, neurons fire and the old man blows wheezily on his tea.

Brown ripples and waves appear on the surface of the tea and behind his watery eye somewhere free, his brain clicks back in time and he's standing on the rocky hillside watching the waves on the surface of the Dubh Loch high above Carnmore Lodge. Ruadh Stac Mor looms, its scree-grey summit slopes streaked with snow.

The old man sitting in the tan-coloured armchair in the cluttered room is unaware of the bracken on the hillside fading to orange and the rowan berries deepening to red. Someday soon he'll escape from the nursing home. Be free to roam the heart of the wilderness below A'Mhaighdean for all eternity.

Suddenly a nerve cell passes an electrical signal to a cluster of brain cells in a deserted chamber somewhere in his mind. In a flickering dream he's driving a car for mile upon mile through the southern highlands along Loch Lomondside, through Bridge of Orchy and Glencoe and all along the western seaboard of Scotland.

Creagh Dhu Cottage white below the Buchaille, the mountain all grey schist and trails of yellow gravel. The old man remembers the way the sun warmed the lichen-coated rocks on Curved Ridge. The scree at the foot of the crags. The birch trees climbing the hillside. The silver spray and granite boulders in the burn. The dragonflies hovering over the peaty black pools. He remembers the way the mountains stood as September dusk fell against a grey sky.

At Gairloch the seagulls are lined up on the beach among the shells and brown kelp. Now the car door bangs shut at the edge of the road across the bay from the white art nouveau house among the palm trees.

He tramps thc long miles past Kernsary and the ruined cottage at the foot of Strathan Buidhe in that golden summer long ago when they made the long walk in to A'Mhaighdean and Ruadh Stac Mor.

Now he's sitting at the writing desk in the bay window of the flat overlooking Great Western Road; drops of rain running down the glass. Chapter 11 almost complete: Loch Maree to Loch Broom; route descriptions and timings for the ascent of twelve Munros in the far north-west of Scotland.

He inserts a fresh sheet of paper into the roll of the typewriter. Smells the graphite smell of the black ribbon. With two fingers starts to type, pressing down the plastic-capped metal keys.

Clack.
Clack.
Clack.
Black smudgy letters on crisp white paper.
((((At the shore of the Dubh Loch the heart of the wilderness is reached and

A'Mhaighdean soars up.......he typed one afternoon long ago as, outside the window, drizzle fell on the pavements of Glasgow. He's lost now, his brain crumbled away, his body wasted but somewhere in his mind, where fragments of memories linger on like strips of pages in a paper shredder, the old man in the tan-coloured Parker Knoll armchair wrote these words and the printer typeset them on page 223 of The Scottish Peaks Over 3000 Feet better known to generations of Scottish hillwalkers as:

THE MUNROS BOOK*

*(As in: We're at the edge of a cliff! Which way did the Munros Book say to go again?)

The book Elena dusts every week, the one next to the pewter hip flask and the silver shield at the foot of the bed in the room in the nursing home with its view to the distant Campsie Fells. The book that lies on the top shelf of the wobbly IKEA unit behind the sofa in the flat on level zero of the high flats in Drumkirk.

Donald always gave a generous margin of time for the walks in his book. He let people think how fit they were, made sure they'd get off the hill before darkness crept along the glen.

A wisp of cloud touches the top of A'Mhaighdean. They need to push on to the summit. The old man bends down to pick his rucksack up from the deergrass and boulder-strewn hillside; his legs twitch and the cup of tea drops, spilling onto the orange, nylon carpet of the bedroom in the nursing home.

23 texts

The texting had started again. TBH it had never really stopped. Even worse he'd been getting phone calls and voicemail messages again too. For a while, around the time he met Jinksie and Danny in the Waterloo and they'd told him in hushed tones Jonnie was back in the Murray Royal again, the voicemails had ceased entirely.

He just got a text ten minutes ago. Thinks, I could go round tae Shamoon's and get a new SIM and a new number but he's done that before and ended up with Jonnie on his doorstep.

He never answers the calls or replies to the texts but still they come. Five – ten – fifteen: there were 23 one day! Sometimes he guesses from the frequency and length of the texts that Jonnie must be on the interminable Megabus journey back to Perth. Bored; resentful; jealous; angry. One thing on his mind: Mickey Bell.

> I just keep getting yer fuckin voicemail  

> v v angry u even did that Mickey dont u think i ve enough 2think about my Mum's having more chemo 2day I need 2 focus

ill tell you what why dont u continue 2 ignore my texts while im stuck on this fuckin bus

u mashed my head up Mickey

Who the fuck do u think u r Mr  

The tone, content and level of aggression of the texts varies according to time of day. Mickey can guess how much Jonnie has had, almost to the nearest can or half torpedo of Strongbow, from the content of his texts. After two litres of cider the messages became shorter and more succinct.

shes in hospital u kno

u fuckin bastard

Cunt

was a favourite late night Saturday one.

the fate of climbing books

))))))£££:££***...Two and a half years I'd been there.... TWO AND A HALF YEARS!... sandwiched between the AA Guide to Rural Britain and Michael Owen's Soccer Skills. Abandoned... forgotten at the end of an inaccessible bookshelf behind a wire basket of CDs and a plastic crate of videos.

It was the long nights that were the worst... after they locked the door at five o'clock. During the day a faint breeze from the Campsies sometimes drifted through the window in the back store room, but at night, the smell of second-hand clothes permeated everything... it seeped, seeped into my covers.

Two and a half years I'd been there.

Before that I was twelve years on a shelf in a bright, sunny, northern-lit room with a view of the ocean where candles were lit at night; the smell of beef bourguignon and glasses of red wine on the shiny, oak table in front of the bookcase.

Those twelve years I was side by side

with Nan Shepherd's The Living Mountain. On my left were the Art Books. I liked them; tall broad hardbacks with glossy pages, the illustrations of paintings by Matisse and Gauguin. They looked down on me though because I didn't have a jacket, just a hard cover and they ignored me when I tried to explain I was printed and bound that way.

I was a present given them when they retired to the house by the sea. I came new from the bookshop, only a month off the press and I was fresh and my new book smell was all around me when my pages were open and my glossy colour photos gleamed and my paper was new and all of a book's life lay ahead of me.

As I was fresh and crisp, my ink just dry, I yearned to have my pages opened, to be on a mountainside, to feel drops of rain on my cover. I wanted annotations in my margins, ticks next to my hills.

I knew if I was an often opened, well thumbed book, over time my cover would become tattered, my spine and binding weak, my pages curled and folded-over but that was a price I was glad to pay because I wanted to be A Real Climbing Book.

Abandoned, forgotten, left on the shelf, unopened, my pages still clean and pristine and untorn, I knew I'd last forever. But I wanted to be a book that's well loved. I wanted to be a real climber's book. I'm THE MUNROS BOOK [ed. D.G. Fraser] and I wanted to be used as my writer intended. For he laboured long, researching and taking photographs for my pages, over many hill days.

That's the fate of climbing books, you see, be used and in time fall to pieces or live forever at the end of a row of books on a forgotten, dusty shelf.

But after a few days on the shiny, oak table in the house by the ocean, they put me on the shelf next to the Art Books. Perhaps I was a project they never got round to in retirement; weaving and embroidery and the community council took all their time.

And then figures on a computer screen highlighted in red, a number beyond the parameters of normal, led to more tests and a visit to a hospital.

They sat down heavily on the couch in front of the bookcase and sighed. And then one of them stood at the big window looking out at the sea for a long time.

The men came in blue overalls and carried the shiny, oak table out while we books watched from the shelves. Then I was at the foot of a cardboard box. The Art Books went into another crate and I never saw them again.

Nan Shepherd's The Living Mountain went into the same box as me but after only two weeks on the shelf of the Oxfam shop she was bought by a new owner. Two and a half years passed and I was there still, abandoned at the end of a forgotten shelf.

Dust motes danced in the shaft of sunlight falling across the open doorway of the shop.

I could almost smell the heather in bloom on the high hills, the yellow tormentil and the alpine saxifrage, the cool breeze off the snowfields.

Wait a minute!

Suddenly I was upside down!

Someone had picked me off the shelf!

He was flicking through my pages, pausing now and again to look at my colour plates. I was being carried across the shop. I was on the counter. Three gold-coloured coins laid down on my cover. Oh happy day I waited so long for! Goodbye Microwave-oven cookbooks! Goodbye golf videos!

I'm in a rucksack.

It's dark in here.

Yuck – who are you?

The Dog's tennis ball?

Well DON'T mess up my cover, please.

Smell of diesel, dusty checked seats. Hot and noisy. Sunshine burning my cover. Fields and copses of trees and hedgerows. Now city streets and concrete and brick.

I'm the only book on this wobbly, IKEA shelf unit behind the faded and frayed blue sofa. In fact I think I'm the only book in the whole house and it's not a house, by the way, it's a flat on the ground floor... but it's way better than the charity shop! It's not the house by the sea but I'm next to a 1988 OS sheet 51 that spent five years in a cardboard box under the bed and there's a chipped Silva compass here beside me. Her black numbers are a little worn between 340 and 10 degrees north but her needle still floats and there's no bubble in her paraffin.

And that first night ((((((someone opened my covers, turned to page 6 and put a tick in smudgy blue biro next to Ben Lomond, 3,196 feet! ##0000£-----------

a big pile of shite

He finishes the last of his pint.

He's had enough.

He wants to leave the bar and the music and the staring, lustful eyes.

He wants to be home – with Tyke – on the sofa.

The air out in the street is cold and sharp as he squeezes past the bouncers and the huddle of smokers standing at the door. He pulls his hoodie over his head, stuffs his hands deep in his pockets as he steps over the pavement cracks and into the city night. On the wasteland by the dual carriageway the urban fox watches Mickey Bell pass by.

11 pm: Late night empty. On the muddy grass outside the high flats Tyke has just seen off the white Alsatian from the tenth floor. Three years old and the veteran of some two hundred and fifty Munros, Tyke is still the puppy at heart, his tough Border Collie genes and intelligence enabling him to outwit, intimidate or outrun the local Staffies and Rottweilers.

That first night, when Mickey'd come back to Drumkirk after six months in Assynt, Tyke had stood stock-still on the grass across the road from the high flats, nose twitching, sniffing the cacophony of smells of the city borne on the night air. Then he ran across and wagged his tail at the jakeys swigging from blue plastic bottles of cider on the benches beside the playpark.

The dog cocks his leg at the smashed TV embedded in the grass. Mickey looks up; in the blue, night sky above the high flats he can see the winking red tail lights of a plane coming in to land at Glasgow airport.

§

They named the hill in the time they call the little ice age. Father Padruig leads the straggling line of raggedy people across the hillside to Loch Callater. Their breath smokes in the freezing air and the ground beneath their feet crunches with frost on blades of grass.

Though it is well into May the frost still grips the land in its claws, the soil hard and unyielding. At the shore of the loch Father Padruig kneels down and crosses himself. Head bowed, eyes closed, he prays for an end to the frost while the silent hills stand all around.

A wisp of mist drifts across the summit of the mountain, a mild flow of air from the west, from the sea. When the priest opens his eyes he sees a drop of water run off a blade of grass and at last the ice begins to melt. And in the days that are to come the people will name the mountain Carn an t-Sagairt Mor, the big hill of the priest.

§

'They were £165 *new* from Nevisport in Sauchiehall Street.'

'You're joking!' Zelda'd said.

'Naw— seriously,' he'd explained, 'it's like car tyres, its no the kindae thing you want tae save money on but.'

A bright and windy day; pine needles and tarmac beneath

the Vibram soles of Mickey's brand new Zamberlans as he crossed the A93.

His new boots: his only two points of contact with the planet. *See I'm no planning on hurtling off the cliffs of Lochnagar – falling heid first through the air – seeing death hurtling towards me from the boulder-strewn floor of the corrie – ma last seconds spent wishing I'd put another seventy quid on ma credit card and no bought boots wi' a crap sole!*

On the far side of the road the wide river glinted between the leaves. A quarter of a mile upstream, six arches of stone spanned the fast flowing waters of the Dee, where Major Caulfeild had used rock and gunpowder to build the bridge after the defeat of the Jacobite army on the moor of Culloden.

The Old Brig o' Dee they called it, humpbacked with segmental arches increasing in size to the centre. Each span had a different size, irregularity dictated by the need to build pier foundations on reefs of river rock and in this asymmetry lay the beauty of the bridge.

Yellow larches towered above the approaches to the old stone bridge. It was the kind of place an elfish warrior on a grey horse might gallop up and set a jewel in the dirt to stop the Black Riders.

Across the bridge on the north bank of the river, Mickey pushed open a gate in a deer fence and found himself in the Ballochbuie Forest. He breathed in the sharp resiny smell of the wood. Blaeberry and ling grew thickly at the base of the hoary old Scots pines. And there were young trees two or three feet high – all furrowed pink-tinged bark and long bluish-green needles. Some of the gnarled Granny pines shading the path in the Ballochbuie Forest were four hundred years old, trees already a century old when the teenage Charles Edward Stuart stepped ashore on to a seaweed-covered rock on the Isle of Eriskay.

Beneath the ancient pines the wood ants, the hunter-gatherers of the insect world, fanned out in legions hundreds' strong from nests in two-foot-high mounds of pine needles. And deep in the Ballochbuie Forest, there lived one of a dying breed. His black fan of tail feathers was speckled with white. His breast a rich green shading to indigo. His neck sheathed in grey feathers, he had a red comb over each eye and his beak was brightest yellow. He fed on berries and the buds and shoots of the Scots Pine. His talons gripped the mossy boulder. He fanned out his black tail feathers and stretched his neck up to the sky and opened his beak of brightest yellow and sang. And when they heard his extraordinary song the Gaels named him the capercaillie, the horse of the woods, for the clip-clop sound they heard when he sang.

Man and dog they followed the path, climbing in steep zigzags up the steep heathery bank beside the Feindallacher Burn. Through the trees an elegant, green-painted, iron footbridge spanned the white Falls of Garbh Allt where once, when Mickey was a child, a teenage princess posed for the Pentax MXs and xenon tube flashes of the paparazzi.

Where the brown lands ended the Stuic rose, a great green prow. As the forest began to thin, the scattered Scots pines took on a look of the Serengeti; a hint of Africa in the Eastern Grampians. Soon the trees dwindled to open moorland and he reached a gate in a deer fence where a large boulder rested among bog myrtle, juniper, creeping azalea, blaeberry and ling.

GO BAK AK-AK!

The sudden mechanical croaking rattle made him jump. A grouse exploded from the heather, lipstick-red mascara above each eye. He watched as cearc-fhraoich flew low over the the stony mountain-top heather in an elaborate display, flapping short distances just above the heather, feigning a broken wing as she lured the dog away from her nest of chicks.

He unbuttoned the top pocket of his shirt. He had three bars of signal on his phone.

He texted Jonnie.

No reply.

Blank screensaver: sulking silence.

After the heather and the open spaces and the yellow tormentil by the Feindallacher Burn, the sun-bleached, twisted, white fragments of aluminium scattered across the smooth, rounded, granite boulders and little plains of gravel and mountain heath came as a shock.

Black rubber tyres and the shiny, metal remains of the undercarriage lay on the hillside. Close by, an entire wing rested in the heather. Wires and cables dangled beneath it, a target-shaped RAF symbol still legible on the sun and snow-faded paint. The strength of the metal frame impacted on the mountain was impressive. He hadn't thought of aircraft being that strong, constructed from aluminium girders now twisted and scattered across the rounded Grampian mountain top.

Long ago when cars had chrome fins, Elvis Presley was young and *That's All Right* played on every wireless set in Memphis, a scientist bit into a poisoned apple and these twisted pieces of sun-bleached aluminium among the woody stems of ling and cross-leaved heath flew gleaming, high in the stratosphere.

Manufactured by the shiny new English Electric Company (in the same factory that produced a washing machine called the Liberator, in a Britain that still made things!) these twisted fragments of metal were once a Canberra bomber. An aeroplane designed to carry a payload of Red Beard hydrogen bombs, enough to wipe out four Hiroshimas.

The jet aircraft was on a night sortie that November day in 1956 and had just completed a controlled descent through cloud when it slammed into the granite boulder-studded heather killing the crew of three young men in fur-lined leather jackets and flying suits and white cotton army-issue boxer shorts even as *Heartbreak Hotel* played in their heads on the remote mountainside.

Leaving Carn an t-Sagairt Mor and the wreck of the aircraft behind, he headed north-east to a wide grassy col. From here he followed the edge of the crags uphill to the Stuic where he found the footpath marked on the map, a worn groove in the grassy mountain top.

Mickey tramped over short-cropped turf. A low rickle of stones stood on the wind-clipped heath; an eroded line of footsteps cut a faint stripe across the green plateau to the south. He followed the footprints in the turf half a mile to the Munro they call the White Mounth. In the distance a herd of red deer grazed on the wide open summit plateau and to the east the rounded Grampian Mountains seemed to go on forever.

Carn a'Coire Boidheach.

Another tick in the Book.

Then, turning northwards once more, he walked back towards the Stuic. On the skyline along the edge of the featureless, stony plateau a line of granite tors came into sight: giants standing on the mountain top. The path climbed another three hundred feet to Cac Carn Mor from where a wide track led a quarter-mile further north. A scramble up the granite tor and then Mickey stood at the trig point and mountain indicator that marked the summit of Cac Carn Beag.

That Saturday afternoon, when Mickey and Tyke sat at the trig point on the edge of the cliffs of Lochnagar watching the cloud shadows move across the hillside and Jonnie lay on the sofa watching Columbo and texting his mum, in the dog-eared book on the shelf on the rickety IKEA unit behind the sofa on level zero of the high flats in Drumkirk there were 277 smudgey ticks in black biro.

He had five Munros left.

Mickey smiled to himself. The night before, sitting in the Fyfe Arms in Braemar making a pint of Stella last an hour, the taste of fish and chips still on his fingers, he'd been reliably informed by the old guy sitting at the end of the bar that the names Cac Carn Mor and Cac Carn Beag meant a wee pile of shite and a big pile of shite.

§

viral load <40 copies
CD4 count 538
meds 600mg abacavir 400mg nevirapine 245mg tenofovir
munros 277/282

§

Fifty yards: the maximum distance a claimant must be unable or virtually unable to walk – without severe discomfort, or at risk of endangering life or causing deterioration in health by making the effort to walk – to qualify for the higher rate mobility component of Disability Living Allowance.

Thursday

1.03 am: Mickey's asleep on the couch. Tyke is stretched out on the shiny carpet among the stains and fag burns, snoring quietly but audibly. His shaggy, black and white coat rises and falls slowly. His ears lift a couple of millimetres off the carpet, his eyeballs flicker beneath their lids, and then his front left paw begins to twitch and then his right paw, then all four legs are going, and his nose and mouth, as in his doggie dreams Tyke relives his run-in with the white Alsatian from the tenth floor.

Buzz!

Buzzzz!

Buzzzzzzzzz!

BUZZZZZZZZZZZZZZZ!

Mickey jolts awake with a stab of anxiety. He stumbles through the tiny, cramped hall of the flat and picks up the entryphone.

'Fuckin open the door, Mickey – you've got to see me!'

He can't think for Tyke's barking. He hesitates for a moment then slams the entryphone back onto its cradle. Tyke's bark has changed to a low resonating snarling growl.

BUZZZZZZZZZZZZZZZZZZZ!

Mickey goes back into the front room and curls up on the sofa in a ball, his fingers stuck in his ears. After a couple of minutes he takes them out and listens; the sound of a car door slamming outside and male voices arguing followed by the noise of a battery on 12.2 volts of charge struggling to turn the starter motor of a second-hand car. Then the engine fires and the driver revs up.

BUZZZZZZZZZZZZZZZZZZZZZZZZZZZZZZZZZZZZ!

Then silence...

Suddenly there's a loud **BANG!**

The wall shudders and glittering shards of glass explode across the front room carpet. A white hand and arm are sticking through a jagged hole in the window. A single drip of blood runs down the glass.

Mickey grabs Tyke by the collar and drags him into the windowless internal kitchen of the flat and slams the door shut.

One – two seconds pass – then Jonnie pulls his arm back through the glass. There's a star-shaped hole left in the window. The white hand and arm are gone. Crimson blood runs down the glass onto the yellowing, white plastic of the window frame.

Mickey throws open the front door and runs across the tiled entrance hall of the flats and out into the street. Jonnie is lying half on the pavement, half in the gutter. Bright arterial blood spurts in a crimson jet from his forearm. One of the Iranian asylum seekers from Flat 12 has taken his top off and is kneeling bare-chested over Jonnie, trying to staunch the bleeding with his T-shirt. A half-eaten bag of chips lies on the pavement. Jinksie and Danny are standing white-faced, looking down at Jonnie. The engine of Jinksie's eleven year-old Vauxhall Cavalier is still turning over with an uneven rattle.

'Fuck's sake!' shouts Mickey. 'FUCKIN HELL!'

Lights are coming on in the flats upstairs. The young Polish woman and her boyfriend, with the beard and the blue Ford Fiesta, are out on their balcony on the fifth floor.

'We were going back to Perth,' stutters Jinksie, 'he made us stop here. He's aff his face.'

It was Thursday night in Glasgow.

The city of the broken windae.

Later, as the paramedics lift Jonnie into the ambulance, Mickey sits on the edge of the sofa giving a statement to the young policeman.

'Name?'

'Age?'

'Occupation?'

'Mickey Bell.'

'35.'

'Unemployed.'

'Do you know the full name of the person who broke your window?'

Mickey hesitates. 'John Paul O'Malley.'

The policeman looks up from his notebook, with a frown. 'Why do you think he broke your window?'

Mickey shifts uncomfortably on the edge of the faded and frayed blue sofa.

'He's been taken to the Royal Infirmary,' the policeman continues. 'I've seen injuries like that before. It's funny – you can put your hand through a glass window and not have a scratch on it. It's when you pull it back through the damage is done. He's lost a lot of blood but I don't think any tendons were severed.'

Mickey looks blankly at the floor.

His mind birling.

His life's default setting: **OUT OF CONTROL!**

If Jonnie's desperate enough tae punch his hand through glass... what the fuck else will he dae?

'Why would he put his arm through your window?' asks the policeman again.

3.15 am: the black bin liner and flattened cardboard box sellotaped across the jagged, star-shaped hole in the front room window rustle gently in the breeze of the warm September night in the city. The orange, flashing lights on the white City of Glasgow Council long-wheel-base van parked in front of the high flats are reflected in the puddles of water on the tarmac. The two workmen in fluorescent green jackets hose down the pavement and the road while the blood washes away into the gutter and runs down the storm drains and into the Clyde.

Common side effects of combination antiretroviral therapy:

nausea
fatigue
headache
high levels of cholesterol
lack of energy
raised tryglycerides
vomiting
abdominal pain

diarrhoea
fever
loss of appetite
skin rash
abnormal liver function tests
flatulence
feeling weak
dizziness

the night station

Eleven months: the life expectancy of a patient with symptomatic HIV/AIDS in the mid-1980s.

8.10 am: Mickey awakens, a fine film of moisture between his skin and the sheets, his head cold and wet in a sweaty dent in the pillow.

Jonnie's last text plays in widescreen across his frontal cortex. The text he got while Jinksie's eleven-year-old Vauxhall Cavalier revved in the street outside, seconds before Jonnie smashed his fist through the window. The phone screen with the message on it is seared to the back of his eyelids. It plays in his head over and over again.

> I grassed u to the dole
> High rate mobility DLA??!!
> C you in jail cunt
> Ha ha ha!!!

Sweat oozes from the base of Mickey's neck. Shining drops of perspiration, like condensation on the side of an ice-cold glass of water, glisten on his forehead. He sees, as clearly as if it were yesterday, Carmen d'Apostolini filling in his claim form in her office that mild February afternoon five years before.

He folds his arms over his face:

Aw fuck!

I wish I'd been mair fuckin careful but.

Fuck!

Fuck!

Why the fuck could ye no jist keep yer fuckin mouth shut aboot the Munros?

Fuck!

FUCK!!

FUCK!!

§

He'd been seeing Jonnie for a couple of weeks. They'd been in bed, had sex in the morning after the pub. When he heard the sound of the letterbox and the scrabbling of the dog's claws on the hall vinyl and Tyke's demented, postman bark, he was standing naked pissing a yellow stream down the side of the avocado toilet bowl.

When he came back from the bathroom Jonnie was sitting up in bed holding a three-page, official-looking letter in his hands. A brown envelope lay torn open on the duvet cover in front of him.

'Dear Mr Bell— '

Jonnie read aloud from the letter in his campest accent.

'Disability Living Allowance – about the amount of money we pay you,' he lisped, 'You are entitled to the higher rate mobility component because you need someone to guide or supervise you when you are walking on routes that are unfamiliar – we will pay – how much?! Fuckin' hell! – into your account—FOR HELP GETTING AROUND!'

Jonnie pulled the duvet up over his face giggling.

'Well you didnae seem to need "help getting around" when you were away climbing that big fuck-off mountain on your ain the other weekend!' he shrieked.

Mickey snatched the letter from Jonnie's hands then slid back under the duvet and lay there on his back with his arms behind his head, heart pounding.

'I ken all your secrets now,' Jonnie said.

Then he reached across and squeezed Mickey's cock.

§

Carmen was on the phone when he tapped on the door of her office, that mild February afternoon five years before. Back then Face West operated out of a suite of rooms at the former AIDS Hospice Waystone House. As Carmen opened the door and beckoned him in, the first thing Mickey saw was an enormous black poodle standing blocking the doorway.

Carmen put her hand over the phone.

'Come on, Roly boy— git out the way!'

He patted the poodle. It sniffed at the crumbs of dog biscuit in his jeans pocket as he squeezed past into Carmen's office. The part-time advocacy worker and benefits adviser reminded him of someone off the telly but he couldn't think who. It was only later, back home watching Babylon Five with Tyke curled up at his feet, that he remembered. Celebrity Big Brother! Carmen d'Apostolini was the spitting image of a younger version of Germaine Greer.

And her approach to his claim for Disability Living Allowance was kind of how he imagined Germaine Greer might tackle the Department of Social Security had she opted for a career in welfare rights rather than radical feminism.

Standing in Carmen's office, listening to her bellowing into the phone, he almost felt sorry for the poor civil servant at the other end of the phone in some anonymous office block in Blackpool. Carmen had the most aggressive phone manner he'd ever heard.

After a few minutes she reluctantly surrendered the phone to him so he could give the dole his permission for her to act on his behalf.

'I used to work for the DSS,' she declared in strident Australian tones, as soon as he put the phone down.

'These claims for DLA are processed by civil servants sitting at desks using a points system. If you score 14 out of 30 you get zilch but if you get 15 points out of 30 – Bingo! You get to keep your benefit money.'

He stared out the window at the trees. The former AIDS hospice had a neglected, run-down feel about it. Last autumn's leaves still lay on the grass. The beige phone on Carmen's desk had rung just once in the hour he'd been in her office.

After a few minutes she looked up from her laptop with a frown.

'And if your claim's rejected,' she announced, 'then we'll appeal it and after that we go to a tribunal – that's when *we* get to start asking the doctors the questions.'

Mickey wondered how kindly Doctor Santos from the clinic would react under cross-examination from Carmen d'Apostolini.

'Now— are you on anti-depressants for this anxiety you suffer from – no – just been left to cope on your own, have you?'

Then she started typing angrily on her laptop once more. After a few minutes she looked up again. 'I think what might really help is if I write a letter of support on your behalf, as your advocacy worker, to go in with your DLA claim form.'

The poodle was sniffing at the pine-framed, glass door which opened on to a mossy patio where weeds sprouted between cracked paving slabs.

'You couldn't take Roly out for ten minutes, could you, while I get your letter typed up?'

Mickey hesitated.

'Aye— OK,' he said, glad to escape the stuffy office but faintly anxious as to what Carmen was writing about his medical condition.

Ach well, he thought, she wis the expert the charity had referred him to – she must know whit she's daein' like.

In the glass-roofed atrium of the building a training session had just broken up. A dozen paint-smattered black plastic chairs were arranged in a semicircle around a flip chart with the words *Volunteer Induction* scrawled across it in green marker pen. Words and phrases like keeping safe, limit testing behaviour, boundaries and communication (this last one repeated several times) were scribbled in red and blue marker pen on multi-coloured post-its which speckled the magnolia walls of the atrium.

On a table beside the glass doors, surrounded by dirty coffee cups, half-opened packets of biscuits, plastic bags of supermarket grapes and a bowl of kiwi fruit, a stainless steel tea urn was just coming to the boil.

He turned right along a brown-carpeted corridor. Roly the poodle padded along behind him. Faded panels of the AIDS memorial quilt hung from the walls of the long corridor. *To my best friend Linda. We miss you.* On another the dates *3/9/61-19/6/95* were hand-sewn in crimson thread below two white doves flying over an embroidered rainbow.

The dead faggots' duvet, Zelda used to like to call it, until someone at a candlelit AIDS vigil threatened to punch him.

Through the dusty glass of the narrow, internal windows beside each doorway he saw that most of the rooms in Waystone House were now offices. Computer monitors and desks, ring binders and half-finished cans of diet coke had replaced hospital beds.

Furniture was stacked in another room: tatty, pastel-coloured sofas and more paint-splattered plastic chairs. Waystone House appeared deserted. The cream-coloured interior walls were grubby with fingerprints and scuffs and the carpets were worn and faded by the sunlight.

Where the corridor widened out there stood a large and solid-looking, built-in wooden console like the reception desk in a hotel. Children's drawings in crayon and felt pen were sellotaped all over it. A bank of beige plastic telephones was recessed into the top of the desk beside a dusty panel of switches with lights and room numbers. He remembered phones like these from when he was a kid. Pre-mobile-phones, thought Mickey; in another world.

Then he realised with a chill, he was standing beside what had once been the nurses' night station. A whole pre-fibre-optic-cable, telecommunications system connected the desk to the hospice bedrooms where a thin white hand, blotchy with purple lesions, might grasp for the wall-mounted phone at the bedside to hear a human voice at the edge of the night.

He struggled to push open a pine-framed, glass door leading out onto a patio where weeds flourished in the gaps between mossy paving slabs. Where patients once sat out to feel the last of the spring sunshine, four raised vegetable plots now stood, choked with bolted leeks and the yellow flowers of broccoli gone to seed.

The building felt as if squatters or new age travellers had moved in. Round the front, near the main entrance, half a dozen rescue battery hens pecked about inside a high, chicken-wire coop, safe from the foxes that had hunted here since before the city tide of bricks and tarmac spread over the woods and fields.

The hospice stood among trees in a corner of what had once been the grounds of the Northern General Hospital. Back in the late '80s the search for a suitable site for an AIDS hospice had taken place in the teeth of furious opposition from local residents and the Glasgow Evening Post.

A quarter of a century later and the Northern General Hospital was long gone. Its extensive wooded grounds sold off to a property developer. The wards demolished or converted into expensive flats during the house price boom that ended with long queues of worried looking people standing outside the branches of a former building society clutching red deposit books in their hands.

A path threaded its way among the oaks and sycamores that grew between the perimeter fence and the mossy lawns in front of the windows of Waystone House. So many had been expected to die: not a family in the land would be spared the toll of AIDS, the leaflet said, the one with a gravestone on the front.

In 1990 Greater Glasgow Health Board spent several million pounds building an AIDS hospice in the year Princess Diana was photographed by the world's media shaking hands with HIV-positive patients at St Thomas' Hospital in London. Yet among the trees Mickey passed only a handful of memorials to people who had died in Waystone House.

Roly the poodle sniffed around a stone slab of sandstone in the grass. Mickey crouched down and brushed last autumn's leaves away then read the words on the cold stone:

grief is not forever
but love is

He walked back along the corridor, past the abandoned night station festooned with children's drawings. The silent building stood as a memorial to medical progress and a monument to fear, a kind of medical Maginot line.

When doctors at the Aaron Diamond AIDS Research Centre in New York observed that giving HIV-positive patients the drugs ritonavir, AZT and saquinavir, all at the same time, halted the spread of the HIV virus in their bodies and allowed them to live a normal lifespan, the AIDS epidemic in Europe and North America was effectively over.

All that fear banished in one bright sunny morning in 1996, thought Mickey, as he walked through the glass-roofed atrium on his way back to Carmen's office. He noticed someone had turned a fresh page on the flipchart and had written in slightly shaky red marker pen: *Facing the Future*.

On page 36 of DLA form 731 Mickey had written he suffered from bouts of diarrhoea. When he got back to her office, Carmen quizzed him at length about this. 'Is the diarrhoea caused by HIV infection or your medication?' she'd asked. She clearly thought she was onto something, another cudgel to wave at the DSS.

'We need to be saying something like after eating and first thing in the morning you have repeated bouts of diarrhoea which leave you exhausted,' she said emphatically, 'When you're filling in the form you need to be saying how your symptoms are on a bad day and I mean a really bad day. That way you'll score enough points to qualify for DLA and you'll get your money.'

Mickey coughed.

He does have repeated bouts of diarrhoea some days and they do leave him feeling tired and washed out but Tyke still has to have an hour's walk each day. The Twin Towers might fall but the dog still has to go out for nine o'clock empty.

'Now, Michael,' the welfare rights adviser stormed on. 'There's a condition where you have diarrhoea accompanied by burning erections which can be very uncomfortable. Tell me, have *you* ever suffered from diarrhoea and burning erections – if you have, we need to tell the DSS because it's highly relevant to your claim for DLA.'

Mickey gawped.

He'd been around the block a few times.

Had a rough paper round, as they say in Glasgow, but even he had never heard of a condition like that.

Diarrhoea and an erection at the same time?

No way!

Carmen didn't even blink.

'Well, never mind,' she continued undaunted. 'What about these sweats you suffer from? How many times a night do you have to change and wash your bedding?'

§

8.42 am: Sleep is gone. He sits on the edge of the bed in checked pyjama trousers, bare-chested. Tyke's tail twitches in anticipation of the new doggy day as Mickey stumbles groggily across to the dog basket in the narrow hall. He kneels down and strokes the dog's back then buries his head in Tyke's rough coat.

'What are we gaunny dae, dog? What the fuck are we gaunny dae?'

He pulls on grey, trackie bottoms and a white vest. As he wriggles his toes into flip-flops, phrases and sentences from Carmen's letter to the dole five years ago keep coming into his head.

'Aw fuck!'

It had sounded nothing like him at all.

§

That mild February day five years before, sitting in the front seat on the top deck of the bus heading back into town, Mickey had looked in horror at what Carmen had written.

'You're entitled to this money, Michael,' she'd declared half an hour earlier as she reached down to the printer under her desk and handed him an unsealed brown envelope containing two copies of her letter in support of his claim for DLA.

Judging by its contents, Carmen had missed her calling in life when she'd gone in for a career in welfare rights and advocacy work rather than as a best selling writer of fantasy fiction. He'd opened the envelope as the bus waited at the lights in Great Western Road.

To Whom It May Concern:

I would be grateful if you would take the following information into account when assessing this gentleman's claim for Disability Living Allowance.

This gentleman suffers from anxiety which is extremely debilitating and frightening; it has meant that he is now unable to leave the house alone without being accompanied as he simply cannot cope. He very quickly becomes short of breath, develops a whole body tremor and cannot move or speak without encouragement or assistance.

An unpleasant side effect of his HIV/AIDS medication is frequent and involuntary diarrhoea/bowel incontinence which happens without warning fairly frequently both at night and in the day. At night this requires bathing and a complete change of bedding which completely exhausts him. When this happens during the day he needs to re-bathe and change and wash his clothing. He finds this very difficult to deal with, exhausting, embarrassing and especially stressful at night or when out. The loss of continence is unpredictable but happens frequently throughout every week.

In addition to the anxiety and diarrhoea he also experiences deep fatigue on a regular daily basis which can mean that he finds it difficult to leave his bed at all some days or at best that he has to rest for a considerable period after any exertion. He still experiences regular and debilitating whole body sweats, which necessitate changing his clothing and absolutely exhaust him.

I hope this letter clarifies the situation with respect to this gentleman's care needs and enables you to arrive at an appropriate decision on his claim for Disability Living Allowance.

Yours Sincerely

Carmen d'Apostolini
Support and Advocacy Worker
Face West Care

He'd slumped forward, his head in his hands banging against the bus window as phrases and sentences jumped off the page at him like the slam of the letterbox as a brown envelope from the Sheriff Court dropped onto the hall doormat.

What the fuck was she thinking of?

He very quickly develops a whole body tremor and cannot move or speak without encouragement or assistance.

He'd wanted to jump off the bus and run back into Carmen's office and get her to retype the letter and tone it down. But she'd just given him a cheery wave as she drove past while he stood waiting at the bus stop on the main road at the edge of the drab, grey, harling-clad '60s housing estate that surrounded Waystone House, Roly the poodle sitting upright on the front seat staring back at him through the rear windscreen of the three-year-old Renault Clio.

His claim form in its prepaid brown envelope addressed to the Department of Social Security, Quarryhill House, Leeds with Carmen's badly punctuated letter of support neatly stapled to page two; *please include any other evidence in support of your claim on a separate sheet* lay on the front seat.

She'd pop it in the post for him on the way home, she'd said.

Fuck!

Fuck!!

FUCK!!!

How the fuck have I ended up like this? Why can I no jist hov a job like every other heid the baw on the planet? It's no like I turned down a career in merchant banking in exchange for a life on fuckin benefits but. Aye right? Its jist ma shitty life took a wrong turn somewhere along the way. Thing is I need the money – Fuck! Fuck! Fuck!

But just then the number 43 bus pulled into the turning circle at the stop in front of the high flats. He crumpled the letter into his messenger bag and walked slowly down the stairs and stepped off the bus and back into his life because in the end he just had to get on with it.

§

11.27 am: *Viramune should be taken with or after food* says the long leaflet in small print that comes neatly folded inside each and every box of tablets. But he can't face eating anything so he takes his five tablets washed down with a glass of orange juice and knows the meds will be rough on his guts.

Seeking a way to blank it all out, he swipes his finger across his phone and starts another game. The red and green lozenges drop from the top to the bottom of the screen in a perfectly ordered, controllable world. He belches and a little of the orange juice and the bitter taste of the tablets returns to his throat.

'Sugar crush,' intones a deep voice from behind the screen. 'Sweet.'

Tyke is curled up in a tight ball beside the sofa. He senses his master's stress. It smells as strong and pungent to the dog as the black bags, the tray of putrid lasagne and the stained mattress piled up at the entrance to the high flats.

It's a pack thing:

Sleep when the pack sleeps,

Fear when the pack fears,

Run when the pack runs.

1.10 pm: He's hoovering up arrow-shaped shards of broken glass in the front room when he feels his phone start to vibrate in the pocket of his trackie bottoms.

His stomach contracts in a watery spasm.

Jonnie?

It has to be.

He pulls the phone out his pocket. The display shows the name of the caller.

Fuck does *she* want?

Then instant guilt floods over him as he remembers childish faces pressed against the windows of the caravan and roasted marshmallows on sticks.

He taps the green phone symbol.

'Hi, Aunty Nora.'

'Mickey! How are you?'

'Ah'm fine,' he lies, 'How are you?'

'Well I'm fine and dandy,' says Nora.

Mickey guesses she's on her second or third large glass of red wine.

'Are you remembering it's our Ashley's wedding this weekend?'

Mickey isn't remembering. He's forgotten all about it.

'They're getting the train up from Newcastle. Be lovely if you could come too.'

Mickey hesitates.

'Where is it they're tying the knot again?' he asks, playing for time.

'Well, the ceremony's taking place on the eighteenth green of the Carrick Country Club and then they're flying by seaplane to—'

He vaguely remembers Ashley's fiancé lives in Cardross and is captain of the local golf club. Golf, for fuck's sake!

'But that's just the happy couple, the best man, the maid of honour and the bridesmaids—'

Aunty Nora prattles away in the background while Mickey despairingly surveys the broken window. The sellotape holding the black bin liner in place has started to peel away from the glass. At least he's got the blood off the window frame, though from the way Tyke's nose is pressed against the carpet there must still be some blood on the floor he's missed.

'So you'll come then?'

'Sorry? What?'

'To the wedding on Saturday, it's at the Lomond Shores Motel – where President Clinton stayed when he came to The Open at Loch Lomond. Oh, and there's a boat trip to Tarbet on Sunday if the weather's OK—'

Mickey's stopped listening again but when he hears the name Loch Lomond, suddenly in his mind he's standing on the shore, gazing across to the ancient oak trees on the eastern side of the loch, the gorse and juniper, the deergrass and heather giving way to frost-shattered, bare rock at the mountain's summit. Ben Lomond… his first Munro…

Suddenly from nowhere the germ of an idea begins to form in his mind.

He'll escape.

Leave Glasgow.

He'll run.

Away.

Run.

Mickey.

Run!

'What did you say the name of the hotel wis again? Does it take dogs?' he asks, finally giving poor Aunty Nora his full attention at last.

Friday

bette davis eyes

The orange light on the meter of the taxi glows and the diesel engine rattles as Mickey pushes the door shut with his foot and places the last cardboard box down on the pavement beside the flat screen TV and the battered travel bag.

As usual the stair door on the corner of Langside Road and Dixon Avenue is jammed open with a half brick. The lighting in the close has been broken for years and though it's bright sunshine outside he has to peer ahead into the gloom to see the steps.

The cream-coloured paint on the walls of the stairwell has yellowed over the decades and is peeling away in damp mushroom-like clumps of blisters. The green-tiled dado is chipped and scratched; three of the cast iron banisters that support the polished wooden handrail are missing and the stone steps, littered with fag ends, feel sticky to the tread.

The first front door he passes on the top landing has a white plastic frame and fake diamond-shaped, leaded window panes but the door at the far end of the landing still has its original Victorian panels and architraves.

When the wooden front door finally opens, only Zelda's head is visible. Mickey catches a glimpse of rolls of marble-white flab and a pair of (seriously unfashionable) size XXL M&S blue briefs as Zelda scuttles back to bed.

Mickey puts the cardboard box down in the narrow hall. His laptop balances precariously on top of a photo frame and a clock radio. The two-room flat, a single end, where wains once played while men worked at the blast furnaces, appears even more cluttered than on his last visit some six weeks earlier.

'Just put your clobber in the boxroom,' Zelda shouts through from the kitchen.

Watched intently by Tyke, he is holding court from an Edwardian brass bed in the alcove beside the fridge. Round tortoisehell glasses perch on the end of his nose and a half-smoked Lambert and Butler hangs from his lower lip.

'I told you she was trouble,' pontificates Zelda from beneath the greasy duvet.

Mickey leans back against the bare plaster wall next to the press cupboard. The door won't close and among the junk spilling out onto the kitchen floor he can see a pair of platform shoes, the head of a shop mannequin and what looks like part of a car bumper.

'There's a tenner in my jeans pocket, pop down to the Booze and News and get some rolls and sliced sausage. Get a pint of milk too—'

Zelda fidgets with the rubber band on his ponytail.

'But not green milk, mind!'

Mickey finishes his sentence for him as Zelda, his bald patch shining, reaches down to the grimy floorboards to stub his cigarette out in a Lalique glass bowl, then flops back onto the pillows, double chins wobbling, a hand clutched melodramatically to his forehead.

Mickey smiles for about the first time since the white hand and arm came crashing through his window. Perhaps it's because he's fifteen years older than Mickey but somehow Zelda always has a way of putting things into some kind of perspective and making him see, maybe just maybe, things aren't so bad after all.

'Cheeky monkey! Tell you what, before you go, make me up a glass of Andrews.' Zelda grimaces. 'I've got an end of the world hangover. And yes, before you ask, I did end up in the Waterloo. My God, they were an ugly bunch in there last night. I said to the barman, never mind salted peanuts, dear – you should be putting out bowls of Pedigree Chum on the bar!'

Mickey steps gingerly across to the rotting sink unit in the window. A sleek black slug is crawling up the disintegrating chipboard. On a square of crumbling lino in the corner between the sink and the New World gas cooker a spider has spun an elaborate sequence of webs over a pair of shoes encrusted with dried-on dogshit. They've been there for two years.

Zelda looks at Mickey over the top of his round tortoise-shell glasses.

'Oh yes, and while I remember, the Gay Toon Planner left an envelope for you in the front room.'

Among the dirty dishes, coffee cups and overflowing ashtrays piled on the draining board stands a red and white tin of Andrews Liver Salts. Mickey takes a sticky teaspoon and rinses it under the cold tap beside the defunct water heater.

'Glasses in the cocktail cabinet,' says the rasping, grating voice from the brass bed.

Mickey walks back through the hall to the front room. The door on the right is ajar; Zelda's flat is one of a handful of properties in Glasgow in the second decade of the twenty-first century with neither a bath nor a shower, just a toilet.

When Zelda does his ablutions he pulls out a large, green, plastic babybath from under the brass bed. After boiling several kettles he tops it up with cold water via a rubber tube attached to the kitchen tap. Then he squats in the babybath, a process he describes as 'having a whore's bath'.

Mickey pushes the front room door open. The woodwork is Farrow and Ball shades of pink. Zelda wallpapered the room himself and never tires of pointing out to visitors to the palace that the dark green wallpaper with its cascading bunches of black grapes is hand-blocked William Morris.

Zelda bought six rolls in a second-hand shop in Byres Road when he was a twenty-three-year-old student at Glasgow College of Art. It took him a good twenty years to get round to hanging the wallpaper and he likes to tell anyone who'll listen it is evidence of his good taste – even when he was young.

Mickey squeezes past four upholstered chairs and a semi-circular drop-leaf table pushed up against the wall. He can hear Zelda talking to Tyke in the kitchen. The Victorian dining room table is covered in finds purchased from the charity shops of Glasgow: a Wally dug, a brooch made from a grouse's claw, a bunch of marble grapes, a melon baller and a ceramic cat and mouse statuette.

Zelda has 'tortured' the layout of the ornaments in the front room. In a tarnished silver frame propped up against an art deco figurine is a photo of a square-chinned woman in Victorian dress: Zelda's mother in costume for an amateur dramatics production in the late 1970s.

On one of the upholstered chairs by the drop-leaf table, a book of black and white celebrity photos lies open at a picture of Elizabeth Taylor and Richard Burton sat groggily at a table covered in empty glasses. Next to it there's a newish-looking paperback with the title *Making Art Pay* on top of a pile of unopened brown envelopes from the Department of Social Security.

On the floor, propped up against the wall, is an unframed oil on canvas of Suilven. The hill is in red and black-grey, the sky in blue-purple and white and the heather, peat bogs, pools and rocks below the mountain in orange and green.

§

Zelda has climbed only one Munro in his fifty years on the planet. It was three years ago but he never tires of telling anyone in the pub who'll listen, about what he calls the Chris Bonington Experience.

A warm July morning, forecast good and promise of sunshine that day. The Gay Toon Planner, an old friend of Zelda's from art college days (*Poor man – he works as a town planner in Cumbernauld!* said Lesbian George) collected Mickey as arranged from outside the high flats in Drumkirk.

Mickey dropped his rucksack into the boot of the Peugeot 308. He smiled. 'Nice day for it.'

A copy of *Diesel Car Magazine* in the footwell scrunched up under his boots as he sat down in the passenger seat. He glanced across at the Gay Toon Planner.

'You still wi' the council?'

'Aye. You still on the dole?'

'Aye.'

'I'll go up and see if she's ready,' the Gay Toon Planner said as he pulled the handbrake on, outside Zelda's flat on the corner of Langside Road.

Mickey watched the stair door through the insect-spattered windscreen.

Five minutes... ten minutes passed.

Then the Gay Toon Planner reappeared, alone. He was frowning.

'She's sitting naked in a plastic babybath drinking a gin and tonic and singing along to Judy Garland on the radio,' he explained with a shrug of his shoulders.

When Zelda finally emerged from the close he was resplendent in faded jeans, denim shirt and knee-length, leather motorcycle boots.

'Morning, girls – oh get her, very butch!'

Zelda cast up and down searchlight eyes at Mickey's

climbing boots and white Adidas football shorts before announcing, 'I have to sit in the front or I'll start hyperventilating.'

The car sank visibly as Zelda plumped heavily into the passenger seat.

Red Audis and BMWs flew past them on the bends on the narrow section of the A82 between Tarbet and Pulpit Rock. The hill was An Caisteal. The sun shone on Ben More and Stob Binnien. A train clacked along through the Scots pines in Glen Falloch.

'Who gave you the book on making art pay?' the Gay Toon Planner asked as a motorcyclist overtook them on a blind corner just before the Drovers' Inn.

'That cheeky witch Madge Beeton,' replied Zelda, 'Having a go at me 'cause I haven't worked since 1993 – don't forget what it said above the gates of Auschwitz, I told her, *Arbeit Macht Frei*. That put her gas at a low peep, I can tell you.'

Mickey knew what was coming next. He'd heard the tale several times before: about how Zelda got sacked from his last job at The Carpet Warehouse after taking magic mushrooms in his lunch hour.

'—all the patterns on the Persian rugs were dancing and spinning around and this old cow from Bearsden was ordering a carpet and giving me the measurements and I was just writing scribbles and gibberish on the order form.'

Zelda lagged a long way behind from the start of the walk, stopping every ten minutes to take a swig of orange juice from a white plastic water bottle. But when he passed the bottle round and Mickey took a gulp, the orange liquid had a bitter aftertaste. It wasn't just fruit juice, he quickly realised. It was more like fifty-fifty vodka and orange.

They made the summit. Sat there on the wind-clipped, grassy heath, they looked west across the blue hills to

Ben Cruachan and Stob Diamh, Beinn Eunaich and Beinn a'Chochuill, Ben Lui, Beinn Oss and Beinn Dubhchreag. To the north lay Ben Dorain, Beinn a'Chreachain, Ben Challum, Beinn Heasgarnich and Meall Ghaordie and to the east Ben Vorlich and Stuc a'Chroin on the shore of Loch Earn and faraway on the glistening western sea, Ben More on the Isle of Mull.

The vapour trails of jets cut white lines high in the resin-blue sky; the air hostesses pushing trolleys along the aisles, the clink of ice in glasses of gin and tonic. Crane flies brushed Mickey's bare legs. A heath bumblebee hovered over the pink flowers of ling. He heard a low reverberating sound. He looked round. Zelda was asleep in the heather, snoring.

§

Mickey's eyes move away from the painting of Suilven propped against the skirting board. The double window, glass dirty, top right-hand pane cracked, sash cords frayed and broken, is framed by pink damask curtains. He sat in this room with Jonnie one Tuesday afternoon watching as the light level dimmed; the sky black turning to purple across the city while forked lighting spiked up from the spires of Glasgow University.

A press cupboard and a stone fireplace, decorated with a faux marble effect painted by Zelda using feathers and sponges, occupy the gable-end wall. On the mantelpiece, beside a digital thermometer that measures humidity and a Japanese paper fan, is a Venus flytrap Zelda keeps as a pet and a pair of tweezers he uses to feed the plant pieces of raw mince.

A frayed, gold-coloured satin curtain hangs across the doorway to the boxroom. Vinyl records in cardboard boxes, a super-eight cine film projector and a screen gather dust on the ancient linoleum under the single bed with its pink candlewick bedspread. A mink stole hangs from a nail in the door frame. For the six months Mickey was Zelda's lodger he slept here staring at the mats of horsehair sticking out the hole in the plaster beside the door frame.

Zelda collects art deco and the prize piece of his collection is the cocktail cabinet that stands against the back wall of the sitting room. Its glass-panelled twin columns recall the frontage of the Beresford Building in Sauchiehall Street and the Empire Exhibition of May 1938 in Bellahouston Park.

Mickey pulls the door of the cocktail cabinet downwards. It folds out to provide a gleaming surface to mix drinks on. As the door opens, the cabinet lights up, illuminating shot glasses, tumblers and decanters.

The interior of the cabinet is lined with purple, water-marked silk and mirror tiles. Cocktail umbrellas, out-of-date jars of maraschino cherries and a box of pastel-coloured Balkan Sobranie cigarettes are stored on its glass shelves. Sticky bottles of Martini, Crabbie's green ginger and Bombay Sapphire gin (empty) are reflected in the mirrored backdrop.

Amongst the clutter on top of the cocktail cabinet is a pink, art nouveau rose bowl. In it is a white envelope. Mickey picks up the envelope, feels the shape of keys inside, then folds it in half and shoves it in the back pocket of his jeans.

He selects a suitably camp, stemmed glass and takes it back through to the kitchen, adds a heaped teaspoonful of white powder from the tin of Andrews, a sgoosh of water from the single cold tap above the sink and stirs. Then he hands the glass of cloudy, white liquid to Zelda who immediately gulps half of it down.

'Well, if they come round here looking for you, I'll say you've taken to the hills,' declares Zelda with a flamboyant gesture towards the double window and the distant green Campsies.

They're sitting at the half-leaf table in the front room – Zelda has cleared a space among the objets d'art and unopened mail – eating sliced sausage rolls dripping brown sauce onto green and gold antique plates. Zelda is still in a grubby, white, towelling dressing gown. Its two o'clock in the afternoon.

'I always said that yin was trouble. Bonny – mind. Beautiful eyes,' he says, taking a puff of Lambert and Butler between mouthfuls of sliced sausage roll, 'Speaking of eyes, there's a Bette Davis film on BBC 2 this afternoon if you're not taking to the heather right this min...'

ON SCREEN: Bette Davis lifts the lid off a cardboard box. She takes out a wide-brimmed hat and stands at the mirror fiddling with her hair and adjusting the tilt of the hat.

The door opens and an unshaven man in a suit, with black circles beneath his eyes, comes into the room.

Bette Davis ignores him and continues admiring her new hat in the mirror. The man stares at the pile of hat boxes and tissue paper on the floor.

'What have you been buying?' he asks, frowning.

'Just some things...'

A look of desperation crosses his face as he says, 'Running up bills I can't afford again? Who'd you think I am – your Uncle William?'

Bette Davis turns her huge eyes on the man. 'Why,' she says, 'I do believe you're even jealous of him.'

Zelda knows the black and white movie line by line. Through the grimy window panes the towers of Glasgow University stand on the city horizon. Ragged, grey clouds scud across a sky shading to white brightness at the edges. Mickey lights a spliff, smokes half, hands it to Zelda then lies on the floor giggling while on the screen Bette Davis raises her huge eyes heavenwards and taps her high heels on the polished wooden top of the Vitrola in tune to the mellow tones of South Sea Rumba.

Saturday

lust

3 pm: Luss. Though for ever after Mickey will think of it as Lust. The tyres of the big yellow and black Citylink coach splash the grey water out the puddles in the potholed tarmac of the lay-by. The door hisses open and Tyke jumps down followed closely by Mickey.

'Cheers, mate!' he says to the driver.

At lunchtime, back at Buchanan Street, he didn't think he was going to get Tyke on the bus. As he weaved his way through the crowds, travel bag over his shoulder, the dog followed at his heels, sniffing at a pigeon feather on the pavement and the beggars sat under their blankets on the shiny tiled floor of the bus station.

They waited at stance 55, *Buses to Inverness, An Gearasdan and Uig*. On the far side of Killermont Street, at a window, in a four-storey office block overlooking the bus station, a man in white shirt sleeves sat at a desk staring blankly at a computer monitor. A door opened, a woman came into the office and handed him a folder. She left the room and the man in shirt sleeves turned back to his computer screen.

'It's no dogs on Citylink,' the driver said when Mickey flashed his National Concession Card. Then he sighed and scratched his head. 'Where are you going to, pal?'

Mickey hesitated. 'Just tae Luss?'

The driver twisted round and asked the other passengers

already seated on the coach, 'Does anyone mind about a dog on the bus?'

Mickey held his breath.

Nobody objected.

'Look pal – just take the dog to the back of the bus, keep him quiet and make sure my inspector disnae see him.'

Beyond the crash barriers at the edge of the motorway, the purple-pink flowers of rosebay willowherb brightened the straggly grass and weeds. A kestrel hung in the air. The grey bridges flickered by on concrete stilts behind the dusty, rain-spattered windows of the coach. The graffiti became a passing blur of colour against the monotone grey concrete: *Angst* in big rounded red and blue letters, *Unthank* in black and silver spray paint.

Near Renfrew the coach moved into the slow lane to take the exit sliproad. Behind the barbed-wire-topped perimeter fence, cargo jets stood lined up alongside the terminal building. The bus slowed as it entered the drop-off zone with its yellow airport signs. Two traffic police leant back against a jeep, casually watching the flow of taxis and cars.

Back on the motorway, high above the Clyde, the stylised towers and steel cables of the Erskine Bridge slid past outside the grimy windows of the bus. To the east the pylons marched across a cityscape of cream and red towerblocks and grey rows of terraced houses. To the west low hills, scrubby bushes and fields of yellow tansies sloped down to the mudflats where the freshwater of the Clyde met the saltwater of the Firth. As the city slipped away, Mickey wondered if Jonnie was still in Glasgow or had gone back to Perth, his lacerated arm criss-crossed with black thread stitches.

5.30 pm: Mickey is standing in front of the full-length mirror in the hotel bedroom. He takes the belt on his sporran in another notch then straightens the folds on his ghillie shirt where it's tucked into his kilt while Tyke licks the last grains of Wilsons Original from his steel dog bowl.

His phone vibrates in his sporran.

'Hi, Aunty Nora.'

'Mickey! Does the kilt fit?'

'Aye – sure does. Size 32. Spoteroonie!'

'And how's your room? Did you find the whisky?'

'Aw thank you – yes, it's magic!'

'My pleasure, pet. Your room's a Corbett same as mine, isn't it?'

Mickey has the feeling someone up there is seriously messing with his head as Nora goes on to explain the standard hotel rooms are classified according to – *fuckin hell but* – hill lists! Mickey and Tyke are in a Corbett class room which he guesses is better than a Graham but (presumably) less luxurious than a Munro.

Corbett or not, it's the best hotel Mickey's ever stayed in. There's a wetroom and in the corner of it a sauna the size of a large wardrobe. There's a double bed with a suede headboard and a leather Chesterfield beside a glass-topped coffee table. The tongue-and-groove pine panelling on the walls does give the room a faintly early President Carter feel or maybe it's been deliberately created by some middle-aged interior designer waxing nostalgic for the decor of a '70s childhood.

'Steve's mam and dad are in an apartment – its lovely,' continues Aunty Nora, 'but you should see Steve and Ashley's room in the President Clinton Suite.'

'There's no a blue dress wi' a stain on it hanging in the wardrobe, is there?' jokes Mickey.

It takes a moment for the penny to drop. Then Aunty Nora laughs. 'Oh, you're terrible, Mickey.'

'And you'd better warn them no tae touch the cigar in

the ashtray,' he goes on as Nora giggles nervously.

'Have you got a view from your balcony?' she asks, keen to change the subject.

Mickey slides open the picture window and steps outside. Screened from the road by trees, the Lomond Shores Motel looks like half a dozen, three-storey blocks of flats crammed onto a narrow strip of foreshore between the A82 and Loch Lomond. His balcony overlooks the hotel's private beach, a narrow strip of sand squeezed between the hotel, the birch trees and the loch. Across the glassy water he can see Ben Lomond, most southerly of the Munros, its summit clear of mist.

'OK – tara for now, pet' says Nora 'don't forget we're having voddies in Linda's apartment at 6 o'clock. Bye now!'

Nora works selling curtains and haberdashery in the last department store in Glasgow. Everyday she passes the statue of Donald Dewar outside the Buchanan Galleries as a light rain falls on the city streets.

Linda Hysterectomy and the rest of the girls from Habby are out on the balcony of their third-floor flat puffing on Superkings as Mickey walks across the suburban, mono-blocked car park below. He hears a wolf whistle and responds with a mock curtsy and twirl to applause and cheers from the balcony. He wonders how many Bacardi breezers they've downed already.

The girls from Habby have really gone to town. On the large table in the kitchen / living room of the apartment there are bottles of red wine and bacardi, Coca Cola, bowls of cashew nuts, pakora, olives and Parma ham.

'What d'you want to drink, Mickey – there's white wine or lager in the fridge?'

Nora thrusts a plate at him.

'Here, try one of these, Linda made them herself – prawn toasts. They're gluten-free, you know?'

She turns and looks pointedly across at an overweight woman with dyed black hair sat on the sofa in the corner. 'Are you going to leave your phone alone for like one whole minute, Linda?' she says, frowning.

Mickey takes a bottle of Sol from the fridge and sits down carefully in a black leather armchair, knees pressed together.

Linda Hysterectomy puts her phone down.

'Just checkin' ma Facebook. You're looking very smart, Mickey. I love a man in a kilt, don't you, Carol-Ann?'

'Oh aye. Wish ma John had legs like that,' giggles Carol-Ann from behind an enormous glass of red wine.

'Was it Ashley's idea to have all the guys in matching kilts?' asks Linda.

Mickey shrugs his shoulders.

'Did she say what they had tae wear under them too?' splutters Carol-Ann.

The girls from Habby all shriek with laughter as Mickey presses his knees tighter together.

'How many Munros have you got left now then?' asks Nora, keen to steer the conversation away from kilts.

'Five,' he answers.

'Aw, that's brilliant! Well done you,' says Linda.

But Carol-Ann's face could curdle milk.

'All right for some – sounds like you've got too much time on your hands,' she says with a scowl.

Mickey catches the sour note in her voice. He knows what she thinks.

There's nothing wrong with him, she's said it to Nora more than once, he should be working.

Then to Mickey's relief the spotlight of the conversation moves away from him and back, inevitably, to talk about work – floorwalks and goods-handling – quite literally, shoptalk.

6.45pm: They step out through the glass doors of the apartment block and Nora slips her arm through Mickey's. As they walk the short distance to the main concourse of the hotel she squeezes his hand. She's like his mum but not his mum. She comes from the same small town in Perthshire at the foot of one of the wide, green, agricultural straths that sweep down from the Grampian mountains - one of those wee Scottish towns where the streets are empty in the middle of the afternoon, in the space between lunchtime and the kids getting out of school. She's like his mum but not his mum. She's warmer, less brittle, less hard-edged and he feels the security of childhood there once was around her.

The girls from Habby clack along behind them, all high heels, short skirts, giggles and expensive perfume. Beyond the oaks and rowans, shadows darken the loch as Ben Lomond catches the last of the evening sunshine and the traffic on the A82 roars past behind the dense screen of birch, hazel and alder at the rear of the hotel.

The bride and groom have taken their places with the family at the top table in the ballroom. The guests with evening-only invitations queue up outside in the corridor (embossed wallpaper, painted beige to dado height, cream above). Staff from the Lomond Shores flit about in black trousers and white shirts.

'What name is it please, sir?'

The first thing Mickey notices about Ryan is his big fat arse.

The waiter looks down at the blue clipboard in his hands.

'Any special dietary requirements, sir?'

It's the kind of bum Mickey could bury his face in.

'You're at table five, just over there by the bar, sir.'

It's not that Ryan is fat or anything – he's good-looking in a kind of chubby way – but his bum is huge.

11.45 pm. Bottles of Sol drunk: 1. Glasses of red wine: 4. Pints of Stella: 5 and a half. Shots: 2. Aunty Nora is asleep in her chair at the table, snoring quietly but audibly above the strains of ABBA blaring from the dance floor.

The cute young guy in the tartan waistcoat from the cash office at Nora's work spewed all over the corridor outside half an hour ago. Lynda Hysterectomy is still checking her Facebook. Ashley and Steve are drunk and repeating themselves.

Mickey leaves the last dregs of the reception around 1 am. It's well past Tyke's usual time for late night empty. As the dog sniffs around the strip of grass beside the shrub roses and monoblock paving in the car park, Mickey catches sight of Ryan the waiter putting his car key into the driver's door of a beat-up, bright orange Citroen Saxo.

'C'mon, dog – it's noo or never— '

And emboldened by five and a half pints of Stella he sidles up to the door of the Citroen and taps on the glass with his knuckles. Ryan winds down the window.

'Hiya!—'

'—ah've got some no bad whisky in ma room – if you fancy a wee shot like?' propositions Mickey.

'Sure – cool,' says Ryan, surrendering with a smile.

He's pretty young, Mickey realises.

'What room number are you – it's just – I'm not supposed to go back to rooms with guests?'

He hesitates.

The night hangs by a thread.

Then Ryan says, 'You go first and leave the door unlocked – I'll be along in two secs.'

'OK – fab – see you in a min,' says Mickey, blood rushing to his groin as his cock presses against his sporran.

Tyke gives Ryan a rapturous greeting when he comes into the room, but quickly settles back down again on his blanket.

Ryan sits on the leather Chesterfield in the corner. Mickey perches on the arm. The pleats of his garish Royal Stewart kilt cascade onto the beige, retro, shagpile carpet.

He pours three fingers of whisky from Nora's bottle of Glenfiddich on the glass-topped coffee table.

'So whit's it like tae be a gay boy in Luss then?' he asks nervously.

'It's cool. Glasgow's half an hour down the road.'

He hands Ryan the glass.

'You stay near here but?'

'Yeah – in the village with my mum – she moved here for work when I was twelve.' He takes a sip of whisky. 'I'm twenty-one now – I was a bit wild when I was a teenager.'

At thirty-five, Mickey's thinking he's nearly, but not quite, old enough to be Ryan's father.

'I'm going to Telford College in Edinburgh in the autumn,' Ryan says proudly.

'What you gaunny study, college boy?'

'Can't you guess?' Ryan brushes his heavily volumised, dyed-blond hair away from his forehead.

Mickey flounders. 'Caterin' – chef —?'

'Hairdressing, stupid,' Ryan says and puts his hand on Mickey's bare knee.

Mickey takes a gulp of whisky. Fuck it, he thinks. 'You gaunny ask me if ah'm a true Scotsman then?'

'Are you a true Scotsman then?' parrots Ryan coquettishly as Mickey gets to his feet and lifts the heavy folds of tartan to reveal pendulous cock and balls.

He sits down again.

'What colour of pants you wearing?'

'Green CKs—' answers Ryan and then he unbuttons and unzips his black nylon waiter's trousers to prove it.

Later: 2 am. In the half darkness the little waves lap the shore of the loch and the trunks of the silver birches glimmer in the light that falls in yellow shafts from the windows of the hotel. Mickey's had his wish. He's buried his face and his tongue deep in Ryan's big fat bum.

Turned out it wasn't just a fat arse Ryan had. He's got a huge cock too. Mickey's lying naked, face down, spread-eagled, a dark brown taste in his mouth, a cold sticky patch of his own cum on the sheet, biting the white linen pillowcase in pain-filled ecstasy as Ryan fucks him up the bum.

Then as Ryan's mouth drops half open, his eyes go blank and he gasps, 'Aw – I'm cumming!'

And pumps five millilitres of white semen into Mickey's rectum (bareback – nae condoms here, see I'm no thinking about the legal implications of love right now and anyway I leave it up tae the other guy whether he wants tae use one or no). Mickey thinks, I'll no be able to sit down in the morning.

Later still: 2.50 am. A few stars speckle the cloudless sky. A light breeze rustles the bracken on the darkened hillside on the far shore of the loch where the leaves of the rowan trees gleam in the moonlight.

He watches from the bed as Ryan walks naked across the shagpile carpet to the ensuite bathroom. His huge fat bum looks like it's chewing toffees.

'I'm working at 8 am,' Ryan says as he pulls up his green Calvin Kleins.

3.02 am: Fully dressed. Leaving.

He turns to Mickey lying naked under the duvet. 'See you at breakfast.'

He blows Mickey a kiss then cautiously opens the hotel bedroom door and looks up and down the corridor.

An aura of what they've done hangs around Ryan as he drives the beat-up, orange Citroen back to the village. As he speeds along the darkened, tree-lined road, reflecting the headlights, a pair of green eyes by the side of the road - a hill fox or an otter perhaps - watch him pass by.

Sunday

10.30 am: There are a few drops of rain on the wind and the cloud is draped in ragged grey curtains across Ben Lomond but the boat trip's going ahead anyway.

Mickey stands on the narrow, cresent-shaped strip of sand in front of the Lomond Shores Motel throwing a tennis ball for Tyke.

His hoodie is pulled up over his head.

He has what Zelda would call an end-of-the-world hangover.

Breakfast in the hotel had been an ordeal. The first thing to confront him at the self-service buffet in the dining room, after a kiss from Aunty Nora, was (a rather less hungover than himself) Ryan cheerily serving up bacon and eggs.

'Would you like a sausage, sir?' chirped Ryan, brandishing a greasy-looking, pork banger suggestively.

Aw naw, thought Mickey, turning green.

He frowned and shook his head.

'Black pudding maybe?' said Ryan with a cheeky grin.

'Mornin',' and a feeble smile was all Mickey could manage as he helped himself to one rasher of bacon and a slice of fried bread.

He sat down at a table in the corner with Nora and the girls from Habby. They were all looking amazing though perhaps their make-up was a little thicker than yesterday.

He sniffed.

And pretty heavy on the perfume too.

'Isn't that our waiter from last night?' asked Nora, glancing across the table at Mickey.

'The one who said he could scare for Scotland?' giggled Carol-Ann.

Aw, swallow me up, earth, thought Mickey.

The *Loch Lomond Queen* is an inelegantly high-sided boat. She looks top-heavy to Mickey's eye. The grey waters of the loch lap against her red fibreglass hull. Banners are tied along her rails. A large blue and white one reads 'Cruise Loch Lomond.'

'Think I done enough of that last night,' Mickey mutters to himself.

The wind has moved from moderate to fresh by the time the grey-haired boatman unties from the private jetty at Luss. With a push of a boathook he sends the *Loch Lomond Queen* out onto the water as he jumps quickly aboard.

Out on the loch, little waves capped with white spray ruffle the gun-metal grey surface of the water. There's a crackle of white noise over the loud speaker above Mickey's head followed by the voice of the tour guide. 'Just coming up on your right on the far shore is Rob Roy's Prison—'

Mickey yawns.

Tyke lies flat, head down, in guarding-the-sheep-in-the-pen position. Nora's been feeding him barley sugars and one is stuck to his coat. As the *Loch Lomond Queen* chugs past Inchlonaig, Mickey tries to remove it but Tyke gives a low, warning growl and bares his white, needle-sharp teeth.

Mickey shrugs.

'I'll jist have tae cut it off with scissors later while you, doggie, have got a chew in your gob – that way I'll no lose a hand,' he says, looking down at the dog.

The Inn at Inverbeg slips past on the left and he glimpses the red-painted eaves of the youth hostel at Rowardennan on the eastern shore of the loch.

'And on our left, Firkin Point,' announces the tour guide to giggles from the girls from Habby.

Mickey's sure they're looking at him. He shifts uncomfortably on the shiny, red plastic seats of the *Loch Lomond Queen*.

Fuck's sake, ma bum's sair.

Worth it, mind, he thinks as he scrolls down to Ryan's number on his phone, taps the screen. *Compose Text...*

11.45 am: 'Yous have got half an hour here,' announces the tour guide at Tarbet as the grey-haired boatman moors the *Loch Lomond Queen* between a yacht and an orange dinghy.

On the pier Mickey hugs Aunty Nora. Tyke jumps up at Carol-Ann, leaving muddy paw prints all down her white cotton trousers. Nora looks down at the dog.

'Now sit, you wee bugger,' she says, 'I've got something for you.'

And from her shoulder bag she produces a tartan dog coat.

'Made it myself on me old Singer,' she says proudly.

'The pattern included a matching hat but I decided you might look silly in that, pet,' she says, bending down to pat Tyke.

'It'll keep you cosy in the mountains.'

Tyke sniffs the tartan fabric politely and Mickey says, 'Aw thanks, Nora,' as he shoves the garish tartan dog coat into the side pocket of his rucksack.

'I went up to Skye once, you know – on a coach tour. It was when I was working at Bainbridges,' she continues.

He smiles. He's heard the story before.

'I thought the Cuillins looked like they could do with a bloody good dusting,' she says.

He hugs Aunty Nora again then, calling to Tyke to follow him, he strides away across the grass towards the turrets and battlements of the Tarbet Hotel. As soon as they're out of earshot he looks down at the dog and says, 'Dinnae worry son, you'll never have tae wear it.'

When he reaches the A83 he brings Tyke to heel and walks half a mile along the grassy verge to Arrochar and Tarbet station. In his pocket he has the keys from the white envelope on Zelda's cocktail cabinet and a purchased-in-advance £11 single to the second last station on the West Highland Line, Ruaidh Bridge.

fire and water

The engines of the class 158 Express Sprinter scream as the four-car diesel multiple unit accelerates up the 1 in 45 Cowlairs incline out of Glasgow Queen Street Station. Above the driver's cab a yellow illuminated sign glows in the darkness of the tunnel and is reflected in the oily sheen of the puddles by the side of the track. The yellow sign reads *MALLAIG*.

Out through the suburbs of Glasgow, rattling and clattering through Westerton and the towerblocks of Dalmuir, passing quickly past stations at Bowling and Singer. Low tide on the wide firth, the stumps of the pier at Craigendoran stand stark and black in the water. Seaweed-coated rocks line the shore, green navigation buoys like beached submarines, the abandoned carcass of a boat on the mudflats at Dumbarton, green-black with weed. Two people walk out across the grey sand at Cardross; a red figure, a black figure and a dog.

A gradient now, a series of tight curves, the squealing of wheels and couplings and brakes, the bottles on the buffet trolley rattle and chink, as the train winds it way through the conifers and birches, out along an embankment on a ledge, across the steep grassy hillside pulling up to Garelochhead.

Coach A is jam-packed with Dutch and German and Japanese tourists, standing in the aisles, taking photos, videoing the crooked pinnacles of the Cobbler on iPads, as the train twists its way along the hillside high above the sea loch. Then fences and fences topped with barbed wire enclosing sinister, rectangular, grassy mounds on the hillside. Each section of fence carries a warning sign. Ministry of Defence: Keep Out. Keep Out. KEEP OUT.

The branches of the silver birches claw and scratch at the carriage windows as the train creaks and rattles along a bracken-covered terrace. Hundreds and hundreds of feet below in the blue-grey waters of the Gareloch, passing glimpses through the yellow birch leaves of grey sheds and black jetties: the Faslane naval base.

Where red-coated soldiers once marched on stony paths, low flying jets scream through the glens and, beneath the salt water of the loch, black-hulled submarines slide in between the hills.

Why didn't they put them in the Thames, these last phallic symbols of an impotent former imperial power? wonders the white-haired man in Coach B wearing a tweed jacket, open-toed sandals and a YES badge pinned to his flat cap.

They won't be here much longer if he has anything to do with it. When he walks briskly through the doors of the primary school with its smell of milk, school dinner mince and crayons and stands in the plywood voting booth scrutinising the ballot paper in front of him, he'll think on this day high above the Gareloch, of the naval frigates and cranes and sheds glimpsed through the branches and yellow birch leaves.

Ten minutes pass. The train is high above Loch Long, three miles south of Arrochar and Tarbet station where Mickey Bell, hangover finally beginning to lift at last, bum still very sore, stands waiting with Tyke among the rhododendrons on the weed-covered platform.

It's a slow haul up Glen Falloch but, as the train reaches the head of the pass, the sun cuts a grainy beam through the cloud, lighting up the Scots pines and the steep flanks of Ben More, speckled grey with rock outcrops and scree. While the train divides at Crianlarich, he gets off and wanders along the platform, puffing on a roll-up.

The sound of a train whistle; between the birch trees a maroon Class 66 diesel-electric appears round the bend hauling a long line of grey metal canisters laden with bauxite to feed the smelter fifty miles to the north. As the long goods train passes slowly through the Highland station, Mickey gazes across the railway sidings to Ben More.

The yellow lights on the doors of the carriages are illuminated and the passengers are starting to drift back onto the train. An American woman in a clear plastic poncho is making a fuss of Tyke, 'What kind of a dog is this?'

Tyke wags his tail politely as the woman tickles him under the collar and exclaims,

'Hey, furry little guy!'

Tyke has climbed onto the seat next to Mickey and is curled up, his warm head resting against Mickey's knee. He puts his arm around the dog and presses his face against the dog's neck and breathes in the smell of the dog's fur. As the train creaks and rattles along the hillside south of Tyndrum, through the dirty window of the carriage, across Strath Fillan, he can see Ben Lui, its great, grassy northern corrie still holding a tiny white remnant of last winter's snow. And he remembers how the dog's wet coat smelt that day in the rain on the mountain.

§

Early June, three years before. In the grey mist, the mountain's summit had been like another planet strangely removed from the world below. Instinctively he'd followed the edge of the cliffs northward. Steep grass and moss fell away into the cloud on his left before the summit ridge widened to a little plateau where a stone cairn trembled on the edge of the cliffs. A cornice of dirty snow, stalks of grass frozen into it, had shrunk away from the summit cliffs like icing falling off a slice of wedding cake.

He was out of the mist, almost back down at the bealach, when the rain came in great sweeping sheets, driven across Glen Fyne by a sudden squally wind. The rain soaked into the green nylon of his rucksack and drops of water glistened on the dog's muzzle. He pulled on overtrousers *(always feel like a kid wearing them – dunno why like)* and climbed the six hundred feet to the summit of Beinn a'Chleibh as curtains of rain lashed the hillside. But over Cruachan there was a blue tear in the grey cloud and almost a brightness as if the sun still shone on Loch Awe.

Crouched down at the cairn with Tyke, his view of the rain-swept mountains framed by the dripping hood of his black SuperDry jacket, he broke off a corner of pork pie and dropped it at Tyke's paws. Then he put his arm around the dog and pressed his face against Tyke's neck and breathed in the smell of wet dog, like the smell of your woolly jumper when you played out in the rain when you were a kid, the smell of wet fur he'd remember every day for ever, the smell of the dog's wet coat would always be in his heart.

§

He leaves the train at Bridge of Orchy. Silence descends on the Swiss-chalet-like station buildings with their wooden shingles and wrought iron. The sound of the train fades as it heads out across Rannoch Moor. Thin beams of sun probe down through gaps in the clouds. The swallows nesting under the wooden eaves swirl around as he walks down the hill towards the 1930s roadhouse-style hotel.

Behind him, a slippery eroded path worn by thousands of pairs of walking boots climbs up through the heather and peat of Coire an Dothaidh to a high col. Beinn Dorain lies to the south, Beinn Dothaidh to the north.

Tyke trots along at his side, not fifty yards ahead of him for once. At the hotel Mickey crosses the A82 then takes the byroad to Forest Lodge. Pied wagtails flit from fence to road to field as he tramps past Inveroran and an hour passes before they reach Loch Tulla and its pine-tree-clad islands shining in the September sunshine.

Where the tarmac ends, a rough track tips down across the moor. It cuts a stony line across the heathery hillside, the main road through Glencoe until surveyors arrived in the 1930s with little round glasses and overcoats and theodolites and notebooks and drew the plans for the new motor road with its concrete arched bridges.

A day of sunshine and showers, of raindrops dancing in the sunlight, swept along on the fresh westerly wind. A day of shining tracks, of walking under rainbows and double rainbows against a dark grey-green sky.

The hills of the Blackmount, Clachlet and Meall a' Bhuiridh rise to the west of the track. At Ba Bridge a fine masonry arch leaps the peaty burn that splashes down from Coire Ba. He stands looking over the low parapet at the yellow water foaming in a creamy-white frenzy around the stone abutments of the old bridge.

North of the River Ba a series of lesser bridges and culverts carry the track over the many little burns that flow down from the Blackmount. Tyke plays a game at each bridge, finding a stick or tearing up a root of heather and dropping it into the burn on the upstream side of the bridge then charging downstream to retrieve the stick as it emerges on the far side. The dog never tires of the game and the miles along the track to the White Corries pass easily enough on grass, on peaty mud, on stony boulders and crunching gravel, Mickey's scuffed boots sending gleaming little shards of mica into the air, where they glisten in the sunlight.

September in the Blackmount and the green of the deergrass is beginning to fade. Soon the hills will be coloured in rich, autumnal shades of brown and russet as the shoots of deergrass, patterned with fawn and orange, die back and winter approaches.

As they pass by, man and dog leave a boot print and a paw print in the soft, black, peaty mud. A little while later a hill fox crosses the path. She sniffs warily at the peaty mud and bald tussocks of deergrass that cling tenaciously onto the eroded track.

Her name is Mhadaidh and she is remembered in the names of many Scottish hills. She has a den in a rickle of stones at the top of a mossy crack in a rocky outcrop on the hillside six hundred feet above the path. The vixen's territory is forty square kilometres, all of Meall a'Bhuiridh, a whole mountain. Mickey won't see her but Tyke scents her droppings on rocks and on the gravel at the edge of the path.

Her fox prints in the peaty mud, neater and more purposeful than Tyke's dog tracks. Both have four toe-pads and claws but her fox prints are longer, more delicate and pointed, almost diamond-shaped.

She smells man and dog on the hill track. Something's afoot, thinks the fox, sniffing the peaty mud, but she never will learn anymore about the journey of the man and the dog and what brings them to the edge of the Blackmount.

As the afternoon draws on and the light shades to evening, Mickey stops to eat a sausage roll and a Cadbury's creme egg. He sits on a line of stones that lie in the grass; a lush, bright green square of ground among the brown heather. Before the First World War these fallen stones by the track were a house, the walls once home to a shepherd.

The shades of the climbers who crowded into the abandoned cottage in the 1930s watch Mickey Bell as he sits on the low wall – all that remains of Ba Cottage. The attic where they kept the rifle long fallen into the tall grass but the shades comprehend what Mickey's about as he rests on his way to the White Corries.

For they too once tramped the long miles, followed the journey of the pipes from the Glasgow of shipyards and factories and foundries. They too once took the penny tram-ride north to Milngavie. They too escaped to the hills in an age of recession and unemployment. They too climbed these mountains once. They too knew the smell of wet earth and bracken and wood smouldering in the hearth of the ruined cottage. For where Mickey steps, the shades of the climbers have stepped along the path before him. The shades watch Mickey Bell and his dog and they reach out their shadowy arms as if to entwine him in a web of ghostly hemp ropes.

The time we shot the stag with the rifle from the attic,
The day we climbed Clachlet,
The moonlight traverse of the Blackmount one June night.
On the Rannoch Wall,
Around the fire,
On the bus back to Glasgow...

The shades remember the days that are gone.

The sun moves behind a ragged grey tear of cloud. A few raindrops blown on the wind rustle the leaves of the old rowan that stands close by the ruined cottage.

Mickey shivers.

'Brrr – someone jist walked over ma grave. C'mon, let's get going, doggums.'

And he shoulders the heavy rucksack and they set off man and dog along the track to the White Corries. Beside the ruined cottage the shades drift wistfully back into the grass and silence falls, broken only by the clack of a stone chat and the song of the skylarks.

The air is getting cool, the sun low in the sky over the hills of Morvern in the west, when they top the rise of the shoulder of Meall a'Bhuiridh that stretches down to Rannoch Moor. The windbreak of pines around the buildings at the foot of the White Corries stands out, a dark green square against the tawny heath.

He sees the outline of the ski lift; watches the chairs move slowly down the hillside. Half a mile away, on the moorland in the shadow of Buchaille Etive Mor, white chimneys rise out of the ochre and russet heather: Creagh Dhu Cottage.

Fifteen minutes later he crosses a single track road and walks down the grassy path to the whitewashed cottage. Tyke skips happily around, sensing they've arrived. Mickey feels a sore, red chaffedness around his shoulders as he slides his arms out of the heavy pack, unzips his top pocket and opens the white envelope containing the keys neatly labelled *Creagh Dhu*.

The smaller of the two keys unlocks a chain on the iron grille in front of the wooden door. There are bars on the windows of the cottage too, all painted in cheery bright-blue paint. He pushes the Yale key into the lock and opens the rickety double door.

It's dark inside the cottage. There's a smell of woodsmoke. Tyke sniffs under the door on the left. Mickey turns the iron handle. It opens into a wood-panelled room. A collection of comfy-looking armchairs are pushed against one wall and a long wooden table occupies the other side of the low-ceilinged room.

Above the fireplace hangs a large black and white framed photo he recognises as the cliffs of Ben Nuivais and a sepia portrait of two determined-looking women in nineteenth-century dress sitting on a boulder, holding alpenstocks. There are black nuggets of coal in a bucket and newspaper and kindling are neatly stacked by the hearth. Clothes pegs hang from a wire stretched across the mantelpiece where generations of damp climbing socks have hung to dry over the fire.

He pulls opens the shutters on the only window in the room. The walls must be two feet thick. Through the six-inch-square panes of glass he sees a rowan tree bent over in the wind. A white mobile home is making its way slowly up the single track road past the cottage. A grey sheet of rain sweeps over the moor drawing a slate-coloured curtain across Beinn a'Chrulaiste.

Back in the narrow whitewashed stone hall he opens the other door. It's the kitchen: gloss-painted shelves with neatly arranged rows of large saucepans; chipped mugs hang from cup hooks in the rafters. He pulls open a drawer. It's full of clean tea towels. The cupboards are stacked with dinner plates and soup bowls. There are wooden shelves and pigeonholes to store food in, a tea urn, an electric kettle and two Baby Belling cookers.

There's a sink but no running water. Instead, an old milk churn with a brass tap on it and a red washing-up basin to catch the drips, stands near the sink. In the fireplace squats a wood-burning stove and two coal-blackened steel buckets.

He closes the kitchen door. In the hall there are two bunk beds at the foot of a wooden ladder that leads upstairs. Under the lower bunk there is a metal trunk with grey woollen blankets poking out the top.

'Stay – Tyke – stay!'

He climbs the ladder up to the attic. He hears the scrabble of Tyke's paws on the lower rungs, then the dog gives up and lies down, waiting patiently for Mickey to return.

There are iron beds with blue plastic mattresses and more grey woollen blankets in the upstairs room. A low door leads into a smaller bedroom containing a wooden dressing table. He presses his face to the glass in the small metal-framed window in the roof, watching the rain sweeping across Rannoch Moor, breathing the dry old smell of the wooden rafters. As he climbs back down the creaky rungs, Tyke's tail thumps on the wooden floorboards.

The rain has stopped. Outside, the thin light is cold and watery. A low whitewashed stone byre adjoins the cottage. He opens the door. It's dark inside, he feels for a light switch. A shovel propped up against the wall; a ton of coal in one corner. At the end of the byre nearest the door, one corner has been partitioned off with sheets of three-quarter-inch plyboard. Inside is the toilet.

What looks like the bilge pump from a boat is mounted on a sturdy length of two-by-two. An A4 sheet of instructions drawing-pinned to the back of the door details the procedure for filling the cistern using the pump which draws water from the stream behind the cottage. As he sits on the toilet gritting his teeth *(fuck – ma bum is still so fuckin sair!)* he reads that eleven slow pumps are needed to fill the cistern. It's the most Heath Robinson plumbing system he's ever seen.

He pulls his jeans up and fastens his belt then slowly pushes the handle of the bilge pump eleven times. Water bubbles up into the cistern. He flushes the toilet. A large plastic container of salt sits on the window sill. He's not sure if September counts as winter in Scotland but he adds a handful of salt to the cistern just in case. There is a tiny steel washbasin. No tap but a long length of copper pipe running from the bilge pump.

He frowns. 'How tae wash your hands but?'

Then he spots a diverter valve on the wall. He turns it,

pumps the bilge pump and cold water cascades down into the basin and all over the cement floor.

Shaking glistening drops of water from his hands he steps out into Glencoe, blinking in the evening sunshine after the darkness of the byre.

Later he takes one of the metal buckets from beside the wood burning stove and fills it with coal from the mound in the byre. Then he takes the three plastic buckets from the kitchen and walks down to the stream behind the cottage. He fills the buckets by holding them side-on in the fast flowing burn.

Creagh Dhu:
Elemental
Fire and
Water.

Back inside, as he empties the second bucket into the galvanised steel milk churn, something moves in the water. A flash of silver against the tarnished metal of the old milk churn.

'Oo ya beauty!' He exclaims in surprise.

'Tyke!'

The dog runs through and jumps up at him, paws on his thighs.

'Ah've only caught a fuckin fish but!'

The six-inch-long brown trout swims round and round the milk churn. Mickey looks frantically round the kitchen. He grabs a plastic colander hanging from a dusty nail in a rafter. Using it as a net he catches the fish and quickly flips it into the remaining full bucket of water. Out the back of the cottage, under the Buchaille, he squats down by the burn and careful submerges the pail in the stream. After a moment the brown trout swims out of the bucket.

'Have a nice life,'says Mickey.

A flash of silver scales among the brown pebbles and the fish is gone.

Across the flat peat hags the great herdsman, Buchaille Etive Mor, looms over the cottage. The wind flattens the blades of deergrass and white flags of bog cotton and sweeps the smoke from the chimney away across the moor and over Beinn a'Chrulaiste.

Inside the cottage he sits by the fire in the wood-panelled front room, Tyke asleep on a grey woollen blanket by the hearth. Behind him on the wall is a shelf of books: *The Carpet Baggers*, *Harry Potter and the Philosopher's Stone, Birds of Lochaber, The Island of Adventure*. He picks up a thin, dog-eared volume with a tattered green paper cover. *The Cairngorm Club Journal*: Printed in Aberdeen, January 1904. He opens it at page 12.

Words words words – cannae be daein wi' reading all that like, he thinks, as he looks at the black and white photo of Braeriach. Then he runs his eyes down the first paragraph of the article on the opposite page, the title in Century Schoolbook font bold, *Storm on the Garbh Coire Crags* by CG Cash, F.R.S.G.S.

Later, The Munros Book lies open on his lap. The flames flicker across the pages lit red and orange, the smudgey biro ticks and dates in the margins. He turns to page 57, Bidean nam Bian, and thinks about tomorrow.

He flicks through the hills, pausing occasionally, trying to catch a trace of the wet earth and the raindrops glistening on the heather from the dry pages of the book. Some hills he has very clear memories of, others he cannae remember much about at all. Section 6: The Grampians. Blair Atholl to Braemar: compleat.

Page 16 Ben More:
Fuck's sake that wis a slog and a half, eh, pups?

The Munros Book

[in a querulous & pedantic voice]

T------------TTTTTTT****Ahem... (clears throat)... Now look here. I am the Scottish Climbing Club's 1991 revised edition of The Guide to the Scottish Peaks over 3000 Feet and you'll pay attention and listen please. Thank you. That's better. Now if you had read page 16 more carefully you'd have found out I warned you about the ever-steepening grass slopes of Ben More when ascended from the roadside by the A85. Very steep and tedious, I said, not to mention the hanging corrie to the south west of The Dyke: A DANGEROUS PLACE IN BAD VISIBILITY OR IN WINTER!! I told you it was a long unrelenting grind... ah, but do people listen to me? Oh no, nobody listens to me these days... Not like it used to be when my writer typed my pages. Ah, but they were a select bunch back then. The Aonach Eagagh not the trade route it is today. Fewer people went to the hills, you see. None of the riff-raff you get camping by Loch Lomond nowadays. Dear me, no. I blame it all on that dreadful long distance footpath. That awful West Highland Way. My writer DG Fraser did not approve of it AT ALL! Not by a long chalk, he didn't. In fact, he made a point of never walking on it. He'd walk on the road in Glencoe, preferring to risk life and limb on the A82 and the possibility of being mangled beneath the wheels of an articulated truck rather than set boot upon the "West Highland Way". Brought all the wrong sort of people on to the hills, he said and I agreed. Anyway, what was I saying?... Yes, if you had read me more carefully you'd have taken the longer, but more interesting approach to the mountain by way of Benmore Glen. As I point out on page 17, a little more effort but well worthwhile. And yes, I do remember to mention the ridge becomes quite rocky and there are a couple of crags but any difficulties can easily be avoided by traversing to the right or traversing to the left. And, while we're on the subject, your navigation's very slapdash, you know.... you really ought to try and be more accurate. That GPS thingamabob is no substitute for good old-fashioned map and compass work. But does anyone listen to me? Oh no... [Sighs heavily]>>>>>>>>>>

Mickey steps over the sleeping dog at his feet and picks up the blackened steel bucket and throws the last of the coal onto the fire. The coal dust crackles and throws orange sparks up the chimney and out into the night. Tyke's ears twitch. The rain clatters at the window of the cottage. In front of the fire Tyke stretches his back legs out and sighs. Mickey turns to section 9, page 100: Carn an Fhidhleir.

'That wis a sgoosh of a Munro,' he says, looking into the flames.

A warm summer's day, he'd hired a bike in Braemar

and jolted along the track by the Geldie Burn from White Bridge. Left the bike at the ruins and strolled up through the crackling dry ling as the air shimmered in the heat haze. And afterwards he'd taken his boots and socks off and bathed his feet in the shallow pools of the Geldie Burn.

If only all the Munros could be as easy as Carn an Fhidhleir, he thinks, reaching down to pat Tyke as he turns the page and his fingers traverse the paper hills and ridges up Glen Lochsie and onto Glas Tulaichean and Carn an Righ where Tyke chased the half-grey, half-white blue mountain hares.

TYKE: I'm the dog I'm the dog I'm the dog sniff sniff sniff snuff snuff snuff... now here's my master, see, sitting by the fire... I've led him up half the mountains in Scotland, led him through mist, sleet and snaw. He thinks it was that wee plastic thingee with the red floaty needle that done it but I ken it was me found the way home. He'd never have found the path without me.

And where in the name of the Big Dog are we supposed to be going half the time? On and on for mile after mile, through heather and peat hag, it's rough on the paws I can tell you, and then we get to a wee heap of stones where, if I'm lucky, there might be a few crisps, usually it's just some stinky orange peel. One time mind there was half a sausage roll. And then we go all the way back doon again. And we never go up the same hill twice. There was a great yin where there were all these big mountain hares but aw naw we've never been back.

I mean, what the hell are we supposed to be doing on these 'walks'? The first time I thought, Fandabbydosey! We're going out hunting. I got away after some deer but that wisnae appreciated, I can tell you. I was barking and yipping. Come on, come on! They've gone this way! Yip Yip Yip! Whoa, wait. Lots of shouting. In the end I had to come back. I'm like, looking up at him, have you cut your paw or somethin'? But naw. He was fine. Seemed kind of pleased to see me and angry all at the same time. Big Dog kens what that was all that about!

Back then, a'ghraidh, I only had the Gaelic and I couldnae understand what the other dogs in Glasgow were saying. It wisnae long after he got me from the farm. Never goin' back there by the way – dae you ken my ma used to root about in black bags of rubbish – talk about embarrassing rellies... and the seven of us went everywhere in a stinky, ancient red van. I love the city, me. I ain't never going back to that farm and that draughty cold barn. Nope, not me.

Do you know what my master does now? I'll tell you... when he smells there's some of they fat wee stupid white deer about the place, he puts me on a string! I'm like, gaunny no dae that and baring ma teeth. Doesn't happen that often mind tho' cos he's got a terrible sense o' smell – he couldn't smell a mhadaidh til it's nearly at his throat with its hot stinkin' breath.

Now here's my master, see. I've led him up half the mountains in Scotland, through mist, sleet and snaw. Ah m'eudail, he'd be lost without me...

I'm the dog I'm the dog I'm the dog sniff sniff sniff snuff snuff snuff sniff sniff sniff snuff snuff snuff

Nightfall in Glencoe, a half darkness draws down over the mountains. Mickey stands in the doorway of Creagh Dhu, smoking his last roll-up of the night, the moon a yellow orb behind the black wall of Beinn a'Chrulaiste. A few stars prick the dark blue sky over the Buchaille. He watches a lorry on the A82 move slowly across the moor, white headlights on the cab, a line of orange lights along the trailer and then the red tail lights.

the second week
Monday

the botox treatment

The red dusty glow of the city sunrise is reflected in the glass panels of the Shard. On the upper level of St Pancras station, the Somalian early morning cleaner on a zero-hours contract pushes a cloth across the marble top of the champagne bar. In Camden a middle-aged woman in a faded silk dressing gown sits on her balcony above the gardens in Oakley Square. The geraniums flower red beside the miniature olive tree in its terracotta pot. Wallflowers sprout from the brickwork behind the trailing spider plants, the breadfruit and the shiny leaves of the Christmas cactus.

The train speeds across the flat plain of Albion. South of Grantham the needle in the cab of the Class 390 Pendolino touches a hundred and thirty-four miles per hour. Fields of cows and churches and canals at the end of hedgerows, copses of trees and bridges give way to isolated industrial units, factories and streets of bungalows as the train flies arrow-like towards the heart of the great city.

From behind a fence on the industrial estate on the outskirts of Stevenage, the urban fox watches the train pass by. The skyscrapers and towerblocks and spires cluster along the river in the middle of the city. The sun rises out of the marshy coastland over the pylons of Tilbury as the red glow of dawn is reflected in the glass panels of the Shard.

The black man in a grey hoodie leaning out the second-floor window of the Camden townhouse smokes a cigarette. A blackbird sings in the elm tree in Oakley Square as the drag queen walks down the steps to his basement flat, traces of rouge and mascara still on his face. Outside the Londis shop in Camden High Street the Bangladeshi owner throws the steel riot shutters up and hauls a box of on-the-turn tomatoes out onto the pavement.

In Eversholt Road the dark, unshaven young man on the top deck of the number 24 bus talks rapidly in Turkish into his mobile phone as the bus passes the Carreras cigarette factory and the Brutalist blocks of Somers Town.

In the alley behind Greek Street in Soho the Bulgarian waiter unlocks the side door and walks through the silent restaurant. The tables are draped with white cloths and set with silver cutlery, sparkling glasses and linen napkins.

Outside Marks and Spencer's in the Tottenham Court Road a neatly dressed man in clean white trainers, with a little rucksack on his back, rummages in a bin at the bus stop. He pulls out a polystyrene MacDonalds carton, opens the lid but discards its contents, a few leaves of frizzy lettuce.

The rush hour is over, the sun high in the sky above Canary Wharf and large groups of Italian and Spanish teenagers crowd the pavements in front of Buckingham Palace. The taxis cruise slowly along The Mall and in Green Park there are deckchairs for hire this balmy morning towards the end of September. The Union Flag flies from the Foreign Office and, round the corner in Whitehall, Japanese tourists peer through the steel gates at the yellow and red brick facade of Downing Street.

Behind the black front door of the most famous address in the great city, the weekly Cabinet meeting had come to an end some ten minutes before. The room has almost emptied now. The Australian special adviser, talking quietly into his phone, leans back against the wall beside the tall sunny double window.

The Prime Minister is squeezing awkwardly out of his chair, trying not to scratch its eighteenth-century wooden legs on the marble fireplace. Standing up, he lifts the chair over the table, taking care to avoid the brass chandeliers that hang from the elaborately corniced ceiling of the cabinet room. The Prime Minister places his chair – the only one with arms in the Cabinet Room, such are the privileges of high office, he reflects – by the window, in front of the blast-proof curtains. The Prime Minister enjoys his little ritual of replacing the chair in the space by the window where it has been kept since at least Harold MacMillan's time. The sash is open six inches and the bombproof netting shifts gently in the breeze.

The Cabinet Room smells of talc and expensive aftershave and instant coffee and biro ink and men's suit trousers. A faint smell of burnt toast wafts down from the flat on the top floor. He straightens his tie and draws the blastproof curtains apart and gazes out at the blazing sunshine and 26 degree heat of twenty-first-century London. How far the climate has changed and altered since the little ice age of the fifteenth century! There won't be stalls and an ice fair on the frozen Thames during his premiership, he doesn't suppose.

He hears a cough behind him and turns to see the skull-like face of John Fraser-Smythe, Secretary of State at the Department of Social Security. The minister in charge of the DSS, known throughout Whitehall as the department for scroungers and skivers, is almost completely bald save for an inch-and-a-half of neatly clipped grey hair around the sides and back of his head. His eyes bulge a little as he contemplates the Prime Minister and First Lord of the Treasury.

Despite having left the army in the early 1980s, the minister still carries a faintly military bearing with him in the straightness of his back, the shininess of his black patent leather brogues and the obsessive neatness with which he arranges pen and notebook, Blackberry and ministerial iPad in front of him during Cabinet meetings.

The PM thinks to himself that the secretary of state is beginning to resemble Captain Jean Luc Picard. He's also pretty certain the minister regards his welfare reform programme as every bit as crucial to the future of mankind as any mission ever undertaken by the crew of the starship Enterprise.

'Could I have a couple of minutes of your time, Prime Minister?' asks the secretary of state.

The PM nods and rests his backside on the polished hardwood of the boat-shaped table installed in the Cabinet Room during Harold MacMillan's renovations of Number 10 in the early 1960s. The table creaks on its pillar-like mahoghany legs as Fraser-Smythe thrusts his iPad in front of the Prime Minister's face. A scanned document, like a poor quality, blotchy, black photocopy appears on the screen. The Prime Minister can make out the DSS logo and the departmental heading: Fraud Investigation Service.

'We've had an advance warning about this case, Prime Minister—'

He swipes his finger across the screen of the laptop. A blurred photo, of a man in a hoodie leaving a block of flats in the rain, appears.

Still waving the iPad in the Prime Minister's face, the secretary of state continues, 'Thirty-five-year-old male – living in Glasgow – been claiming the high rate mobility component of DLA for the last five years—'

Though he doesn't remember it now, indeed he probably forgot about it over dinner at Gleneagles the same night, the secretary of state, while in opposition, had once visited Drumkirk and promised great things. But when it came down to it, as you walked past the boarded-up shops, Greggs and Cash Generator on your way to sign on, nothing had changed since the shadow minister, now a cabinet secretary, had worn a little of the soles of his patent leather brogues off on the mean pavements of Drumkirk.

The Prime Minster raises a finger.

'Remind me. Which one is DLA?'

The Prime Minister is still rather hazy about the labyrinthine British benefits system. He remembers an adviser once telling him there were only three civil servants in the entire country who understood exactly how the welfare and tax credits system worked. DLA, ESA, JSA, Attendance Allowance, Child Benefit, Income Support.

Dear Lord!

There were so many of them. But then social security benefits weren't something he could reasonably be expected to know much about. After all, at Eton they had trust funds.

'Disability Living Allowance, Prime Minister. Supposed to be for people unable, or virtually unable, to walk more than fifty metres without severe discomfort or the risk of endangering their life,' explains the secretary of state.

'OK – got it,' says the Prime Minister.

'Well, the NBFH got a tip-off about this Jock.'

The PM raises an eyebrow.

'The National Benefit Fraud Hotline, prime minister – this Glaswegian chancer was awarded DLA five years ago because he was HIV-positive.'

'Can't be easy—' interjects the Prime Minister, seeing in his mind's eye Tabatha's junkie brother who wasted away and died skeletally thin in St Thomas' Hospital in the mid-nineties while it seemed every bus shelter in London displayed the Benetton AIDS patient ad.

'The informant told the benefit fraud hotline the suspect's medical condition is now well controlled,' the minister continues coldly. 'Some little poofter in Glasgow takes it up the shitter and the taxpayer's expected to support him for the rest of time. The voters of North Kent don't like it.'

The Prime Minister frowns. Truly, he does lead the Nasty Party. He feels a faint fading shadow of Super Mac and the One Nation Conservatives drift across the Cabinet Room table and out the tall double windows.

'Get to the point, man!' he snaps, losing patience. 'I've got Tabatha's beautician giving me a facial at half eleven.'

Ah – Tabatha's beautician – she works three mornings a week in the perfumery department on the ground floor of Harvey Nicks: the white marble tiled floors, the island counters, Lancome, Givenchy and Elizabeth Arden. A fourteen-year-old girl sits on a chrome and leather stool as Tabatha's beautician in her white coat expertly wields a tiny makeup brush, applying delicately shaded layers of foundation and blusher. As the hands on the art deco clock in the vast atrium of the department store click the minutes round to 11 o'clock, the girl's make-up is complete and she has the face of a twenty-five-year-old.

Tab's beautician fascinates the Prime Minister. Her make-up is a work of art, a painted mask of a face, a smell of eyeliner, foundation and anti-wrinkle cream drift into the room with her. She'll place the black leather case containing her set of six chrome syringes on the sofa in the pokey little flat on the top floor where Margaret and Denis heated up tins of tomato soup and gave the order to the submarine commander two hundred feet below the icy South Atlantic to sink the Argentine battle cruiser.

'The point is – sir.'

The military demeanour again. Fraser-Smythe slips back into it when he's stressed.

'The point is his medical condition is now so well controlled he's been climbing the Munros.'

The Prime Minister raises a quizzical eyebrow. 'He's been what?'

'Climbing the Munros – they're the Scottish mountains over—'

'You don't need to tell me what a bloody Munro is, man!' the PM interrupts, 'Dicky Arbuthnott's got one slap bang in the middle of his deer forest in Perthshire. Bloody nuisance it is in the stalking season. Do you know they can't shoot on Carn Gorm at all anymore?'

Scotland, he thinks, bloody buggery Scotland. Feels himself like George III during the American War of Independence taunted by the Prince of Wales, only a few cobbled streets from where he now stands, over the loss of England's North American colonies.

During his weekly audience at Buckingham Palace the previous day, the Queen had gone on at length on the subject of Scotland, though she had seemed less concerned about the loss of one third of the territorial land mass of the Disunited Kingdom than the potential loss of use of her holiday home for her great-grandchildren.

A master politician that snake oil salesman, Scotland's charismatic first minister. Never one to miss an opportunity to exploit weakness in a political opponent or a chance to play upon the Scots' resentment of the English. It was his misfortune, the Prime Minister reflected, to be in office at a time of constitutional turmoil and to have to deal with a once-in-a-generation political operator.

'Hundreds of 'em, aren't there?'

The secretary of state frowns.

'Sorry, sir?'

'Munros – mountains over three thousand feet.'

'282 to be exact and, according to the tip-off the fraud line received, this chancer from Glasgow has climbed – hang on, I'll just check—' Fraser-Smythe swipes his finger across his iPad again, '– 277 of them,' he announces triumphantly.

Why is the secretary of state telling him all this? He thinks of Neville Chamberlain standing on the tarmac at Heston aerodrome in his long overcoat and wing collar and black tie – a faraway country of which we know little.

'The SNP have us on the backfoot over welfare reform,' Fraser-Smythe explains.

So that's it then – the political and presentational catastrophe of the bedroom tax. He sees again in his mind's eye the nightly TV news reports: people in wheelchairs pouring red paint onto the pavement at the gates of Downing Street, bailiffs holding eviction notices in leather-gloved hands while police held placard-waving, shouting protesters in woolly hats back behind crowd-control barriers.

'This could be our chance to spin the welfare reform debate back our way in Scotland, Prime Minister. Show the man on the Glasgow omnibus what people on benefits really get up to – scroungers versus strivers and all that.'

He's less than comfortable with it. This kind of manoeuvre inevitably backfires. Think Jennifer's Ear. He'll be accused of homophobia. All his efforts on gay marriage wasted. He keeps seeing the Benetton ad from the '90s, the one with the AIDS patient dying in hospital, as he hurried up the the tiled escalator from the tube station at Green Park; Tab's brother's skeletal hand clutching the white sheet.

'The fraud investigation service are tailing the—'

The secretary of state starts to speak but he is interrupted by Leyton Crossfire, the Prime Minister's Australian special adviser, 'Get pics of him climbing a mountain, *YouTube* videos – that kind of thing.'

The Prime Minister glances at his spin doctor.

'People in the UK hate scroungers on benefits. Skivers versus strivers plays well with Sun-reading white van man in Essex,' the Australian explains.

The Prime Minister can see why Fraser-Smythe is attracted to this. The unpopularity of welfare reform north of the border is driving voters towards independence for Scotland. Jesus Christ! He doesn't want to be a page on Wikipedia, a question in Trivial Pursuit: *Who was the last Prime Minister of the United Kingdom?*

He stands up and draws the blastproof net curtains apart again and gazes out at sun blazing on yellow London brickwork. He thinks of Churchill on the roof of the Foreign Office watching the German air raids during the Blitz. On the scrambler phone to Roosevelt twice a week in the war rooms under fifteen feet of concrete.

Christ, he's lucky if the President remembers his first name.

The Prime Minister is filled with a wistful sense of regret tinged with nostalgia. Where once his predecessor fought a world war from the basement of the Cabinet Office, he's spending his premiership trying to stop the United Kingdom falling apart and wasting time dealing with suspected petty benefit fraud in Glasgow.

He hesitates for a moment before he says, 'Liaise with the Scottish Secretary – do what you can with it.'

Then he picks up his Union Jack mug from the table and walks out between the Corinthian pillars and up the stairs to the flat on the top floor to await his botox injection.

nae dugs

CD4 count 572
viral load <40 copies/ml
Munros 279/282

Striped with black bands and studded with yellow warts and short black bristles, the malachite-green caterpillar inches his way across the stony path. He starts life as a caterpillar but his destiny is to become Iompaire Chorcaraich. In the long light days of the Highland summer the caterpillar feeds on the ling. As the days grow shorter on the steep hillside he spins a tough, bottle-shaped cocoon deep inside a tussock of deergrass. Safe inside his cocoon he undergoes metamorphosis and, when the snow and ice have melted in spring, he will emerge as Iompaire Chorcaraich. His wingspan will reach the length of a finger, the eye-like spots on each wing a camouflage he'll use to deceive hunting, predatory eyes.

Five hundred miles to the north of the great city, as the Highland sun dips low in the sky over Beinn a'Chrulaiste and the shadows stretch long, grey fingers across the scree of the Aonach Eagagh, Mickey crests the top of a low rise in the heather and stands, a little wearily, at the edge of a black peat hag.

Sron na Creise, Stob Dearg and Stob na Broige guard the entrance to Glen Etive. A mauve-grey mist is settling over the moor. As he looks across the bleak, wind-scoured heath towards Creagh Dhu, he sees there's a red Ford Focus parked outside the cottage. Not across the road in the big potholed lay-by where the campervans park up overnight - the red Ford is right outside Creagh Dhu and there is a figure on the roof of the whitewashed cottage!

Aw fuck!

He'd been looking forward to lighting the fire, making a pot of tea and munching a Tunnock's snowball before slipping upstairs and into his red and black sleeping bag for an hour's kip.

As he and Tyke draw nearer to the cottage he can see the figure on the roof is an extraordinary looking woman in her seventies in an auburn wig with clumsily slapped on make-up and crimson lipstick, wearing thick, round-framed glasses and a flapping, brown, janitor's coat. She's straddling the apex of the roof and holding onto a chimney pot while below her on the track in front of the cottage a butch middle-aged woman in a blue boiler suit is leaning on a pickaxe.

A timid-looking woman with mousey brown hair and a Rab jacket is holding a blowtorch connected to a blue camping gas cylinder via a length of perished orange rubber tubing. The encrusted layers of paint on the iron gate of the cottage are bubbling up into blisters and an acrid smell of melting gloss paint taints the crisp moorland air.

The woman at the gate puts the gas torch down on the stone doorstep and stares at him as he walks down the track. The woman in the wig and janitor's coat holding onto the chimney stack greets him. The voice is pure Kelvinside:

'Are you the chap who's staying here – from the mountaineering council?'

The accent is plummy and posh

'Aye, that's me,' he replies.

Tyke eyes the figure on the roof suspiciously.

Meanwhile the manly-looking woman in the blue boiler suit has inserted the pickaxe beneath a muddy boulder embedded in the grass and is grunting and puffing away.

'C'm here, mate,' she calls, 'Give me a hand with this rock. The President pranged her exhaust on it at the Easter meet – got to roll it off the track before the next lot of rain.'

'Typical Glencoe weather,' declares the septuagenarian on the roof, 'Fair one minute – foul the next.'

He pushes the boulder with all his might but he's no match in strength for the woman in the blue boiler suit. With one great heave she rolls the granite boulder, that had lain at the foot of the Buchaille since the Ice Age, off the track and into the heather. She straightens up and brushes glittering shards of mica from her hands.

'I'm Pat, by the way,' she says and profers a suntanned hand with dirty fingernails.

'Mickey Bell,' he replies as she gives him a finger-crushing handshake.

'All hail Mickey Bell from Glasgow,' calls the septuagenarian from the roof and she bows low while holding onto the whitewashed chimney stack.

'Scottish Women's Mountaineering Club maintenance party –' explains the mousey-haired woman as she strokes Tyke's head, 'we're here to fit a cowel to—'

The figure on the roof interrupts her. 'You can't bring that dog into the cottage you know. Club rules! Etta May's Westie fought with the Hut Custodian's golden retriever at the 1995 New Year meet. Dogs been banned ever since. Now hand me up the electric drill please'

Mickey pulls the black plastic tap on the urn forward and lets an inch of steaming water warm the tannin-stained steel teapot. He searches around for teabags, milk and sugar. 'So yous are all in the same climbing club then?'

'Yes we're all in the SWMC,' says Pat, 'We're just here for one night. Tomorrow we're driving up to Invergarry to meet Moira.'

'She of the teeteringly high rucksack,' the mousey-haired woman adds.

'We're going to be doing a three-week stravaig from Glen Shiel to Cape Wrath.'

And as they talk he recognises the names of many of the remote glens and bothies around Loch Mullardoch and Loch Monar.

While Mickey munches a Tunnock's snowball the mousey-haired wielder of the gas torch says, 'You know the sepia photo next to the fireplace in the front room, of the two determined-looking ladies in Victorian dress sitting on a boulder —?'

Mickey nods.

'Well, that's Ethel Buglass and Jean Inglis Drummond, our first President and Secretary. The club doesn't own the cottage,' she explains, 'it's leased from the White Corries Estate.'

Mickey pours boiling water onto the three teabags in the metal teapot while the mousey-haired woman goes on to explain how, back in 1947, the SWMC decided they should have their own hut.

And how, from Creagh Dhu Cottage at the foot of the Buchaille, generations of formidable women have set forth to scale the Glencoe hills.

When he climbs down the wooden ladder and goes into the kitchen an hour later he finds the three women gathered around a large double-handled saucepan bubbling on top of the wood-burning stove.

'Pat's making one of her famous veggie stews,' explains the mousey-haired woman.

Mickey's heart sinks.

'Found it!' cries the septuagenarian who is crouched down rummaging in a cupboard. She holds a tin of okra in one hand and a can opener in the other. She opens the lid and tips the contents into the saucepan.

'Ladies' fingers – just the job.'

A half smile plays on Mickey's lips.

Pat dips her thumb into the stew and licks it. 'Hmmmmm—' She digs about in a plastic carrier bag. 'Root of ginger – spice it up a wee bit.'

The three women take it in turns to stir the veggie stew while Mickey fantasises about steak pie and chips.

'And now for the pièce de résistance,' cries the septuagenarian, thrusting a chipped enamel colander under Mickey's nose.

'Don't they smell gorgeous?'

He hesitates, then frowns.

'Toadstools?'

'Nooooo! Bay boletus mushrooms,' says the septuagenarian, 'picked 'em myself on the way up here.'

After they've eaten, he sits with the three women beside the fireplace in the wood-panelled front room of the cottage. They pull the worn armchairs with the home-sewn cushions close to the fire as orange-red flames weave above the coals and the wind moans in the lum. Outside smoke swirls from the chimney of Creagh Dhu cottage and the line of lorries and cars with their red tail lights moves slowly across the moor half a mile away.

Maybe it's the red wine or perhaps it was the toadstools in the veggie stew but time seems to have a fragmented quality to it now. The older woman with the janitor's coat and the auburn wig picks up Mickey's copy of the Munros Book and opens it.

'So what's the plan for getting these Skye ones you've got left ticked off then?' she asks.

'Ah dinnae really know but,' says Mickey uncertainly. 'Just have tae see when I get there I guess.'

The butch middle-aged woman in the blue boiler suit is peeling the foil off an unopened bottle of Bunnahabhain. 'Just ask around the campsite when you're up there – I'm sure you'll find someone who'll chum you up onto the ridge – we've had help from folk in the most unexpected places on our stravaigs, haven't we?' she says with a glance at the other two women.

After a long silence the woman in the auburn wig and crimson lipstick puts the Munros Book down, looks at Mickey and states with emphatic certainty:

'I predict you'll finish your Munros this year.'

There is silence again.

Then the mousey-haired woman asks, 'So what're you doing after Skye?'

'Lookin' for a job if I can find one,' replies Mickey.

'Och, you'll be fine – you're young, you're smart, you're independent, there's nothing to stop you – I'm know for a fact you'll get something.'

Silence falls again. The coals flare. The wind roars in the chimney. Mickey swirls the smoky, peaty-tasting Bunnahabhain around his mouth. Then the mousey-haired woman speaks again, 'Well I wonder when we three will meet again?'

'The hurly-burly of IndyRef'll be done by then – battle lost or won and all that,' says the septuagenarian in the auburn wig, 'what d'you think's going to happen then?'

'Hmmm – I reckon it'll be a narrow win for Yes,' says the butch woman in the blue boiler suit as she reaches into the blackened scuttle with the tongs and drops another nugget of coal onto the fire. The three women sit gazing into the flames, trying to see the future in the embers, and they wonder how Scotland will stand, as the birch leaves slowly turn to orange and the stags roar across the corries and the first dusting of snow whitens the top of Bidean.

11 pm: Tyke is barking.

Determinedly.

Very determinedly.

Doggedly in fact.

He knows this is a battle he can win.

Woof! Woof!

Wear the humans down until they relent and let him take his rightful place on the blanket in front of the fire.

'Woof! Woof!'

If he can't sleep then neither will they.

Nessun Dorma.

'Woof! Woof! Woof!'

'Bark!'

'Bark!'

'Bark!'

11.24 pm: The hinds corried doon among the peat hags 2,700 feet up on Meall a'Bhuiridh hear the small black and white dog barking outside the whitewashed cottage under the Buchaille. As the moon rises over Beinn a'Chrulaiste the door of the cottage slowly opens. A figure in a flapping janitor's coat and an auburn wig emerges and unties Tyke from the gate, puts a finger to her lips and leads the dog into the cottage.

Tuesday

taghan

On a branch high in the old Scots pine that stands beside the stone bridge, Taghan crouches, watching. Dark-coloured, cat-sized, with a long snout, a creamy-white bib and a bushy tail, his eyes are like black, shining beads. With loping, bounding gait he hunts in the woods along the river taking voles, birds, beetles, squirrels, rabbits and the red berries of the rowan. Always an opportunistic feeder, as the years have gone by Taghan has learned to scavenge from the rubbish bins round the back of the hotel.

Trapped and snared by gamekeepers, when the iron roads cut through the forest only a few isolated groups of Taghan's kind survived in the far north-west. But over the last fifty years the pine martens have returned to their ancestral forests across the Highlands and to the woods along the River Ruaidh.

Taghan's claws grip the hoary bark of the branch at the top of the old Scots pine. His white-tipped ears twitch as he crouches there watching the man and the dog. He sees the blue-green luminescent glow of the phone in the man's hand and smells the tobacco smoke that drifts up through the branches as the man stands on the bridge looking down at the river, then flicks the cigarette end off the parapet of the bridge. Taghan watches the glowing red tip as it twists through the air and is lost in the dusk.

the key above the door

For centuries an inn had stood on the site of the white-washed Victorian hotel with its crow-stepped gables and green-painted wooden eaves on the spit of land where the two rivers meet in the shadow of the mountains they call the Grey Corries.

Maybe there was once a taigh or a whisky house here where the River Ruaidh, at the end of its fifteen-mile journey from the snow fields of Creag Meagaidh, beneath the oaks and rowans at Brunanachan and the ruins of Achavady, flows over the stones to join the Cour at the long tongue of shingle the Gaels of Scotland's western seaboard called a stron.

In the cold, late spring of 1689 Bonnie Dundee led his army north through the mountains by the high pass of the Lairig Leacach. They crossed the River Cour at the Stron and his standard bearer the poet wrote: *At last our march is ended, and Dundee plants his foot on level ground, and presses with his heel the verdant bank...* of this place where the two rivers meet in the shadow of the Grey Corries.

Today the word Stron is commemorated in the name of the public bar of the Ruaidh Bridge Hotel. A corrugated iron extension at the rear of the Victorian building, it was erected over the course of a weekend during the cool, damp July of 1890 by navvies working on the West Highland railway line.

Every year the swifts return to nest under the wooden eaves of the Ruaidh Bridge Hotel. The swifts who feed on the wing, sometimes mate on the wing and even sleep on the wing. The swifts that in a lifetime will fly over four million miles; the swifts some of the last migrants to arrive in Scotland and the first to go. Few are seen in Ruaidh Bridge before the end of April or after the middle of September. The swifts with their long scythe-shaped wings and short forked tails, the swifts black in flight against the sky, the swifts who alight on the ground only to nest or when the storm is at its fiercest.

Malcolm calls them by their old name, lum screamers, and on summer evenings they fly screeching around the white-painted chimney stacks of the Ruaidh Bridge Hotel. He says each pair mate for life, meeting up at the same nest site each spring.

Malcolm is a big man in his early sixties. His hair the colour of low cloud on the Grey Corries, there's a mole on his left cheek and his face is weathered by the soft Highland rain like the crags in Monessie Gorge. He's invariably dressed in beige chinos and a short-sleeved checked shirt. When Mickey walks into the Stron, Malcolm is sitting in his usual place on a stool behind the bar polishing his spectacles with a white hanky.

'Ah, good to see you again,' he says, thrusting a sheet of paper across the bar as Mickey drops the heavy rucksack onto the stone-flagged floor.

'I've been working on this,' he explains, 'it's my interview for Camra, you know, the real ale folk, my favourite film, book, why people should come in here…'

Andrea bangs through the door at the end of the bar, a tray of coffee cups in her hands; late forties, thin-faced and tired-looking, her dyed blonde hair, its colouring less obvious in the Stron than outside in the daylight. Always dressed in dark flared trousers and a white blouse, she's often to be found propped up against the wall at the door of the hotel, smoking an Embassy Regal.

Originally from a small town in central Scotland, Mickey knows she is the second Mrs Malcolm. And she loves Mickey. Curled up on the sofa on wet afternoons in Camelon while the oil refinery beside the wide firth thrust a red tongue of flame up into the darkening sky, she'd watch the DVD of *My Best Friend's Wedding* over and over again.

The movie starred Julia Roberts; Andrea always longed for a gay best friend like the urbane Rupert Everett. A bit rougher at the edges but Mickey's the best gay friend, realistically the only gay best friend she's ever going to have in Ruaidh Bridge.

Long chats and heart-to-hearts in the car park while Mickey made a roll-up or she crashed him a Regal till the midges gathered in swarms around them as the rain drops fell on the puddles and finally drove them back into the fuggy, beery warmth of the bar.

He knows Andrea had a fling with Polish Andrew last summer. Malcolm had become suspicious about the length of time Andrea and Polish Andrew were taking to clear up the kitchen while he was stuck upstairs guarding the till behind the bar.

After they'd loaded the dishwasher, wiped down the work surfaces, checked the temperature of the fridges, hung the tea towels to dry on the Rayburn and mopped the floor, with the air still thick with the smell of bleach and deep fat frying, she would unbutton her nylon blouse. Polish Andrew untied his food-stained apron, slid his blue checked chef's trousers down a few inches, pulled out his white Polish penis and fucked her over the stainless steel table in the centre of the kitchen where earlier in the day they'd prepared the lasagne.

Red scratch marks among the black hairs where her

painted fingernails dug into his buttocks. Afterwards while she fastened her bra they giggled at the sweaty outline of her bum like a Rorschach inkblot on the stainless steel surface of the table, before going upstairs to have a drink at the bar before last orders.

Mickey looks around the pub. Judging by the preponderance of young female waitresses he reckons Malcolm picked the temps this summer.

Taking no chances then, Mickey smiles to himself.

The only male is the chubby, ugly Portugese bloke with the thick glasses. Mickey reckons Zelda, who rates potential trade on a scale ranging from a one pint job (very attractive) all the way to a twelve pinter (very ugly and old), would rate Mr Portugal a seven pinter. At any rate he's no Polish Andrew.

'My Dad worked on the dam in Glen Nevis,' Malcolm's telling the Geordie couple sitting at the bar.

Mickey's heard the story before.

'He came over from Donegal to work on the hydro schemes when he was fifteen – bought this place in 1957.'

Mickey looks around, taking in the wood-panelled walls toned a rich golden brown in the decades before the smoking ban and the tartan curtains, watermarked with a tideline of black mildew halfway up where they stick to the condensation on the windows. The stone-flagged floor of the Stron is dappled with years of beer spills. The inn is heated by a forty-year-old, oil-fired, white-enamelled Rayburn in the kitchen. Andrea does the lasagne in it and it keeps the kitchen warm when the ice forms at the edge of the pools on the River Ruaidh.

'Pint is it?' asks Malcolm reaching up to a row of gleaming tumblers stacked on brass racks above the bar. He selects a tulip-shaped glass and holds it under the Stella tap.

The marble-topped bar is guarded by two griffons that perch, wings outstretched, high above each corner, their varnished wooden talons grip the bar gantry and their carved, bearded faces glower down on the bottles that line the shelves; Glenfarclas and Glenmorangie, Aberlour and Dalwhinnie, Bowmore and Bruichladdich. Malcolm keeps more than one hundred malts behind the bar. In the middle of the rows of dusty bottles on the varnished wooden shelves is a 1951 Glen Grant he sells to American tourists for £30 a nip.

Malcolm prides himself on his real ales and the Camra newsletter on the bar carries glowing accounts of the beer in the Stron but the food's another story. Mickey's never seen Malcolm or Andrea eating anything. Andrea appears to draw all her sustenance from wine glasses of Baileys Irish Cream which she starts on around teatime.

A stuffed pine marten with a frozen snarl stares out from a glass case above the fireplace. The stuffed head of a red deer hind is mounted on a wooden shield over the door to the Ladies and a royal stag with twelve-point antlers over the entrance to the Gents with its three tall Victorian urinals, smell of blue bleach cubes and battered cubicle door. There's been no lock on it for years so if you need a dump you've got to be brave or not care. One busy Saturday night Mickey pulled the door open to find one of the local shinty team sat on the toilet, jeans and red boxer shorts around his knees. He smirked as Mickey shut the door red-faced.

The wooden tables and chairs in the Stron don't match. The smell of stale beer is overlaid with the sulphurous tang of smoke from the coal fire with its pair of brass lions that crouch, one each side of the grate. Pewter candelabras encrusted in dripping red wax stand on each wooden table.

At weekends JT from the village sits in the corner by the fireplace playing the piano accordion. His range extends all the way from 'The Blue Blanket' to 'New York New York'. Elton John's 'Sacrifice' is playing on the Wurlitzer juke box in the corner of the bar next to the pool table. Come closing time it'll be the Red Hot Chilli Pipers and 'Flower of Scotland'.

The handful of locals standing at the bar are surrounded by a big group of canoeists in expensive-looking fleeces and Jack Wolfskin jackets. They'll be staying in the bunkhouse behind the hotel. Mickey rests his elbows on the bar and looks furtively at the tall blond guy in combat shorts and flip-flops then looks quickly back at his phone before the guy can catch his eye.

Mickey Bell, Mr Discreet in a Highland pub, he thinks to himself. Well kindae.

The white-haired stalker stands halfway along the bar. Dressed as always in plus fours, Harris Tweed jacket and deerstalker, he takes a relaxed attitude to the drink-drive laws, downing several nips and halves of heavy each evening before walking briskly out to his Land Rover in the car park and driving the five miles home along the narrow single track road up Glen Ruaidh.

The family of overweight English tourists are studying the dessert menu. The Spanish couple in the corner by the fire are playing cards.

And then there's Kyle.

Kyle's been working for Marine Harvest this summer. Every afternoon he takes the inflatable out to check the salmon pens in the loch across from the burned-out farmhouse. Twenty-seven, dyed blond hair, pierced nose, komodo dragon tattoo on his left calf, each evening after he's finished work Kyle sits straddling a bar stool in the Stron.

'All right, mate? How you doin'?' he'll say with that cheeky smile.

And when he leaves, the bar seems a little dimmer, the

lager a bit flatter and Mickey feels a wee bit older.

He first met Kyle in the birch woods along the banks of the Cour. Kyle was fishing. The kind of fishing that involved spending a lot of time with his hands stuck down the front of his black Adidas trackie bottoms. Naw, seriously, he did have a rod and reel, and yards of white nylon line trailing in the turgid waters of the Cour, as well as a plastic tub brimming with squirming maggots. But enough happened and didnae happen that Saturday afternoon three years before for Mickey to know Kyle won't ever be happy living in a Barratt home in Banavie with a pretty blonde wife and a baby in a buggie.

See some folk, they dinnae like Kyle... they say he's wide, cheeky like but it's no his fault – his mum fed him full o' tablets when he wis a kid. She done it so she could keep claiming DLA for him being hyperactive but. Then she fucked off back to Ayr, as soon as he turned fifteen. Seeing as whit a bad time he's had o' it – he's turned out no bad like. No exactly minted but job and a motor, like.

Nothing's happened since though. But then this is the Central Highlands and it's a bit like being gay in the 1970s: a couple of car parks off the A9 at night or moving to Glasgow to go to college when you're eighteen. Kyle's brother lives in Glasgow. Is he gay too? Mickey fantasises sometimes.

There's one weil kent car park on the dual carriageway just north of the Kessock Bridge, another on the outskirts of Aviemore. Face West has an outpost in Inverness from where a Geordie health promotion worker distributes leaflets and condoms and sachets of water-based lubricant in the Gents toilets among the dripping silver birches at a number of lay-bys along the A9 corridor.

Naw... dinnae like car park trade. It jist disnae appeal. Never really tried it TBH. Well no havin' a motor's a bit of a disadvantage tae start wi'. And I dinnae like Grindr...

never hov. Ah guess I jist dinnae like the idea of some fuckin weirdo turning up on ma doorstep but. No up here anyroads – lonely 64-year-old kilt-wearer in Drumnadrochit looking for a special friend. I dinnae think so… Naw…

No: Mickey likes to think he prefers an old-fashioned barroom pick-up so, as far as Ruaidh Bridge goes, there's just Kyle.

He puts his empty pint glass down on the bar and reaches up and touches the polished, wooden claw of the nearest of the two carved griffons that perch, wings outstretched, on either side of the bar gantry.

'Aye, you be lucky now,' says Malcolm, discretely topping up the half-pint glass he keeps under the bar from the Three Sisters tap.

The Ruaidh is roaring down under the bridge next to the inn. Headlights shine through the low windows of the bar as a car splashes through the puddles. The smell of coal smoke hangs in the misty September air.

Scraps of grey cloud, like puffs of smoke from a cannon, drift across the Grey Corries as the door of the Stron bangs shut behind him and Mickey dodges between the puddles in the hotel car park.

Thirty feet below the high stone arch of the bridge that carries the road over the River Ruaidh, the dipper perches on a rock in the middle of the fast flowing water. Gobha-uisge is her name and she has a nest on a ledge high on the stone abutments of the bridge.

Her territory extends half a mile downstream to the shingle Stron where the Ruaidh flows into the Cour. A truck rumbles across the bridge and the short-tailed, dumpy bird flies away, whirring low over the black peaty water.

Where it passes through Ruaidh Bridge, the A86 is flanked by an avenue of tall oaks and beeches. At the grey, stone primary school Mickey turns down the narrow lane that leads to the railway station and the River Cour.

He stops on the humpback bridge across the railway tracks and stands looking over the iron parapet. On the platform below a solitary passenger awaits the arrival of the last train from Glasgow Queen Street.

The line here is single track and green spikes of mare's tail sprout among the stagnant puddles in the ballast. The station buildings eaten away by spores of dry rot, demolished decades ago and replaced with a Perspex bus shelter scored and slashed with graffiti. Only the station master's house remains, wood smoke rises from its hint-of-art-nouveau chimneys.

To the west on the shores of Loch Arkaig the sky is turning to yellow behind Beinn Bhan while to the east the tracks stretch in a straight line for a clear mile until the rails curve round into Monessie Gorge. On the south bank of the Cour the slopes of Beinn Chlinaig catch the last of the evening sunlight. On the steep flanks of Stob Coire na Ceannain the quartzite screes that run like raked gravel down the mountainside are washed with pink as dusk falls over the Grey Corries.

The yellow illuminated sign on the front of the three-car diesel electric unit reads *Mallaig*. Mickey watches the carriage roofs slide under the bridge. The red tail light of the train disappears around the curve in the tracks and into the birch woods.

He hears the train whistle as he passes the white-painted wooden fence at the top of the steps that lead down to the station platform. The sound of the train fades as it crosses the green-painted iron girders of the viaduct that spans the Ruaidh. The silver birch trees and birdsong close in around him as he walks on, down the byroad, towards the river.

He breathes in a smell of leaves and wet earth. Tyke cocks

a leg over a clump of mare's tail at the edge of the tarmac. Simple, primeval and ancient, the plant grows all along the verge. Sown by Victorian engineers to stabilise the railway embankment, over the 125 years since the line opened the mare's tail has slowly spread down the lane. In another century it will reach the banks of the Cour.

Near the river, where the tarmac road ends, he takes a narrow path through the head-high bracken. Tyke sniffs at something on the ground. Black, twisted and pointed at one end, the dog is mesmerised by its musky, jasmine smell: a pine marten scat. He smells the Earb that live in the woods along the river too, the bucks with their short, waxy antlers and gleaming points and coats that shine foxy-red, sleek and glossy.

When nightfall creeps between the trees the Earb scrape away at the ground to sleep on a bed of bare earth, but the Fiadh high on Beinn Chlinaig lie down in the long grass on the open hillside and in the grey dawn the only sign of their passing is a patch of flattened grass.

The twisted roots of the oaks and rowans criss-cross the path like the veins on the back of an old man's hand. Half a mile into the woods, just off the path, screened by hazel, rowan and dense, apple-green blaeberry stands the old caravan. Painted in blue Dulux gloss to window height and white above, a rusting sign on its steel chassis reads *Eccles*.

Its roof is green with lichen that drips from the leaves of the silver birches and hazels that grow thickly around it. The caravan has been repaired at the two front corners with silver, tar-backed roofing tape from B&Q. Its chassis rests on four concrete breeze blocks, one at each corner, its tyres cracked and split by the Highland sun and the ice in winter. The autumn storms hurl hundred-mile-an-hour gusts down from the Grey Corries and chains secure each of the four rusting corner steadies to steel dog-tethers corkscrewed into the ground. Bullfinches and goldcrests crowd around a bird-feeder tied to the guttering.

In the late 1960s, in its glory days when it was shiny and new, the caravan had been towed along the seafront at Nice on the French Riviera from Juan-les-Pins and along the Cote d'Azur to southern Spain and the remote fishing villages of the Costa del Sol.

A mother, a father and their three young daughters went on holiday in the caravan and when they parked up in the centre of a French village, a crowd of curious locals looked on, while the mother handed plates of stew out the window.

The caravan had been towed from Yorkshire to Loch Lomond and to the Edinburgh Festival and along the narrow single track road beside Loch Maree. Retired to a croft in Argyllshire as a holiday home for the grandchildren, the caravan had taken its last journey thirty miles north to Ruaidh Bridge in the late 1990s, towed behind a rusty dormobile driven by Dutch blacksmith Lute van Steeman and discretely located among the birch trees on a two-mile-long strip of heather and blaeberry of uncertain ownership between the A86, the railway and the river.

After the ice retreated and the glacier that spread its long tongues out from the frozen Atlantic along Loch Arkaig and over Glen Ruaidh had melted, tribes of people settled along the coast and slowly moved inland.

They farmed the fertile ground along the banks of the River Cour. And in autumn the birch leaves turned to orange.

The scratch of quill pen on parchment in twelfth-century Scotland; a hand clutches the wooden arm of the throne. The warlords stand with bowed head before the king. The land along the banks of the Cour is made the subject of a feudal charter; the land along the Cour was stolen.

And still in autumn the birch leaves turned to orange.

The Prescription Act of 1617 conferred the title for land to those who had possessed it for a period of forty years. The establishment of the Register of Sasines in the same year allowed Donald MacDonnell of Keppoch to register a legally defendable deed for the stolen land along the Cour he had inherited from his father.

And still in autumn the birch leaves turned to orange.

In the warm, balmy September of 1663 young MacDonnell of Keppoch and his brother Ranald were murdered by their cousins. They forced Ranald to watch while they took his brother by the hair, pulled his head back and cut his throat with a dirk. Then they pulled Ranald's white linen shirt up over his head and slit him open from rib cage to groin and watched his guts spill out onto the stone-flagged floor of the mansion house at Insch.

Revenge was swift. The seven murderers lived but a few days more before their necks were on cold stone and a notched axe sharpened. The seven heads were wrapped in a tartan plaid and presented at the feet of MacDonald of Sleat, high chief of the clan. But first they held each head by the hair and washed the blood away in a spring on the shores of Loch Oich known for evermore as Tobar-nan-Ceann, the well of the seven heads.

And still in autumn the birch leaves turned to orange.

After Alexander MacDonnel of Keppoch was killed by a musket ball through his left eye at the Battle of Culloden in 1746 his lands, which by now stretched as far east as the Corrieyairack Pass, were seized by the British government and managed on behalf of the crown by the Commissioners of the Forfeited Estates.

Thirteen years later, in 1759, his son Ranald Og successfully petioned the British crown for the return of his estate on the grounds he had loyally served in King George's army at the siege of Quebec.

And still in autumn the birch leaves turned to orange.

With the family estate safely back in his hands, Ranald began the process of establishing himself as a Highland laird and member of the British aristocracy. Unfortunately for the MacDonnells, his son Alexander ran up such vast gambling debts at the gaming tables of London that in 1831 the estate had to be leased to a sheep farmer from Peebles.

A decade and a half later, in 1847 the land was bought by a Mr Player, a cigarette manufacturer from Nottingham, who spent a great deal of his money building a shooting lodge on the hillside high above Monessie Gorge. And on his orders the estate's ghillies and stalkers toiled over a number of summers as, surrounded by clouds of biting insects, they constructed an iron deer fence all along the boundaries of the estate.

And still in autumn the birch leaves turned to orange.

In 1991 the eastern part of the estate, from Monessie Gorge to the Corrieyairack, was purchased by Smersh Holdings, a Bahamas-registered company part-owned by Sheikh Bin al Assad of Dubai.

And still in autumn the birch leaves turned to orange.

Some local people say the strip of land beside the river was acquired from the Player family in the 1920s by the British Aluminium Company when it bought the fishing rights on the Cour. Once one of the great salmon rivers of Scotland, its upper reaches were reduced to sluggish midgey pools of dark peaty water after the construction of the dam at Laggan.

And the title deeds? Lost down the back of a rusty filing cabinet in a derelict brick outbuilding at the smelter in the town twelve miles away.

Still others claim the Caledonian Railway bought the two-mile-long strip of riverbank in the 1890s when they pushed the line west out of Monessie Gorge to reach the western seaboard at Loch Linnhe.

And still in autumn the birch leaves turn to orange.

And so it seems Mickey Bell's claim to the square of dense blaeberry, rowan and birch where the old caravan stands is as good as everyman's.

'You'll always find the key above the door.'

He can hear Zelda's grating, lisping tones in his head as he reaches up onto the roof of the old caravan. He turns the key in the rusty Yale and pulls opens the door. The faint familiar whiff of Calor gas. Tyke hops up onto the step then jumps onto the bed.

The interior of the caravan is lined with varnished plywood finished to the exacting standards of a 1960s cabinet maker. The red and white checked curtains, the Gay Toon Planner ran up on his antique Singer sewing machine while its black-painted iron legs made little dents in the sanded floorboards in the sunny bay window of his flat in Hyndland, are tightly closed. Windshields, deck chairs and welly boots poke out from under the caravan and inside the lockers are stocked with tins of corned beef, ravioli and meatballs, sprouty potatoes and UHT milk.

Where, in the '60s, there was a wardrobe with a mirror on the door (to adjust your hat before stepping out onto the beach at Cannes) there squats a small, pot-bellied wood-burning stove (£99.99 from Machine Mart in Great Western Road). Tiles are cemented to the caravan floor to form a hearth and one breezy April day Mickey stripped a rectangle of the varnished plywood lining back to bare aluminium then cut a neat circular hole in the wall out of which sticks a six-inch British Standard flue pipe.

A dented and blackened kettle stands on the stove. An armful of twigs from the woods heats the caravan so efficiently, half the time Mickey sits in just his boxer shorts and T-shirt. Nearby are the deep pools of the Cour or he can climb the fence behind the toilet block at the caravan site in the village and sneak into the showers.

The caravan had been South African Pete's mother's originally. When Pete realised things had changed since the '90s and that, without a British passport, the welfare state wasn't going to pay his rent and the cost of getting his teeth fixed, he'd gone back to Jo'burg to be with Jolene and had left the keys for the caravan on the veneered top of Zelda's cocktail cabinet. Zelda had visited Ruaidh Bridge once, reacted badly to a cleg bite, been rude to the locals in the Stron (*bloody Highland teuchters!*) and had sworn never to return.

Before he turns off the black plastic valve on the camping gas lantern that sputters on the scratched, varnished tabletop, Mickey lifts the Munros Book down from the overhead locker.

He turns to the final pages.

Section 17: The Islands.

He turns to Skye where as yet several of the pages are still pristine, not yet spidery with black biro ticks and smudgey dates.

Then he opens the caravan door and steps out into the soft Highland night. Over the hunched dark shoulder of Beinn Chlinaig, a yellow moon is rising. He leans back against the corner of the caravan, a roll-up in one hand, a can in the other. Back in Ruaidh Bridge, back in the north.

Ruaidh Bridge: the place in the Highlands he set out to climb so many Munros from, a place to escape to in the forest at the foot of the mountains, the stress and fear of the city falling away as he gazes across to the Grey Corries. Over the past three years the old caravan has been Mickey's basecamp. The place the dreams were dreamed and the plans were laid. Everest might have the Rongbuk Glacier and the south col but Mickey Bell will always have Ruaidh Bridge and the Grey Corries.

The night is mild and still and he can hear the river; moonlight gleaming on whirling black eddies and white waves. He wishes he was here for a week not just one night. The stars stand out sharp, the Milky Way cuts a pearly-white swathe across the sky, a darker blue against the black of the woods and the hills. A grey shape flickers erratically between the silver birches. Ialtag the bat, dodging and twisting at great speed, chasing insects in the night air.

The moths flutter around the shaft of light that falls from the open door of the caravan. The smell of woodsmoke drifts between the birch trees. Patches of mist, the owl hoots in the woods across the river. The way the weather changes here: a front's swept in from the Atlantic in the two hours since he got back from the Stron. Now standing under the trees, he sees already the night is darkening, high cloud covering the stars and the wind is mild and from the west. He knows it'll be raining by morning.

Wednesday

mr f

Even as the hot July sun blazes down from an azure blue sky and the cattle lie down beside the slow flowing waters of the Cour, the first chanterelles appear in the woods around Ruaidh Bridge. The dusky orange mushrooms push up through the yellow birch leaves and tangles of spongey sphagnum moss among the roots of the silver birches. In the grass, under the hazels and oaks by the banks of the little stream that flows down to the gorge, the slugs have been eating the mushrooms and the orange caps of the chanterelles are a thin lacework of holes.

The first drops of rain smatter the windows of the old caravan and the wind rustles the branches of the rowan trees. Butter melting on hot toast soaking up the juices of fried sausages. Mickey lies on the bunk. The sun cuts a shaft of light across the blistered varnish of the table. Tyke gnaws a hide chew on a cushion on the floor.

The rain has stopped; Mickey locks the door of the caravan. No much point really, he thinks. It wouldnae exactly be difficult tae break in. Andrea told him thousands of pounds' worth of leather saddles and horse bridles had been stolen from Laggan along with a sit-and-ride lawnmower from the village. But naebody's going to be interested in the old caravan and so he reaches up and puts the key above the door.

In spring the woods along the River Ruaidh are yellow with primroses even as there is still snow on Beinn Chlinaig. The white wood anenomes open, then the ferns unfurl before the first bluebells appear under the oak trees and then in June the green fronds of the bracken.

The waxy leaves of the blaeberry bushes brush against his legs as Mickey follows the track between the silver birches further into the woods. Tyke's lagging fifty yards back, sniffing around in the bracken. Mickey pauses for a moment and stands quietly. A flicker of movement, brown wings speckled with white, a buzzard flaps lazily between the trees.

See last summer, the Polish boy who wis workin' in the kitchen at the Stron showed me which mushrooms you can eat from the woods like. Aw but the dog wis bein' a right fuckin pain that day and kept bringing us sticks and droppin' them at oor feet and barking while we were crouched doon lookin' at all they toadstools. He showed me how the skin of the bay boletus feels tacky when it's wet like. And then he gets this knife out he's got with him and he slices this toadstool open and it's got these yellow pores and they turn blue when you cut intae it. Ah wis all polite like and listened tae him cos he's dead pretty like but totally hetty (fuckin waste ha ha!) and I didnae want tae say I dinnae really like mushrooms, no even the ones in blue plastic trays you get from the supermarket but...

An accelerating low rumble, a flash of blue and glass through the trees, the sound of a train whistle. The railway line runs through the woods. He knows all the trains: they whistle to clear the deer and sheep from the track. The 8.02 south to Corrour, the 11.47 west to the Fort, the 15.48 from Glasgow and the 18.03.

Suddenly, Tyke shoots forwards towards a tall pine tree beside the path, nose to the ground. Mickey catches a glimpse of a red tail, white belly and tufted ears as Feorag Feoirag races across the ground and up the tree. He scuttles twelve feet up the far side of the trunk then presses himself flat and motionless against the bark. Tyke stands up on his hind legs, one front paw resting on the tree trunk, transfixed.

Long spiral twists of stripped bark, the husks of acorns and chewed pine cones that look like apple cores: there are signs of the Feorag in the woods all along the Cour. In autumn as the first frost dusts the grass with white and the trees that line the River Ruaidh turn rich shades of gold, burgundy, russet and umber, the hazelnuts drop onto the ground beside the old caravan. Most contain a juicy nut but sometimes the shell is empty or the kernel shrivelled and inedible. But the Feorag can choose between good and bad nuts just by holding them in his paws. One day in April, rummaging in the gas box of the caravan, he found one of the Feorag's stashes: a little pile of split halves of hazelnut shells hidden under Zelda's boule set and the pink frisbee.

A mile from the old caravan he crosses a strip of marshy ground and finds himself in a clearing in the forest. An ugly 1970s bungalow and a faded arrow reading *Manager* stand surrounded by wooden pallets, car batteries, old tyres and rusting washing machines.

Nearby, among the dripping birches, six damp, mournful-looking timber chalets circle a square of hard standing where half a mile of dirt track road leading from the A86 ends. On a gate is a sign in Gaelic. Mickey smiles: translated it means *The Little Houses*. A nice name for the tourists but in Gaelic 'the little house' is also a euphemism for the toilet.

Each chalet is surrounded by timber decking. Above each door a wooden disc, green with moss: Loch Clunie, Loch Arkaig, Loch Lochy, proclaim the signs. The chalets have a neglected, down-at-heel look to them. TV aerials point skyward out of the brambles and nettles. A toppled whirligig clothes drier lies on the ground. Plastic garden chairs sit in the long grass. A tattered curtain is pulled halfway across a window. Through the glass he can see a wall-mounted electric heater.

On the proprietor's website there are photos showing the chalets or rather 'lodges' in a flattering light: cosy log cabins in the woods with a view to the distant snow-capped peaks of the Grey Corries. *A great place to relax and unwind! Affordable self-catering holiday accommodation in the heart of the Highlands! Click here forTariff. Click here.*

A nylon washing line is strung between two of the chalets, walking boots and waterproof trousers are hung over a wooden picnic table. A square of grass has been cut in front of each chalet but elsewhere the owner of *The Little Houses* has given up on the unequal struggle to strim back the encroaching brambles and bog myrtle that grow verdant and jungle-like in the mild and damp West Highland climate.

Outside Loch Arkaig Tyke ignores a woman with long dark hair opening the rear doors of a Fiat Doblo van with Italian number plates. The dog runs in a straight line towards the collection of motorbikes parked up in front of Loch Garry. Tyke dodges between the Harleys and Triumphs and up the wooden steps in front of the chalet to where a dozen bikers in oily jeans and leather jackets are sprawled across the decking.

The bikers range in age from late thirties to late sixties. There are shiny bald heads and grey beards and tattoos and earrings and red kerchiefs around thick necks. They're sat in white plastic garden chairs swigging from bottles of Becks in the late morning sunshine. A smell of oil and rubber lingers in the air, a hint of melted tarmac clings to faded denim.

Walking through the woods and coming suddenly upon the bikers with their grey stubble and leather jackets you might turn hurriedly back into the trees, before they see you. They have a scary look to them; like they could be the

Hells Angels coven pledged to kill the Rolling Stones after Altamount in '69, still on the road and still on the run.

Tyke though sits down at the feet of the biggest biker of them all, six foot two with an impressive walrus moustache and grey, fuse-wire beard. His oil-stained jeans have a rip in the left knee just above his studded motorcycle boots. He wears a black cap-sleeved T-shirt and on the exposed, brown suntanned skin of his right upper arm is a circular blue tattoo. Motorbikes and leather belts entwine around the acronym MSC. For these are not Hells Angels, this is the Eindhoven Chapter of the Motor Sports Club of Holland.

The big daddy biker's just finishing a story: '—and then ve rolled a joint while the ambulance men wheeled the dead transvestite in the wedding dress out on a stretcher!'

As the laughter fades, he looks down and sees Tyke at his feet then turns around and waves, a look of surprise on his face.

'Mickey!'

The bikers come to Ruaidh Bridge every summer, driving north from Folkestone then roaring up the A1 to Newcastle. Thunder in the glens as they roll over the stone bridge across the Teith at Doune and past the tourists eating chips and licking ice cream cones in Callander; dodging the potholes and stones on the A84 by Loch Lubnaig, then on through Strathyre and Lochearnhead, Crianlarich, Tyndrum, Bridge of Orchy and the Blackmount.

'You've brought the sunshine veev you, Mickey.'

'I always dae, Mr F!' grins Mickey.

The Motor Sports Club of Holland is part of a Europe-wide network of 'motor sports clubs' first established in the early 1970s for men with an interest in motorbikes and leather and men.

'Mickey – you come and see my new wheels.'

Mr F jumps down from the decking and leads Mickey

between the motorbikes parked up in front of the timber chalet.

'Here she ees,' he says, pointing at a gleaming chrome and red trike. 'Eesn't she's a beauty?' He runs his hand along the trike, caressing the carriagework. 'Supercharged – 1700cc – naught to sixty in 4.5 seconds – with my bad heep I find a bike too heavy these days. And look,' Mr F twists a chrome handle under the gleaming luggage rack. 'Eet's even got a boot! I take you for a spin – yes? – room for you too, pups. Up you go!' he continues, lifting Tyke up onto the leather double rear seat of the trike.

'You vant a Becks? I'll get you one from the fridge—'

Mickey shakes his head. 'Bit early for me, Mr F. Gottae leg stretch the dog across the river. I'm off on the bus tae Skye later on but.'

'Ah – ve had a great run up that way yesterday – up to Loch Carron and over the Applecross Road but I'm tired now.'

Mr F lifts Tyke down from the trike. 'You are going alone?' he asks.

'Aye, just me and Toots,' replies Mickey, ruffling the dog's thick shaggy coat.

Mr F frowns. 'You be careful up there, Mickey.' Then he says, 'You vant to borrow a sling – or a harness?' The old biker's eyes bulge salaciously.

'Only if it's a climbing harness, Mr F,' Mickey banters back. Then he grins as he repeats Zelda's old line, 'Ah'm more climbing slings than slingback shoes, me.'

And he remembers back to the first time he got talking to Mr F: the story he told in the Stron of how he came by his name; the music throbbing across the dancefloor of the club in the disused warehouse in Amsterdam; the air heavy with crystal meth and ketamine and poppers. On the packed dance floor, leather queens dripping chains, propping up the whitewashed brick walls of the club, as outside the sun sank low over the cranes and shipping containers and the competition to elect Mr Fuk Holland 2012 began.

'It was a clapometer for the voting, Mickey, and when I walked up onto that stage and said *I'm sixty four and I'm still getting eet* the clapometer went off the scale.

'I won! I am Mr Fuk Holland 2012!'

the grave in the woods

It was autumn again, when the birch leaves turn from yellow to orange and then to brown and snow dusts the top of Aonach Mor, when he first came to the grave in the woods. The sun low in the sky; the glint of water between the mossy trunks of the oak trees; the river flowing in slow pools at the foot of the steep fifty-foot bank. A narrow, leafy path leads down the slope to the water's edge.

He's reached the Cour. He's been here before.

On the flat ground at the foot of the bank stands a simple cairn of stones gathered from the riverside. Fronds of fern shade the cairn and a foot-high sapling of oak grows out between the mossy boulders at its base. Many small pebbles have been placed in the gaps between the larger rocks and stones. A flat, oval-shaped boulder tops the cairn. Carved on it, in faint childish letters, is a Gaelic name.

An air of sadness hangs around the cairn, a sense of dreams dreamed and lives lived. Once he found a single bluebell carefully laid on the flat stone. He'd asked Malcolm in the Stron about the cairn in the woods.

'Perhaps it's a dog's grave,' Malcolm had said and it tears at Mickey's heart as he watches Tyke racing between the patches of sunlight and tall fronds of bracken beneath the silver birches.

He crosses the broad shallow river, stepping on the dry boulders that protrude from the slow flowing water. Balancing carefully, for the rocks below the waterline are slimy with green weed, he follows a line of stones diagonally along the middle of the river until he stands roughly two thirds of the way across. Then he steps onto a slab of smooth rock near the far bank before he splashes through the shallow gravelly pools where shoals of tiny silvery minnows scatter.

He pulls himself up the overhanging bank where the licheny oak trees grasp the pebbly soil with twisted roots. He's only crossed the river yet it always feels different, remoter somehow, over here at the foot of Beinn Chlinaig.

He can hear sounds of laughter and car doors slamming on the north bank of the Cour, breaking the silence under the mossy branches of the oak trees. But he's crossed the river and entered an older world. He feels the Highlands past pressing in all around him. He felt the same at Barrisdale standing beside the eighteenth-century house beneath Luinne Bheinn and Ladhar Bheinn, sheltered behind lichen-green, stone walls from the sea gales hurled along Loch Hourn. And he feels it now on the far bank of the Cour as the dragonflies whirr in the heady, late summer air.

He squeezes through a hole in a rusty, iron deer fence and climbs up between the sycamores and rowans, following a narrow line of hoofprints in the dry, peaty soil. A whirr of wings and long curved beaks as two brown and grey-speckled woodcock fly up from the ground and disappear between the trees.

On the steep grassy hillside above the gorge of the Allt Beinn Chlinaig, a lone telegraph pole stands on the hillside, wires long gone but white ceramic insulators still intact. He climbs up to a level terrace cut into the flank of the hill. A length of rusting iron rail lies in the grass. He's reached the tramway.

Tufts of wool lie on the short cropped turf between the patches of bracken. Two sheep and a lamb bolt into the undergrowth as he and Tyke approach. The dog walks past the sheep, to heel, a sulky, recalcitrant air about him, a glint of mischief flickers in his blue-green eyes.

The level solum of the tramway makes for dry, easy walking and, where the wet flushes, yellow with bog asphodel, cut down the steep grassy hillside, the marshy ground is imprinted with the pattern of long gone railway sleepers. A stump of concrete stands high on the hillside. The remains of a Blondin, a cable lift once used to haul stone and rubble and spoil across the river.

He follows the line of the tramway towards the lip of the gorge of the Allt Beinn Chlinaig. A flat terrace cut into the hillside curves round into the birch and rowan trees that line the steep-sided ravine. A two-foot-diameter length of pipe and a rusted pump lie among the bracken and long grass where the terrace ends at a locked iron gate at the entrance to a tunnel. Carved in the rock above the gate are the words ADIT No.5.

He peers between the iron railings into the dank, dripping tunnel. Puddles of rainwater stagnate on the ground and white stalagmites drip down from the ceiling. In the darkness, two hundred feet further along the shaft, the adit ends abruptly at a wall of brick and concrete. Behind the wall, inside the mountain, lies another deeper shaft. Wide enough to take a railway train, it runs from the dam at Laggan, beneath the Grey Corries and Beinn Nuivais to the smelter on the shore of Loch Linnhe.

He holds onto the bars of the iron gate, staring into the darkness, imagining the trillion gallons of water from Loch

Treig surging through the dark in the rocky shaft deep inside the mountains to the pumphouse high on the hillside, plunging down through four great pipes to the smelter on the shores of the loch. He feels the power of Loch Treig spinning the turbines, generating the electricity, powering the machines, turning bauxite into alumina to make the aeroplanes that cut white vapour trails across the azure blue sky.

When they built the tunnel the hillside above the Allt Beinn Chlinaig was torn open, stripped back to bare rock and earth. A corrugated iron pump-house and a steam crane were erected on the hillside; locomotives hauled men and materials up to the adit, a seeping open wound on the flank of Beinn Chlinaig.

But in the second decade of the twenty-first century as he stands looking through the rusty gates of Adit No.5, only faint traces are left: the rusty pump in the long grass, the stump of concrete pillar on the hillside, the rotting telegraph pole. Verdant nature, the jungle-like way plants and trees and green things grow in the West Highlands, has healed the scar on the hillside. The bracken and the deergrass have spread over the spoil heap and the roots of the silver birches have knitted the wound back together.

The hillside is healed.

But the waterfall is gone.

He turns and looks across at the dank, dripping, black cliff face where once a white waterfall cascaded down the hillside. The water pours through a steel grate in a concrete dam higher upstream now, the waters of the Allt Beinn Chlinaig stolen by the tunnel to drive the turbines to generate the electricity. The price: the waterfall that is lost.

Somctimes though, when the burns are high and the tunnel overflows with Lochaber's abundance of rainfall then the lost waterfall on the Allt Beinn Chlinaig reappears for a night or a day and white water cascades over the black cliff and the lost waterfall is seen again, a ghost waterfall glimpsed between the leaves of oak and rowan.

He retraces his footsteps; then, pulling himself up on tree roots and clumps of heather, emerges onto the open hillside above Adit No. 5. He sits on a rock; Tyke comes and leans into him. He feels the warm sunshine on the dog's coat as he looks out across the wide valley of the Cour.

Below him the tramway curves round the hillside into the deep gully of the Allt Beinn Chlinaig. An iron bridge straight out of the Wild West, topped with a deck of rotten railway sleepers, spans the gorge.

A mile further west the tramway threads its way through the stumps of felled conifers at the foot of the pass of the Lairig Leacach. A dirt track road runs through the pass today, a narrow path four hundred years ago when Bonnie Dundee led his army down the Lairig to cross the Cour at the Stron.

The crag-studded slopes above the pass sweep up through scattered birch trees to the grassy slopes of Beinn Bhan where a deer fence, at the edge of the dark conifer forest, stretches across the hillside. Cattle graze between the Grey Corries and Sgurr Inse and around the stone bothy at the foot of Stob Ban. The door's ajar and inside, in the darkness, there's the smell of woodsmoke.

Five thousand feet above on Beinn Nuivais the last section of the route across the stony summit plateau is still a white sheet of crystalline spring snow. The cliffs of the north-west face fall away in great soft cornices. A trail of bootprints leads to the summit.

The climber touches the cairn three times then walks across the snow and sits down among the ruins. The temperature is three degrees, cold enough to chill the water in the bottle in his rucksack as he sits watching the snow buntings flit around the ruins of the Victorian observatory. A group of walkers pulling red *Beating Bowel Cancer* T-shirts over their heads are having their photo taken. The cloud is brushing the summit of Scotland's highest mountain but through the mist the climber can make out Loch Linnhe 5,012 feet below.

Where the wide river flows into the sea at the broad isthmus of the sands of Caol, at the end of the flat plain of the Lochy, crouch the blue sheds of the smelter. The machinery to make bauxite into ingots of alumina fully automated now and the workforce reduced to one hundred and fifty humans to tend the machines. The blue sheds at the foot of the hydro pipes that plunge down the mountainside are quiet now, the hum of machinery undisturbed by human voices at the foot of Ben Nuivais.

The town is a sprawl of grey bungalows and industrial units spread across the boggy, green birch- and rowan-fringed plain. In the '60s the Highlands and Islands Enterprise Board (back then central economic planning and the last vestiges of socialism lingered still) built a car factory at Corpach; the new Hillman Imp would be assembled on the flat heathery plain of the River Lochy. A factory with a glass tower on the edge of the sea at the place the Gaels called the field of the corpses where the birlinns once floated on the sea loch with black sails and the corpses of kings laid out on the wooden planks of the deck.

And they built houses too. The workers at the factory would live along the fringe of sand the Gaels named Caol. The pile-drivers sank the concrete fifteen feet deep to reach the sand and gravel below the black peat that had covered the land since the ice age.

And DG Fraser five thousand feet up on the grey scree slopes of Scotland's highest mountain would say the tower's design was modern with much glass and later, sat at his typewriter in the flat in Byres Road, would write 'it looked surprisingly well' seen against Ben Nuivais from across Loch Eil.

Over to the east the broad glen of the Cour stretches out in front of Mickey. The road and the railway snake along by the river. Across the glen lie the rounded hills of Glen Ruaidh and Braeruaidh Lodge where the public road ends and beyond: Meall na Teanga and Ben Tee and Creag Meagaidh still with a white lip of snow.

At his feet, down in the forest at the foot of the hills, lie the rooftops of the houses of Ruaidh Bridge. The grey slated slopes and whitewashed chimney stacks of the hotel poke out above the canopy of trees. Andrea leans back against the wall by the plastic tables and chairs. She brushes a strand of dyed blonde hair away from her eyes as she lights an Embassy Regal from the pack on the table and stares across the car park at the birches and rowans.

At the bus stop beside the community garden the air is warm, sultry even, and midges hover in the shade of the undergrowth across the road from the yellowing harling of the 1930s council houses in Aonachain Terrace.

The farm collies chained to their kennels outside the narrow-windowed stone barn at Keppoch are barking. The gleaming solar panels on the corrugated iron roof of the village hall flash black in the sunlight and the sign above the door of the shop next door reads *Established 1957*. He hears the faint shouts of the nine children in their red sweatshirts playing football in the school playground.

The English owner of the Ruaidh Bridge holiday park astride his motor-mower circles round and round the green clearing of grass in the woods by the river. Seen from the hillside, the white gravel hardstanding pitches of the caravan site writ like Inca runes in the desert.

The plain, slate-roofed, stone church stands on a brackeny rise by the bend in the river, high above the village. The road and railway twist along side by side by the shingle flats of the floodplain of the Cour. The tourists stand at the door of the church, breathing the scent of the honeysuckle that winds itself around the wire fence enclosing the graveyard.

Behind the studded wooden door the altar and pews are dimly lit by bare bulbs on the stone interior walls, damp prayer books and incense, the smell of a church. Outside, graves surround the stone kirk, the oldest mere human-sized bumps in the mossy turf. Others have simple unmarked headstones, boulders in the grass, sprouting beards of white and lime-green lichen.

A. Stewart 1st Lovat Scouts 26th January 1916. There are Camerons here and MacRaes too. The sands of time slip through a lichen-crusted hourglass below a skull and crossbones. Words in Latin carved in sandstone: *Sailor drowned at Barrisdale*.

Beyond the wire fence, on the grassy hillside, sheep graze among the bracken and spiky clumps of soft rush. Past the yew tree, by the cement path, a woman in a headscarf stands by the foot-high granite obelisks, linked by rusty green chains that cordon off a square of gravel. A white-winged marble cherub, arms crossed in prayer, stands among baskets of pink plastic roses. The woman turns to look at the soft toys, their soggy fur matted by the rain. She reads the inscription on the stone at the cherub's bare feet: *Here Lie God's Holy & Beloved Innocents*.

At the edge of the trees, behind the grey granite presbytery, the old black Austin rusts in the long grass outside the tumble-down woodshed. The white-haired priest sits at the dark polished wooden dining table, half a dozen copies of a slim paperback volume stacked neatly in front of him. He picks the top one up, opens it at a random page, reads the words, his words, for the priest wrote the book, paid to publish it privately, one hundred copies: the story of a doctor, a scrap of tartan and the aftermath of Culloden. Gently, almost tenderly, he lays the book back on the pile and turns to look out the double window across the trees.

the fifth floor

'Thirty-five minutes stuck on the bloody sliproad before the bus even got onto the motorway!'

Nige is standing beside the team leader from IT support as he fastens his clip-on tie, in the narrow, unisex changing room with its rows of battered grey lockers. He likes to be at his desk by 7.30 am each morning. In fact sometimes he's there at 7.10 am. Nigel's a commuter. He takes the train home but on a level 5 salary he can't afford to travel both ways by rail. But he still likes to be at his desk by 7.30 am.

Nige was born just as the 1960s became the seventies, just as Simon and Garfunkel released their final album *Bridge Over Troubled Water* and Rolf Harris was number one with *Two Little Boys*. Johnny Cash performed at the White House for President Nixon and Jimi Hendrix was found dead in his room at the Lonson Hotel.

Nigel's own musical era was the '80s. He's a big fan of the Thompson Twins and Howard Jones. His James Bond was Roger Moore and his Doctor Who, Tom Baker.

His neatly swept-back hair is flecked with grey, his face a little flabby with grey bags beneath his eyes. Something of a workaholic since the break-up of his marriage, when he's not in the office Nige likes to spend the days at his timeshare on the coast, where the sea sweeps across the estuary faster than a man can run. In the warm summer weather he wanders around in shorts and boots and a sun hat, showing off his beer belly. Afternoons whiled away sitting in a deckchair with a bottle of cheap white wine reading the latest Andy MacNab. When the sun drops low in the sky over the sandy estuary he ignites the fire pit. The timeshare is Nigel's little piece of heaven.

Nige is relentlessly cheerful. As he often says to Gina, for him it's a case of, 'If we didn't do it someone else would 'ave to.'

The file open on his desk. The single mother on income support jailed for taking a ten-hour-a-week cleaning job to pay for new shoes for her kids. Even before he applied for the secondment at the FIS, Nigel learned never to answer, 'I work for the DSS,' when asked at parties what he did.

In the awkward silence and ensuing discussion, verging on aggressive argument, over single mothers or work capability assessments or whatever current controversy the DSS was embroiled in, Nigel felt duty-bound to defend the department.

Now he just says he's a civil servant. Further probing elicits the response, 'In finance,' which, he's discovered, closes down that line of conversation very nicely.

Like he says to Gina as they queue for sausage rolls and cartons of milk at Greggs in the shopping centre across the road from the office,

'Someone's got to do it. If we resigned tomorrow there'd be a queue of people waiting to take our jobs.'

Gina Hazelwood: head of section at the Department of Social Security's Fraud Investigation Service, late fifties, very overweight. Walking behind her down the corridor to the canteen for his fifteen-minute morning break, Nigel is mesmerised by the huge girth of her thighs, wobbling like Zeppelins in loose-fitting black flares.

Dyed blond hair: her face has a coarse, hard-bitten look to it. Her skin, even under make-up, has a puffy, flushed, broken-veined,bottle-and-a-half-of-white-wine-every-night-in-front-of-the-telly look to it.

Divorced: single for several years then she'd tried internet dating. Filled in the online form, made up a user name, BlackpoolGirl39, entered her password Holiday11 (twice) and began scrolling through profiles. She hit gold, black gold to be precise, with date number three.

Jaap from Denmark: working out of Abertay as a geological surveyor in the North Sea. Brown hair and glasses, he spoke English with a mild Danish accent. Sometimes his bonuses from working on the rigs were more than Gina's annual salary after fifteen years at the DSS.

Gina was smitten: within a year they were buying a bungalow near the airport and she was boring everyone is the office with the minutiae of the transformation of bland 1960s concrete box to love nest. Early in their relationship Gina and Jaap discovered a shared interest in spiritualism and spent many long, happy hours trying to identify cold spots and haunted corners in bars, shops and friends' houses.

Gina was infatuated: Jaap was twenty years younger than her. And he was in a very well paid job. She had no worries about his facial tic and his tight foreskin.

The team meeting takes place every Wednesday morning in Gina's office high above the shopping centre. Nigel has been at his desk since 7.19 am. He's secretly hoping to be promoted to head of section when Gina retires or takes redundancy in the next round of civil service cuts. As she's always telling people, Jaap earns so much money she doesn't even need to work.

Nige goes down for breakfast with Gina and her pal from occupational health. He takes a croissant from the basket by the till then pushes his green plastic key into the drinks machine.

Your balance is £3.74 flashes across the top of the screen.

Nige presses: Cappuccino. Stronger. Milk. Sugar. More.

Flashing dots complete a pale-green, semi-circular arc across the screen. *Your drink is...............100% ready.*

Nige helps himself to a tangerine from the bowl of fruit at the end of the counter. Gina is on the 5:2 diet and just has an espresso.

The talk at the corner table with its chipped Formica top and view of the traffic on Quarryhill Road is all about last night's episode of *You're Fired* and the impending royal baby. They did names last week. Nige thinks Wills and Kate should call their third born Jason or Darren or Kylie. Give it a nice common touch, get close to the people.

Nige leaves Gina and her pal from occupational health in the canteen. He climbs the two flights of concrete stairs to the third floor to set up the chairs and flip chart in meeting room 5: cramped, windowless, stiflingly hot in summer; cold and draughty in winter.

Nige flicks through his green ring binder. He's due to open the team meeting with some preliminary results from this year's Employee Happiness Survey. Each year the Department of Social Security carries out a survey of its employees. Three pages of questions followed by the Verbatims: blank spaces where staff get to write anonymously about how they feel about their job and their colleagues. All questions must be scored on a scale of 1 to 10 where 1 is very dissatisfied with (my level of pay) to 10 completely satisfied (my line manager values my contribution). Promotions are made, pay rises depend and careers can be broken by the results of the Employee Happiness Survey.

Nige has just written *I feel my voice is heard in the organization* in big green loopy childish felt pen letters. He's getting near the end of his feedback on Employee Survey. He's turning the page over on the flip chart, and wondering if organisation has an *s* or a *z* in it, when the door opens and Marc Paine enters the room.

Marc Paine from the fifth floor!

People from the fifth floor don't usually drop in on team meetings unannounced; Nige wishes he'd got his good suit back from the dry-cleaners. The trousers on the one he's wearing definitely need a wash and the jacket's frayed at the pockets.

Five minutes later Nige winds up his section of the meeting, '—and finally, during our migration to omnichannel operating systems,' he garbles in his best business speak, 'going forward, that reflects the fantastic capability across the department.' Then he adds, almost as an afterthought, 'Well, thanks for listening to me.'

As he's putting the tops back on the marker pens, Gina heaves herself to her feet and waddles over to the flip chart. 'Now, I'm sure you all know Marc from steering group. Marc's going to be joining us for the first part of this morning's meeting.'

Marc gets to his feet. 'Hi guys,' he gushes, 'I'd just like to say I've heard some great things this morning – really great things. I just think Employee Survey is such a great tool for team building. The improvement in those scores for "I experience personal development" since last year – fantastic!'

'Thank you, Marc,' simpers Gina with a flutter of mascara-encrusted eyelashes.

Then, glancing down at her clipboard, she addresses the team, 'Okey dokey – Marc's got to leave at half past so we're going to start with item three on the NBFH printout—'

A hand goes up at the back of the room.

Gina frowns. 'Yes, Debbie – it's OK I *am* remembering – the Morris dancer? Um – he's up in court next week, isn't he? Now, where was I?' She looks down at the clipboard again. 'Yes – Nige's the FI on this one, it's not got a FRAIMS number yet but it will have one just as soon as I can get logged onto the system.' Gina raises her eyes heavenwards before continuing, 'The suspect is a thirty-five-year-old male claimant living in the Drumkirk area of Glasgow. He's been in receipt of the high rate mobility component of DLA for the last – er – just over five years – probably the right decision at the time. DLA awarded by an adjudicator on appeal following a report from the claimant's GP and a letter of support from an advocacy worker in the voluntary sector.' She hesitates, squinting at the clipboard. Gina hates public speaking.'Carmen de something?'

She turns to Nigel. 'How would you pronounce that, Nige? A-pot-oh-leeni?'

Nigel nods as Gina continues.

'The informant – an ex-partner – surprise, surprise.' A muffled ripple of cynical laughter goes around the training room. 'The informant alleges the suspect is now in good health and – this is a new one on me, I have to say – spends most of his time climbing the highest mountains in Scotland, the – er – *Mon-roes*?' She falters, looking down at the clipboard again. 'That's the 3,000 Scottish mountains over 282 feet – no, I'm sorry, I think that's 282 over 30,000 feet...' She tails off. There are giggles from the back of the training room.

Gina turns pink and bristles, scowling at the empty front row of plastic chairs. 'Anyway, the height doesn't matter!' she snaps. 'What's important is it's a failure to report a relevant change in circumstances—'

Then Marc Paine from the fifth floor chips in. 'The secretary of state's following this one, so please, guys, let's try and show the department in a good light. I'd just like to remind you of best practice in a case like this. It goes without saying careful surveillance and recording are vital and don't forget the department is subject to Scottish law as the suspect lives north of the border and Scottish law—'

Here he pauses and looks hopefully at the staff crammed into meeting room 5.

'Needs corroboration,' several voices mumble on cue.

'Also, guys, the minister is very keen we get good video footage of the suspect.'

Marc Paine pauses.

He glances across at Nigel.

'At the risk of stating the obvious, this is going to be a bit more complicated than the usual outdoor surveillance procedures.'

No hiding in the shrubbery behind the clubhouse filming claimants hauling golf buggies and swinging clubs then, thinks Nige.

'This needs someone halfway up a remote Scottish mountain filming the suspect climbing.'

Marc looks down at the orange carpet tiles that cover the concrete floor of meeting room 5. He remembers his only holiday in Scotland: the incessant rain, the midges, the surly owner of the caravan site, the terrifying overtaking on the road to Inverness. What a place! Thank Christ he can afford to go to Spain. Wouldn't worry him if the Jocks decide to go it alone – good luck to 'em. And it would save the department a pile of taxpayers' money too. Let them pay their own welfare out their bloomin' oil money they're always going on about...

He's drifted off: stopped talking. The air conditioning unit on the ceiling at the back of the room hums noisily. He can hear the painters in the corridor outside talking about the value of an eight-year-old Vauxhall Astra. He looks up and sees Gina looking expectantly at him.

'So – er – that's the outline of the case under investigation.'

He continues at last.

'The tip-off checks out as genuine and, like I say, Whitehall are following this one. Gina's agreed to be SPOC contact and, given the nature of the case, it's a bit out of the ordinary – it needs someone who can cope in the great outdoors – maybe someone from a forces background?'

Gina looks at Nigel.

Nigel looks at his feet.

'You did the Pennine Way Challenge a year or two back, didn't you, Nige – raised all that money for the kids' hospice? That was you, wasn't it?' asks Marc Paine.

'And he was in the Marines,' pipes up Gina.

Nigel shuffles his feet uncomfortably. He's beginning to wish he hadn't gone on so much about his time in the army. 'Well – er—' he mumbles. 'It was a very long time ago— '

tinned fish

On a bend in the road between the ugly, grey, scree-like shores of Loch Cluanie and the steep-sided, grassy hills of Glen Shiel the bus brakes suddenly. A red BMW is stopped in the road, its orange hazard warning lights blinking urgently. A caravan and car are stopped too and craning his neck along the aisle of the coach, Mickey can see a long tailback of cars stretching as far as the series of sharp bends before the Cluanie Inn.

There's no traffic coming east on the other side of the road and people are getting out of their cars: elderly women in cardigans, men with beer bellies in polo shirts, bikers in leather trousers and a ten-year-old boy carrying a West Highland terrier. A young guy with a beard and red skinny jeans climbs up the heathery embankment at the side of the road to try and see what's causing the hold-up.

On the sun-warmed tarmac Home Counties accents mingle with German voices and Edinburgh tones, the sound of the wind in the grass and the clicking of contracting metal as hot engines cool.

The breeze whips up little waves on the grey surface of Loch Cluanie. Near the austere stone lodge on the far side of the water, a green Land Rover moves slowly along the dirt track road on the southern shore of the loch.

Tailgates are opened. Flasks of coffee produced and sandwiches unwrapped; hard boiled eggs peeled. Mickey's sure he can smell tinned sardines. The word is: a motorbike has hit a car on a bend just before the Cluanie Inn.

Two cyclists with bulging panniers and fluorescent green jackets pedal slowly past the queue of stationary cars, vans, mobile homes, lorries and minibuses. Every so often two or three motorbikes whirr by, making their way to the head of the traffic jam. After an hour and a half a flatbed recovery truck, with *West End Motors Fort Augustus* painted in red and silver on its cab, drives quickly along the deserted eastbound carriageway, past the four miles of stationary traffic, orange lights flashing.

He walks Tyke along the verge of the road as far as the stone bridge over the Allt a Chaorainn Mhoir. The traffic shows no sign of moving. A green square of conifers stands out on the smooth flank of Am Bathach. Old iron posts and the rusty wires of a deer fence trail in the heather at the side of the road. Beside a gate stands a Scottish Rights of Way Society signpost. The white letters picked out on green paint read *Alltbeithe 5 miles*.

'Aw clever dog but—'

Tyke sniffs the ground, remembering the dank smell of the stones at the base of the iron signpost and the path that climbs the long green glen between Mullach Fraoch Coire and Ciste Dubh before losing itself in the peat hags at the head of the pass then dropping down to the suspension footbridge over the River Affric at Alltbeithe where a wind turbine spins by the old farm buildings. A lonely rowan stands close by, its roots gripping the black peaty banks of the burn that flashes and gurgles down from Coire na Cloiche. Around the stone farm buildings (reclad in sheets of green corrugated steel) the grass is long and deep. Bracken and clumps of soft rush encroach on overgrown fields where other dwellings once stood, low ruins in the grass. The mountains stand all around the empty glen: Ben Attow and Sgurr Gaorsaic, An Socach and Mam Sodhail.

§

A July day two years before, they'd taken the path by the burn behind the ruined cottage. It led up past a black plastic water tank that lay in the long grass. Where the track crossed the stream he stepped quickly over the white lichen- and moss-covered boulders. Beside the burn grew green fronds of ferns and the purple heads of devil's bit scabious. In the sunshine the peaty water cascaded over the grey schist rocks down frothy white falls into brown peaty pools.

Pink cross-leaved heath and bog myrtle thrived on the wet ground. Plum-coloured bells of ling hung on woody stems among tussocks of deergrass by the banks of the stream. Gold spikes of bog asphodel glittered among red cushions of sphagnum moss. A green caterpillar striped with black bands and dotted with yellow spots crawled across a white paint-like splash of lichen on a granite boulder.

He gained height quickly. The timber on the gate in the deer fence bleached white by the rain and the sun. He unhooked the latch and Tyke squirmed through, leaving a tuft of tan and white dog hair on the wooden slats of the gate. When he stopped and turned to look back, the buildings at Alltbeithe had shrunk and the River Affric was a narrow blue seam in the grassy floor of the glen.

The sun shone on the hillside. Tyke lay down in a shallow pool in the burn. The golden flowers and cactus-like leaves of alpine saxifrage, clinging to the wet peat at the side of the burn, reflected in the dog's green eyes like little yellow suns.

The path led on into the grassy bowl of the upper corrie; white bog cotton shivered in the breeze; cracks of black peat fractured the grassy hillside. A line of boulders stood on the ridge guarding the skyline. Streaks of scree swept down from the upper slopes of Sgurr nan Ceathreamhnan.

;;;;;::::::::And long ago as the rain beat on the windows of the flat in Byres Road, DG Fraser pressed the keys of the typewriter.

Page 2 2 1 .

Clack clack clack.

Smudgey typeface.

"The mountain is in a very remote and wild situation, making it one of the great prizes for the hillwalker."

And then he wound the frayed black type-writer ribbon forward....__________

From the ridge Mickey looked across the desolation of Gleann a' Choillich to Gleann Sithidh. The steep flank of Mullach na Dheiragain was seamed with lumpen green bulges. Deergrass long ago spread its roots over the rock slip on the steep mountainside. Ten thousand years had passed since the hillside slid down into the glen like a collapsing sandcastle as the tide of ice receded.

He stood there watching the grey shadows of clouds move across the steep grassy scarp of Carn Eighe. The mountains swept down to the desolate mudflats at the head of Loch Mullardoch where a track led west down to Iron Lodge and then on to the sea at Killilan.

The path, a thread of shattered white quartzite, twisted through the mossy crags of the east ridge as he put suntanned hand to boulder on the narrow rocky top of Stob Coire na Cloiche. Among the folds of rock and grassy heath lay a shallow peaty pool where dragonfly larvae buried themselves deep in the mud in winter. Tiny white petals of mountain thyme and the yellow flowers of alpine lady's mantle trailed from cracks in the grey rock. To the south across the glen at the end of An Caorann Mor, Loch Cluanie was a triangle of blue between Ciste Dubh, Mullach Fraoch Choire and A'Chralaig.

The summit of Sgurr nan Ceathreamhnan was the size of a couple of tables pushed together. There was space for a cairn but not much else and there was a strong smell of tinned sardines. The smell of fish was coming from a grizzled hillwalker who was sitting on the cairn eating a can of Waitrose sardines in tomato sauce. Mickey hated tinned fish. Behind the cairn was a sheer drop down to the stony, grass-filled bowl of Coire Allt an Tuirc and he had no choice but to sit down next to the grey-haired hillwalker.

Like a high rampart on a mountain fort the airy summit ridge of mossy schist boulders swept round to the west top. Below his feet Am Gorm-lochan gleamed in a wrinkle in the corrie floor. The sky was clear and from the mountain top he could see from coast to coast, all across Scotland. The North Sea a blue-grey line beyond where the hills ended at the flat lands around Beauly. To the west at the foot of Glen Elchaig the Atlantic Ocean lapped the weed-coated rocks and the sea pinks among the shingle under the Scots pines at Killilan.

He had that sense again of Scotland the island floating on a blue planet in dark space; that feeling he'd had on Ben Lomond four years before but more intense now as he stood at 3,800 feet on a remote mountain high above upper Glen Affric.

'Ah, he's a lonely old fellow out there, the old Mullach,' said the grizzled hillwalker putting down the tin of sardines and nodding in the direction of Mullach na Dheiragain out on a long, scree-dappled ridge to the north.

The Abhainn Sithidh snaked along Gleann Sithidh. The dark peaty hill lochans tucked into the folds of the mountains glistened. Loch Mullardoch was a blue streak at the foot of Beinn Fionnlaidh and at lonely Iron Lodge the piece of hardboard fixed across the broken window flapped in the breeze while the starling fed her young in the nest at the top of the broken drainpipe. Mickey dropped crisps for Tyke. The grizzled hillwalker said not another word and he was sitting there still as Mickey stepped between the quartzite boulders down the north-east ridge making for the hill of the falcon.

&&&&&&&????????? NO! NO! NO! NO... you mustn't walk along the edge of the path like that... you'll widen it into A Muddy Morass. Yes I do know it's a quagmire already but walking along the edge of the path like that will only make it even wider and that could lead to UNSIGHTLY EROSION of the hillside.

The climber must remember at all times to: minimise the Erosive Effects of one's passage.....>>>mullach na dheiragain 982m the hill of the falcon Page 16888888888

Stop! Put that stone back... do you not understand, son? If you do that it will lead to an UNSIGHTLY PROLIFERATION OF CAIRNS ON HILLS and that will detract from the feeling of wildness.

Oh yes… You've forgotten, haven't you? Just like all the rest… It's September and you should have telephoned the stalker's house to ask permission to go on the hill. It's the stalking season you know and INTERFERENCE in this activity should be avoided. Of course you don't like reading and so you skipped pages 3 to 9 of my Introductory Chapters. Had you taken the time to read Chapter Two, The Climber and the Mountain Environment, you'd know that it is essential at all times to consider the sporting and proprietary rights of landowners. I'd strongly recommend consulting the factor or gamekeeper before taking to the hills next time.

Right, well now we're clear about every... uh oh! Wait a minute... you're not taking THAT up the hill with you are you? For Heaven's Sake! It's not even on a lead. See Page 5: Dogs should be kept under close control at all times and not taken on the hill in March, April or May for that is lambing time.

Finally I have to state that as the guidebook I can accept NO LIABILITY for personal injury resulting from the use of any route described wwwwwwwwwithin my pages.---------------------"″////////,,,,

clink clink lap lap

The orange plastic aerobie flies through the salt-tanged air, twenty feet above the glistening white sand. A straight line of regularly spaced pawprints follow arrow-like across the wet sand. Front pawprints at two-foot intervals – then a great scrape in the wet sand where the dog jumped three feet into the air in one great leap to catch the aerobie between gleaming white teeth.

Tyke runs back across the white sand towards where Mickey stands at the far end of the bay. The tide is out, the smell of ozone and seaweed in the air. The little wavelets break onto the pristine wet sand swept cement-smooth as the moon waxed and the tide ebbed. The sea is Seychelles green. The rocks at the far end of the bay are daubed with lime and white and ochre lichen. Drifts of brown kelp lie stranded by the tide. Sheep graze on the machair at the far end of the beach beside the path to Coire Lagan.

The sun warms the salt water in the rock pools left behind by the retreating tide. The Viking harbour lies at the end of the low green and brown promontory; Askaval and Ainshval on Rum, blue arrowheads in the ocean where the sea ends and the sky begins.

Where the sun on the brown heather and the sea-cooled air meet, a light thermal lifts the aerobie ten feet higher on the next throw and it sails over the beach, across the dunes and onto the strip of machair at the edge of the campsite where a handful of tents are pitched among the maram grass. The orange plastic disc lands beside the man and the woman sorting climbing gear on the yellow, tormentil-studded grass. The clink clink of runners and nuts and steel figures-of-eight over the lap lap lap of the wavelets breaking on the white sand. The aerobie lies on the grass, the shiny orange plastic disc haloing a cluster of sea pinks.

'Tyke! Fetch yer 'robie!' cries Mickey from the red sandstone rocks at the far end of the bay a hundred metres away.

Tyke picks up the orange aerobie with his sharp pointed white teeth and throws it down at the feet of the female climber. The orange disc rolls like a wheel and lands beside her. She laughs and throws the aerobie along the beach. The dog brings it straight back to her and flops down in sheepdog-guarding-the-pen mode, his wet coat matted, trailing in the sand, muscles, sinews tensed, blue-green eyes fixed on the aerobie.

Mickey's bare feet in the wet sand follow the arrow-straight line of pawprints across the crescent-shaped bay. When he gets to the dunes Mickey bends down, picks up the aerobie and grins.

'Great dog, mate,' says the male climber with a smile, his glance taking in the green-blue sea and the sun and the warm rock.

Sat there on the machair under the great broken rock ridge of the Cuillin, all cliffs and scree-strewn ledges and flights of gabbro boulders, they talk. He tells them about the motorbike crash and the coach driving down Glen Shiel in a thunderstorm, brown water in deep puddles spraying up over the windows while forked blue lightning broke over Aonach air Chrith. The banks of white, cottonwool-like fog out in the sea between Kyle and Broadford; the bus bouncing along the road past Kyleakin and Breakish, Harrapool and Strollamus, Luib and Sconser; racing to pitch the tent at Glen Brittle while the thunder rumbled over Scaraster.

And they talk mountains and Munros and dogs till the midges gather like silver flecks and the sun drops orange and yellow and blue behind Rum.

Thursday

going commando

The Leeds branch of Pennine Outdoor occupies three floors of a formerly family-owned department store on the corner of Eastgate and Albion Street. At 9.30 am on a Thursday morning the only customer in the shop is a white-haired man in a green Barbour coat. Open shoe boxes, scrunched-up tissue paper and unlaced climbing boots lie scattered across the carpet.

'These Zamberlans have got a lot of give in them,' a rosy-cheeked young sales assistant tells the white-haired man as he stomps up and down a three-metre-long strip of artificial path complete with boulders and a miniature stone bridge.

Why oh why did you have to go and open your bloody big mouth? Nige asks himself as he pushes open the chrome-handled doors of the shop. He'd told Gina about his army days after one Black Russian too many on a DSS staff night out at CoCo's Super Bar in Great George Street.

He had been in the Marines. For two weeks and one day to be precise, before he was summoned to the sergeant's office and told he wasn't commando material. He'd spent the next five years peeling spuds and scouring saucepans in the catering corps before taking redundancy in the 1999 round of defence cuts.

His knowledge of the Highlands of Scotland he'd slightly

exaggerated too. He'd once spent a long weekend with a soon-to-be-ex-girlfriend in a bed and breakfast on the Isle of Arran. Still remembers the row of white houses along the shore and the sandstone church tower at Lamlash looking out across the flat seascape to the lighthouse on Holy Island.

On the Saturday morning Nige and his girlfriend had taken the bus into Brodick and climbed Goatfell. He remembers sitting on a granite boulder halfway up the hill watching the white wake of the ferry coming in to dock at Brodick pier. The path was hard to miss and every few hundred yards they passed another Glaswegian family making their annual ascent: women in suntops and cut-off denim shorts and sunglasses; men in jeans and trainers and Scotland football tops; one wee boy in a yellow Brazil strip.

It was misty at the top but they kept to the path and reached the trig point on the boulder-crowned summit of Goatfell in less than three hours. They did have a bit of difficulty, he recalls, finding the start of the path back down and the map he'd bought wasn't much help, but then they'd heard voices and a few minutes later a family emerged out of the clammy mist dressed in see-through plastic macs, shorts and flip-flops and carrying a carrier bag full of yellow cans of Tennents.

'Morning, need any help?'

A long-haired shop assistant with a beard lounges behind the counter on the ground floor. Pennine Outdoor is a retail temple piled high with gleaming cooking stoves, red hollow-fibre sleeping bags and rainbow-coloured waterproof jackets.

Wouldn't be surprised if the bleedin' carpets are made of Gore-Tex too, thinks Nige as he picks up a pair of loose-weave socks and turns over the shiny, red, laminated price tag. At £17.99 they're the cheapest item he's seen in the shop. Many of the products on the shelves and racks carry a price tag of £300 and upwards. He's not worrying though. His shiny black credit card with its silver hologram is tucked in a leather pocket in his wallet. This is all going on expenses.

'Just mind and keep the receipts,' Gina had said as they sat in Costa Coffee in the shopping centre eating jam doughnuts and caramel frappuccinos.

Nige picks up a set of pots and pans, a Bear Grylls kettle, a thermos insulating mug and six *Beyond the Beaten Track* mountain meals in white plastic-coated foil wrappers.

He reads the label on the top one. 'Tender chunks of chicken and sliced mushrooms in a creamy white sauce served with pasta... a real adventurist pack... contains a main meal, spoon, wetwipe and flameless ration heater.'

Then he picks up six sachets of *Rev-Up* (instant energy drink powder - just add water!) and three large bars of Kendal mint cake. And for dessert there's sticky toffee pudding, chocolate cake in cream sauce and he smirks, thinking of Gina again: spotted dick.

He's still smirking when he spots the display of multi-coloured Bawbag Cool De Sacs Technical Boxer Shorts. Company motto: *Keeping 'em Tidy since 2007*. Hmmm. He can almost hear Gina giggling: *you won't be needing them, Nige!*

He runs his fingers along the flysheet of a yellow tent, its guylines gaffer-taped to the shiny, laminate wood-effect floor.

'Lightweight four-seasons, you could use it at the South Col on Everest.'

He hadn't noticed the long-haired shop assistant with the beard standing there. After crawling inside, Nige adds the tent to the silver foil survival bag, the hand sanitizer, the four-pack of biodegradeable toilet roll, the miniature, wind-up radio and the head torch he clutches in his arms.

'I'll need a sleeping bag too,' he says.

Should it be three seasons, four seasons or – wait a minute – five seasons?

Hollow-fibre, micro-warm or down, he wonders?

What on earth's a thermorest?

Maybe he should get a campamat too.

It had never occurred to him cooking stoves would range in price from £27 to £399.

'D'you want gas or multifuel?'

Nige frowns. The shop assistant confuses him with baffling talk about butane, propane and Meta tablets.

'Really,' he says 'you'd be best going for a jet-fired stove with aluminium wind protection and piezo ignition.'

How many cylinders of gas will he need?

By now Nigel has two shop assistants in tow. He looks around for the largest rucksack he can find. The labels are confusing. 'What exactly does 60 litres plus 20 litres mean?' he asks the long-haired shop assistant with the beard who wishes he was in Chamonix.

The shop assistant looks at Nige with barely concealed scorn. 'What are you planning to use it for? These are bio-flex rucksacks, you know. Have you used one before?'

Christ, a rucksack's a rucksack, thinks Nigel.

'Thing is I'm not happy selling you all this gear if you don't know what you're doing with it —'

Then the other sales assistant pipes up. 'Do you do a lot of climbing?' he asks. 'Or are you more of a weekend rambler?'

Jesus! How far would you get with this kind of attitude in Tesco, Nigel wonders? Imagine being asked at the checkout, 'Do you do a lot of pizza eating sir, or are you more of a weekend pizza eater?'

Nige circles a rack of brightly coloured waterproof jackets as the assistant explains the benefits of the new fabrics incorporated into Pennine Outdoors own-brand range of overtrousers. It seems to Nigel that every product in the shop breathes and wicks. Maybe if he stands still long enough he'll be able to hear the waterproof outer shells and the baselayers breathing and wicking quietly away to themselves.

'Sure—' the shop assistant says, 'an entry-level jacket will do the job most days but for another £150 you'll get this—,' He holds up a red Arctic Alpha SV jacket, ' a really great piece of kit. Most of the folk I know swear by them.'

Nigel swithers. 'It's an awful lot of money,' he says feebly.

On the way to the till he grabs a metal toast-grilling attachment for the camping stove and an inflatable pillow. As he stands at the counter looking down at the little grey screen, waiting for the chip and pin machine to process his transaction, one of the shop assistants asks, 'Off somewhere nice then?'

'Climbing a Monro,' replies Nige with a nervous smile.

The long-haired shop assistant with the beard helps Nige carry the half-dozen large carrier bags, emblazoned with the snowy peak and ice axe logo of Pennine Outdoor, to his car.

'Have a good trip,' says the long-haired shop assistant with more than a hint of sarcasm in his voice, thinks Nige, as he bangs the tailgate of the car shut in the concrete-pillared, underground car park.

aw, fuck!

Mickey is at the back, sweating up the red scree ridge above the Glen Brittle Memorial Hut, a dry metallic taste in his mouth. An hour earlier the sun had risen mistily out of a leaden sea. The Cuillin ridge is washed in a pink light over the grey tiers of dawn. A bead of sweat runs down his spine between his skin and his wickable Helly Hansen top. The rock climbing ironmongery and the rope make the straps of the rucksack cut into his shoulders.

Aw fuck, whit've I let mysel' in for? he wonders, watching Kristoff's girlfriend's bum wobbling in black lycra as she climbs the path up ahead of him. It had seemed like a great idea the night before after four cans of Budweiser in the tent. But now it's all scarily real as fifteen hundred feet below the mist lies over the dark green rectangles of conifers beside the road down in Glen Brittle.

Sitting on the toilet in the cubicle in the shower block at the campsite at 7 am that morning, watching an earwig crawl across the chipped Formica surface of the door, he'd tried to think of excuses not to go. The dog was always a good one.

But when he came out of the cubicle and went to wash his hands Kristoff was brushing his teeth at one of the row of chipped avocado-coloured basins.

'You still up for Mhic Coinnich and the Pin?' he'd asked, spitting white Colgate foam into the basin.

'Sure am, bud,' Mickey Bell had said but inside he was shaking, his stomach churning.

11 am: they're sitting in a circular stone shelter at the foot of a staircase of shattered gabbro boulders that leads up onto the rooflike ridge of Sgurr Mhic Coinnich. The dry mouthful of cheese and tomato roll is stuck to the roof of Mickey's mouth.

Aw fuck! I am brickin' it, he thinks, as they sit looking along the serrated, broken-backed, twisting, knife-edge ridge of the Cuillin.

And three thousand feet below, on the flat floor of the glen where the sea plane once landed, the two red tractors criss-cross the yellow field behind the dunes, as they will all that day, even as the dusk gathers, racing to bring the harvest in while the settled spell of high pressure lasts.

Friday

the beast of tianavaig

The otter flies across the bay with doglike front crawl strokes, cutting a white wake through the mirror-smooth sea loch. Then he halts, head up, just breaking the surface of the saltwater. The otter's whiskers twitch as he turns his head first one way and then the other, sniffing the early morning Highland air.

He sees the yachts on the moorings, the deserted jetty of the Tianavaig Inn and the white houses climbing up the hill. He sees the waves lapping at the seaweed and yellow lichen-coated rocks along the shoreline and the little orange tent pitched among the scrubby bushes between the roadside layby and the seashore. The otter's whiskers twitch again. A ripple of bright water and he is gone.

The sun blazing through the flysheet of the tent awakens Mickey to a thick-head, sticky-mouth, summer morning, cider hangover. He lies sprawled face down on top of his sleeping bag. He opens a gluey eye and looks through a hungover haze at the orange wall of the tent, slowly beginning to reconstruct the events of the night before. He gropes around for the bottle of Irn Bru. Drinks. Then unzips the tent and struggles outside in boxer shorts and T-shirt and pisses into a gorsebush. As he stands there, a spider, at the centre of a perfect silver web glistening with morning dew, stares back at him.

Last night: he would have recognised Dougal Anderson from the Wheelhouse Bar, Lochinver, anywhere.

§

As West Pilton is to Edinburgh and Glasgow has Easterhouse, in Abertay there's Torrilands. Tell the taxi driver you work in Torrilands and he'll say you've got a big heart. Poor housing, unemployment, drugs, child poverty, heroin, alcohol addiction, glue sniffing, joy riding, prostitution, fights outside the pub. They all happened in Torrilands.

And the worst street in the whole scheme was Sandybanks Crescent. A drab, curving strip of dirty grey harling three-storey council flats ending in a square of muddy dog shit and litter-strewn grass behind the chippie on Great Northern Road. Only a mile as the herring gulls swirl from the university and the beach, the discovery in 1969 of oil in the Montrose Field of the North Sea changed little in Torrilands and it was here among the burnt-out cars and the roaming Alsatians that Dougal Anderson grew up in the early 1980s.

He was brought up in a thirties council flat on the third floor. Every Saturday morning a red-headed youth would come round the doors selling lemonade and crisps. The youngest of five boys, Dougal learned from a young age to lash out first and ask questions later.

One Friday afternoon as northern light flooded through the frosted glass window on the top landing, Dougal closed his two-year-old fists around the red-painted railings in the close and jammed his head tight between the iron banisters, the better to gaze into the drop down the well of the stairs.

Four-year-old Dougal pushed his scooter along the hall.

The metal painted red, the handle grips white plastic and the tyres black rubber. He will remember how the grips on the handle bars felt even as he picks his way along the icy corniced ridge high above Coire Lagan, the metallic scrape of crampons on gabbro under powder snow over the incessant bleeping of the phone in his pocket.

He pushed the scooter along the vinyl on the hall floor with its strong rancid smell when he lay flat and pressed his face to the smooth, cold surface. Strands of fibre frayed along the edges where the floorlayer had cut it to fit along the skirting board. Dougal reached up, stretching on tip toe to release the shiny knob on the Yale catch high on the front door, the spring inside the lock worn and loose.

He pushed his scooter out onto thc landing. Vinyl gave way to damp concrete and a smell of bleach. The old woman in the top flat opposite still mopped her landing and the top flight of stairs every Friday. Dougal pushed the scooter until he reached the top of the flight of concrete steps leading down to the second floor. The front wheel over the edge of the top step now, the white plastic hand grips pressed into his soft child's palms. His feet in white ankle socks and red sandals pushed off. The scooter and Dougal hurtled down the concrete stairs.

At the end there was blood where Dougal had cracked his head off the railings but he stood, eyes shining, left hand holding the scooter by one white plastic-gripped handle bar, his right arm raised triumphantly aloft with clenched fist.

Years later, at the end of his first ascent of the north face of Les Droites, Dougal would stand on a rock pinnacle at the summit, right arm raised aloft with clenched fist.

Small and wiry and black-haired with a typical rock climber's build he first came to the island to work for an industrial rope access firm carrying out a structural survey of the Skye Bridge. That first summer he was nursing a couple of broken ribs sustained falling out of a four-hundred-year-old oak tree while evicting a crusty, dreadlocked tree hugger from the route of the Didswell bypass.

His days on Skye spent hanging from a cable below the deck of the bridge, his weekends dangling from a rope on Cioch Direct. Dougal loved the island, a world away from Abertay and Torrilands. When the contract working on the bridge came to an end, Dougal stayed on living on supplies shoplifted from the Co-op in Broadford and sleeping in his car at first and then in a caravan in exchange for working mornings helping the emaciated, wasted junkie who ran the campsite shop.

Pretty soon he'd established himself in a nice line of work guiding frightened hillwalkers, desperate to complete the Munros, along the Cuillin ridge. Dougal had no formal qualifications for guiding but that didn't stop him. He took clients out in all weathers. Rain or snow, it was the grey wind that stopped him most often.

So what if the clients were wearing jeans and trainers, Dougal would get them up and along the ridge. He undercut the prices of the other guides operating on the Cuillin. It didn't exactly make him popular but as Dougal liked to say, did he look like he gave a flying fuck about that?

The money rolled in. Munro-bagging was at the height of its popularity, yet to be superseded by sea-kayaking and mountain biking. He had savings from previous lucrative contracts in the North Sea and pretty soon he'd earned enough from guiding to get a mortgage on a plot of land. Working midweek when there were fewer clients in need of his 'guiding' services, he set about constructing a self-build kit house in a field near the road with a view out across Loch Tianavaig.

The kit house came from an outfit called Highland Homes which supplied everything bar a concrete base to put the house on. With a couple of rock climbing mates who doubled as assistant guides (despite their very limited knowledge of the Cuillin) Dougal built the timberframe of the house over a fortnight in May. Helped by the driest summer on record they had the house wind- and watertight in time for the first equinoctial storms of autumn.

Over the long, dark Highland winter he kitted out the inside, sawing plasterboard, squeezing silicone sealant from a gun and assembling flatpack kitchen wall cupboards. He paid an electrician and a plumber from Portree who turned up when it suited them (and never on Fridays) to sort out the bathroom and the hot water system.

In a corner of the garden, still a weed-strewn, muddy wasteland, stood a little building with a shop window Dougal planned would be the head office of the Skye School of Mountaineering.

Life was good for Dougal. He loved his job. But men formed ninety per cent of his clients and he got fed up hearing male orgasm-type grunts as yet another terrified hillwalker from Edinburgh hauled himself up the bad step on Am Basteir.

It was the women Dougal liked to guide. He knew just the right moment to take advantage of their euphoria after climbing the In Pin; when to slip an arm around a shoulder, just brushing a nipple, while asking if they were single or not. Sometimes Dougal would give a female client a quick 'accidental' grope while he checked the adjustment of her climbing harness.

On hot days he led the way to the Fairy Pools, leering at the women in wet T-shirts and knickers before appearing on a rock, camera in hand. A few pints at the Tianavaig Inn after a climb and more often than not he got an invite back to a tent or a hotel room.

Sometimes Dougal's young wife cooked for him and they ate in the light, airy, picture-windowed, open-plan room with its view out across the sea loch. Some days she put jelly babies in his packed lunch box. Every night was spent in the Tianavaig Inn. Dougal started with a couple of pints of Stella about five o'clock then moved onto whisky later in the evening.

The next morning, smelling strongly of alcohol, he would stride briskly if rather sweatily ahead of his anxious clients as he led the way up the steep path beside the Allt Coire na Banachdich. As he handed out helmets at the foot of the In Pin he'd cheerfully admit to clients, he liked his whiskies.

§

The night before the thick-head, sticky-mouth, summer-morning, cider hangover Mickey had been sitting at a table in the corner of the backroom of the Tianavaig Inn. On the oval-shaped plate in front of him: yellow chunky chips, perfectly round green Birds Eye peas, orange breaded scampi, shredded iceberg lettuce and a white slick of tartare sauce. Tyke was stretched out under the table. He knew all about pubs.

'Fuck's sake! I'm sae hungry I could eat a scabby dug! And speaking o' scabby dugs...' Mickey reached down to pat Tyke. 'Pure dead brilliant day, eh pups?'

The Munros Book lay open at page 240. He slid a blue biro out his back pocket and carefully placed a tick on the page next to Sgurr Dearg, The Inaccessible Pinnacle and another next to Sgurr MacCoinnich, 948m.

'Oo ya fucker!'

One Munro left.

'Ya beauty!'

He washed a mouthful of salty prawn and breadcrumbs down with a swig of Stella.

Fuck you, Mr Wonga! Ah'm treating myself but.

Putting it on his maxed-out credit card before the direct debit bounced at the end of the month and his card stopped working.

He'd been lost in thought about the In Pin and credit cards and debt and whit the fuck was he going to dae for money when he became aware of raised voices, then shouting coming from the bar of the Tianavaig Inn. Tyke barked. Mickey slid his chair across the floor the better to see through the doorway from the backroom into the bar.

A woman in her mid-thirties with dirty-blond hair, wearing a Harris Tweed jacket and sunglasses, was standing over a group of three men sat at a table near the window. She held a full pint glass in one hand and with the other she stabbed the air with her finger.

'I paid to be guided up the In Pin not to be groped and then stalked for a year, you fuckin creep,' she shouted.

Heads were beginning to appear around the doorway that led from the backroom to the bar.

'Just fuckin leave me alone!'

And with that she emptied the pint of Pinnacle Ale she held in her right hand over the head of the nearest of the three men sat at the table in front of her. He jumped to his feet and strode past Mickey's table on his way to the toilets, wiping sticky white froth from his beard. Mickey felt a twinge of pain in his right rib. He would have recognised Dougal Anderson from the Wheelhouse Bar, Lochinver anywhere.

§

The girl was sitting on a flat rock right at the water's edge with her arms hugging her knees when he walked down onto the rocky shore of the sea loch where pink-flowered thrift grew among the pebbles. Suddenly he didn't want to be in the pub anymore. He wandered along the high tideline collecting sticks and tearing pieces of bleached, white driftwood out from the dried tangles of seaweed.

The embers glowed in the sand and the pieces of driftwood crackled and spat in the flames. Tyke wagged his tail as the girl walked past the fire. Without the dark glasses Mickey could see she had black shadows under her eyes and her face had deep lines around the mouth. She stopped and crouched down and stroked Tyke's thick shaggy coat.

Looking up at Mickey, 'Hey – can I bum a roll-up off you,' she asked in a husky, throaty voice.

'Sure.' He smiled as he pushed the green Golden Virginia tin towards her.

Her hands shook as she opened the lid.

'D'you want a can of cider too? Look like you could dae wi' wan.'

Sat there on the orange and white lichen-daubed rocks, squeezing the pods of brown kelp between forefinger and thumb as the planks of fishbox and blue nylon rope burned on the rocky shore of Loch Tianavaig, Mickey tossing clumps of seaweed onto the driftwood fire to keep the midges away, he listened and she told him her story.

§

It was when she got the first phone call at work Tamara knew she had to stop him. She'd just got back from the meeting with the book designer, desperate for a cup of coffee, when the phone on her desk started to bleep: number unknown. Shoving sketches and drawings back into the worn red leather folio case she'd had since college with one hand, she picked up the phone with the other.

'Hullo, it's Dougal Anderson,' said a thick Abertay accent at the other end of the phone.

Silence.

Tamara fiddled with the Winnie the Pooh badge on her folio case.

'I'm down in Edinburgh for my business and I was wondering if you wanted to meet up for a drink.'

'Please – leave – me – alone. I've had nearly a year of you texting and hassling me like this. I've told you. I'm not interested.'

Tamara could hear a tremor in her voice and her hand shook as she pushed the door shut with her foot. She didn't want the intern overhearing. Christ, the intern would know what to do – how to get rid of this creep. Christ, the intern would probably shag him.

'Aw, come on darlin'—'

The droning Abertay accent again.

'I'm all on my own here. I could do with some company.'

'Fuck off!'

Tamara slammed the phone down and the flimsy plastic base unit crashed off the back of the desk knocking over a chipped Greenpeace mug full of biros and dried-up felt pens. She was trembling as she knelt down and picked the phone off the floor and replaced it, and most of the pens and pencils, on the desk. She felt like bursting into tears but she wouldn't do that at work.

She needed to do something though.

The bastard was practically stalking her.

She thought she'd stopped it when she flushed her mobile down the toilet.

Tamara had been on Skye the summer before with a group of friends. Not walkers. Well, not the kind that climbed mountains. Their idea of a walk was a stroll down to the old bridge at Sligachan after a venison burger and a few pints of Pinnacle in the Slig.

Tamara was meeting her family on Iona to babysit her sister's kids for a few days. She had an extra couple of days on Skye after her friends left, and the forecast was good. They were all sat in the Tianavaig Inn on the last night. The food wasn't bad though it wasn't that good either but the pub beside the loch had a friendly atmosphere. They'd eaten mussels and crispy confit of duck washed down with a bottle of house red. Tamara had the veggie curry with organic naan bread. Waiting to be served behind a man with a long grey beard and a thick fisherman's oiled wool jumper, she noticed a pile of business cards on the bar.

DOUGAL ANDERSON
Mountain Guide

Make the very most of your visit to the Isle of Skye, and enjoy an experience you will never forget!

Employ the services of a professional mountain guide to lead a walk, scramble or serious climb.
Parties of 2 to 20 catered for.
Phone 0782 0112 999
Established 2008
Dougal Anderson is a member of Skye Mountain Rescue Team

She picked up one of the cards and shoved it in her back pocket before returning to the table with another round of three pints of dark, malty Black Cuillin, a Kronenbourg and a glass of white wine. Half an hour later she dialled the number on the card. A man's voice with a strong Abertay accent answered.

Dougal arranged to meet her in the car park of the Sligachan Hotel about 9.30 the next morning. She paid for one day's guiding up front by PayPal using the hotel's free wifi.

The next morning the tops of the Black Cuillin were clear of even a shred of mist and Loch Sligachan gleamed in the sunshine. The tide was out and the briny smell of the sea drifted across the moor on the light breeze. Sgurr nan Gillean and Am Basteir stood dark grey-green against a blue sky flecked with high white cirrus.

Tamara parked the Love Shack in the shade under the trees beside the kiddies' playpark. The smell of frying bacon drifted from the hotel kitchens at the rear of the building. She laced up her boots, hauled her bright pink daysack out the car and shoved her Gore-Tex jacket in the top. She locked the Love Shack and attached her keys to a plastic clip in the side pocket of her rucksack and then walked slowly up and down in front of the whitewashed hotel.

A yellow Citylink coach was just pulling up at the bus stop. Two Japanese girls and an anxious looking man in his forties got off. She watched as the white-shirt-sleeved driver opened the boot and dragged a large travel bag and rucksack out. As the bus pulled away with a hiss of air brakes the man heaved the heavy-looking rucksack onto his back. Tamara fiddled with the CND symbol on her charm bracelet as he wheeled the travel bag across the main road and down the track to the campsite.

In the quiet between the roar of passing cars and vans she could hear the birds cheeping on the heather moorland. Glancing down at her watch she saw it was twenty to ten. Could the red Renault Kangoo be her mountain guide? It was slowing down – no – taking the byroad to Tianavaig not heading into the hotel car park… 0950 came and went… as did 0955. By five past ten Tamara had given up and gone back to the Love Shack. Dougal Anderson, it seemed, wasn't coming.

But at half past two that afternoon her phone pinged. Sorry, babe! He'd had a mountain rescue call out – that's why he hadn't made it to the Slig. He'd take her up the In Pin first thing in the morning, Dougal promised.

§

'See, Mickey,' she said, her fingernails scraping through the dry sand, digging a hole down to the wet sand beneath, 'When I was little I always smelt of bleach – my mum used to wash my clothes in Domestos. D'you know why?'

He shook his head, staring at the sand.

'Because I was abused when I was a kid – she knew it was happening and it was dirty and she tried to wash it away with bleach—'

Tamara's voice was a husky croak.

'I didn't understand what was happening to me then. But I knew it was wrong. D'you know how that made me feel? I said I'd never let anything like that happen again. It took – well – forever but I'd reclaimed my life. I was doing OK till I came up here last summer and that bastard groped me and then started texting and hassling me...'

He reached across to his rucksack, took out another two cans, handed one to the girl. Distant music and the sound of laughter drifted across the rocky shore from the Tianavaig Inn. Tongues of yellow flame licked at brown, rust stains around brine-corroded nails on the smouldering driftwood.

The sandflies hopped towards the fire.

He cracked open his can of cider and they sat there watching the Milky Way as the stars dropped off the edge of the sky. He looked at the wavelets lapping the kelpy shore for a long time then he glanced across at the girl.

'I've got an idea,' he said.

hasta la vista, baby

As the sun drops low in the sky over Loch Brittle and the light level falls, she emerges. She lays her eggs and after a few days they hatch. Her larvae burrow into the soil and mature during the autumn and winter: thousands and thousands of maggots squirming and wriggling in one square metre of soil. A short pupal stage and then they emerge as flying adults and they mate and the whole cycle begins anew.

She is a tiny fly.

She undergoes metamorphosis.

She is the Highland midge.

She likes warm, humid weather.

She's light-sensitive.

She keeps out of the bright sunshine.

She appears in still, overcast weather and in the evening when the sun sets.

She needs damp conditions to survive and reproduce and finds an ideal habitat in the

Highlands and islands of the west coast of Scotland.

And she bites.

Because, for her eggs to develop,

She needs to feed on blood.

'Bring your climbing gear,' she'd told him.

Tamara, it turned out, was a natural when it came to acting a role. The Skye weather helped too, for once. She'd texted Dougal and arranged to meet him at the Glen Brittle Memorial Hut, outside the red telephone box, to be precise.

The sun is low over the Rum Cuillin as she stands outside the ugly, white-painted building wondering if Dougal will show up. Ten minutes pass then she sees the blue and white van appear around the last bend before the suspension footbridge that leads to the cottages on the west side of the River Bhreatail, just where it broadens out and the fresh water of the river meets the salt water of Loch Brittle.

'Nice night for it,' says Dougal, getting out his van. Then, cockily, 'You've changed your tune since last night. Midnight stroll on the Cuillin is it?'

Tamara reaches out and takes his hand.

'It's so beautiful,' she says quietly, her voice husky and throaty, pointing to the sparkling waves and the peaks of Ashkival and Ainshval glowing a faint pink against the dusky blue sky.

She glances at him.

'Sorry about last night in the pub and the pint and all that.'

She brushes a strand of dirty-blond hair back behind her ear.

'Aw, nae worries darlin'.'

'C'mon,' she says, 'I've always wanted to watch the sunset from the Cuillin but I'm scared to go up there on my own...'

'It's getting' late – I don't know.' There's doubt and unspoken questions in his voice.

She drapes her arms around Dougal's neck. Her skin smells faintly of patchouli oil.

'Well, if you put it like that,' he says, a look of surprise on his face.

They climb the stile behind the red telephone box and walk up the footpath towards Coire na Banachdich. White gravel scrunches under their boots as they climb the steep rise by the hut circles where the Pictish farmers tilled the sides of the glen but found no agricultural value in the scree and crag-girt Cuillin. Not even for grazing animals was there a blade of grass and they christened the mountains, the Cuillin, the worthless hills.

They stand looking across at the white falls of Eas Mor where the Allt Coire Banachdich splashes down through silver birch and rowan. She squeezes Dougal's hand then kisses his cheek. The golden yellow spiky flowers of bog asphodel; bliochan, the people who once farmed in Glen Brittle called it, grows among the deergrass at the edge of the path. Where their feet leave bootprints in the wet peaty soil, the pale pink bell-shaped flowers of cross-leaved heath shine.

'I had it all wrong about you,' she says, fidgeting with the string of amber worry beads around her wrist, the ones from La Caleta.

At a bend in the path white feathers lie scattered, the site of a kill by a bird of prey. The moorland ends where a red scree ridge claws down from the Cuillin. Sweating now, they climb the west shoulder of Sgurr Dearg. They pause only briefly, for the midges gather in swarms as soon as they stop for more than a few moments.

A blue-grey haze is settling into the corries but, above, the sky is saffron, scarlet and pink. The air is warm and the September night in the northern hemisphere so light, the father in his tent at the campsite in Glen Brittle can still see to read a bedtime story to his eight-year-old son:

> The door swung open at once. A tall, black-haired witch in emerald-green robes stood there. She had a very stern face and Harry's first thought was that this was not someone to cross.
>
> 'The firs'-years, Professor McGonagall,' said Hagrid.

The ridge narrows and they climb a giant's staircase of gabbro boulders. She feels dry rough rock under her hands. Little yellow flowers of alpine lady's mantle and starry saxifrage cling on among the volcanic rubble. Saxifrage the stone-breaker, growing on the bare rock, a crack in a basalt slab bringing the plant all the moisture and nutrients it needs; like all its names, its Gaelic name, clach-bhriseach-buidhe, has stone in it too.

Dougal climbs quickly on ahead of her. He's been up here so many times he could walk it blindfolded. Suddenly one last pull up onto a boulder and they're on the ridge.

'This'll do, won't it?' he complains, losing patience, keen to get back down for a pint at the Tianavaig Inn.

Tamara has anticipated this. She unzips her pink rucksack and produces a bottle of white wine, drops of condensation still frosting the chilled glass.

'Let's go to the foot of the In Pin,' she pleads.

'I'm no climbing it in the dark,' moans Dougal.

Ten minutes scrambling warily along the narrow ridge where scree, crag and cliff plunge hundreds of metres down to the floor of Coire Lagan and suddenly there it is: a black tower against the blue night sky. Most notorious, most feared of the Munros, the unfeasible blade of rock that forms the highest point of Sgurr Dearg: The Inaccessible Pinnacle.

They stand on the rocks that top the red scree ridge looking across to the In Pin. Tamara takes Dougal's suntanned hand. She kisses him and says quietly in his ear.

'Dougal?'

'What?'

'I want to – you know – um – with you.'

He hesitates, looking around at the scree-strewn mountain top.

She points at the implausible column of basalt thrusting up into the evening sky.

'What? No on top of the In Pin?'

'No, stupid – up against the side of it,' she explains.

Dougal swallows, mouth dry with excitement, heart racing as she takes his hand and leads him down the steep scree and across the overlapping plates of basalt to the base of the In Pin. To where in daylight the mountain guides tell their clients to put their helmets on. Figure-of-eight knots are tied and nervous hillwalkers fiddle anxiously with helmet straps and sit-harness buckles.

Tamara pushes Dougal back against the basalt rock of the In Pin and sticks her tongue down his throat. Then she peels his Helly Hansen top off.

'Take your clothes off,' she commands.

In an ecstasy of fumbling, Dougal unties the laces of his boots and pulls his socks and Craghopper trousers off. He's naked under the In Pin. Something hard and metal, not the volcanic rock of the pinnacle, is sticking into his back.

Tamara runs her tongue around the inside of his mouth again then steps back and tips Dougal's rucksack upside down. Coils of yellow climbing rope spill out. She hands him a climbing harness complete with runners, slings and carabiners.

'You're a bit kinky, aren't you?' he pants.

'You wish — put it on,' she instructs.

Dougal pulls the harness on and, hands trembling with excitement, tightens the belt. Teasingly she kneels down and unclips two cord slings from the harness then stands up and runs a carabiner across his chest, dangling the cold metal over his nipples.

'Belay me, Mr Rock Climber,' she breathes as she takes one of the cords and twists it once, twice in a tight Prusik loop around his left wrist.

Holding him by both arms, she presses him back against the rock and (quick! quick! quick! she and Mickey practised this in the afternoon at the foot of the seacliffs as the gulls screamed over the white surf and the Atlantic breakers rolled the shingle on Tianavaig beach).

Click!

She snaps the cord sling tied around Dougal's wrist onto the open screw-gate carabiner on one of Kristoff's two spare cams Mickey jammed into a crack in the basalt flank of the In Pin two hours earlier.

Dougal looks momentarily surprised.

'What is this, doll?' he asks, 'Fifty shades of grey?'

Suddenly there's a shaggy black and white dog on the ridge. It stops and sniffs the crisp evening mountain air. The creature has a faintly disreputable air about it. It has the look of a poacher's dog, thinks Dougal, as it trots down across the scree and sniffs around his rapidly shrinking cock. There's a sound of rocks and scree shifting and grinding and then a climber appears from the far side of the In Pin.

'All right, mate?' he says and, seizing Dougal's remaining free arm, he pins it back against the rock while Tamara ties a second Prusik loop tightly onto his wrist, snaps a carabiner on and clips it to the second cam.

'What the fuck?' exclaims Dougal, trying to kick out as the climber binds the coils of yellow rope round and round his ankles.

Then the mysterious climber takes out his phone and snaps several pictures of Dougal tied to the In Pin.

'For Facebook,' he explains with a grin.

Tamara steps back, laughing.

The mysterious climber with the dog who appeared from nowhere: he's seen him somewhere before.

Fuck! Fuck! Fuck!

It's that wee poof from the Wheelhouse Bar in Lochinver.

The more Dougal struggles, the more the Prusik loops tighten around his wrists. Meanwhile, Tamara gathers up his clothing and climbs back up to the crest of the ridge one hundred feet away. She throws his trousers and then his Helly Hansen top off the edge.

'See her, pal—'

Mickey looks Dougal straight in the eye:

'She disnae miss and hit the wa'!'

Dougal's Craghoppers float away down towards the boulder-strewn floor of Coire na Banachdich but his stripey boxer shorts catch on a spike of gabbro and hang there until the first equinoctial gale at the end of October shreds them to rags.

The girl, the poof, the dog they're picking up their rucksacks – they're leaving...

'Where the fuck are you going?' he shouts, 'You can't fuckin leave me up here. I'll fuckin kill yous!'

'Hasta la vista, baby,' pouts Mickey, blowing Dougal a kiss as, with Tyke at his heel, he and Tamara head off down the rocky ridge, back to Glen Brittle.

The light of the two head torches dipping and bobbing along the ridge fades. Silence falls. The rocks and scree settle back into place. It's a warm, humid night and already the midges are beginning to swarm around the naked man tied to the In Pin.

They're back down at the Love Shack in less than an hour. It's dark now, high cloud covers the night sky but Venus is still a blazing white orb above the dark trees. On one of the steep hairpin bends where the road climbs out of Glen Brittle a baby barn owl sits in the middle of the road. Its round, moon-like face gazes at them with flattened beak and eyes of shining black jet before it spreads its orange wing feathers and rises up over the fence at the side of the road.

The dark squares of conifers stand black against the night sky, the road quiet. By a field of cows, near the junction signposted Cul nam Beinn 8 miles Tianavaig ½ mile, Mickey has Tamara stop the Love Shack at a lay-by.

'Wait here,' he tells her, 'back in five.'

Tamara frowns. 'Mickey?'

'Whit?'

'Where are you going? We need to get out of here.'

He's got the door open.

'Mickey? I'm serious!'

He jumps down from the Love Shack and climbs over the barbed wire fence at the side of the road and walks quickly between the cowpats and clumps of soft rush. He squeezes through a gap in the fence at the far side of the field and into the muddy area of grass and earth that surrounds Dougal Anderson's newly built home.

The house is dark. Dougal's wife and the other guides must be in the Tianavaig Inn. He doesn't know why he's here. Then a red mist descends in front of his eyes as he remembers lying in the car park of the Wheelhouse Bar with a broken nose and three cracked ribs. And he remembers Tamara's description of her childhood: the Stricher family bungalow on the edge of the dusty hillside of scrubby low bushes and the little girl in Winnie the Pooh pyjamas, lying in the half-dark, heart pounding, waiting for the bedroom door to slowly open.

In a corner of the muddy ground in front of the house stands a cement mixer. Sacks of top soil, plastic crates and wooden planks are piled in front of it; the debris of the builders. He picks up a scaffolding pole from the heap and half walks, half runs towards the house with its floor-to-ceiling picture windows looking out across Loch Tianavaig.

He swings the scaffolding pole and the glass fractures with a crack and a hiss.

As he smashes the second of the three picture windows, he can see the guy with the polo neck and furry-hooded Parka from Channel 4 standing in front of the house talking to camera, 'These double-glazed units arrived on a lorry from

Germany this morning. They're millimetre perfect—'

Crack! Hiss. He can still hear Kevin MacLeod in his head as he swings the scaffolding pole for the third time.

'—each specially made in a factory in Hamburg to the architect's precise dimensions. These babies come in at around £4,000 per unit.'

Then he drops the scaffolding pole and runs back through the field of cows to Tamara and the Love Shack. He's shaking, tears streaming down his face as he pulls open the door and climbs up onto the passenger seat.

The stencilled flowers and hand-painted rainbows on the body panels of the Love Shack vibrate and rattle as the needle on the speedometer wobbles just above 46 miles per hour.

The iPod hanging from the rear-view mirror on a string of wooden beads swings gently from side to side. The Fratellis are playing through the retro fitted speakers mounted on squares of chipboard screwed to the dashboard.

'Na na na na na na na na na na na na na!' sings Mickey. Then, raising his voice over the music and the motorbikish scream of the Volkswagen engine, 'Bit conspicuous as a getaway vehicle, is it no? Can you no make it go any faster?'

Tamara laughs. 'You wish.'

They're roaring across the Skye Bridge at 51 miles per hour when Mickey dials 141 and the number for Dougal Anderson Mountain Guiding.

Dougal's wife answers.

'Hiya!' says Mickey, grinning across at Tamara.

'Who is this?'

He can hear the clink of glasses and the sound of voices in the background. Like he thought, they're in the pub.

'Dougal's stuck on the In Pin,' Mickey tells her.

Silence on the other end of the phone.

'Sorry? Who *is* this?'

Mickey glances across at Tamara again.

'He's no hurt like but he's in a very exposed position,' he says before pressing End Call and collapsing onto the white sheepskin rug covering the front seat, arms around Tyke in a fit of semi-hysterical laughter.

§

Eddie Barraclough, dour Lancastrian and longtime leader of Skye Mountain Rescue Team usually co-ordinates mountain rescues from the comfort of his swivel chair and mug of Nescafe in the MRT post in Glen Brittle. He's not often to be found joining the team climbing the ridge up to Sgurr Dearg on a Friday night but this is one incident he's determined to attend in person.

The first call had come from Mike, deputy leader of the mountain rescue team about 9.30 pm while Eddie and his wife were comfortably ensconsed on the sofa at Cuillin Croft, watching the latest Scandic noir police drama; the one about the coeliac detective with the teenage Goth daughter.

'Hi, boss – you're not going to believe this one. We've had a report Dougal Anderson's stuck on the In Pin.'

Eddie scratches his beard.

'Is he injured?'

'Nope – his missus got a phone call from some bloke saying Dougal was unhurt but in a very exposed position. That's all the guy said. Then he hung up.'

'I don't get it,' says Eddie. 'Dougal's been up and down the In Pin hundreds of times guiding clients —'

'There's more, boss,' continues Mike, he's loving this, nothing ever happens in Tianavaig. 'She's had to get the police out from Portree. Someone smashed three windows at their new house.'

'Ah—' says Eddie. He hadn't seen this one coming but now it's happened, he can't say he's surprised. 'Pissed someone off, 'as he?'

'Well, you know Dougal,' replies Mike.

He knows Dougal all right: knows all about the long list of guiding clients who paid up front only for Dougal not to show up on the day because he was too hungover. Dougal's standard excuse in this situation – it worked a treat, he'd found – was the one about having been on a mountain rescue call-out. Or the terrified clients who went out with Dougal once but were too petrified ever to set foot on a mountain with him again. Like the group he was leading the day he took the wrong descent route from the Bealach Coire Lagan, getting them stranded on a cliff on the west face of Sgurr MhicChoinnich, unable to move up or down.

The group eventually abandoned Dougal and made their own way back up onto the ridge and the safety of the Coire Lagan screes. In the furious exchange of texts, emails and then letters that ensued, Dougal refused to give the group a refund or to admit he'd made a serious navigational error.

'I was only two metres out,' he'd protested. But on Skye two metres was the difference between being on the path or lost in the mist.

On the ridge or in the abyss.

Two metres was a long way on Skye.

Then there were the hoteliers he'd antagonised as traumatised guests cut short visits to the island. Zero chance of enjoying the whole package of your trip to Skye if you'd picked Dougal as your mountain guide: you'd have paid up front on Paypal of course.

He led groups of tourists in trainers and jeans up the In Pin. Gung-ho some called him. Plain dangerous was Eddie's opinion of Dougal's boasts that he was the only guide who'd go out in gale-force winds and his habit of hurling loose rock from the ridge down into the corries below.

And there were the clients who found the strong smell of stale alcohol on their guide's breath distinctly unreassuring when he checked their climbing harnesses as they prepared to be led up the In Pin by him. Dougal was quite open about this aspect of his life.

'I like my whiskies,' he'd say, in that cocky way he had.

Eddie's own run-in with Dougal had been alcohol-related. He'd kicked him out of the mountain rescue team the second time he turned up for a call-out straight from the Tianavaig Inn, reeking of drink. But this hadn't stopped Dougal continuing to prominently display across the top of his website the statement 'Dougal Anderson is a member of Skye Mountain Rescue Team.'

Eddie raged inside that Dougal used the mountain rescue team's name falsely to promote his business. But this was a small island community and mostly tensions and anger seethed beneath the surface. Until Mickey Bell set foot on the island, that is.

And then there were the dozens of husbands and boyfriends of women on the island: the fish farm workers, the teachers, the barmen, the bin men, the bed and breakfast owners, the crofters, the policemen and the paramedics. Dark-haired and good looking, working the irregular hours of a self-employed mountain guide, ensured Dougal had plenty of opportunities to bed wives and girlfriends while their husbands weren't around. Eddie had heard Dougal was in the habit of carrying a carabiner in his pocket (to use as a knuckleduster) and couldn't go to the north end of the island anymore because the stalker at Uig had threatened to shoot him after finding out he'd deflowered his sixteen-year-old daughter during an eighteenth birthday party at the Slig.

All this runs through Eddie's mind as he perches on the

edge of the wicker chair among the spider plants in the porch of Cuillin Croft, pulling his boots on and tightening the laces. As he closes the door he takes out his walkie-talkie and glances up at the black outline of Sgurr Dearg in the darkness.

'This is Cuillin Eddie. Come in, deputy team leader.'

The green screen lights up as the radio crackles into life.

Mike's voice: 'Roger, Cuillin Eddie, this is deputy team leader. Go ahead. Over.'

'I was just wondering – do you think we need back up on this one? Over.'

'Can't be too careful. Over.'

'Best let the other guides know then. Over.'

'Already have, boss – they wouldn't miss it for the world. Over and out.'

Saturday

In the narrow, cramped kitchen of the Tianavaig Inn the grease-spattered radio blares out from the top of the fridge. The crashing electric chords of the bass guitar fade to a soft West Highland accent.'Well, that was Rainbow with *All Night Long* and I'm Kenny John Munro bringing you all the hits here on Three Lochs Radio 106.4 FM. Well there's only one story we're all talking about here in the studio today and that's the strange tale of local man Dougal Anderson found handcuffed to the In Pin late last night – a dangerous stag night prank or a wee bittie of S&M gone wrong? We'll be asking Mike Tomkins, deputy leader of Skye Mountain Rescue Team for his thoughts on this bizarre episode in just a moment.

'Meanwhile, in a separate, apparently unrelated incident, several windows at a house in Tianavaig were broken in the early hours of this morning. A bit later in the programme we'll be talking to community councillor for Lochs and Glen Brittle, Jean MacDonald and asking: is a crime wave sweeping our island? Let's be having your texts and tweets on that right now.

'And after some of these and a word from our sponsors at Thomson Aggregates, I'll be back with Billy Ray Cyrus and then we've got some Robert Palmer for you – ah – see *you ain't so tough...*'

The minute hand on the clock mounted on the wooden tongue-and-groove pine panelling above the bar of the Tianavaig Inn moves from two minutes to three to one minute to three. Creamy white froth runs down the side of the pint glass as the barman tilts it under the Guinness tap.

'Did you hear what happened when they got up there?' he says to the only customer in the bar at one minute to three on a Saturday afternoon.

'Aw Christ, aye! Mike Tomkins said they could hear him shouting and swearing ages before they got to the foot of the In Pin.'

The barman places Lachie's pint of Guinness on a beermat.

'He said Matt had got there before them.'

'Which one's he again?'

'Works for Island Guides – Dougal headbutted him at the Slig not last New Year but the one before.'

'Oh aye, I remember—' the barman nods.

'Well he had this portable rescue arclight thingee with him. Mike said it was like daylight up there and Matt was filming the whole thing on his phone. There was just like this huge great black cloud of midges swarming around the In Pin.'

'And was Dougal OK?'

'Mike said his wrists were chaffed and he was a wee bittie cold – but going mental like.'

'Dougal can't come to the phone right now he's a bit tied up!'

'Aye, he was seriously underequipped for being up there,' Lachie adds, smirking as he slurps his pint.

But the barman's determined to finish his story. 'Then Eddie Barraclough walks up to him. He's holding a silver foil survival blanket. He looks Dougal up and down and then he says – is that a cleg bite on your tadger? They can be nasty, I'd get some cream on that if I were you.'

Lachie splutters and chokes on his Guinness.

§

The yellow flower shines like a golden starfish in the black peaty mud at his feet. Wherever Saint Maolrubha touched his staff upon the earth the strange looking plant would grow, they said. Butterwort was one of the names they called it. And if a traveller carried nine roots of the strange looking flower with him he would safely reach his journey's end: so said the Gaels of the western seaboard of Scotland, when the world was young.

The Love Shack is parked up in a big grassy lay-by at the head of Glen Docherty where the road sweeps in broad curves down to Loch Maree. A faint smell of burning rubber lingers in the air and a few drops of Scotland's oil have seeped from the sump onto the sun-warmed tarmac. The silver iPod hanging from the string of wooden beads wound around the rear-view mirror is playing the Killers.

Slioch the spear mountain dominates the scene, a sandstone arrowhead set on a plinth of gneiss. Tamara lies propped up on one elbow, threading a daisy chain necklace. Mickey is making a roll-up one handedly, with unconscious skill.

'Mickey?'

'Whaaaaat?'

'Make a spliff if you want, there's stuff in the tin in the glove compartment,' says Tamara.

He hesitates a moment. Then coughs:

'Na, it's too early but. I dinnae want tae be wrecked by lunchtime.'

He lights the roll-up and spits out a strand of tarry tobacco and gazes down Glen Docherty towards the line of mountains guarding the eastern shore of Loch Maree: Ben Airigh Char, Ben Lair and Slioch. The peaks of the wild west so different from the rounded heathery hills of the Grampians far to the east.

When the ice sheet that covered Scotland for ten thousand

years retreated at the beginning of the time geologists call the Holocene, it left behind the scoured and flattened eastern hills and the jagged and pointed peaks of the wild western ranges, the landscape of the Scotland of today.

In the east the long tongues of ice had softly licked the land and when the glaciers melted many of the features of the pre-glacial period, the gentle rolling slopes, rock tors and wide rivers remained. But in the west where the snowfall was heavier and the ice thicker, the glaciers ripped and clawed at the mountains. And when the steeper, faster-flowing western glaciers melted they left behind the jagged and notched peaks of the west coast.

Dust motes float in the shaft of sunlight that falls on the Munros Book lying open on the scratched table of the Love Shack at Page 126 (Section 8: The Cairngorm Mountains) and on the photo DG Fraser took of Beinn Mheadhoin with his Pentax MX one chilly morning in April decades before.

**********IIIIIIIIIIIII'm the guidebook all print and pppppppppaper and ink. I sell well even in these days of web pages and hillwalking apps (good heavens! ...what on earth are they? Some ghastly thing to do with the internet, no doubt.)

Trust me and my routes above all else for I'm the guidebook, the distillation of the days and weeks and months my writer spent in the hills. He poured his knowledge into me, and you can trust me, you see, for I'm the guidebook.

I'm the guidebook. I age and go out of date quicker than you. Forestry plantations spring up blocking paths I loved in the time between my first and second editions. Deer fences will be strung across my open hillsides and wooden footbridges swept away in winter spates.

Don't stray from my red colour-coded routes, you could get lost if you wander from the ridges I recommend. You love it when you catch me out with a mistake though, a misprinted grid reference or a wrongly spelt mountain name. I'm the guidebook though and I KNOW BEST. And if you tire of me you need only close my pages and put me back on the shelf.

I'm the guidebook. Ah, flick through my pages, read my phrases, skim over my sentences. Traverse with me the mossy ridges and boulder-strewn summits... with my timings calculated on the basis of four and a half kilometres per hour for distance walked, plus ten metres per minute for climbing. I think you'll find it A BRISK PACE.

I speak disdainfully of one much frequented route and make disparaging references to the much trodden path leading to the summit. I WARN the reader: descent of this ridge should be treated with respect... in misty conditions, route finding may be confusing and that this is a long and serious mountain expedition. That hanging corrie on the north-east face... a dangerous place in winter or poor visibility. No, an ascent up the very rocky hillside is not recommended and furthermore there are circumstances when it may be positively advantageous to find overnight shelter in the hills. A little mild rock climbing if desired... Ah, but the airy ridge becomes quite narrow and well defined with some very pleasant and easy scrambling over rock towers. A short pitch that cannot be easily avoided. A rocky bluff. Ah...

[Sighs wistfully]

The tie-dyed curtains of the Love Shack billow gently in the light breeze. The shadows of the clouds chase patches of sunlight across the grassy hillside above Glen Docherty. He flicks open the scratched brass Zippo lighter. Half reads the spidery engraving: *To Michael with all my love.* He's never been Michael, always been Mickey. Jonnie gave it him. A whiff of petrol. He lights the roll-up. Inhales. Lies on his back gazing down at Slioch and the islands of Loch Maree shining in the sunlight. Tyke is sniffing around in the long grass and bracken.

'Mickey?'

'Whaaaaat?'

'You're just goin' to love Sanda Mor. We'll pitch up on the sand dunes – nothing between us and the Outer Hebrides.'

The usual flow of traffic up and down Glen Docherty, slow-moving mobile homes, coaches, motorbikes and caravans towed by estate cars driven by timid middle-aged couples, is interrupted by the BMW X5 jeep and the black Range Rover driving in convoy at speed from the south.

If Clamhan the buzzard riding the thermals high above the glen were to turn his keen, wide-ranging, near-perfect vision on the tinted windows of the fast-moving BMW he'd see in the driver's seat, florid-faced and tweed-suited, Sir Gideon George Oliver Brokenshire, multi-millionaire, absentee landowner of the vast Torran estate, up in Scotland for the month of September for the red deer stalking. The buzzard, sensing a threat, would fly higher, sweeping away across the glen and out over the water to the remote eastern shore of Loch Maree.

The Romanian cleaner or the dark-haired barman moonlighting at the Kinlochewe Hotel might just recognise the bald-headed, wizened, walnut-like face of the eighty-year-old man in the expensive Savile Row dark blue overcoat sat stiffly upright in the passenger seat, from TV news and a score of media-watch websites, as the billionaire business magnate often described as the last old-style press baron in the world and universally known in political circles as the Canadian.

The second car in the convoy, the black Range Rover, is driven by a broken-veined, red-faced, middle-aged man with bad skin. An ex-policeman, unmistakeable in the way policemen are. In the front seat, dressed in a middle-of-the-range suit from middle-England's favourite department store, sits a thirty-something, bearded man with black, trendy geek-type spectacles. He looks sharp, intelligent, astute and has something of the journalist about him.

But if the sheep, grazing by the side of the road in Glen Docherty, were to raise their heads for a moment. Or the Czech backpackers sitting on their rucksacks, killing time waiting for the 15.40 to Kyle of Lochalsh, were to look up from their Kindles as the convoy sped through Achnasheen, they would see in the rear seat the balding head topped with close-cropped hair and curving folds of double chin; the unmistakeable portly outline of the First Minister of Scotland.

Mickey stubs out his roll-up and lies on his back watching the clouds drift across the sky over Slioch. On the iPod the faint rough voice of Rufus Wainwright singing *Across the Universe*.

He looks over at Tamara, a smile playing on the edge of his lips. 'Aw please – nae mair fuckin cheese. Can we no have some Kylie?'

She sticks her tongue out at him.

Lying on the grass in the warm sunshine he feels dozily horny and his mind drifts back to Ryan pulling his green Calvin Klein's up in the hotel room, while outside the little waves lapped the shore of Loch Lomond. He swipes his finger across his phone, taps the screen. *Compose Text....* A light breeze rustles the fronds of the yellowing bracken.

Suddenly two things happen very quickly. He hears a piercing, squealing, frenzied yelping: a sound he recognises with a cold, gnawing, twinge in his stomach.

He leaps to his feet.

'Fuck!'

'Tyke!'

'Tyyyyyyyke!'

But it's too late. Already a shape like a black shadow is racing across the hillside, burning through the heather, three thousand years of collie dog genes playing out as Tyke snaps at the hooves of five sheep running in a line across the grassy flank of Glen Docherty.

In the same instant he sees Tyke chasing the sheep he becomes aware of two fast-moving black vehicles approaching along Glen Docherty from the south.

'TYYYYYYYYKE!'

He shouts, his voice beginning to break into a sob. At that moment the sheep scatter: two break away, scudding hooves in the black peaty mud as they head back up the hillside. In a crazily calm part of his mind he thinks, Tyke, you'd lose points on *One Man and His Dog* for letting they two get away.

But then in a great sweeping curve – *go way off!* – generations of Tyke's ancestors carried out this manoeuvre, on the slopes of An Riabachan, on the high hills above Loch Monar before the hydro board flooded the glen, the dog brings the sheep back together. As he watches Tyke successfully complete the manouevre Mickey's horrifed eyes see the dog chase the frightened sheep right across the road.

The BMW slams to a halt. German smart-chip-assisted braking technology gripping Highland road, tested to its limits. The Canadian media mogul has spilt the coffee he bought at the hotel in Achnasheen all down his dark blue Savile Row overcoat. Then the black Range Rover skids to a halt inches behind the BMW.

Unable to see the reason for the sudden, unexpected stop, the First Minister's driver already has his 9mm Glock halfway out its shoulder holster. His eyes scan back and forth across the hillside and the empty road, the image of the crumpled Mercedes in the Alma Tunnel flashes before him but all he can see is some young guy in a hoodie dragging a wild-eyed shaggy dog along by its collar and five sheep huddled together higher up the grassy hillside.

'You're a bad dug!' Mickey shouts in the dog's ear.

Tyke is panting. Great trails of saliva drool from his mouth. There's a wicked glint in his eye, a spark of his Viking ancestry.

Brokenshire gets out of the BMW. 'You fucking idiot! Get that bloody brute under control.'

The First Minister winds his window down. A smell of bog myrtle drifts into the Range Rover.

'Christ, you're welcome to this bloody country of Weegie tinkers!' mutters Brokenshire.

Then he turns and shouts at Mickey, 'Get that blasted dog on a lead. If I see it on my land again, I'll —'

An ASDA delivery van and a Citroen Picasso towing a Freedom caravan are stopped behind Brokenshire's BMW. He gets back into the jeep and slams the door then accelerates away aggressively.

The black Range Rover follows along behind at a distance now.

The First Minister winds up the window.

'Fine-looking dog,' observes his bodyguard from behind the wheel. 'Beardie collie crossed with a border collie, I'd guess.'

'Aye,' says the First Minister. 'Reminds me of a wee dug I used to see around Linlithgow when I was a laddie.'

Through the shimmer of heat haze Mickey watches the convoy speed on down Glen Docherty towards Kinlochewe. Looking down at the tyre tracks in the peaty mud where the black Range Rover swerved onto the verge to avoid Tyke and the sheep he sees a yellow star of butterwort right at the edge of the tyre gouges, its two mauve flowers perfect and unscathed.

ooh, ya!

On the far north-western seaboard of Scotland, south of Ullapool, north of Kyle, between Loch Torridon and Loch Broom, two great promontories jut out into the Atlantic Ocean. The Rubha Reidh and the Rubha na Lice Uaine: the red point and the green stone point. Somewhere on the smaller of the two promontories, behind the shelter of the low hill marked on maps as Meall an Udrigill, lie the handful of remote crofts, scattered around the crescent-shaped bay of Sanda Mor.

The sand martins are the earliest of the swallows to come back to Sanda Mor in spring. Every year they return to nest at the same place in the steep bank of the Sand River where dozens of narrow tunnels lead to scooped out chambers lined with grass and feathers. All summer long the sand martins sweep low across the machair flying ceaselessly in and out of the sandy tunnels to feed their fledglings with insects caught on the wing.

When the Love Shack (Tyke in disgrace in the back, forbidden from riding up front with Mickey) finally pitches up on the dunes at Sanda Mhor they do have a view of the Outer Hebrides but it is the serrated, broken-backed peaks of Skye that dominate the foreground. Somehow the jagged teeth of the Cuillin look angrier and more sinister than ever.

'Aw fuck, it's Skye,' he mutters to himself, frowning as

he hammers another plastic tent peg into the maram grass, seeing in his mind's eye a small uruisk-like figure, a Highland leprechaun, running up the steep flank of Sgurr Alasdair: Dougal Anderson in a murderous rage.

The scent of burning incense sticks drifting across the sand dunes mingles with the smell of ozone and kelp. Tyke scampers across the grass to the half-pitched tent.

'You're gaunny love it here but, dog,' he says, as Tyke licks his face.

A low peaty headland cradles one side of the bay; the rocks are black with seaweed below the highwater mark. The red sandstone outcrops that fringe the shore are daubed with lichens the colour of lime and tangerine. A square of wind-bent Scots' pines shelters the old schoolhouse at the end of the promontory; sheep graze in the overgrown garden.

The waves boil over the rocky skerries that thrust black knuckles out from the sea. The white houses huddle on the low hillside above the sandy bay. Daisies, buttercups, cranesbill and meadow rue speckle the machair. The sand martins fly low over the dunes on their ceaseless hunt for insects. He can hear birdsong over the sound of the wind through the maram grass. But what draws his eye north, beyond the Summer Isles and Achiltibuie on its long headland, is the line of mountains lit like painted theatre scenery: Quinag, Suilven, Canisp, Stac Polly, Ben More Assynt, Conival, Ben Mor Coigach, Beinn Ghobhlach and An Teallach. He puts his arm around Tyke, pressing him close to his side as he whispers in the dog's ear. 'That's home there, doggie – yer puppy days at Torbreac.'

And they watch as the red and white ferry slides smoothly across the panorama of sea and mountains and islands as if hauled by wires across a stage.

§

Mickey's bare bum has a blueish shade to it in the moonlight and the seawater. The swallows fly low over the waves. The oystercatchers stand in a line at the edge of the sea. The fire flares up. Ash frosts the smouldering pieces of driftwood. Stubbed out roll-ups and crushed green cans are scattered around. An empty bottle of red wine lies horizontal on the sand. A small pipe with a silver bowl, its blue barrel embossed with an Aztec eagle, lies on a rock.

Tyke leaps over the white breaking wavelets. Mickey dives forward but stands up after three seconds, spitting out saltwater.

'Ooh ya! It's fuckin freezin'!'

He avoids looking at Tamara's dangly tits. Doesn't think she's looking at his shrivelled cock.

But she can't resist. 'Is your willy always that small, Mickey?'

'Fuck off!' he cries and splashes her with cold northern hemisphere seawater.

Tyke barks. The moonlight streams down onto the crofts of Big Sand and the little shingle cove at North Erradale. A fishing boat with red navigation lights chugs towards Gairloch harbour while over the Cuillins the sky turns a darker shade of black.

see me

See me. I'm the wee black and white collie at the end of the lane.

I'm the wee collie gnawing a bone behind a stack of wooden barrels when Mary Stuart put a satin slipper on the cobbled setts at Leith as she stepped ashore from a French galley.

I'm the wee collie running with the Edinburgh mob as the parcel of rogues signed the Act of Union in Queensberry House.

I'm the wee collie hid under the pines as the red-coated soldiers burnt the croft.

I'm the wee collie trailing along at Rabbie Burns' heel.

I'm the wee collie asleep under the table as the wax dripped down the brass candlestick and he penned A Man's a Man for a' That.

I'm the wee collie in the oil painting that hangs on the wall of the gallery in Princes Street.

I'm the wee collie ran a hundred miles home from the Falkirk Trysts.

I'm the wee collie peering over the edge of the deck watching Loch Linnhe slip by from the ship anchored in Caol bay.

I'm the wee collie whimpering while the piper played and

the ships waited to sail for America on the high tide.

I'm the wee collie guarded the farmstead the first winter in Manitoba in the snow drifts.

I'm the wee collie fought the wolves howling at the edge of the darkness.

I'm the wee collie waiting at the door for my master who'll never come back from the trenches.

I'm the wee collie lying under a deckchair watching Lord Brocket and Von Ribbentrop on the lawn at Inverie.

I'm the wee collie ran off down the street as the bombs fell on the tenements of Clydebank.

I'm the wee collie chased the sheep on Arthur's Seat.

I'm the wee collie dozing behind the sofa among the empty cans of Tartan Special when Archie Gemmill scored in 1978.

I'm the wee collie smelled the burning paper when they set a match to the warrant sale notice.

I'm the wee collie sitting in the van outside the village hall when my old master hitched up his frayed grey suit trousers and said, 'We have won the land'.

I'm the wee collie sniffing the lamp post at the corner of Charlotte Square when the First Minister slipped and cracked his heid on the stone steps.

I'm the wee black and white collie in the crowd in the Canongate the day the Queen came to open the Parliament.

I'm the wee collie tied up outside the supermarket while the old wifie does her shopping.

I'm the wee collie you stroke on the heid as you get off the bus.

I'm the wee collie in the soaking deergrass half way up Stob Binnien.

I'm the wee collie chasing a tennis ball in Pilrig Park.

I'm the wee collie licking your face on the sofa as you watch the telly.

I'm the wee collie mooching crisps in the pub.

I'm the wee collie sat on Arthur's Seat watching the helicopter begin its long slow drop down to the waiting TV cameras.

I'm the wee collie splashed in the pools in front of the parliament the September night the lights burned late.

See me, I'm the wee collie asleep in front of the fire, dreaming.

Sunday

CD4 count 598
viral load <40 copies per ml
Munros 281/282

Just past Crocodile Creek with its buckets and spades, surfboards, fishing nets, inflatable sharks and baskets of sun hats and flip-flops outside on the pavement, a handwritten cardboard sign is tied to a wooden gate at the edge of the village: *Strath Sheepdog Trials Today Sunday*.

Tamara inches the Love Shack up the steep track to the Sandpit Field. At a second gate a red-haired man in a blue boiler suit and wellies is leaning against a pick-up truck. He ambles across to the Love Shack, a roll of pale blue cloakroom tickets in his hand.

'We take three pounds for the parking,' he says in a West Highland accent as soft as a smirr of rain on the hillside.

Then seeing Tyke sat up on the front seat he asks, 'Are you running a dog today?'

'No fear, mate!' grins Mickey as he reaches into his pocket and hands over a fiver.

Then, as Tamara drives off across the field towards a line of Land Rovers, pick-up trucks, mobile homes and half a dozen motorbikes with Dutch numberplates, Mickey collapses in a fit of giggling. Burying his face deep in Tyke's shaggy coat, he rolls about laughing on the front seat of the Love Shack. 'Are you running a dog? Hee hee hee! Wouldnae exactly be One Man and His Dog would it?... and next it's Mickey wi' Tyke from Glasgow, well I dunno whit he's daein' now... aw naw, he's chased the sheep out onto the road... aw shite! He's bitten one of the judges but...'

Tamara parks the Love Shack between a galvanised metal sheep trailer and a muddy pick-up truck with the tailgate down. Three working collies bark furiously from behind a mesh grille.

Mickey's still giggling as Tamara pulls the handbrake on with a grinding creak of rusty cable. She pokes him between the ribs. 'C'm on, ya big Jessie. I'll take Tyke, you go and get me a bacon roll from the tent over there.'

'Thought you were a veggie and all?'

'I am – I just fancy a bacon roll – OK?'

Mickey grins then throws Tyke's lead at her.

The Sandpit Field slopes at a 30-degree angle down from the Poolewe road to the shoreline at Strath. A red van is parked at the top of the slope and a dozen sheep are corralled in a wooden pen nearby. About halfway down the slope are two gates set twenty feet apart and there is a flag on a post near a second wooden pen at the lower end of the field where a line of spectators are standing behind the fence that separates the parking area from the Sandpit Field.

Mickey and Tamara are leaning against the fence eating bacon rolls. Half of Gairloch must be here. Mickey had to queue for ten minutes in the white marquee where the local ladies of the WI were serving up filled rolls and a mouth-watering selection of homemade scones, chocolate brownies and Dundee cake. An urn steamed on a table: 50p for a cup of tea, £1 for a sausage roll.

There are tourists with expensive cameras, tweed-clad hunting-shooting-fishing types, bikers in oily jeans and leather jackets, crofters in muddy wellies and kids with runny noses.

'It's a no bad bacon—' he starts to say but he's interrupted by an ear-splitting burst of feedback from the loudspeaker system.

'Next up is Alec Macrae from Bundalloch with Mist.'

Alec is a red-faced crofter of around sixty in mud-spattered trousers and an old blue fleece. Mist is a big collie with a broad snout and a black and white coat with a streak of tan down his chest. He trots to heel behind Alec who stops beside the flag at the foot of the field. A hush descends on the crowd. Mist is poised, still, immobile, his eyes fixed on Alec. Then Alec makes the smallest of gestures with his right hand and whispers, 'Go way off,' between clenched teeth.

Mist sprints away, up the Sandpit Field, like the wind in the grass. He heads to the right of the two wooden gates and runs on up towards the red van at the top of the sloping field before lying down twelve feet in front of the pen containing the sheep.

Mist's tail swishes slowly from side to side in anticipation. The odour of frightened sheep fills the dog's twitching nose. A man with a shepherd's crook opens the gate and releases three ewes. Out in the open field, faced by Mist baring his teeth, the sheep huddle together. First they step to the right, then they walk six feet left before stopping. Alec sticks his fingers in his mouth and whistles. Mist advances on the sheep and they move off down the hill heading straight for the gap between the two gates.

'Aw! Pure dead brilliant! Eh?'

Mickey smiles then he bends down to pat Tyke.

'Straight in tae the pen – bet you'd've been a braw sheep dog, pups.'

Tamara looks at him over the top of her sunglasses.

'In your dreams, Mickey Bell,' she says.

Next dog up is Rags from Antrim in Northern Ireland. Rags is a lean, rough-coated collie. He makes a good start of it on the outrun and lift but on the way down he sets the sheep running at too fast a pace and they go to the left of one of the gates instead of through the gap between them.

This seems to spook Rags and it takes a good ten minutes of whistling and hissed commands from his grizzled, grey-haired Arran-sweater-clad master before the wooden gate of the pen nearest the spectators finally bangs shut with a prod from a shepherd's crook.

A stocky, middle-aged woman is approaching the flag marking the starting point. Mickey's mouth drops half-open in surprise.

'She's got her sheepdog on a lead!'

He whispers to Tamara.

'Nae street cred there but – you cannae take your dog to a sheepdog trials – on the lead!'

He can almost hear the farm collies in the back of the muddy pick-up truck behind them sniggering.

'Think I'll miss this one,' he says. 'Tyke could dae wi' a leg stretch – back in a flash.'

He strolls through the crowd. The dog trails along behind him, sniffing the grass and hoovering up flakes of pastry and bits of sausage roll. Tyke was always last in line at the battered steel dog bowl in the barn at Torbreac. When he got to Glasgow he was quick to learn about triangles of day-old pizza and dropped kebabs served fresh from the pavement.

'Aye, you like yer street treats, eh pups?'

He bends down and ruffles Tyke's shaggy coat affectionately. As he does, out the corner of his eye he sees the big Highland Constabulary Land Rover parked behind the tea tent. He looks around as casually as he can. A policeman in white shirt sleeves is standing beside the Love Shack examining the tax disc. As Mickey watches he runs his hand along the crumbling bodywork above the rusty wheel arches then looks down at the number plate hanging off the back bumper. The policeman reaches into his trouser pocket and takes out his notebook.

Mickey feels a watery looseness in his guts. Tyke's still

sniffing at something in the grass. He drags the dog back to where Tamara's standing at the fence.

Another squealing burst of feedback.

'Next dog up is Mac from Inverurie,' says the announcer, 'but before that please give a big hand for two great wee pipers.'

A ripple of applause runs through the crowd in the Sandpit Field.

'What's wrong with you?' asks Tamara seeing Mickey, white-faced, clutching the dog by the collar.

'The polis are lookin' at the van – is it unlocked?'

Tamara nods, a scared look on her face. She brushes a beaded hair extension away from her eyes.

'You stay here and keep hold o' Tyke,' he says.

Then he creeps around the back of the line of parked cars and motorbikes. Crouched down he half-walks, half-crawls over to the pick-up truck parked next to the Love Shack. A white collie with a black patch around one eye is tied to the towing bracket at the rear of the truck. A shiny steel dog bowl half full of water lies in the grass nearby. The white collie's tail thumps the ground as Mickey approaches.

He squats down in front of the pick-up truck and looks through the dusty nearside window. The policeman is walking back to his Land Rover. The rusty side door of the Love Shack slides open with a squealing, grinding noise. The interior smells of patchouli oil and insence.

On his hands and knees he crawls under the table and pulls out his rucksack. Then he climbs down from the Love Shack and slides the door shut then walks as casually as he can between the cars, back towards the line of onlookers at the fence.

He stops to hoist the rucksack onto one shoulder. As he does so he can't help glancing across at the police Land Rover. The policeman's in the passenger seat – on his radio.

Just as Mickey looks away the policeman looks up and their eyes meet for a second. Mickey panics and runs across to where Tamara is standing by the fence.

'Mickey?'

He grabs Tyke by the collar.

'Fuckin shifty-shufty dog!'

They sprint down towards the gate that leads onto the road.

Tamara calls after him, 'Text me!' Then quietly, to herself, 'I'll miss you, Mickey Bell.'

The heavy rucksack bashes into his back. Tyke has a wild-eyed, fearful look in his blue-green eyes. They reach the Shore Road and run along the pavement. The tide is out and ripples of flat wet sand and lines of brown kelp stretch out towards Skye. Sweat drips down his face as he half walks, half runs up the incline leading to the main road.

A German family, mother and father and two blond little boys, all eating ice creams, give him a strange look. He's reached the road junction opposite Strath Stores when he hears the siren. Glancing back over his shoulder he can't see the police Land Rover but imagines it forcing its way through the crowd in the Sandpit Field. He runs past the Spar delivery truck parked on the pavement, engine running. At the doorway of Strath Stores he collides with a burly figure in a leather jacket emerging from the shop.

'Mickey!'

It's Mr Fuk Holland 2012 from the log cabins at Ruaidh Bridge.

At that moment the police Land Rover appears at the junction of the Shore Road and the A832. Mr Fuk sees the police jeep, blue lights flashing, stopped at the junction and he sees Mickey drenched in sweat. Behind them the Spar delivery truck, white rear lights shining, reverse warning alarm bleeping, is doing a three-point turn and blocking the main road.

'You een trouble, Mickey?' asks Mr Fuk, shouting to make himself heard over Tyke's barking. 'Quick, you come with me.'

Mr Fuk grabs Mickey by the arm and half-drags him across the dusty car park of Strath Stores. The chrome handlebars and red paintwork of the chopper gleam in the sunshine. Mr F straddles the trike and stamps his heavy leather boot down on the kick-start lever. The cylinders turn over with a whirring wheeze. Then nothing.

'Put the rucksack een the pannier!'

Mr Fuk shouts over his shoulder.

Tyke springs unbidden up onto the rear seat of the trike as Mickey bangs the lid of the pannier shut and twists the chrome handle. Mr Fuk kicks his boot down again. A cough, a whirr then the 1700 cc engine fires with a low throaty rumble. Mickey jumps on behind Mr F, clutching the edge of the seat with one white-knuckled hand and Tyke's collar with the other as the trike lurches over the potholes and out the car park of Strath Stores just as the police Land Rover, blue lights flashing and siren wailing, mounts the pavement to get past the Spar delivery truck.

Mr Fuk forces the trike round the bends on the hill leading up to the Gairloch Hotel. The police jeep is fifty feet behind them. Mickey clings to Tyke's collar.

When the destroyers lay at anchor in the sea loch, the wartime despatch riders carrying Ministry of Defence telegrams in leather messenger bags, anxiously awaited by men in navy greatcoats and white Arran sweaters who paced up and down outside the austere stone frontage of the Gairloch Hotel never went as fast as this.

The nearside rear wheel of the trike lifts clear of the tarmac on the sharp right-hand bend just before the garage. The foreign driver of a hire car pulling out into the road slams his foot down on the brake pedal as the trike flies over the crest of the blind summit. Mickey has a two-second glimpse of shocked white faces pressed against the windows of the car.

At the tight corner at the top of the hill leading down to the town beach and the nine-hole golf course, sudden G force pushes Mickey's face against Mr Fuk's worn black leather jacket with the MSC Eindhoven badges hand-sewn on the back. He starts to slide forward in the seat. He tries to keep back, away from Mr F, pressing his feet against the footpegs, using his thigh muscles to control his position on the seat. And all the while clinging onto Tyke's collar.

'Scheisse!'

The trike's brake pads bite into the discs as Mr Fuk swerves to avoid smashing into the line of stationary cars, vans and mobile homes fifty yards ahead.

The traffic is moving at walking pace. The police Land Rover is two hundred yards behind them. Mr Fuk roars along the wrong side of the road past the traffic jam then bumps the trike up onto the pavement. A procession of fifty people is following a hearse down the hill to the white church and graveyard by the wide, sandy bay.

A Highland funeral: the mourners at the back ruddy-faced, dressed in ill-fitting black suits. A balding thirty-year-old man in a kilt walks behind the hearse with two little boys holding his hands. In the back floral tributes propped up against the coffin spell *GRANNY/MUM*.

It's at this point in the crazy morning there comes to Mickey's ears the most plaintive bagpiping he's ever heard. Just inside the iron gates in the low drystone wall that surrounds the graveyard a man in a scruffy black jacket and black trousers that aren't part of a suit, stands playing the bagpipes at the edge of a freshly dug grave.

This is no shortbread tin piper playing for the tourists on Princes Street or for the coach parties arriving at Eilean Donan castle. The man at the graveside is playing a lament.

He's playing the way the pipers played *Lochaber No More* as the people boarded the emigrant ships that rode the waves in Caol Bay in the shadow of Ben Nuivais, waiting to sail for America on the high tide. Even the stubbly young gravediggers standing under the trees in hoodies and French Connection T-shirts, cigarettes dangling from their lips, turn to listen as the sound of the lament drifts across the loch and echoes from Sidhean Mor over to Flowerdale House.

The trike skids and bounces along the grassy verge then scrapes along the mossy drystone wall of the graveyard.

'Bloody tourists!' shouts one mourner.

The police jeep is stuck behind the hearse, its siren respectfully silenced by the disapproving scowls of the mourners.

Clear of the funeral procession at last, the trike screams out past the *Failte Ghu Gairloch Please Drive Carefully* sign and the humpback stone bridge that leads to Red Point. They fly along the single track road spraying gravel from a lay-by as Mr F swerves to avoid a startled-looking Booker Foods truck driver.

Mickey inhales the smell of pine. Road and trees flicker by as the trike roars up Kerrysdale. They say the waterfall that once cascaded down the crags at the head of the glen was more dramatic than the Falls of Glomach. But fifty years ago the beauty of the torrent splashing down through rowan, birch and oak was lost. The riverbed is dry, the old waterfall a mere trickle and between the pine trees at the side of the road Mickey sees a large green pipeline on concrete stanchions.

The single track road with its passing places lies behind them now. As the trike rumbles over the cattle grid at the Red Barn, Tyke barks and Mickey catches a glimpse of Baosbheinn and Beinn an Eoin rising Suilven-like above the boggy moorland. The birch trees beside the River Kerry flash by and then they're on the long straight two miles of road leading down to Talladale.

The road cuts a black asphalt line through the Scots pines. Tyke stares straight ahead. His furry black ears fly back in the wind. The spear-shaped rock faces of Slioch loom across the blue-grey water. Mickey looks over Mr Fuk's shoulder. Through blurry, watery eyes he can just make out the red needle on the speedometer on the chrome handlebars wobbling just below 129 miles per hour.

Mr Fuk slows the trike to take the series of bends where the road runs close by the shore. Eilean Ruaridh Mor, Garbh Eilean and Eilean Dubh na Sroine; the low, flat, pine-clad islands lie spread out before them on the pewter surface of the loch. As Mr F opens the throttle to accelerate out of the last tight bend before the Loch Maree Hotel, Mickey, eyes wide in horror, sees a red deer hind, her coat moulting and matted, standing spindly-legged in the middle of the road.

'Mr Fuk has no braking distance,' whizzes through Mickey's mind, followed by, 'Aw fuck, man, I'm gaunny die.'

Two seconds.

The hind looks straight at Mickey with soft brown eyes then takes a couple of panicky steps towards the nearside verge. Mr Fuk misses the deer by millimetres. They pass so close to the animal, Mickey can smell the same disinfectant-like odour he remembers from the hollows of flattened grass where the deer lie down at night on the slopes of Beinn Chlinaig.

His arms are trembling, knuckles white where he grips Tyke's collar and the edge of the seat. He feels sick but, fuck it, he thinks, I'm no gaunny give up now. He taps Mr F on the shoulder.

Mr Fuk pulls off the road at a signpost with a picture of a picnic bench. There's only one other car parked in the lay-by.

'You stay here, Mickey,' says Mr Fuk. 'You keep hidden

in the woods and I'll draw them off. How d'you say eet – like a red herring. Ja?'

Mickey climbs shakily off the trike.

'C'mon, dog – move! Skedaddle aff!' he cries.

But Tyke just sits there, looking suspicious.

Mickey drags the dog off the trike, grabs his rucksack, hugs Mr Fuk then walks quickly down the track towards the shore of Loch Maree. Through the trees he can hear Mr F revving the trike then accelerating out of the parking place and back onto the road. Already he can hear the distant sound of sirens.

There are more parking spaces down near the loch and, among the silver birches, oaks and hazels, a Bedford campervan is parked. The door of the van is open and inside he can see a bottle of Lagavulin next to a pile of hillwalking guidebooks and a Roberts' radio. Ordnance Survey maps spill out of a cardboard shoebox and a dozen or more yellow boxes with Kodak emblazoned on the side lie scattered across the floor.

A canvas rucksack lies in the grass. A pair of walking britches and a cagoule hang from a washing line strung between the slender lichen-encrusted branches of a silver birch. Tyke rushes around to the other side of the campervan to greet its owner who is seated in a deckchair sewing a patch onto a pair of canvas gaiters. He puts down the needle and thread and strokes Tyke's head.

The owner of the campervan is lean and wiry with bright blue eyes. His hands are liver-spotted but he looks tanned and fit. He's wearing brown corduroy trousers and Merrell trainers. White hairs stick out from the open top button of his checked shirt.

'Well, you're a friendly one,' he says rubbing Tyke's ears.

Tyke offers a paw then licks the old guy's hand.

'You remind me of Storm, you do, doggie,' he says quietly.

As he runs his hand through his silver beard and looks between the rowans and birches and out across Loch Maree, it seems to Mickey the old man is seeing another time long gone, far beyond the distant shore of the grey loch. He's seeing something from the past. And there's a moistness in the corner of those blue eyes. Mickey is sure.

The old man looks up from stroking Tyke. His blue eyes take in Mickey standing there among the silver birches. The old man looks sharp, like he'd not take well to fools or chancers. Mickey feels gauged, assessed, appraised, quickly read all in that one look. On the road two hundred yards away through the Scots pines and yellow whin the police Land Rover tears by, blue lights flashing, siren wailing.

'They're in a hurry,' observes the old man in a level tone. Then, seeing the rucksack on Mickey's back, 'Where are you headed, fella?'

'Over there,' replies Mickey, pointing to the spear-shaped rock faces of Slioch on the far eastern shore of the loch.

'It's ma last Munro,' he blurts out.

It just slipped out. He hadn't meant to tell this stranger.

But the old man's face lights up. Once more, Mickey senses, he sees into a world Mickey can't see: the days that are no more.

'That's a grand dog. He really is.' Then, to Tyke, 'How many Munros have you done then, fella?'

Mickey senses there was a dog in the days that are no more. 'Two hundred and countin',' he says proudly.

The old man smiles but doesn't say anything. Somehow he's not as impressed as Mickey expected him to be.

The sound of sirens fades into the distance replaced by the cheeping of the blue tits, chaffinches and wrens that flit between the branches of the rowans and aspens on the shore of the loch. The old man looks up at him again.

'How're you going to get there?' he asks, pointing at Slioch a mile away across the grey waters of Loch Maree.

'I havnae really thought about it, tae be honest,' says Mickey. 'Walk round tae the head of the loch I guess.'

The old man frowns.

'But you'll be all day doing that – and the weather going to close in later – mind.'

The old guy gets up slowly out of his deckchair and points towards a little bay fringed by oak and Scots pine.

'My canoe's down there, son. You can borrow it if you like.'

Mickey hesitates.

'Aw thanks, mate, but how will ye—?'

The old guy interrupts him, 'Just leave it on the far side of the loch and I'll drive round to Kinlochewe and pick it up tomorrow.'

'But you'll have tae walk miles back?' protests Mickey.

'No, I can just cycle round and paddle back,' says the old man, pointing to a fold-up commuter bike strapped to the back of the campervan. 'After all, I've got all the time in the world.' A reflective look passes across his face and he adds, 'Or perhaps none at all.'

The old guy leads Mickey and Tyke down through the trees and along a path orange with fallen birch leaves and spangled with yellow tormentil and white wood sorrel to a little bay on the shore of Loch Maree, a miniature beach of gravel and boulders.

The 'canoe' is pulled up on the grass. It's nothing like the red fibreglass boats they practised Eskimo rolling, in the blue chlorine water of the school swimming pool at Our Lady of Lourdes High.

It's nothing like the canoe he helped the Dutch people carry up the jetty at Dornie the summer before last. The guy, blond hair and beard, pulling off his wetsuit top, all muscles and wispy blond hairs on his chest, told him they'd paddled the big red and white sea kayak all along the seaweed- and barnacle-crusted skerries off Arisaig.

Mickey looks dubiously at the old guy's canoe. The black rubber stretched tightly across its wooden frame is riven with tiny cracks, but the alternative is struggling through four miles of boggy woodland along the side of the loch then wading the Kinlochewe River. He has no choice. He daren't take the road. It's the crazy way the day's going. He never envisaged his last Munro would be like this.

'Bought her from a PE teacher in Cardenden in 1983,' the old guy is saying, hands on hips. 'She gets some strange looks these days.'

Tyke sniffs the perished rubber hull of the canoe suspiciously.

'You can stow your rucksack at the back,' the old guy continues, pointing out a space under the rubber skin of the canoe. 'And plenty of room for you, pups, up front.'

He bends down to pat Tyke. The dog sits, looking up, hoping for a biscuit.

'Leave the canoe somewhere over the other side – just make sure you pull her well up out of the water.'

Mickey unlaces his boots and takes his thick woolly socks off and rolls his trousers up to the knee. His toes look white and the black hairs stand out on his skin. He pushes the canoe into the water. Ice cold. His feet tingle then go numb. Still the loch in winter.

'Tyke! Here!'

Tyke looks at Mickey.

Mickey reaches into his pocket for a dog biscuit. Tyke's holding a stick in his mouth. His furry head goes down and his tail goes up.

'Aw, no now but—,' says Mickey.

'Come on, dog,' says the old man, attempting to shepherd Tyke into the canoe.

Big mistake: Tyke's not having it. He wants to play stick among the crisp brown autumn leaves in the dappled patches of sunlight under the silver birches. Each time the old guy approaches, the dog lets him get within two feet then runs away in a wide arc. Tyke races around the shore and under the trees in wide joyful circles. Mickey knows from experience the dog can keep this up for an hour at a time. He can hear Zelda's voice in his head, 'I told you so – training a dog's not easy, you know.'

He blames himself; him a first time dog owner and Tyke a born leader, an alpha dog always jockeying to be pack leader, always pushing the boundaries, always edging his way up onto the sofa.

'He's a character,' says the old man as Mickey unzips the side pocket of his rucksack. Usually he doesn't get too worried when Tyke has one of his strops but it's different today. They have to get away from the road.

'Emergency measures, mate,' he winks, brandishing a plastic squeaky toy in the shape of a half-eaten apple core.

'WHIT'S THIS, TYKE?'

The dog stops running in mad circles. Mickey holds the plastic toy aloft and squeaks it furiously.

'Tyke! Herc!'

The dog trots over to his feet

'Tyke! Sit!'

He fumbles in his pocket. As the dog crunches the biscuit, Mickey snaps the lead onto his leather collar. He drags Tyke to the water's edge then lifts the sullen dog into the canoe.

'Tyke! Stay.'

He pushes the canoe out into the water then climbs in. It wobbles then his weight grounds it on the stony bed of the loch, the thin rubber hull scraping rocks that have lain by Loch Maree since the last glacier melted.

The old guy hands Mickey the paddle. He balances it across his lap, his hands walking through the shallows as he pushes against the slimy stones. The old man gives the canoe a shove and suddenly they're floating, clear of the shore.

Mickey dips the paddle deep into the clear, cold water of Loch Maree.

Right-hand side.

Then left-hand side.

Cold, peaty water pours down his arms, soaking his sleeves. He finds his rhythm, ploughing a straightish, slightly shoogly line across the loch, steering well to the right of the white house at Letterewe.

There's no spraydeck and soon half an inch of chilly water is sloshing about in the bottom of the canoe.

'Aw, naw!' he says under his breath. 'Ah've got fuckin wet pants but.'

One hundred feet out into the loch he turns the canoe carefully around so it faces back towards the shore. He rests the paddle across his lap and watches as two sleek, black-throated divers glide across the sheeny surface of the loch.

The old guy is standing at the water's edge staring across at the far shore where the arrowhead cliffs of Slioch are capped by low cloud: gazing, gazing back into the past again. Mickey raises his arm in a wave then dips the paddle into the water, turns the canoe and paddles towards the distant oak trees on the eastern shore of Loch Maree.

The old man turns away and walks back through the silver birches and rowans, back to the campervan with its slide boxes of memories of hill days held in dog-eared notebooks and yellow Kodak slide boxes. Behind him the ripples spread out across the loch, the low cloud scuds across the mountains and the grey heron flies slowly over the bay.

§

Mr Fuk Holland 2012 was finally stopped by a police motorcyclist at a lay-by near the Tore roundabout, seven miles north of Inverness.

'Don't worry, mate – we'll throw the book at him.'

The young traffic cop had assured his colleague in Gairloch, speaking over the radio ten minutes earlier. But when it comes to it and he gets off his motorbike and walks slowly across the lay-by, doubt has already begun to seep into the edges of his mind.

Mr Fuk sits astride the trike with his helmet under one arm and his grey ponytail blowing in the slipstream of the passing lorries. His denim waistcoat is unbuttoned to reveal a dragon tattoo snaking out from beneath the belt of his leather trousers. A one-inch diameter brass ring hangs from his left nipple and a bent silver nail protrudes from the grey-haired biker's lower lip. To the young policeman's eyes the gay Hell's Angel appears to have multiple piercings to every orifice the cop can see and most likely to those he can't too...

'Good afternoon, officer. Ees there a problem?'

Mr Fuk's eyes bulge salaciously as he looks the young traffic policeman up and down with searchlight eyes.

'Can I see your driver's licence, sir?'

'Sure – I'll just get eet.'

The young traffic cop looks on as Mr F opens the panniers on the rear of the trike and rummages about inside.

'Eet's here somewhere,' says Mr Fuk, bending over the trike.

A moment later a leather whip and then a set of handcuffs fall out onto the asphalt at the edge of the A9. A light breeze off the Beauly Firth stirs the dead grass at the edge of the lay-by. The sun glints on a clear shard of plastic roadside debris. The traffic policeman glances down at the tarmac. Then he frowns. There's a big wobbly black dildo lying at his feet.

Mr Fuk looks up and winks at the traffic cop. Three

youths in a red Ford Fiesta with a thick exhaust and a rear spoiler slow down. The driver shouts something out the open window and toots his horn.

'Ah, here eet is.'

A bead of sweat runs down the inside of the traffic cop's helmet. He examines the driving licence gingerly. One corner of it is sticky with something he hopes is just lubricant. He looks around anxiously. A pile-up on Scotland's busiest trunk road is beginning to look a distinct possibility as rubber-necking drivers slow down to witness the spectacle of the sixty-six-year-old gay Hell's Angel and his collection of sex toys spread out across the lay-by and the young policeman, now desperately wishing he was back home with his wife and two young children in their '90s semi in Milton of Leys.

Three days later as the side screw propellors churn the briny water and the car ferry manoeuvres ponderously out of Ramsgate Harbour, Mr Fuk leans over the white-painted rail and tears the Highland Constabulary fixed penalty speeding ticket into little pieces. He watches the scraps of white paper floating among the petrol rainbows on the oily waters of the English Channel and he thinks of Mickey Bell.

goodbye iPhone, hello ptarmigan

'Listen, I know it's your country and all that, mate, but I still don't want to have to show me passport at Berwick everytime I come up 'ere.'

Nigel is seated on a green tartan stool at the bar of the Kinlochewe Hotel, a large white cup and saucer in front of him, a tideline of cappuccino foam around the rim. Torn-open paper sachets of brown sugar lie scrunched up on the saucer. Nige is wondering if it's too early to have a drink.

'Anyway, enough of politics – d'you know what I saw this morning?'

The barman shrugs.

'Only a bloomin' golden eagle! It was sitting on a fencepost right by the road at the edge of the village.'

A stray midge hovers over the optics. There's something odd about the hillwalker staying in room 8, thinks the dark-haired barman as he dries a pint glass from the dishwasher and puts it away on the shelf behind the bar.

'Is that right?' he says. He knows full well what Nigel's seen is a TE; a bird of prey, yes, but only two thirds the size of an eagle and just 20 percent of its weight. Real deal golden eagles don't sit on fenceposts by the road. But buzzards do and that's why the locals call them Tourists' Eagles.

Nige starts another game of Angry Birds on his iPhone then he notices he's got a text. It's from Gina:

Hi babes Miss u Mountain man 😀 xXx

He's about to text her back when he hears the scream of Mr Fuk's trike as it roars through the narrow street of white-painted houses and rattles the window panes of the hotel.

'Bloody hell –'e's travelling, all right!'

A few minutes later the Highland Constabulary Land Rover, with siren screaming and blue lights flashing, awakens the investigator in Nige.

'Put the cappuccino on me room tab,' he says, sliding off the bar stool and pulling on his brand new Arctic Alpha SV jacket.

He walks quickly out through the residents' lounge, squeezing between the brown leather Chesterfields and the coffee table with its stack of back numbers of Scottish Field.

His feet crunch on the gravel in the courtyard behind the hotel. A blue Triumph Spitfire is parked in the corner by the open door to the kitchen where he can see a man with a beard in chefs' whites standing at a steel table, chopping carrots and parsnips on a wooden block.

He clicks the car key in his hand and the hazard lights on the silver Avensis blink orange at him. He pulls open the driver's door and slides onto the black plastic upholstery, starts the engine and reverses the Toyota out the courtyard. He feels it in his guts as he passes the garage and the Tipsy Laird Café. There's something going on, he thinks, as he hits sixty, three hundred yards before the national speed limit sign at the edge of the village.

The road runs close to the shore and the blue-grey waters of Loch Maree flash past between the Scots pines. Above the tree line white shattered quartzite scree sweeps down from the notched ridge and pinnacles they call the Black Carls of Eighe. On an impulse Nigel pulls over into a lay-by. He bangs the door of the Avensis shut and crosses the road.

Through the trees he spots the rubber kayak heading out across the loch and he sees the small collie sat bolt upright in the bow of the canoe staring straight ahead, watching the far shoreline.

'That's gotta be 'im,' mutters Nige, running back to the car. A quick three-point turn, narrowly avoiding a Highland Council dustbin lorry that peeps angrily, while a man in a high-vis jacket in the cab gesticulates furiously at him, and then the Toyota's speeding back through the Scots pines towards Kinlochewe.

Once in the village again, he turns left at a signpost to Incheril and onto a single track road where he abandons the Toyota in a car park hidden by a belt of young larch trees.

He struggles to haul the rucksack out the boot of the Avensis. He gets one strap over his shoulder then has to fight to get the other one on. He'd barely managed to squeeze his jeans and trainers and spare T-shirt into the top and the straps on the back are extended to maximum length. The cumbersome, teeteringly high rucksack pushes his head forward, making him look like a hunchback. It unbalances him too and he jars his hip in a pothole in the tarmac.

The orange birch leaves of autumn cover the ground and the sun glints between the trunks of the rowans and aspens as he opens a gate in the deer fence at the back of the car park and hurries along the track beside the river that empties into the southern end of Loch Maree.

Ahead stretch the flat fields of the plain of the Kinlochewe River. Scots pines climb the lower slopes of Meall a'Ghiubhais on the far shore. A wisp of cloud brushes its stony summit. Sweat pouring down his face, Nige stops to catch his breath at a little burial ground just past the house at Culaneilan on the flat river plain beneath the Black Carls of Eighe. The gravestones and crosses on the yellow turf stand starkly against the backdrop of the silver-white and grey quartzite mountain.

'Jeezo! Take it easy,' says a voice inside his head, '—don't want to end up pushing up daisies, Nige, old son.'

The path twists on along the foot of the brown, heather-covered hillside before disappearing into a plantation of oak and beech on the banks of the Kinlochewe River. Sheep graze by the path and the fronds of bracken are turning yellow along the margins of what were once well tended fields on the fertile alluvial plain of the river.

He glimpses blue water and creamy-white foam between the lichen-encrusted tree trunks. Near the mouth of Loch Maree the river broadens out into wide stretches of shingle like a sea loch. On the north bank six-foot-tall bushes of whin, densely armed with inch-long rigid spikes, encroach on the white shingle. Foxes make their dens in the middle of the impenetrable thickets which blaze with golden-yellow, almond-smelling, sweet-pea-like flowers. Nige remembers his Nan standing in the garden of her brick back-to-back at the edge of the fields that ran down to the Tyne telling him an old rhyme about the whin:

When the gorse's not in flower,
Kissing's out of fashion.

And he repeats the lines to himself as he walks along the shore of Loch Maree: a charm to ward off the threatening cloud-capped mountains that stand all around.

The path over short-cropped turf along the side of the loch is easy walking and he makes good time though something, it feels like it might be the wind-up digital radio, is sticking into his back. After an hour he reaches the woods at Coillie na

Dubh Claise and the bridge over the Abhainn an Fhasaigh.

He stops.

'Jeez! That's better,' he says to himself.

Ah – the relief from the rucksack straps not cutting into his shoulders but he can't stop for long. He needs to keep ahead of the suspect. He has a quick glance at the map. He's at the bridge near the ominous sounding Cladh nan Sassunach, a name the dark-haired barman in the Kinlochewe Hotel had gleefully translated for him the evening before as meaning The Englishman's Grave.

On the far shore of Loch Maree cloud streams across the white quartzite screes of Beinn Eighe. Beyond the wooden footbridge at the gloomy entrance to Glen Bianasdail the track starts to deteriorate into a muddy, peaty, boggy, slippery hillwalkers' path. The cliffs on the far side of the glen are in shadow, the rocks and crags thrust sideways by ancient geological forces.

He takes the Cicerone guide he bought as an afterthought out the pocket of the Arctic Alpha SV jacket the long-haired assistant with the beard at Pennine Outdoor had persuaded him to buy.

'Follow the grassy gully up between Meall Each and Sgurr Dubh,' the book says.

'Sgurr Dubh must be the rocky lump over there on the left,' Nige mutters to himself as he plods on up the path towards the grassy boulder-studded rim of Coire na Sleaghaich. Clumps of deergrass cling tenaciously on in the middle of the eroded path and there are dozens of bootprints in the black peaty mud.

He tries jumping over the boggy bits.

But his jarred knee cartilage twinges with little stabs of pain.

'Won't be doing that again, will you, Nige?' says the voice in his head.

Sweat dribbles down between his shoulder blades.

'Jesus Christ this rucksack's friggin' heavy!'

He can feel a sticky damp patch on his back.

Maybe he should dump some of the stuff behind a rock?

But technically it's the department's property and they're incredibly strict about printer paper and rolls of sellotape and he had that terrible row with Gina last year over a stapler.

Low cloud obscures the summit of the spear mountain. It spills down the hillside in great white billows. He hums the opening lines of Peter Gabriel's Solsbury Hill. Then, remembering Arran, he takes out his iPhone. The screen glows cheerily with its host of friendly icons. There's a text. It's from Gina:

> Hey mountain man 😀 guess what? Jaap's got a job in Norway looks like bye bye FIS for me... miss u honey bunny xXx

He brushes his forefinger across the screen and selects Location Services. A map appears: Slioch, Sgurr Dubh and Glen Bianasdail. A flashing blue ring indicates his position at the edge of the corrie to within ten metres and a purple line running off the edge of the screen points the way back to his car, four kilometres east at Incheril.

Perfect! Isn't technology great?

Along the foot of the screen is his position in co-ordinates:

57.6561°N 5.3239°W

He frowns.

Hmm? That'll be longitude and latitude then?

But the numbers along the edge of the map are different to the figures on the screen.

What's the rule for a grid reference? he wonders. They did it at school, last period before lunch while the smell of shepherd's pie wafted along the corridor.

'Is it up the stairs and along the corridor or along the corridor first and then up the stairs and does it matter which way up the map is?' he asks himself.

A few drops of rain blown on the wind. Still the phone and its glowing screen reassure him. He taps the S of Slioch and a drop-down menu box appears, offering him *Navigate To* and *Route Options*. He taps *Navigate To* and a reassuring flickering arrow appears, pointing the way ahead.

On the screen of the iPhone a fleck of rain glistens; the shiny screen, clipped onto the base unit of the phone in the factory on the giant industrial estate where there were only paddy fields ten years ago. The woman on the assembly line was tired, the sixteen-hour shift, the long bus journey back to Zhejiang. She snapped the screen onto the phone and it wobbled off down the conveyor belt and the next base unit was lying there in front of her. She reached for another screen. The phone moved further down the line of white-coated workers, beginning its long journey across the planet, to end up here in the heather and mist of a Scottish corrie.

Where the path becomes fainter and begins to lose itself in the peat hags at the entrance to the grassy bowl of Coire na Sleaghaich, Nige takes off the heavy rucksack and drags it through the deergrass towards a trio of lichen-spattered boulders each one the size of a small car, that stand in the heather one hundred yards from the path.

In a little hollow among the boulders, sheltered from the freshening north wind, the apple-green foliage of blaeberry and the segmented leaves of cloudberry sprout among the grey schist rock. On one of the boulders a few small, dark-coloured, sausage-shaped, white-tipped, bird-like droppings lie among the ochre lichen.

In a hole in the dry peaty soil beneath the largest of the boulders, Nathair Chasach sleeps curled up (for more than half her length is tail). This morning she lay in a gap in the heather facing south, looking out towards the mountains of Torridon, waiting for the sun to warm the dry black peaty soil with refractive heat and the air with reflective heat. As soon as she had absorbed enough warmth from the sun to raise her body temperature and move quickly, she wriggled out to hunt the spiders of Coire na Sleaghaich.

Soon she will hibernate and until March stay curled up in a crevice in the dry peaty soil beneath the boulders where the temperature always remains above freezing level even as the snow lies a foot deep on the hillside. This morning she basked on a rock in the unseasonably warm autumn weather but as the wind changes and grey cloud covers up the sun the lizard feels a sluggish cooling in her blood.

Nige too feels the cold edge of the strengthening north wind as he drags his rucksack into the little hollow among the boulders; he pulls up clumps of heather, roots black with peat, and lays them over the rucksack to conceal it.

Lying flat in the heather at eye level with its small purple flowers, he sees its tiny leaves grouped in fours, overlapping like the slates on a roof. Down among the boulders in his khaki waterproofs he blends into the brown and ochre shades of the grassy floor of the corrie.

He has a clear view of the path climbing up to the lochans high on the southern shoulder of Slioch, a thousand feet below the summit. He slides the Leica (20 mega-pixel, 50 x zoom) out of its waterproof case. George Lazenby in *On Her Majesty's Secret Service* (the one where the baddie falls into the snow blower and the snow sprays out red) would've given anything for one of these back in the '60s. He zooms in on the path, hearing the electronic whine of the autofocus over the rustle of the deergrass. He practises focusing on a rock. He hums a few lines of Howard Jones. And then he waits.

After ten minutes something moves in his field of vision. A set of antlers appears over the heather and then a line of red deer coming up from Meall Daimh: the stags at the front and the hinds and calves trailing along at the back. Heads down, the animals graze their way slowly across the lush floor of the corrie until they surround the boulders where Nige lies hidden. A smell like TCP fills Nigel's nostrils. Scotland: a place where wild animals still roam.

Christ, it really is another country, he thinks to himself.

The red deer of Coire na Sleaghaich, though, are but stunted shadows of their ancestors who dwelt deep in the forest when the world was young. Long ago when the Great Wood of Caledon covered Scotland, the red deer grazed beneath the trees but then the climate changed, the tide of forest receded and the red deer were forced to live on the bare hillside without shelter. They survived but they grew smaller and there is today no stag in the Highlands with the size and splendour of antlers of the deer Mary Queen of Scots hunted on the slopes of Beinn a'Ghlo five hundred years ago.

At their offices in the cobbled street in Edinburgh the scientists of the Deer Commission estimate the population to be around 350,000 beasts, double what it was in 1965 when the old man in the nursing home with the view to the distant Campsies wandered the hills and the young father in his black donkey jacket told his wide-eyed children about the day he rounded the bend on the way to the ferryman's house at South Shian and there, standing in the middle of the road, was a stag.

After five minutes the Leica switches itself off and the lens contracts with an electronic whine. The deer lift their heads, momentarily frozen and fearful of the man-made sound in the deserted corrie. Then they move nervously away on their long legs, disappearing higher up the scree- and boulder-strewn slopes of Sgurr Dubh.

§

The rubber hull of the canoe scrapes on the rocks. The north shore of Loch Maree is suddenly just six feet away. His arms ache and he has a searing pain in his right shoulder. He steps gingerly out of the canoe and onto the slippery, brown, weed-coated boulders. The sky is overcast now. The morning sunshine by the sea in Gairloch has gone and the wind has a cold biting edge to it.

The sound of the canoe bumping over the rocks and up the gravelly bank under the oak trees breaks the quiet that presses in all around. As he turns the canoe upside down and leaves it wedged between the mossy roots of a tall beech tree, out of sight of the road on the far side of the loch, the silence of the deserted north shore closes in again.

The roots of the oak trees clutch the eroded, earthy, pebble-studded bank where blue harebells and white wood sorrel flower. An old grassy path winds along the side of the loch between the hazels and rowans.

In the seventeenth century, in the industrial revolution, men in white-powdered wigs came and burned the thick oaks in stone furnaces to smelt iron. By the path under the broad-leafed trees in the old wood, the past is only a fold in time away: a glimpse of a scarlet frock coat through the silver birches, black shoes with buckles, a sword in a scabbard catches on a leafy branch.

He feels the silence like when he was a child on holiday once. The kids cycled to the end of the track and the heat and the silence settled all around them while a dragonfly hovered in the air. The atmosphere was heavy, sultry with the scent of gorse and bog myrtle.

He feels the same brooding silence here on the north shore of Loch Maree as he sits on a white lichen-spattered rock drying his feet with his socks and lacing up his climbing boots.

He opens a bag of crisps, tastes sweet artificial flavours and salt in his mouth. Then he bites into an apple.

Tyke waits expectantly.

'Gimme a paw!'

Tyke lifts his left paw then crunches the apple core given him; Mickey shoulders his rucksack and sets off east following the old grassy path along the shoreline below the stone, arrow-shaped cliffs of Slioch.

Peeiou!

Peeiou!

Peeiou!

A plaintive cry sounds over the loch. Clamhan the buzzard circles in slow lazy flight on his endless search for prey: rabbits, sheep carrion, caterpillars and beetles from the fields and moorland on the fringes of the mountains. When the white blindness came to the glen, the rabbits disappeared and Clamhan's kind struggled to survive the harsh Highland winter but now there are rabbits in abundance again, the laws of men protect the buzzard and Clamhan thrives.

The bird of prey circles on the thermals high above Glen Bianisdail. At the foot of the grey scree slopes of Sgurr Dubh, the buzzard sees the speck among the boulders that is Nigel the investigator lying in the heather. Then the bird sweeps out over the Abhainn an Fhasaigh and where the peaty yellow burn empties into Loch Maree he sees another dark speck preceded by a smaller black and white dot moving slowly towards the boulder-studded rim of Coire na Sleaghaich.

The cold comes creeping up from the ground, stretching tendrils of chill around Nigel's Gore-Tex-clad body. He pulls his down jacket on, noticing as he does it still has the price tag attached. £349.99 scored out, £299.99 scored out and, scribbled over in red biro, the figure £279.99.

While Nige waits in the heather, the small brown birds of Coire na Sleaghaich flit from rock to rock. A meadow pipit, then a flash of white as a wheatear flutters past. Brugheal they used to call him in Gaelic and, where there are boulders and short turf, there will usually be a pair of wheatears.

A noisy bird with his squeaky, warbling song, Brugheal builds his nest of grass, lined with moss, animal hair and ptarmigan feathers on the bare hillside. It's September now. Most of his kind have left for Africa already and soon he too will be gone.

After thirty minutes of waiting, the cold has crept into Nigel's bones and he pulls on his black balaclava, fantasising he's back in the marines, special forces preparing to storm the Iranian embassy, grenade in hand as the TV satellite vans wait on the far side of the city square. Like when he's playing SAS Zombie Assault on his phone in the car, waiting to photograph the single mother on income support at the end of her cleaning shift at the bingo hall. Like when the whole office went paintball wargaming in the field by the sycamore wood beside the motorway last Christmas and his team won.

His stream of thoughts is interrupted. There's movement on the path. He presses the red button. The screen on the camera lights up. A small black and white dog is sniffing along the edge of the track.

'Target engaged,' says the cyborg commander in Nigel's head as he presses Record.

A minute or two pass. Then the suspect appears, striding along the path. The small black and white dog halts, sniffing the air, ears pricked up, looking intently at the boulder where Nige is concealed. The dog takes a few steps off the track and into the heather. Nige holds his breath but the suspect checks the dog and they walk on along the path.

The red R on the screen flashes at regular, pulse-like intervals. Nige holds the camera steady. He zooms in on the subject, panning along the hillside, taking in the rough terrain and the large rucksack the suspect is carrying. The lens whirrs as Nige zooms in on the dog. This is good. More evidence: the claimant is able to care for a pet and exercise it on a daily basis.

'Chuck – chuck – chuck!'

A sound like two stones tapped together. Then a robin-sized bird, with a black head, white collar and reddish front, flies low over the grass and lands on a nearby rock. The stonechat watches Nige watching the man walking up the corrie path.

Even as he sees the flashing red R on the screen, in his head Nige is already completing his fraud investigation surveillance report, carefully filling in each section, scrolling the tab key to right and left, checking for typos.

He sees himself back at Quarryhill House handing the report over to Gina. It'll be digitally scanned and an email attachment sent electronically from Leeds to the department's headquarters in Whitehall. Then they'll go for cappuccinos and jam-filled doughnuts at the Costa Coffee across the road. Nige sees his report lying on a leather-topped desk; tucked in among other government papers in the minister's briefcase.

He sees himself standing up in the witness box. 'No, the defendant did not display any difficulty walking over rough terrain for a distance considerably in excess of fifty metres.'

Scroungers and skivers: Nige approves of the UK government's rhetoric. He sees the minister's tiny, crablike handwriting in the margin of his report. At the Department of Social Security only the secretary of state is allowed to use green ink. Once and only once in his career in the civil service has Nige seen a letter in green ink: it had been printed by a laser printer admittedly but the text was in green. In his twelve years with the department Nige has often fantasised about seeing the minister's handwriting in green ink in the margin of one of his reports.

The suspect and his dog are out of sight now, nearing the foot of the steep slope leading up to the pair of hill lochans that sit high on the southern shoulder of Slioch. Nige touches the red button. The flashing R vanishes from the screen. He presses Play to check the recording worked but, even as he slides the camera back into his pocket, a sliver of doubt creeps into his mind.

The department's best practice manual recommends gathering as much evidence as possible and, looking at the flickery video on the camera screen, he thinks it could have been taken anywhere, right next to the road even.

He looks around. The cloud has lifted and the summit of Sgurr Dubh is almost free of mist. There's even a hint of sun brightness again behind the grey sky. Through a tear in the curtains of cloud he glimpses the summit of Slioch; the top two hundred metres are white with fresh snow.

Nige picks up the heavy rucksack and strides on up into the corrie, renewed energy and vigour driving him forward. He sees the minister looking at a video of the suspect climbing up through the snow. He sees the camera panning across a line of snow-capped peaks. Just like that video Gina got a couple of years back of the wheelchair-user snowboarding. It got her promoted, was the gossip around the office. And Nige's desperate to get above Level 5. He wants a Level 7 job before he's the wrong side of forty-five. And now Gina's retiring...

So he pushes on up the hillside, drops of sweat running down his face while the straps of the rucksack cut red weals into his shoulders. He's careful to keep the suspect well ahead of him. He could be just another hillwalker but it's better the target is unaware of him. He hears Gina's voice in his head, 'Remember, you can't speak to a suspect – not without a CHIS.'

Nige doesn't plan on wrecking his chances of promotion by landing the department on the receiving end of a claim for a breach of Article 8 of the European Convention on Human Rights.

In places the path up to the lochans is a storm channel cut feet-deep into the hillside. His boots slither on sliding scree and gravel. From time to time he glances down at the iPhone in his hand. Once or twice, rather disconcertingly, the map screen has gone blank and a message flashed up: *Weak GPS Signal*. It only lasts a minute or so though, before the reassuring blue circle reappears.

After half an hour of sweaty toil he reaches the first of the hill lochans at the foot of the summit ridge of Slioch. Broken crags run down into the tormentil-fringed pool. Grey-green cladonia lichen grows among the rocks at the edge of the lochan: a little piece of the Arctic tundra in Scotland.

Through the clear water he can see the black peaty bed of the lochan. The wind is stronger here than down in the corrie. It whips up little wavelets on the grey sheet of water and drives the cloud across the hillside fifty feet above the surface of the lochan.

A line of eroded steps leads up a steep grassy slope into the mist. The suspect is out of sight, hidden by the low cloud and, inside Nigel's head, Annie Lennox is singing *Here Comes the Rain Again*.

The mountainside above the lochans is far steeper than he expected; he feels the leaden weight of the rucksack. He feels the attraction of gravity pulling him backwards off the hill. The gravity of Slioch pulling him in, the gravity of the planet pulling him out. If he falls, he'll be accelerated down the mountainside like a ball bearing down a runway in that physics experiment they did in sixth form.

Behind the stones at the edge of the path and among the blades of grass, flakes of snow have accumulated into miniature drifts on the leeward side of the tufts of fir club-moss that grow in the cracks between the rocks. Another two hundred feet and he's able to follow the line of bootprints in the centimetre-deep snow covering the path:

left
boot

two
neat

front
paws

two
neat

back
paws

right
boot

Nige stops and takes a couple of digital photos of the line of prints in the snow. Clicks a couple more pictures of rocks and mist for background. Puts the camera back in his pocket, then checks the GPS screen on the iPhone.

No way?!

Nige screws up his face as he looks in disbelief at the phone in his hand as the mist now flecked with tiny granules of snow flies past. A message in a white font on a blue background has appeared on the screen: Warning! Low Battery. Connect to Charger.

HOW CAN IT BE?

He can use the phone for two whole days at work before it needs charging. It was fully charged when he left the hotel this morning. He'd only played five minutes of Angry Birds and sent a couple of texts from the bar, before he heard the police sirens on the road outside.

A new message flashes insistently in the centre of the screen:

Warning! 5% of battery remaining. Connect to Charger.

Oh right, thinks Nige, here at 2,500 feet up a Scottish mountain. Maybe if he goes and looks behind that boulder over there there'll be a three-pin socket he can plug it into.

He's still got the map though and an expensive Silva compass the shop assistant in Pennine Outdoor persuaded him to buy. Trouble is he's not sure which way up to put it on the map. He started reading the instructions in the hotel bedroom but then *Britain's Got Talent* came on and now he's not sure he can remember all the stuff about lining up the red lines on the compass with the blue lines on the map.

What the hell? He wants pictures of the suspect on top of a snowy mountain. The technology has let him down but all he has to do is follow the line of boot- and pawprints in the snow to the summit of Slioch (it can't be far now?). Once he's down below the snowline there's a clear path all the way back to the car.

While these thoughts and images are processed by electrical signals, chemical neurotransmitters and synapses in Nige's brain, the last of the battery's power, flattened by the near-freezing temperature at 800 metres, dissipates, the screen goes black and the iPhone in Nige's hand dies.

'Bollocks!'

He curses the mist and the rocks and the snow-clad mountainside as he shoves the phone deep into the inner pocket of his jacket.

§

It wasn't how he thought his last Munro would be. He'd kind of imagined people gathered around the cairn. A last Munro party. A handsome, dark-haired man in a kilt sat on the cairn playing the bagpipes. Half bottles of whisky produced from rucksacks and passed around as someone brings out a cake in the shape of the mountain. A hipflask engraved with the date. Then back to a warm, cosy Highland hotel; drinks in the bar, a shower, a meal, a speech, champagne in an ice bucket.

Serious reality check: it's just him and the dog and the cairn in the mist. He bends down and kisses the summit cairn of Slioch and then kisses the top of Tyke's head, in that order. He takes a slug of Aunty Nora's Glenfiddich hoarded for this day. The whisky burns in his throat as he toasts the cairn and the dog and the mist and the snow. 'Ah done it pups! Ah fuckin done it!' He punches the air. 'Ah fuckin done it but! Two hundred and eighty-two Munros, pups!' He hugs Tyke. 'Mickey Bell – A Compleat Munroist,' he says in his posh voice.

Mickey Bell finally done something with his shitty life.

Two hundred and eighty-one times before he's had this moment: knowing he's going to make it to the top. Fifty metres to go. He remembers climbing Ben Lomond. Drenched in sweat, gasping for breath, reaching the eroded bare rock of the summit, punching the air and silently shouting:

'Mickey Bell – one! HIV – nil!'

He sits on a flat stone with his back to the cairn eating a Spar tuna and sweetcorn sandwich washed down with slugs of whisky as the first heavy flakes of snow start to fall.

He delves into his rucksack and produces a small, cylindrical, silver package. Tyke stretches his neck forward and sniffs.

'Stay!'

Tyke sits obediently as Mickey unpeels the layers of cling-film and silver foil.

'Congratulations! Gie me a paw—,'

The dog hesitates.

'Whit's wrang wi' you now dog? Eh? Whit's bothering you?'

The Dog: I'll tell you what's bothering me, MAISTER (sarcastic like). *There's someone following us, that's what, ya dozy cunt, tae parliamo Glesga, so to speak. And I dinnae think it's cos he's after your body either. No like that waiter you shagged. He's trouble, maister, I'll tell you that for nothing.*

'Tyke – gie me a paw or I'll niver play stick with you again.'

And, as Tyke reluctantly lifts his paw, Mickey hands the dog a cold cooked sausage.

MICKEY: I can remember the magazines in the waiting room see, old copies of OK and Hello magazine. I was kindae half expecting, half dreading the result. I lay there hearing the plastic phials of blood dropping into the foil tray but I jist could never hae imagined how things would end up – the way the cards of time and chance would fall – I expected tae be deid no standing on top of a mountain in the snow. Its funny but, sometimes yer life turns on an instant. Whit like would ma life have been if the virus hadnae been there, lurking among the bottles of poppers, the sticky cans of cider and the ashtray of fag ends on the bedside table at four in the morning. Whit like would ma life have been if I hadnae contracted the HUMAN IMMUNODEFICIENCY VIRUS in the dark, hungover half-drunk wee small hours before the buses start tae run? It was the virus done it all, led me up here like. Would Mickey Bell from Drumkirk be standing on the summit of Slioch in the snaw if the virus, and it's still there, ma doctor says, hiding in ma belly, in ma brain and in ma baws – if the virus hadnae led me up here. It's like the particles of virus have changed the world and now, if I look back, I cannae see whit might have been. But you cannae regret the times that have never been. I'm jist happy tae be here alive, on the mountain – the fuckin last one on the list. And right now, in this moment, I wouldnae have ma life any other way. The last two weeks? Aye well – things change. I cannae go back tae being the person I wis before. I'm jist gaunny have tae take the risk, see how the cards fall. So now I'm like, whit's next from the strange hand I've been dealt in life. But you know what, I wouldnae change a thing but. The partyin', the staying up all night, the druggies, the shaggin' Arthur and Martha, the mashheidedness of it all cos it was just like the best fun ever. There's gaunny be changes in ma life – they're comin' soon – they're here now. I cannae go back to the person I wis before. I cannae go back to Glasgow. Cannae go back tae the flat but. Thing is tho' I feel like at last I've achieved something in ma life. I feel like I've got some of the old self-confidence back. The old like I-feel-OK-inside. Self-esteem they call it. Mine's was like laying face down in the gutter. But like now I jist feel like I've been and done something wi' my life. The strange roads I've followed tae end up here on Slioch at five o'clock on a Sunday afternoon but. The viral particles in ma blood have changed me but the mountains have changed me more. The raindrops and the heather and the air at three thousand feet – sometimes these days I only feel alive if I'm on a mountain. It's the only fuckin thing that's real and matters. See climbing – it's like getting wasted and sex and a night in the pub wi' friends. The rest o' it's all shite. Like the man said: choose a life… choose a motor… choose a fuckin big television. Fuck but I'm sitting here on top of a snowy mountain and there's like £42 quid in my wallet and where the fuck am I gaunny sleep tonight? but that disnae matter cos I've fuckin done somethin' big. I can stand on ma ain two feet now and look the rest of yous in the eye. Ah've got nothing but I feel minted. Fuck the cunts at the DSS! Fuck being on benefits! Fuck it! Fuck it! Fuck it! I'm gaunny be independent but.

He sits with his back to the cairn, double hoods up against the cold and mist. As the snow flakes form a white coat on Tyke's fur he takes the Munros Book out his rucksack and opens it at page 202, section 14, Loch Maree to Loch Broom. He places a slightly shaky blue biro tick next to Slioch; 980m; (OS Sheet 19; 005688); *from Gaelic sleigh, a spear*.

Breathe in, breathe out.

Step by step, one foot in front of another.

The page is ticked.

The mountain climbed.

Every hill in the book has its own gravitational field. Once they called it the attraction of mountains and an astronomer built an observatory high on Schiehallion and at night followed the stars through his zenith telescope. Humans are sixty percent water, gravity moves the world's oceans; Mickey's cerebral fluid a rain drop in comparison. The attraction of mountains has changed him for ever.

He knows he won't die, not of AIDS. It's after the war now and he feels like the veteran of Vietnam returning to the small industrial town at the edge of the Rockies.

He's come through it.

He's survived the war of the virus.

And sometimes these days he has a disconcerting sense of seeing how the world works; an uncomfortable feeling of being able to see the binary digits behind the infinitely vast screen in the sky. Where once how the world worked was a mystery to him, now he can almost see the algorithms.

But what to do with his life, with his days in the world? With this life he thought he might never have? A man's time in the world no longer the eternity of childhood he once saw sitting on the front step by the garden gate, watching an insect crawl across the paving slab at his feet. Sitting at the summit of Slioch as the snow falls late afternoon in mid-September, Mickey searches for a way back into the world, a way to stop running, a way home.

And there's regret tinging the edge of joy on the top of this, his last summit; the Munros such a part of his life for so many days and weeks and months and years. All that rock under his boots: schist, gneiss, sandstone, quartzite, granite, gabbro, basalt, dolerite. Suddenly so much of life is behind him: the days that are gone, the days that will come no more.

The world on the top of a mountain is very simple.

It's the world down there beneath the clouds he's frightened of.

The heavy snowflakes are forming a layer of white on the dog's shaggy coat. He spins the plastic dial of the compass, scrolls through the pages on the GPS, selects Tracbac and a reassuring arrow appears, pointing the way back down.

The hills he's climbed an unseen panorama in front of his eyes. If the mist were to be suddenly swept away like when the screen goes blurry and then clear in the flashback sequence of an old black and white Bette Davis picture, the view from the summit cairn would stretch from the Summer Isles to Sanda Mor and across the sea to the Outer Hebrides to An Teallach, Beinn Chlaidheimh, Beinn Tarsuinn, Sgurr

Ban, Beinn Dearg, Meall Ceapraichean and Mullach Coire Mhic Fhearchair.

Beneath the cloud, down through the mist three thousand feet below lie Loch Maree and its islands. The campervans and the motorbikes, the cars and the coaches move slowly along the lochside road. September and the rowan berries beginning to glow and the heather in bloom turning whole hillsides purple.

The dark-haired barman dries another glass and reaches up to place it on the shelf behind the bar in the Kinlochewe Hotel. The crofter drives his three cattle half a mile along the main road. A car and caravan, a people carrier and a motorbike crawl along behind as he waves his stick and shouts at the beasts.

Seven stone steps lead down to the sea from the white-painted lighthouse at Rubha Reidh. The ocean swell washes across the slanting sandstone slabs. The gannets plummet into the white surf.

On a rock on the beach at Sanda Mhor, Tamara sits, reading *Comet in Moominland*, her Harris Tweed jacket buttoned up tight. *The Rough Guide to Greece* lies in the sand at her feet. The old climber cycles his commuter bike under the beech trees on the narrow road down to Incheril. The black rubber, wooden-framed canoe lies hidden among the roots of the ancient oaks at Furnace.

The three women reach the bothy by the ruins at the foot of Beinn Dronaig on the reedy shore of Loch Cruoshie. Mr Fuk and the bikers ride in convoy down the A1, heading south past Alnwick and Alnmouth and Bamburgh while the sand dunes on Holy Island shine white in the sun.

Dougal Anderson stands in the mist on a slab of gabbro seamed with basalt high above the Bealach a'Bhasteir, his hand gripping a terrified client by the wrist as he leads her, head down, off the west ridge of Sgurr nan Gillean.

Zelda dusts the Lalique vase on the mantelpiece in the cluttered front room on the corner of Langside Road. The leaves on the beech trees in the grounds of Waystone House rustle gently in the breeze as Carmen d'Apostolini gazes at the screen of her laptop. In the kitchen the cook chops carrots and onions for soup for the last patient of the deserted AIDS hospice.

The minute hand reaches five on the town clock in the square in Gdansk and the apostles appear from a wooden studded door while the skeleton Death rings out the hours. Elena opens the curtains to let the sunshine into the empty room while she clears the last of the books into a cardboard box in the nursing home where the distant Campsies are a green line beyond the towerblocks.

In Whitehall the black horse swishes its tail as the Japanese tourists take photos of the red-coated soldiers in shiny breastplates. Behind the black front door the Prime Minister and his spin doctor flick through the newspapers on the coffee table. The hands on Big Ben across the brown waters of the river move to one minute to the hour.

The oil rigs rust in the North Sea. A snell wind cuts along Loch Broom as the ballot boxes are loaded onto the ferry in the harbour at Ullapool. The Kinlochewe River empties into the sea under the stone bridge by the black rocks. The wild salmon turns back at the edge of the Arctic ice sheet.

Ryan, travel bag over his shoulder, slides the car key into the driver's door of the beat-up, bright orange Citroen Saxo by the square of low stone cottages at Luss. Jonnie sits on a plastic chair next to the photocopier in the day room, waiting for the volunteer psychology student who pushes the library trolley. In Glencoe the whitewashed cottage at the foot of the Blackmount stands empty and padlocked, waiting for the climbers in the dusk.

The heron flies at treetop height along the edge of the

woods by the River Ruaidh. The siskins flash yellow between the green branches. Behind the windows of the powerhouse the brown peaty water cascades through the turbines. The collies at the farm at Keppoch lie sleeping at the end of their chains.

Behind the Stron Malcolm feeds the hens from a plastic bucket. Beside the Cour the bullfinches and yellowhammers sing in the birch trees by the stone cairn. A pool of sorrow lies around the grave in the woods. The barn at Torbreac is empty now and the waves still lap the white sands of Achmelvich.

The pedals of the bike revolve slowly as the balding long-haired man in filthy combat trousers and worn leather jacket cycles down Byres Road. And at Lindertis, in a quiet corner of the overgrown garden of the demolished mansion Sir Hugh Munro lies in his grave.

'Fuck's sake, dog!' Mickey jumps to his feet. 'Look at all the snow! It's a fuckin white-out! Time tae get the fuck oot of here, pups. Which way is it again?'

Mickey crouches down and puts his arm around Tyke. The heavy snowflakes lie thickly on the dog's fur. He hugs the dog tight, pulls his gloves on, gives the cairn one last, lingering touch, then picks up his rucksack and walks through the snow, leaving a trail of bootprints behind him as he begins his long descent to the world below.

£2&&&***********___________?? Page 202: Slioch 980m. The/my last tick! I am compleat and annotated. At last, at last I feel the raindrops brush my open pages... I feel the cool breeze from the snowfields. The cold mountain air banishing the fousty smell of

the charity shop. I have lived, been bound, printed,typeset and published just for this.
Ah! But I feel my pages swell with damp, my binding loosening, the glue in my spine dissolving... I need the dry wood of the bookshelves again–
*##! My back cover's falling off
My back cover's falling off
[screams]
Put me back on the shelf!
Put me back on the shelf!#####888"″″

On the rock-strewn summit of Slioch, where the soil is thin and the protective snow cover frequently blown away by the black wind that sweeps down from the Arctic Circle, hardy species of plants are to be found growing. Plants that are adapted to withstand both freeze and thaw. Plants that grow prostrate on the ground or in cushions and low tussocks. Alpine clubmoss garbhag an t-sleibhe is one such plant, its spiky leaves and stems like miniature conifer branches, like something left behind from a primeval, lost world.

For the last twenty minutes Nige has been gripped by a growing sense of unease. Just as the ground at last begins to flatten out, at the top of the steep slope above the lochans, the line of footsteps in the snow fades. He stops and looks around him. The wind has blown the snow into crenellated ridges like the icing on a home-made Christmas cake.

Snowflakes whirl through the air, spinning wildly, trembling, careering, spiralling. They land on Nigel's sleeve and melt into his Gore-Tex jacket. The loneliness of the mountain closes in around him as he sees the line of bootprints he's been following fill with spindrift snow crystals whipped along by the wind. He lost sight of the suspect twenty minutes ago; knows he should've turned back, down in the corrie.

In life, in his forty-four years on the planet, he's never experienced this degree of solitude before. Nothing has prepared him for the cold and isolation and emptiness of the summit of Slioch in winter. The loneliness of the mountain is like a physical presence brooding over the ice-encrusted rocks and the frozen stems of deergrass.

When he opened the bedroom curtains of childhood, the snow that had fallen overnight had created a magical landscape outside the window, coating the lamp posts and rooftops and cars and pavements in white: snow for making snowballs and snowmen and sledging.

But the snow on the summit of Slioch is a wilder, more elemental, primeval kind of snow. In the mountain snow is a little of the Arctic in Scotland, a lingering shade of the faded power of the ice age that gripped the land ten thousand years ago.

He takes the map out from the side pocket of his jacket, where the long-haired shop assistant with the beard at Pennine Outdoor in Leeds showed him to keep it. Only three days ago but it seems like another lifetime now. The outdoor shop with its gleaming displays of walking poles, ice axes and climbing boots, the fitted carpets, the blast of warmth from the fan heaters above the doors. Like another planet, thinks Nige, looking despondently around at the ice world where he now finds himself.

On the cover of OS sheet 19 Gairloch and Ullapool is a photo of the beach at Sanda Mhor under a cobalt-blue sky. The tide is out and the sand has been raked into rills and streams by the receding tide. One broilingly hot fortnight in Crete Nige read *Touching the Void*. On the scorching beach while the Meltemi whipped the sand around, he sat in blue nylon swimming trunks on a white towel borrowed from the apartment, reading Joe Simpson's account of crawling down a glacier in the Peruvian Andes. Looking down at the cover of the map, Nige senses the reversal of situation; the change of circumstances.

He struggles to unfold the map with gloved hands. Drops of melting snow from his hood soak into the paper, blurring the brown contour lines, green forests and blue streams. Nige frowns and trys to think logically. He reasons he must be on the flat ground at around 900m roughly 250 feet below the summit of Slioch. According to the map the trig point should be over to the left a bit, about half an inch, whatever that is on the ground in metres. He wonders what the blue squares on the map mean. He attempts to unfold it to see the scale along the bottom edge but the wind twists and flaps and tries to snatch the map from his hands.

Confusingly, a little to the north-east of the trig point he can see the spot height 981m hidden among the black squiggly crags and cliffs on the precipitous north-west face of Slioch, drawn by the draughtsmen of the Ordnance Survey with sharp, delicate inkpens to the background hum of computers in their warm, quiet offices in Southampton.

Well, the trig point's got to be at the summit of the mountain and if he can find the top he'll know where he is, he reasons, as he folds the map up as best he can. Already it's lost the crisp, sharp folds it had in the outdoor shop and the fibres of paper are beginning to soften. Wrinkles have formed and small holes are starting to appear where the vertical and horizontal folds intersect.

He shoves the soggy map back into his pocket and sets off towards the trig point. He places his feet carefully. The exposed surfaces of the rocks are slippery and the voids between them filled with soft snow.

'Don't want to sprain your ankle up here, Nige old son.'

The voice in his head again.

He walks for just over ten minutes, the ground rising gently as he approaches the summit. He squints into the blizzard, looking out for one of the friendly, white, concrete pillars he remembers from the Pennine Way.

Then the ground starts to level off again.

This doesn't feel right.

Where the hell's the bloody trig point?

The air is full of spinning white snowflakes and there's an empty howl on the edge of the wind. Suddenly a roaring updraft: a twisting column of spindrift stings his face. He can barely see three feet ahead but animal instinct, the baby inside him crawling across the glass floor in Piaget's psychology of perception experiment, senses he is standing on the edge of a void. Below his feet are only snow and ice and the screaming wind.

He steps quickly backwards, stomach turning over in testicle-tightening terror. Somehow he's missed the trig point in the mist and snow. He's standing on the edge of the cliffs at the top of the north-west face of the mountain. Below his feet the broken crags fall away through the cloud to the lochan-studded moorland two thousand feet below.

The cold is beginning to slow and blur his thought processes. In his mildly hypothermic state there's no doubt in his mind.

'Jesus Christ!' he says out loud and the wind tears his words away.

There's no doubt in his mind. The suspect must have plunged to his death over the cliffs in the white-out.

Nigel shudders.

An image flashes into his brain: climbers with beards melting snow in a pan on a gas stove. Must have been something on telly – that programme about Everest maybe?

Now he's stopped moving, he notices how cold he is.

'Only one thing for it, Nige old son,' he mutters to himself,

'Get the tent up and wait till the weather clears and you can get down off this godforsaken mountain.'

He retreats back the way he came. The malicious grey wind hasn't quite had time to obliterate his footsteps entirely. In a little hollow where dry granules of snow have accumulated into a drift, Nige lays down the heavy rucksack. With his boots and gloved hands he clears away the snow. With frozen fingers he fumbles with the straps and drawstring of the rucksack, takes out the stove (still with its price tag on it) and tucks the campa mat and thermo-rest under the rucksack lest the malign spirit that lurks in the icy wind spin them away over the cliffs.

At least he learned something during those two traumatic, gruelling weeks in the Marines. He struggles to fit the slippery aluminium poles together with clumsy gloved hands then takes his mittens off. He stands with his back to the wind, shakes out the flysheet of the tent, locates the doorway and weighs the back down with two snow-encrusted boulders. With numb hands he pushes red pole to red sleeve, green pole to green sleeve.

Suddenly there's a tent where moments earlier there was just a heap of silicone-coated nylon flysheet and tangled guy lines.

'More rocks – Quick! Before the whole bloody thing takes off,' he mutters to himself.

He hammers in a tent peg using a piece of shattered quartzite for a mallet. It goes an inch into the ground then buckles and snaps. He moves the guyline six inches to the left and the peg slides into the half-frozen earth.

A combination of rocks and aluminium pegs keep the tent tethered to the top of Slioch as Nige heaps snow in a low wall around the edge of the flysheet. The open door flap cracks in the wind. Nigel crawls inside, drags the rucksack after him and zips the door flap shut.

Then he seals himself into the inner tent. He's escaped the windchill. Drops of condensation form on the yellow nylon fabric. He unrolls the campa mat and breathes deep dizzy-making gulps of oxygen to inflate the thermo-rest. The sleeping bag expands out of its stuff-sack. Nige unlaces his boots. Grey lumps of slush melt onto the groundsheet. He zips himself into his sleeping bag and, cocooned in a warm fug of condensation, exhausted, he drifts into sleep while outside a million crystals of spindrift blown on the wind pile up against the little yellow tent.

In the first dazed moments of waking, staring at the yellow fabric four inches from his face, Nige can't remember where he is. The walls of the inner tent breathe in and out in irregular gasps like a marathon runner at the finishing line. For a moment he thinks he's in the hotel in Kinlochewe or asleep on the sofa at home. He looks at his watch. He rubs his eyes and sits up.

He's eaten nothing since the scrambled eggs and smoked salmon for breakfast at the Kinlochewe Hotel. He pulls the cooking stove and pots out of the rucksack, finds the chicken curry sachet, tears it open and squeezes the runny, yellow contents into the medium-sized saucepan. He unzips the inner tent to a blast of icy air. He unfolds the legs of the gas stove, places it in the snow in the tiny porch of the tent and screws on the gas cylinder. The piezo ignitor click click clicks. Heat from the gas flame warms the tent. In two minutes the chicken curry is bubbling around the edges. He eats from the pan, greedily scooping the curry sauce up with pieces of naan bread. He finds the sticky toffee pudding and heats it up in the small pan. The sauce is hot, the lumps of sponge still cold in his mouth but it's food on a mountain top.

He lies in his sleeping bag, eating squares of chocolate

and turning the handle of the wind-up digital radio. But the sound of the theme music from *The Archers* emanating from the little yellow tent in the gathering darkness, when some time later he ventures outside to urinate, adds immeasureably to his sense of isolation up here on the mountain top, three thousand feet above the world.

He feels lonelier with the radio on than alone with the sound of the wind and the flapping flysheet of the tent; the south-of-England accents of the announcers so distant-sounding up here in the snow and ice. When *Moneybox Live* comes on, he twists the blue plastic dial on the side of the radio but gets only static and faint Scottish country dance music. He switches the radio off and listens to the patter of the snowflakes falling on the tent, quite different to the sound of raindrops.

Outside, a line of bird tracks and a solitary white feather among the rocks lead to a drift of snow fifty metres away from the little yellow tent on the top of Slioch. The ptarmigan is dug into the snowdrift, insulated from the cold like a climber in a snowhole. A bird of the high mountain tops, she lives her whole life around the 2,500 feet contour line.

Only the fury of a winter storm will drive her down into the relative shelter of Coire na Sleaghaich. The most arctic of Scottish birds, she lives most of the year on the summit of Slioch, surviving the winter by feeding on heather and blaeberry shoots protruding from the snow. Like lichen-covered rock in summer, white as snow in winter, the ptarmigan is perfectly camouflaged.

And the shades of history linger up here among the ice and snow. In the panelled library at Downing Hall, Thomas Pennant dips his quill pen in the inkpot on the wooden desk and writes:

'In winter, their plumage is of a pure white, the colour

of the snow, in which they bury themselves in heaps, as a protection from the rigorous air.'

At ten to midnight, Nige gives the handle another 100 turns and switches the radio on to listen to the weather forecast. The ptarmigan burrowed into the snowdrift fifty yards away hears the chimes of Big Ben for the first time as it bongs twelve from the little yellow tent half-buried in the snow. Illuminated from within by an LED head torch, the tent looks like a giant Chinese lantern fallen to earth on the mountain top, its waxy candle still flickering away in the dark.

The news is dominated by the impending referendum on Scottish independence. Nigel's ultimate boss, the UK government's secretary of state for social security, John Fraser-Smythe, has been speaking to business leaders in Perth, the Fair City once represented by Winston Churchill in an era which, seen from a twenty-first century perspective, seems to belong to a lost world of Scottish politics. Tory MPs in Scotland being almost as extinct as dinosaurs.

As Still Better Together's lead in the opinion polls has shrunk, the Unionists have taken a relentlessly negative tone. The secretary of state's speech is the standard Project Fear message. Words like *loss*, *worry* and *uncertainty* repeated over and over again.

The supporters of the Union, regardless of their politics left or right, are the more affluent in society. People who've profited out of the present constitutional set-up and see no reason to change it.

The Yes campaign, determined to stay positive and upbeat, have been picking up a lot of under-the-radar votes from the dispossessed and the marginalised in Scottish society. From people on benefits, carers, students and teenagers and from the people who crowd around the chiller cabinet in the supermarket where the reduced items are offered for sale stickered with yellow price labels. The people hit hardest by the austerity policy of the UK government, by the bedroom tax and the cuts in benefits. The governments of the '60s and '70s called it social security. Now the London politicians like to call it Welfare.

People in work doing OK don't like to think about it, but they are only ever a GP and a consultant appointment away from ending up on out-of-work sickness benefits, struggling to exist in a shadowy world of ATOSA medical examinations and work capability assessments.

The London government cares nothing for the dispossessed and marginalised in society. They have gnawed away at people's empathy for those in less fortunate circumstances than their own. And if we lose our sense of empathy then what is left of society?

Supporters of Scottish independence have coalesced around the idea of a Scottish Common Weal, a concept first put forward by a left-leaning think tank. They always show the same fuzzy clip on TV: men in black-framed glasses with long sideburns and boiler suits crowd around the speaker. The cranes stand immobile in the background, silent onlookers in the shipyard on the wide muddy river. A lock of Brylcreem-ed hair falls across the forehead of the leader of the work-in as he speaks.

The occupation of the shipyard seen as a crucial event in modern Scottish history and one that seems to be influencing the independence debate. The think tank named after the shipyard workers' leader has published a paper outlining the principles of a Scottish Common Weal.

An independent Scotland, they say, will be organied like the Scandinavian countries. An emphasis will be put on good quality, secure, well paid jobs and decent rates of benefit for those out of work. All paid for by higher taxation. As he listens to the radio, it occurs to Nige that the debate around

Scottish independence is less about flags and nationalism and more about social justice and how to create a fair and equitable society.

The UK government of multi-millionaires has no qualms when it comes to welfare handouts for its backers in the zombie banks and the financiers of the City of London. It has created an edge-of-the-cliff Britain where those in work survive but those who lose their jobs, through misfortune or ill health, are immediately plunged into an abyss of debt, poverty and trips to the food bank.

Such is the state of the land after three hundred years of the union between Scotland and England.

As the gap in the opinion polls between the Yes campaign and Still Better Together has narrowed, a mounting sense of panic has filled the offices of the London government. In Whitehall the sun still shines on the red-coated soldiers in their shiny silver breastplates and helmets and plumes. The black horses at the gates of Whitehall still swish their tails as the Japanese tourists take photos. The crowds of Italian students still peer through the railings of Buckingham Palace and the black tulips still bloom in Regent's Park. But, though the sun still shines on the Cenotaph, inside the buildings of Whitehall, not since Charles Edward Stuart and his Highland army reached Derby, three days' march from the capital, has Scotland caused such a sense of mounting panic among England's ruling elite.

The Mayor of London hadn't helped matters with his attack on whingeing Jocks and his plan for London to become an independent city state with armed border patrols around the M25. For the mayor did not seem to grasp that the inhabitants of London would still need food to be grown and livestock reared in the fields of England if the people of the great city were not to live on money alone.

Rumours had surfaced on Twitter of a blazing row in the

corridors of St James's Palace after a private dinner hosted by the Prince of Wales. The heir to the throne of the Disunited Kingdom was overheard berating the Prime Minister. Not since the Prince Regent taunted George III over the loss of England's North American colonies had the portraits of aristocrats hanging in the corridors of St James's Palace witnessed such an unseemly shouting match.

Reports of secret meetings between the American ambassador and senior figures in the Scottish National Party further fuelled the febrile atmosphere of paranoia swirling through Whitehall as late summer turned to early autumn and the leaves of the birch trees turned from orange to gold and the deer sought the high ground.

The radio fades to a quiet crackle of static. Nige gives the handle another twenty turns. The BBC's political editor is explaining what is at stake. The United Kingdom faces losing ten per cent of her population, a third of her territorial landmass and all her nuclear weapons.

The predicament the British Prime Minister finds himself in is the subject of a certain amount of mirth in the corridors of the Elysée Palace. And when the Chancellor takes a stroll under the lime trees on Unter den Linden, the German leader finds the policies of the Scottish National Party much closer to her own Christian Democrats than to those of the Conservative Party, which in much of Europe is increasingly viewed as akin to Rochester's mad wife locked in the attic, with the British Prime Minister cast in the role of Grace Poole.

Whatever the result of the referendum, concludes the BBC's reporter in Edinburgh, it seems clear the tide of history is running with the Scottish National Party. Win or lose the referendum, Scottish independence is the issue that won't go away.

Nige falls asleep as the newsreader's soothing tones fade into the sound of flapping flysheet and the gentle patter of the falling snowflakes.

He awakens with a start fifteen minutes later just as the newsreader is saying, '—and now over to Darren Bett for the weather forecast.'

'Thanks, Dan – I'll start as usual with a look at yesterday's weather – the highest temperature was recorded at Aviemore in the Scottish Highlands where the mercury soared to 24 degrees centigrade and the most hours of sunshine were on the Island of Tiree. But, I'm afraid to say, the Indian summer, northern and western areas of Scotland have been enjoying, is well and truly over now. Snow is expected over the Scottish hills and there may even be some snowfall at lower levels in more northern parts. I'll begin as usual with London and the south-east of England.'

Over the next four minutes the weather forecaster works his way up from the south of England through the Midlands, skips across the Bristol Channel into Wales before reaching north-east England and then jumping across the Irish Sea to Northern Ireland.

'And finally,' says the weather forecaster, 'to Scotland.'

'Now, as I mentioned at the beginning of this forecast, parts of Scotland have been experiencing unseasonably high temperatures, however, over the next 24 hours, a band of cold weather will sweep in from the north-west bringing the first snow of winter to the Scottish mountains—'

Nige pulls the sleeping bag hood over his head and zips it up to his chin. He falls into a fitful sleep, awakened every two hours by the cold ground aching into his hip. He turns over and dozes again. Around 6 am, as the first pale grey light brightens the sky over A'Mhaighean and Ruadh Stac Mor, Nige dreams to the sound of the flapping flysheet and the gentle patter of the falling snowflakes like a thousand spiders dancing on the tent roof.

Monday

inside a victorian gentleman's tweeds

The snowflakes have ceased to fall from a sky the colour of grey lead. The mist has lifted to around the 2,500 foot contour line and for the first time in the fifteen hours since he reached the top of Slioch, Nige can see a wintry Loch Maree far below through white tears in the cloud.

Hastily stuffing random items into his rucksack but not even attempting to take down the frozen tent half buried in drifted snow, he sets off in the direction he came up onto the mountain top the day before. After fifteen minutes he reaches the top of the steep snow slope.

'This is definitely right, Nige old son.'

Then he realises he's talking to himself again.

The snow is soft. He can kick steps in it and he can still see Loch Maree three thousand feet below.

Soon though the mist closes in again and a fleck of snow lands on the sleeve of his jacket. Then a bigger flake of snow and another and another. Soon it's snowing heavily and he halts, uncertain of the way down.

While he stands there at the top of the steep snow slope the loneliness of his situation overwhelms him as the snowflakes spin and spiral around. The mountain and the silence are beginning to spook him. He tries not to think of the tales of the coffin roads told him by the dark-haired barman at the Kinlochewe Hotel.

In what seems now to have been a life lived a long time ago on a planet far, far away, the weekend before last he'd watched a documentary on Sky about the 1923 Everest expedition. Was Mallory the first to make it to the top before perishing on the descent? He tries not to think about it but the image of Mallory's mummified corpse sitting upright in the snow at the foot of the fall line from the south-west ridge of Everest, just where Reinhold Messner said they'd find it, flashes unbidden into his mind.

At that moment a figure appears out of the mist some fifty metres below him.

Help at last.

Thank God, thinks Nige.

But then: there's something strange about this climber. The figure clambering uphill towards him is clad in a tweed jacket and plus fours with what Nige vaguely recognises from his army days as puttees wound around a large pair of hobnailed boots. The climber wears a balaclava and goggles and is encrusted in hoar frost and carries a three-foot-long Victorian ice axe.

Nige feels a tightness in his chest; little childlike knife-stabs under his sternum. He remembers the framed sepia photos in the bar of the Kinlochewe Hotel. It can't be – but – this apparition looks like Sir Hugh Munro arisen from his grave in the garden of the demolished mansion at Lindertis, roaming the hills again in a bid to compleat a posthumous second round of Munros.

'Calm down, Nige old son,' says the voice inside his head.

But fifteen hours of mild hypothermia and dehydration have clouded his capacity to think logically and he turns and begins to run back up the steep slope, floundering, slipping and falling in the foot-deep powder snow.

He must be hallucinating. He forces himself to stop and look back. The figure is coming after him, waving the long Victorian alpenstock. In blind terror Nige stumbles uphill following the line of footprints back to the yellow tent half-buried in the snow. When he reaches it, he unzips the flysheet and crawls inside then quickly zips it up again while outside the snowflakes rapidly obliterate all trace of his footsteps.

The figure in Victorian dress with the three-foot-long ice axe stops when he reaches the top of the steep snow slope. Out the pocket of his tweed plus fours he pulls out a red spotted hankerchief and wipes his glasses, then checks the antique compass he holds in his Dachstein mitted hand and glances at the fob watch in his ice-encrusted waistcoat.

'Fifteen minutes at 316 degrees north-west,' mutters the apparition. 'Funny, that bloke taking off like that.'

For he is not the ghost of Sir Hugh Munro: he is in fact Mr Alex Roddie, writer of mountain fiction and erstwhile employee of the Carphone Warehouse in Skegness. The author behind the blog *Inside a Victorian Gentleman's Tweeds*, he spends his annual leave days recreating early ascents of Scottish mountains, dressed in period costume.

Mr Alex Roddie has been featured on BBC Radio Scotland and has almost four thousand followers on Twitter. Today he is repeating Lawson and Ling's 1899 ascent of Slioch. Every detail of his Victorian climbing outfit is correct, from his antique compass and canvas knapsack, to his hand-knitted wool socks and voluminous white cotton underpants. If Nige had been less panicked and hypothermic, he might have observed that 'the ghost' was carrying an expensive-looking digital camera with which to record every detail of the recreated climb of 1899 for his blog.

On reaching the summit of Slioch, the ghost fishes in his knapsack for a Mars bar and sits at the cairn, eating a bag of cheese and onion crisps and lamenting the lack of a view. Through the swirling clouds of snowflakes there is little chance of him noticing the yellow tent in a peaty hollow half-buried in a snow drift two hundred metres away.

aw naw, kedgeree

Breakfast at Coulin House is set to be a grander affair than usual this morning towards the end of September when outside the deergrass on the lower slopes of Sgurr Dubh is white with frost and on the track leading up to the Coulin Pass the imprints of dozens of walking boots are frozen solid in the black peaty mud.

Breakfast is served in the dining room. Green and gold tureens are arranged on a Morphy Richards electric hotplate on the long Victorian sideboard adorned with the brass heads of Greek gods. A blue and white coffee pot stands next to a stack of green and gold plates. Not one of the five Victorian dinner services at the lodge is complete. One has saucers but no tea cups. Another has dinner plates but no soup bowls. Side plates are always in short supply.

In the kitchen the part-time housekeeper is making sure breakfast will be a grander affair than usual. She stands at the island unit in the centre of the kitchen with its drawers full of tattered and splattered cook books. Sixty-five years old, she lives with her husband the stalker in the lodge house at the gates by the bridge over the Coulin River with a Jack Russell, two terriers and a placid Weimaraner.

The kitchen is dominated by an enormous country-house-size, blue enamel, diesel-fired Aga with four ovens. The housekeeper's niece is holding a wire grille contraption with four slices of white bread in it. She places it on the hot plate of the Aga. The red needle on the dial on the front of the main oven door sits between 180 and 200 degrees.

'Is that bacon ready yet? No! No! No! Poached eggs, not fried.'

The housekeeper tuts away to herself. 'The First Minister likes a cooked breakfast but he'll need to be watching his cholestrol. I told you that. Here, put another couple of those venison sausages on,' she tells her niece, who's helping out in the big house before she goes back to the University of Dundee to complete the last semester of her degree in ethical hacking.

Secretly the housekeeper is a great admirer of the First Minister. Her employer, Sir Gideon George Oliver Brokenshire, exists under the comforting illusion that his housekeeper and her husband are the last of a dying breed, working class supporters of the Conservative and Unionist Party, 'salt of the earth' types who, in the halcyon days of the 1950s, gave the Tory party a majority of the parliamentary seats in Scotland.

The housekeeper nods along with her employer and his family when they wax nostalgic for the days of Margaret Thatcher's reign, as the port decanter comes round for the third or fourth time. But behind the curtain, in the privacy of the voting booth, she places her cross in the box for the Scottish National Party.

In the dining room the guests are beginning to emerge. The First Minister's spin doctor looks the brightest-eyed as he bounces down the wooden staircase that leads from the first floor landing where the bedrooms are situated, down into the hall where faded floral-patterned sofas encircle a marble fireplace. A smouldering peat fire belches eye-watering smoke into the room, a consequence of down-draught caused by the proximity of the chimney stack to the steep flank of Sgurr Dubh behind the house.

The guests and their host are all a little hungover and sticky-mouthed with tired legs this chilly and overcast September morning with the cloud still low over the mountains of Torridon. They'd started with cocktails at five o'clock. Dinner had been served with the best of Brokenshire's wine cellar: dusty bottles from the back corridor beside the boiler room, the chest freezer and the downstairs toilet.

Really it had been a good night, the spin doctor reflects, and they'd managed to stay off the subject of politics. But, as he'd expected, the Canadian media mogul had remained characteristically inscrutable as to the editorial stance of his Scottish titles on the impending independence referendum.

When the spin doctor enters the dining room, the First Minister is standing beside the Victorian sideboard, pouring coffee, a little shakily, from an elaborate white and gold coffee pot into a floral-patterned green cup on a blue-striped saucer.

He puts the coffee pot down and lifts the lid off a grand-looking blue tureen. A strong smell of smoked fish and boiled egg wafts out as he hastily replaces the lid.

'Christ—' says the First Minister, 'think I'll give the kedgeree a miss this morning.'

The papers won't arrive from Kinlochewe until after they've left at lunchtime, which is probably a blessing, the spin doctor reckons, avoiding screaming headlines about scrounging Jocks and the soaring welfare bill not to mention the imminent independence referendum.

And, indeed, breakfast passes off as harmoniously as dinner the night before. As the housekeeper and her niece begin to clear the dirty dishes through the hatch into the kitchen, Gideon Brokenshire leads the way to the gunroom.

bendo

'Are you all right in there, mate?'

A gloved hand knocks the snow off the sagging flysheet.

Silence.

Then there's a rustling sound from inside the little yellow tent.

Thank fuck, thinks Bendo from Kilmarnock (Instagram profile: paints folks' houses and climbs mountains). He's done 132 Munros and got exactly 150 to go and he'd been shiteing himself because he really didn't want to unzip the tent and find a dead body in it.

But when he does unzip the tent, he is sufficiently concerned about Nigel's condition and hypothermically-challenged frame of mind to immediately get his phone out and check how many bars of signal he's got.

Hands shaking, Bendo opens his first aid kit and skim-reads the laminated *Emergency Procedures: In the Event of an Incident* card he's carried about in the bottom of his rucksack for three years.

The card says he's to keep calm and assess The Situation.

He's to consider The Options.

Should he and the casualty:

A. Descend to safety

B. Take shelter

C. Stay put or

D. Seek help?

Well, the tent is providing shelter, reasons Bendo, so it seems to be a case of options *c* or *d*, *a* is definitely out.

Bendo presses a button on his watch and scrolls through the screens to get a grid reference. He gets the map ready then swipes his finger across his phone, taps the keypad and dials 999.

The signal's breaking up a bit but he can make out, 'Emergency – which service do you require?'

He glances down at the laminated card in his trembling hands and says, 'Police and mountain rescue.'

§

The hissing, fizzing, swirling orange smoke from the flair held aloft in a gloved hand sparks, spins and twists away downwind. Bendo hears the whirring, clattering, thumping blades of the yellow Sea King approaching along Loch Maree long before he can see it. He sets the beam of his head torch to a rapid pulsating flash and turns his face skywards.

The yellow Sea King hovers in the air opposite Slioch, the blaze of its front headlights bathing the wintry summit in white light. Bendo can read the words RAF Rescue on the fuselage. The winchman stands at the open side door of the helicopter, the luminescent stripes on the arms of his flying suit glowing in the fading late afternoon light.

Call Sign 137 climbs another hundred feet until it is directly over the hissing silver-orange flare. The down-draught from the helicopter sends a white plume of spindrift high into the air. Bendo has a brief view of the underside of the aircraft and the spinning tail rotor before the rear floodlight dazzles him.

The pilot steadies the Sea King, aware of the up-draught

from the wind roaring up the icy gullies and crags on the north-west face of Slioch. The red and blue rucksacks and the little yellow tent the only colour on the white, boulder-studded mountain top.

He can't tell where the mountain ends and the sky begins. He has only limited fuel and thirty minutes winch time. He feels the fear of the crew of the Liberator bomber on that dark night in 1944. The war almost over, the Liberator in the darkness over the mountains, losing power, attempting to ditch in the sea off Gairloch, clipping the mountain top and leaving its bomb bay doors there on the mossy summit of Slioch before crashing into the heather moorland above Badachro just a thousand metres short of the sea. The engines lie to this day at the edge of a peaty lochan half in and half out of the water.

Bendo looks up at the Sea King. A figure is sitting on the edge of the open side door, then the spindrift flies into Bendo's eyes, blinding him. When he looks again the figure is being lowered on a cable from the helicopter. The winchman spins in time and space a hundred feet above the snow and ice-encrusted summit of Slioch. Half a minute passes and he's down in the snow.

Nigel stumbles over the icy boulders, dragging his rucksack behind him. The winchman makes a cut-throat gesture with his forefinger and mouthes, 'Leave it!'

But Nige pulls the camera out the top of the rucksack and shoves it in his pocket and with frostbitten fingers pulls clumsily at the zip fastening.

Another two minutes and he's in a climbing harness. His teeth are chattering with cold and fear. The winchman gives him a thumbs-up sign.

'Don't worry, mate,' he shouts, his voice lost in the screaming roar of the Sea King's two massive Rolls Royce Gnome turboshaft engines, 'You could lift a transit van with this.'

He pulls Nige forward and clips him onto the steel cable with a screwgate carabiner. An exchange on walkie-talkies between the mountain rescue team on the hill and the helicopter crew and suddenly Nigel's off the ground, spinning in time and space fifty feet above the snow and ice-plastered summit of Slioch.

He catches a glimpse of the little yellow tent and Bendo standing in the snow, gazing skyward, as the hydraulic hoist hauls him and the winchman up towards the open door of the aircraft.

Suddenly a roaring icy blast buffets the helicopter and throws Nige and the winchman spinning out over the cliffs of Slioch in a sensational vertigo exposure. Lumps of snow fall away from the winchman's boots and spiral thousands of feet down to the dull, grey surface of Loch Maree. Nige shuts his eyes tight.

The helicopter pilot sees the green and white radioactive paint on the needles and the dials in the Liberator's cockpit glowing in the dark. The wrenching, grinding of tearing metal. The terror filling the men, thrown forward as the bomb bay doors were sheared off.

The pilot pushes the throttle forward to steady the Sea King, glancing across at the reassuring green electronic glow of the retro-fitted Cossor GPS as the two men on the winch spin in circles out over the ice cliffs of Slioch.

Nige opens his eyes. Between his snow-encrusted walking boots he can see the islands of Loch Maree and little white horses on the steel grey surface of the loch three thousand feet below. The climbing harness cuts into him, pushing up his Helly Hansen base layer, his Paramo fleece and his red down jacket and exposing bare rolls of his white flabby stomach to the freezing air.

The helicopter stable again, the winch operator presses a green plastic button blackened with thumbprints. The cable holding Nige and the winchman jolts as they're hauled up through the sky towards the open side door of the Sea King.

Nige feels a hot blast of exhaust fumes in his face and his ears fill with the roar of the helicopter's Rolls Royce engines. As several pairs of hands reach out to pull him onto the steel floor of the Sea King, his red down jacket rides up and the camera is squeezed out of his half-unzipped pocket. It tumbles out into the night, bouncing off one of the helicopter's tyres before dropping through the freezing air for two hundred metres and smashing onto a rocky schist outcrop at around the 2,700 feet contour line. Fragments of the Leica explode across the mossy cliff face. The memory card pops out and drops into a crevice in a gully of shattered quartzite scree where it comes to rest on a blue-green cushion of moss campion. A few moments pass then a spider scuttles across the square of black plastic with its gleaming gold-plated contacts. When the snow melts in a sudden thaw at the beginning of October, the cliff runs with water and the memory card is washed down into a dripping crack in the cliff face where it will lie until the next ice age.

the grey one

Liathach the Grey One looks down silently. She wears a necklace of crags and a veil of scree swept across her heart of stone. The man and dog on her lower slopes like the brush of a mayfly. The petty disputes and battles of men are nothing to the Grey One. She has seen far mightier warriors than these men in suits and black motor cars. For the Grey One remembers the great Cuchullin brought to nought; Cuchullin who once hunted on the mountainside with his mighty hounds Bran and Sceolan.

scotch on the rocks

Where the carefully tended lawn in front of Coulin House gives way to heather moorland, a dry peaty footpath leads off through the ling towards a long, low, flat boulder that lies like a giant's tweed cap in the heather half a mile from the house. Some two hundred yards beyond the low, flat boulder stands a tin silhouette of a stag; shiny metal gleams through the faded paint, much dented by rifle bullets.

Gideon Brokenshire in tweed plus fours and deerstalker, the Canadian media mogul in a powder-blue tracksuit, body-warmer and baseball cap, the spin doctor in Barbour coat and green wellies, the ghillie in camouflage Gore-Tex waterproofs and the First Minister resplendent in sheepskin-lined car coat, blue blazer, saltire-patterned tie and garish tartan trews. The four men surround the strangely flat, coffee-table-like boulder on the level moorland at the foot of the Coulin Pass.

On the flat boulder, a little precariously, it seems to the spin doctor, stands the Derbyshire Tantalus on eighteenth-century walnut legs, slightly gammy now from nearly a hundred years of damp West Highland air and the high humidity of Coulin House. The glass doors of the tantalus are gleaming. The housekeeper's niece has even had a go at the stained green leather on the fold-down door at the front of the cabinet where half a dozen crystal glasses and an ice bucket stand on a silver tray, glinting in the pale

September light. In front of the tumblers stands an antique glass decanter two thirds full of an amber liquid the colour of the River Coulin in spring.

'Damn good stuff,' declares Brokenshire, taking the glass stopper out the decanter. 'Fifty-year-old Macallan – a bottle went for $10,000 in the States last year. Scotch on the rocks anyone?'

He raises his glass to the First Minister who chinks his glass with the ghillie and then the spin doctor.

'Sláinte!'

Brokenshire drinks then deposits his empty glass on the green leather surface of the Derbyshire Tantalus. The walnut cabinet wobbles slightly on the granite seamed with mica boulder as the ghillie hands Brokenshire and the media mogul a rifle each.

'Winchester – bloody good piece of kit,' says Brokenshire, looking approvingly at the grey gunmetal in his hands.

'Reminds me of my army days – popping the Argies.'

The First Minster winces then takes another sip of fifty-year-old Macallan. Brokenshire's right about one thing, he thinks. It's bloody good whisky.

Sir Gideon George Oliver Brokenshire raises the rifle to his shoulder and puts his eye to the sights. The crack of the rifle shot echoes around the sullen, brooding mountains. A puff of smoke, an explosion of paint flakes and the deer-shaped target has a new dent one inch above the stag's eye.

The rifle shots make the silence in between more intense. The spin doctor can hear the song of a meadow pipit and the Coulin River tumbling over the smooth, rounded boulders. Brokenshire puts the rifle to his shoulder, pulls back the lever and takes aim.

At that moment the silence of the Coulin Pass is broken by distant shouting and then much closer, by a high-pitched, squealing, yipping barking.

Brokenshire looks like he's going to explode. 'What the hell?'

From the old Scots pine plantation behind the house two red

deer hinds and a young stag emerge at a gallop. Right on their heels is Tyke in full sheepdog mode. He chases the two hinds and the stag out of the wood and across the moorland, right in front of the metal target, now obscured by real live red deer.

'It's that bloody dog again,' shouts Brokenshire, his face turning an apoplectic shade of purple, 'Right, that's it!'

And he presses the rifle sight to his eye framing a small shaggy black and white dog in the cross hairs.

Mickey's running along the track on the opposite bank of the River Coulin from the house, the outbuildings and the plantation of old Scots pines at the foot of Sgurr Dubh when he hears the shot.

Tyke had been trotting along quietly at his heel, occasionally falling back to sniff the twisted roots of an old rowan or a mossy boulder at the edge of the private road that leads down to Coulin House from Glen Torridon.

Blinks of sun glinted on the still waters of Loch Coulin. A rowing boat was moored out on the loch. The Scots pines on the shore by the boathouse cast reflections in the black peaty water. The sun warmed his bones, cold and stiff from the night bivi under the boulder stone by the pony track on the hillside above Kinlochewe. In a weak, grey, dawn light as the dogs barked at Cromasaig he'd traversed the rough moorland on the lower slopes of Beinn Eighe, screened from passing cars by the scattered birch trees along the side of the road in Glen Torridon.

He was lost in his thoughts, mind drifting from the snow-covered summit of Slioch to the beach at Sanda Mhor to Ryan the waiter walking naked across the brown shagpile carpet in the bedroom in the Lomond Shores Motel.

Suddenly Tyke wasn't there.

Gone.

Vanished like a black shadow.

Just a flicker of movement: a flash of a white-tipped tail

disappearing around a bend in the track. Mickey broke into a run.

'Tyke!'

'TYKE!'

Near the bridge over the River Coulin he heard the high-pitched, yipping, squealing bark he knew meant the dog was in full scale pursuit mode.

'TYKE!'

Then he hears the shot.

He's running. Great drops of sweat flying off his forehead.

His heart's pounding so hard he thinks:

Fuck! I could have a heart attack.

He calls Tyke's name again but his voice cracks to a sob.

Despite his girth, Scotland's First Minister was not normally a clumsy man but, just as Brokenshire starts to gently squeeze the trigger of the Winchester, the First Minister suddenly and inexplicably turns and his enormous tartan-trewed arse collides with the Derbyshire Tantalus which teeters for a fraction of a second then topples forwards onto the rocky ground at Brokenshire's feet with a terrible crash of shattering eighteenth-century glass. Brokenshire jumps in surprise and jolts the gun. The crack of the rifle shot sends the hoodie craws up out of the trees in the plantation of old Scots pines at the foot of Sgurr Dubh.

Brokenshire swivels round and looks aghast at the overturned cabinet and bright gleaming shards of glass and splinters of walnut in the heather. The whisky decanter's somehow remained intact but the stopper has fallen out and rolled away and the fifty-year-old Macallan is seeping away into the peaty soil.

Tyke and the deer are gone.

Upstream from the bridge leading to the big house, the River Coulin wanders down through dark peaty pools overhung by Scots pines and spindly rowans on little crags. The waters run so deep and slow, only the spin and glide of the yellow birch leaves prove the current's flow.

Out of nowhere a young stag with stubby, unbranched antlers and two hinds come skiting down the crags on the far side of the river, their hooves skidding on gravel and mud as they crash down through the bracken then gallop through the three-foot-deep pool showering gleaming, clear, crystal drops of water into the air. As he watches, they lumber up the steep bank and across the track before leaping a barbed wire fence and disappearing into a dense conifer plantation.

A small, black shaggy creature stands panting at the top of a crag on the far side of the river. Six-inch-long trails of foamy, frothy saliva drool from its mouth. A twig of bramble is tangled in its fur. But in the dog's eyes there is that flickering blue gleam of consciousness as Tyke stares across the River Coulin at Mickey.

The dog doesn't look hurt, thinks Mickey.

And the river water and the sky and the branches of the Scots pines and the pebbles on the path and the boulders in the river are all suddenly brighter, sharper, more intense than moments before as he walks quickly upstream towards a rocky linn. He knows Tyke won't cross. Not deep fast flowing water. Not since he fell in the River Kirkaig when he was a pup.

'Tyke! Here!'

A couple of nimble bounds over the slippery, green, weed-coated rocks and the dog's across, back on the track. Mickey crouches down, buries his head in Tyke's thick shaggy black coat and weeps.

last tango at stronphadruig lodge

He can hear the sound of traffic on the A835 though he guesses he's still about a kilometre away from the road. He opens the rucksack at the edge of the unsurfaced forest road while Tyke sniffs about the drifts of pine needles. He changes into jeans and baseball boots, puts his hoodie and down-filled puffa jacket on top then pulls out a lightweight black travel bag and slides the muddy rucksack inside and zips it up.

Next he takes Aunty Nora's tartan dogcoat and lays it across Tyke's back. The dog wriggles and squirms and snaps but, after a couple of minutes and several dog biscuits, he fastens the ties on the dog coat. The wild shaggy border collie is gone. Instead the dog has a lurcher-meets-whippet look to him. Anyway, he doesn't look much like Tyke, which is the effect Mickey's after.

And, to a passing hillwalker or forestry worker happening to see the figure making his way cautiously down through the head-high, waxy-green rhodendrons on the hillside above Achnashellach station, Mickey the climber is gone too. The man in a hoodie, headphones in his ears, staring at his Android phone, travel bag over his shoulder, waiting for the 11.47 to Inverness, on the platform of the semi-derelict station, might be a young local guy returning to work after a visit home or maybe a Pole or a Romanian earning a living waiting at tables and washing dishes in a Highland hotel.

He can hear the train's whistle further down the glen several minutes before it pulls into the moss-covered platforms of Achnashellach station. He steps quickly onto the train and sits down in the nearest empty window seat, pushing Tyke under the table, out of sight, kept busy with a hide chew.

The overweight female ticket collector had a blazing row with her girlfriend in Alness that morning and has been in a foul mood all day. She hardly glances at him, staring distractedly out the window of the train as she prints out a ticket and hands him change from the second last £20 note in his wallet.

The train accelerates along beside the River Carron. A bull stands in a field. Through the carriage window he follows the line of the path zig-zagging up the lower slopes of Sgurr nan Ceannaichean. Twisting his head back the way, he snatches a last glimpse of the cliffs of Fuar Tholl and the grey screes of Beinn Liath Mor.

'This train is for Inverness.' An electronic-sounding female voice. 'This train will call at Achnasheen, Achanalt, Loch Luichart, Garve, Dingwall, Conon Bridge, Muir of Ord, Beauly and Inverness.'

The River Braan: glimpses of brown and white water. Mossy rocks and ferns in a gorge, as the train clacks between the silver birches and rowans.

'This is Achnasheen.'

The electronic-sounding female recorded announcement again.

'Please mind the gap when alighting from this train.'

Achnasheen: a hotel, a boarded-up garage and a scattering of bungalows beside the road; gravel moraines by the river and an old stone bridge downstream from the new concrete road bridge and roundabout. A white line slices down the green hillside, the Allt Achaidh na Sine tumbling down from a spaghnum-moss- and dragonfly-infested pool high on Fionn Bheinn.

An insistent bleeping as the doors close and the train leaves Achnasheen behind; road and railway side by side through the wide bare strath where the River Braan meanders through the tawny moorland.

'We are now approaching Achanalt. This is a request stop.'

The train speeds up as it rattles downhill past Loch Sgamhain and across the brown moorland at the foot of Moruisg. A ruined cottage stands beside the line. Deer flee across the brown heather moorland at the sight of the oncoming train. Swallows flit around the log stack at the gable end of a remote house by Loch Luichart. A cottage renovated by a climbing club over many weekends of unpaid labour stands alone and empty across the river, windows shuttered, door padlocked.

He has an hour and a half between trains in Inverness. He walks out the doors of the stone-built railway station and into the busy street. Good to be in the city. Glad to be anonymous among the crowds of shoppers. He walks round the back of the station along the pavement by the dual carriageway. Across the industrial estate, beyond Halfords and Quik Fit, the piers of the Kessock Bridge span the Moray Firth and Ben Wyvis is a green wall to the north.

The train south from Inverness is packed and he has to squeeze into a table seat with three other passengers. Tyke curls up comfortably on two sets of feet, a furry-legged, tartan foot-warmer. The Irish couple opposite smile and pat the dog as Mickey hoists the travel bag with the rucksack inside it onto the overhead luggage rack.

A trolley clinking with bottles of Britvic orange juice, cans of cider, miniature bottles of wine and chocolate brownies in plastic wrappers is bumped up onto the train through the double doors behind Mickey's table seat. He slumps back, head turned towards the window, trying to look invisible.

A young woman in a blue Scotrail uniform with immaculately straightened, dyed blonde hair fiddles around with coffee pots and cartons of milk. Working the buffet trolley with her is a young guy with an Inverness accent and a dark, almost Spanish-looking complexion. He spends the whole journey standing at the trolley telling the girl with dyed blond hair a long anecdote about how he was sitting watching TV in his tighty-whities but Mickey can't hear the rest of the tale over the rattling squeal of the train.

§

Mickey leaves the train and Mister Tighty-Whities at Dalwhinnie. He stands on the bridge and watches until the red tail lantern on the rear coach disappears around the bend in the track. Then he climbs down the iron steps of the footbridge. Hanna, Donald and Wilson: Paisley 1898, reads an oval-shaped plaque on a lamp post. The hunched, rounded shoulders of the A9 Munros huddle around the pass of Drumochter: Sgairneach Mhor and Beinn Udlamain, Geal-charn and A'Mharconaich, A'Bhuidheanach Bheag, Carn na Caim and Meall Chuaich.

Dalwhinnie: the highest station on the British rail network. Long grass grows over the sleepers and rusting rails in the sidings where the platform ends. Once in wartime the field marshal's armoured train, with its flatbed wagons and Bren guns, stopped in the sidings here for three days. The field marshal's staff shuffled maps, notes, files and reconnaissance photos of beaches and the Normandy coastline. In his head the field marshal sees a floating armada of landing craft crossing the channel while he tramps across the heather to the distillery and back, along the dusty road past the white ponies in the field opposite the hotel.

From the blue-and-white-painted station building Mickey, travel bag over his shoulder, sets off along the single track road towards Loch Ericht. Any passing driver who saw him, but there is no one, there are no cars on the road, might take him for a Balfour Beatty sub-contractor working on the line of super-pylons strung over the Pass of Drumochter like skeletal steel Ents marching across the moor.

But there is no one to see, only the swallows lined up on the telephone wires see Mickey Bell pass by.

The dirt track road curves on for five miles between glacial moraines overlaid with brown heather, and firebreaks cut through rectangles of Sitka spruce. The mountains stand all around: Ben Alder and Bheinn Bheoil, Geal Carn and Aonach Beag, Beinn Eibhinn, Carn Dearg and Beinn a'Chlachair.

In the summer of 1845, at the height of railway mania, the top-hatted, silk-waistcoated directors of the Caledonian Northern Direct and the Scottish Grand Junction Railway proposed a direct line from Glasgow to Tyndrum and on north-east along the shores of Loch Ericht to join the Perth and Inverness Railway at Dalwhinnie. But then the bubble burst. No road or railway ever penetrated the empty lands west of Ben Alder and many long wilderness miles lie between Dalwhinnie station and Corrour Halt on the West Highland line.

All that day as Mickey tramps along the overgrown track, in the sky overhead skeins of geese in great V shapes, flying east, calling and calling.

A rotting wooden sign bolted to a fence post encrusted with grey-green lichen stands in long grass at the edge of the track. In faded, black-painted, near-illegible letters he can just make out the words: *Stronphadruig Lodge 3 Miles*.

The sky has a leaden greyness to it of snow about to fall as he turns the cold iron door handle at the back of Stronphadruig

Lodge. The maroon paint is peeling and blistered, the door faded by the heat of a Highland summer and the ice and snow of winter.

There are slates off the roof and in places the sarking is exposed to the wind and rain thrown down in lashing squalls from Ben Alder. Sections of corroded iron guttering lie in the tangled grass, the lead flashing above the double bay windows at the front of the Lodge is split and torn and the rones are sprouting moss and grass.

Sparrows nest in the top of the cracked drainpipes and each summer swallows make the three-thousand-mile journey to nest under the white-painted wooden eaves. Just as they did when people lived at Sronphadruig Lodge, still they return each summer.

The harling on the outside walls of the building is cracked and blistered. Two-foot-square sections of it lie in the long grass beneath the windows. He pushes the red-painted door. It opens into a small hallway with a rusty electricity meter in a wall cupboard. There is a smell of soot and damp.

A white-panelled door on his left opens into a scullery with a stainless steel sink. White-painted shelves on the wall are supported by ornate iron brackets which once held saucepans, china and glass when the house was a hunting lodge filled with the cream of Anglo-Scots society, there for the stalking season.

The tan 1980s vinyl is pulled up in one corner. Great blooms of black mould grow on its once pristine white backing. The floorboards have rotted away and the joists are visible where the floor covering has been torn up. There's a hole in the ceiling too where the slatted lathe is exposed. It's the same on the floor above.

In a winter some twenty years before, a pipe in an upstairs bathroom froze then burst in the thaw as the first snowdrops appeared at the base of the tall oak tree in the yard; water cascaded through this part of the house for days until the brick-built water tank on the hillside above the lodge was empty.

He walks past the scullery into a hallway where a plain, wooden staircase, still covered by a thick red carpet, leads to the upper floors of the Lodge. On his right a half glass, half timbered door gives access to the main part of the house. He doesn't open it. Instead he turns left into the kitchen.

The Lodge must have been done up shortly before it was abandoned: the kitchen units have a 1980s look to them. Every single wooden handle on the doors is missing as are the ornamental wooden balls from the banisters on the staircase in the hall. There are chairs and a bench around a table in a wood-panelled corner of the kitchen. Bare wires protrude from the walls where light switches have been ripped out.

A mop and a sweeping brush stand propped up in one corner of the kitchen. On the back wall stands an oil-fired Rayburn. The enamel is corroded but the chrome lids still gleam. A rusty spark, heavy oil seeps into the burner, a smell of scorching dust, a glow of blue flame. He feels the heat that once emanated from this beast of a stove, warming the entire house and providing hot water as a byproduct. He thinks of the clean tea towels drying on it, the smell of toast in the mornings, the undergamekeeper's bum resting against it while he flirted with the housekeeper and the kitchen maids. Mickey zips up his down-filled puffa jacket, it's still freezing in the kitchen of Sronphadruig Lodge.

The iron north wind blows in through a broken window pane repaired with a sheet of hardboard. Peering through the dirty, cobwebbed panes he can see deer grazing on the steep, grassy hillside behind the lodge. Even as he watches they look up, wary of people, sensing his presence in the derelict building.

An old, well-thumbed, greasy pack of playing cards lies

on the kitchen table next to an ashtray full of roaches. On the dusty work surface next to the Rayburn there's a plastic lemonade bottle with the base cut off and a pile of dead matches. Someone's been chasing the dragon at Stronphadruig Lodge.

An empty vodka bottle sits on a shelf.

'Jimmy the Line's dossed here,' he says to Tyke and the mice and the empty building.

Jimmy – fiftyish, with grey hair, jeans and a leather coat – got his name because he walks the West Highland line sleeping the night in the huts and old linesmen's cottages that lie empty beside the railway. He sits by the tracks in the doorway of a shed built of railway sleepers sipping vodka and orange from a glass lemonade bottle as the night train to Euston rumbles past in the blue darkness.

Mickey picks up the brush from the kitchen and takes it into the room with the fireplace at the foot of the staircase. The deluge of water that cascaded through two floors of the lodge damaged this room too and debris is scattered across the carpet and heaped beside the fireplace. He clears the fallen plaster from a corner of the room and unrolls his sleeping mat and puts it down on the clammy beige carpet. He pulls his sleeping bag out and lays it on the mat. Then he goes outside.

A triangle of yellow larches to the west of the house shelters the empty building from the prevailing wind. Tyke sniffs around the base of the tree trunks. The branches of the larches creak and sigh in the wind as Mickey walks beneath the trees, gathering twigs and sticks.

He drops an armful of firewood at the backdoor of the lodge then walks across the yard to a wooden shed with a red, iron tank on brick stilts adjoining it. The blackened remains of a bonfire lie scorched into the grass. Charred planks broken off the front of the shed lie scattered on the ground.

Inside, mounted on a concrete plinth, is a diesel generator the size of an engine from a Lancaster bomber. Jerrycans lie on the ground and the shed smells of oil and creosote. The metalwork of the generator is painted in British racing green. He puts his hand on the polished wooden starting handle, thinking how it was when the generator throbbed away and yellow light poured from the windows of Stronphadruig Lodge.

Back indoors he hangs his SuperDry jacket from a brass wall light then takes a firelighter, carefully wrapped in silver foil and clingfilm, from his rucksack and places it in the grate. He lays pine needles and a few scrunched-up sheets of newspaper from the kitchen on top. The young model's perfect, pert breasts and pink nipples, tinged with brown, point back at him from the mouse-gnawed newsprint.

The fire burns in the grate, the flames lick at the twigs of larchwood. Fire in the wilderness, the flames will keep the wolves in the snow outside at bay. Tyke lies so close to the fire his head is almost resting on the grate. Mickey crouches down and strokes the dog. His fur is scorching hot.

'Move yer heid – you daft mutt.'

Mickey sits down beside the stretched-out dog by the fire and pours a whisky from the plastic waterbottle in his rucksack. He picks up the greasy pack of cards from the kitchen, takes out the jokers, shuffles the pack and deals himself seven cards. He arranges the cards in a row and turns over the first card on the left; the seven of spades. Then he deals himself another six cards. The wind rattles the broken windows of Stronphadruig Lodge as Mickey deals himself a jack of hearts–solitaire in the wilderness.

Later, before it gets dark, he climbs the creaky wooden staircase and wanders through the upper floors of the house. Most of the rooms are empty but, in one, a wooden chair stands forlornly in the centre of a bedroom with a cast iron fireplace. There is an ironing board set up in another but what would you iron at Stronphadruig Lodge, he wonders?

In a room further along the corridor there is a rotting armchair and the drawers of a wooden dressing table are pulled open. He stands in front of the looking glass, his stubbly reflection gazes back at him, black semicircles under his eyes, face red and wind-beaten.

With Tyke at his heels he walks down the grand staircase of the house, a sweeping arc of carved wooden banisters and peeling lincrusta, yellow squares on the mildewed wallpaper where paintings once hung. At the foot of the grand staircase, beside a pillared fireplace in a wide hall, panelled double doors lead into another empty room.

A scraping sound as he pushes open the doors: rusty hinge pins screech. The fading light of dusk through the tall double windows illuminates the room. He looks around him, taking in the high ceiling and elaborate cornice embossed with bunches of grapes and sheaves of wheat. From a star-shaped ceiling rose hangs a spider's-web-encrusted chandelier, furry with thick coatings of plasterdust. The floorboards are bare and, at the far end of the room under the tall windows, a grand piano stands slowly rotting in the cold damp air.

He walks across and writes his name in the thick layer of dust covering the black satin-varnished top of the piano. He lifts the lid and runs his hand along the keys. The wood beneath the ivory is swollen with water ingress. He plays a chord. The noise echoes eerily around the empty house.

He takes out his phone. Then he places his head torch on the dusty lid of the piano, slides the switch and points the beam at the chandelier. Gleaming dust motes float in the blue column of LED light. The beam rises to the ceiling and the crystal droplets of the chandelier sparkle again.

Mickey plays a scale on the piano. He looks down at the dog.

'Would sir care for tae dance?'

The dog cocks his left ear and tilts his head to one side quizzically.

'Why do I even talk to you, dug?' Mickey says.

Then he presses Play on his phone. Synthesised violins, trumpets, a throbbing bass: the strains of *Your Disco Needs You* fill the empty rooms and corridors. He bows low to Tyke then sweeps the dog up into his arms and man and dog they dance in circles to Kylie: round and round the mouldering ballroom under the chandelier and the grapes and sheaves of wheat on the crumbling plaster cornice, while outside on the steep hillside behind Stronphadruig Lodge the deer graze in the gathering dusk.

canedolia

CD4 count 750
viral load <40 copies/ml
Munros 282/282

The Real Madrid players are peeling off their football shirts on the widescreen TV above the bar in the Stron. Mickey feigns interest in the match as Malcolm loads the dishwasher.

'They were Mary McKillop's cows—' Malcolm is saying.

He's is in the middle of a long tale about when he was a little boy at the stone-built primary school across the road.

'Me and my pal used to have to round up the cows from the woods along the River Cour and take them to the byre on the croft where the caravan site is now—'

Mickey listens with half an ear while eyeing up Cristiano Ronaldo's bare chest.

'How you daein', Mickey?' Andrea greets him. She's carrying a tray piled high with plates of half-finished portions of scampi, abandoned chips, uncooked onion rings, grizzly bits of steak and flapping lettuce leaves. She puts it down on the bar.

'Malcolm? I'll have a Baileys please.'

She turns to Mickey.

'D'you want a pint?'

'Aw thanks, Andrea. How wis Falkirk?'

'It was great. I saw my boys.'

Later, outside, smoking, Andrea says, 'So that's the waiter guy you met at your cousin's wedding then?'

Mickey exhales a puff of blue cigarette smoke and looks across the car park at the rain bouncing off the roof of Ryan's beat-up, bright orange Citroen Saxo.

'Aye, he's just up here for a couple of days like.'

'He's a bit young for you, isn't he?' She jabs her elbow into his ribs. 'Just kiddin'! He really likes you, ken?'

Mickey stares at the ground. The rain's bouncing off the road. The Ruaidh is roaring down under the bridge next to the inn. Headlights shine through the low windows of the bar as a car splashes through the puddles. The smell of coal smoke from the fire hangs in the misty September air.

'I'm serious—'

A faint flush appears under Mickey's skin. He's been telling her about Jonnie and the dole and everything.

'And like I said, you can do kitchen porter now Polish Andrew's away. Malcolm'll pay you cash in hand.'

'Aw– thanks Andrea. I'm done wi' fuckin benefits. They dae ma heid in but. From now on I'm gaunny stand on my ain two feet. If everyone else in the world can – well, so can I. I'll no let yous down – ah promise.'

He takes a sip of ice-cold Carlsberg while watching the shifting images on the TV mounted on a bracket high on the wall, between the door to the Gents and the stuffed pine marten scowling from its glass cage above the fireplace.

The football's finished now and the news is on: footage of Edinburgh, spires and crags; a helicopter shot of the Scottish Parliament nestled in the shelter of Arthur's Seat.

The camera closes in on the pools and paving stones in front of the parliament where the grass and gorse bushes of the Queen's Park blend seamlessly into the turf roofs of the parliament, the vision of the Catalan architect who designed the building he saw as emerging out of the very rock of the city built on seven hills.

A long line of production vans and generator trucks, satellite dishes and outside broadcast cameras is lined up in front of the Scottish Parliament. BBC Scotland's wheelchair-bound, political editor is telling the news room anchorwoman the world's media have gathered in Edinburgh to witness this moment in Scottish history. 'They've come from Canada, Spain, Ukraine and as far away as Taiwan....'

Mickey reaches down from the bar stool and tickles Tyke under his collar. 'Aw, does that feel nice – good dog – lie down.'

Malcolm is looking up at the TV.

'Did you vote?' he asks Mickey.

'Aye – ah done it ages ago, some folk came round the doors wi' postal votes.'

'Well, I'll not be staying up to watch it,' says Malcolm, giving a glass a polish with a British linen tea towel.

When Mickey looks back up at the screen the pictures are from Aberdeen. Union Street, twirly grey granite towers and oil-support vessels lined up in the harbour.

The reporter is standing outside the glass doors of the airport terminal; behind her passengers are sitting on suitcases or milling about the white marble-floored concourse with its yellow airport signs. Mercedes and Kia Sedona taxis are dropping off passengers in front of the steel and glass building.

The camera pans along the road that leads from Dyce into the airport. A flash of blue lights as a police motor cycle outrider stops the traffic of minibuses and private hire cabs.

Then a black Range Rover followed by a mercury-grey Lexus pulls up. The back door opens and Scotland's First

Minister and then his wife get out. The First Minister hurries forward with a beaming smile to greet the airport staff in their dark trousers and white shirts and tartan waistcoats.

Then the camera sweeps over the barbed wire perimeter fence of the airport and closes in on the white Learjet that sits, engines idling, on the tarmac near the end of the runway.

The screen changes to a shot of a deserted Downing Street. The black door of Number 10 is closed but the camera focuses on a shadowy figure standing behind a white curtain that sways gently in the breeze at an upstairs window.

Mickey picks up his pint glass. Somehow, almost without anyone noticing, Scotland has changed and nothing will ever be the same again.

The face of the First Minister fills the screen.

'A moment comes, which comes but rarely in history,' he thunders, 'when we step out from the old to the new, when an age ends, and when the soul of a nation, long suppressed, finds utterance… If not now, when? If not us, who?'

It's very Scottish. There are no cheering, flag-waving crowds. No cars circling George Square with supporters hanging out the windows waving banners, yet there is a tension in the air. Like when Scotland play in the World Cup and in a grimy close in a street in Leith a small girl in pink shorts and a grubby white top leans back against the cracked, peeling paint of the stair door and coyly, shyly tells the couple going into the chipshop, 'Scotland have scored.'

More clips: the silver-bearded leader of Still Better Together speaking, the Mayor of London and the Prince of Wales, the paint-splattered mobility scooters of the bedroom tax protesters and, finally, an aerial shot, white breakers crashing against cliffs, fishing boats rolling in the Atlantic swell, the River Clyde and the cranes, Stirling Castle on its rock then line after line of peaks and corries and glens and mountains streaked with snow, fading to the blue saltire *Scotland Decides* logo.

The bar is empty now. Last orders long past.

'Don't yous worry,' says Andrea to Ryan and Mickey, the last customers in the bar. 'Nae police from the Fort the night.'

Malcolm has gone out to check on the hens and look at the stars over the Grey Corries. When he opens the back door a black shape, an otter from the deep pools of the Ruaidh, slinks away over the fence into the birch woods, its round eyes green discs in the moonlight.

Alone at the bar now, Mickey leans over a little clumsily and sticks his tongue down Ryan's throat. Sat on his bar stool he snogs Ryan as the carved wooden griffons, wings outstretched, glare down. Tyke sleeps curled up in front of the coal fire, dreaming the dreams of collie dogs, his furry head resting on the Munros Book sticking out the top of Mickey's rucksack.

A few minutes later, coming back behind the bar with a tray of glasses, Andrea smiles at the two boys, Ryan and Mickey, snogging at the bar. And outside the silent mountains stand all around as blue shades to darkness and night falls over the Grey Corries.

acknowledgements

Special thanks to Paul Eden and Liz Marshall who read and gave valuable feedback on the manuscript and also to my editor Keira Farrell for all her hard work. I am indebted to Sue Collin and Creative Scotland for both practical and financial support during the writing of this book and to Keara Donnachie and all the team at Sandstone Press. Thanks to Bob Davidson and Moira Forsyth for taking on a first novel and to Gavin MacDougall for suggesting I write fiction. Also thanks to Alan Bissett, Janice Galloway, Andrew Greig and Chris Townsend. And finally, to Alex Roddie for playing along and not taking himself too seriously.

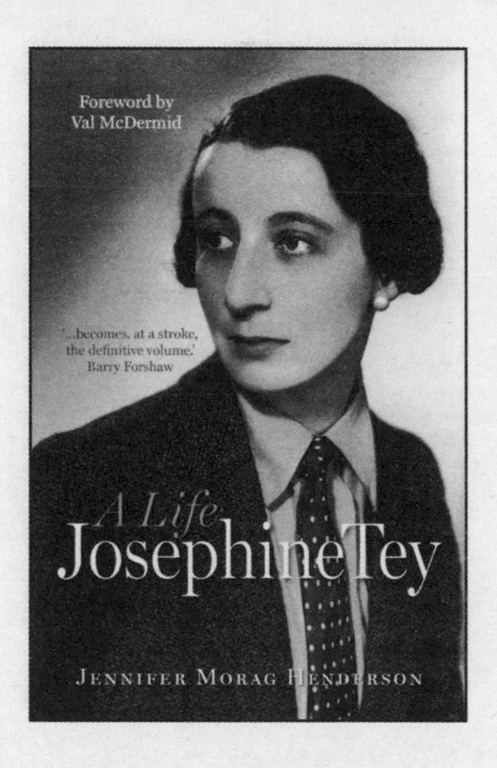

'Tells the moving story of a major leading Scots writer for whom the detective novel became "a medium as disciplined as any sonnet".'

The Observer, Best Biographies of 2015

Elizabeth MacKintosh lived several 'lives': best known as Golden Age Crime Fiction writer 'Josephine Tey', she was also successful novelist and playwright 'Gordon Daviot', and even wrote for Hollywood – all from her home in the north of Scotland.

Paperback ISBN: 9781910985373 RRP: £9.99
Also available in eBook

www.sandstonepress.com

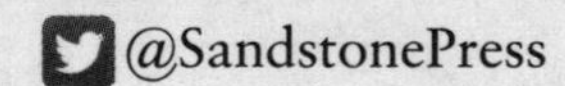
facebook.com/SandstonePress/

@SandstonePress